PRAISE FOR
THE ALCHEMIST'S APPRENTICE

"This book is fun . . . There's humor and adventure, mystery and magic, all rolled up in one package . . . *The Alchemist's Apprentice* can be enjoyed by both mystery lovers and fantasy fans."
—*SFRevu*

"Duncan mingles arch fantasy and a whodunit plot in this alternate version of old Venice . . . Nostradamus and Alfeo's adventures provide more amusement than chills in this charming farce, which comments lightly on class prejudice, political chicanery, and occult tomfoolery."
—*Publishers Weekly*

"Dave Duncan's wit shows a distinctive intelligence, a clear-eyed vision that's both irreverent and astute."
—*Locus*

"Duncan's latest novel launches a new series set in an alternate Venice and filled with the author's customary touches of humor, light satire, and fast-paced action. [Duncan] shows his mastery of both storytelling and character building."
—*Library Journal*

ACCLAIM FOR DAVE DUNCAN
AND HIS PREVIOUS WORK

"Dave Duncan knows how to spin a ripping good yarn."—*SFRevu*

"Duncan is an exceedingly finished stylist and a master of world building and characterizations."
—*Booklist*

"Dave Duncan is one of the best writers in the fantasy world today. His writing is clear, vibrant, and full of energy. His action scenes are breathtaking, and his skill at characterization is excellent."
—*Writers Write*

"Duncan excels at old-fashioned swashbuckling fantasy, maintaining a delicate balance between breathtaking excitement, romance, and high camp in a genre that is easy to overdo."—*Romantic Times*

"Duncan can swashbuckle with the best, but his characters feel more deeply and think more clearly than most, making his novels . . . suitable for a particularly wide readership."
—*Publishers Weekly* (starred review)

THE
ALCHEMIST'S
CODE

DAVE DUNCAN

ACE BOOKS, NEW YORK

THE BERKLEY PUBLISHING GROUP
Published by the Penguin Group
Penguin Group (USA) Inc.
375 Hudson Street, New York, New York 10014, USA
Penguin Group (Canada), 90 Eglinton Avenue East, Suite 700, Toronto, Ontario M4P 2Y3, Canada
(a division of Pearson Penguin Canada Inc.)
Penguin Books Ltd., 80 Strand, London WC2R 0RL, England
Penguin Group Ireland, 25 St. Stephen's Green, Dublin 2, Ireland (a division of Penguin Books Ltd.)
Penguin Group (Australia), 250 Camberwell Road, Camberwell, Victoria 3124, Australia
(a division of Pearson Australia Group Pty. Ltd.)
Penguin Books India Pvt. Ltd., 11 Community Centre, Panchsheel Park, New Delhi—110 017, India
Penguin Group (NZ), 67 Apollo Drive, Rosedale, North Shore 0632, New Zealand
(a division of Pearson New Zealand Ltd.)
Penguin Books (South Africa) (Pty.) Ltd., 24 Sturdee Avenue, Rosebank, Johannesburg 2196,
South Africa

Penguin Books Ltd., Registered Offices: 80 Strand, London WC2R 0RL, England

This is an original publication of The Berkley Publishing Group.

This is a work of fiction. Names, characters, places, and incidents either are the product of the author's imagination or are used fictitiously, and any resemblance to actual persons, living or dead, business establishments, events, or locales is entirely coincidental. The publisher does not have any control over and does not assume any responsibility for author or third-party websites or their content.

First edition: March 2008

Library of Congress Cataloging-in-Publication Data

Duncan, Dave, 1933–
  The alchemist's code / Dave Duncan.—1st ed.
     p. cm.
  ISBN 978-0-441-01562-7
  1. Nostradamus, 1503–1566—Fiction.   2. Prophets—Fiction.   I. Title.

PR9199.3.D847A79 2008
813'.54—dc22

                                                           2007046574

PRINTED IN THE UNITED STATES OF AMERICA

10   9   8   7   6   5   4   3   2   1

For Jessica,
my favorite
granddaughter

Notice Neptune, though,
Taming a sea-horse, thought a rarity,
Which Claus of Innsbruck cast in bronze for me.

—Robert Browning, *My Last Duchess*

THE
ALCHEMIST'S
CODE

PROLOGUE

I hate prologues. When I go to a theater I want action, dialogue, dancing, singing. I resent some long-winded actor coming out to lecture me at length on what the play is about or how great the performance is going to be. In real life, prologues are more interesting but rarely recognizable. This was like that—at the time I did not realize I was in a prologue, but it is relevant to the story and I promise to keep it brief.

"Saints preserve us! Alfeo Zeno!"

That was how it began.

The time: early on a September evening, sweltering hot. The place: a narrow *calle*, packed solid with people emerging from a doorway to spill off in both directions. And me, squashed back against a wall. All that endless, baking summer I had been saving my tips so I could take Violetta to the theater when she returned from the mainland, and the afternoon had been a great success. I had every hope that the evening would be even more so.

As we were trying to leave the courtyard, though, she was hailed by a tall man whom I recognized as *sier* Baiamonte Spadafora, one of her patrons, so I tactfully squirmed

away. I could not love a courtesan if I did not have my jealousy under control, but Baiamonte would be shocked to see
her being escorted by a mere apprentice, which was how I
was dressed. In the Republic people's costumes define them
exactly.

That works both ways, of course. While I waited for my
lover to catch up with me, out in the *calle*, I amused myself
by watching the throng squeezing by, identifying clerks and
artisans and shopkeepers, male nobles in their black gowns,
doctors and lawyers in theirs, even a couple of senators in
red. Venice finds nothing odd in its ruling class mingling
with the common herd. They live cheek by jowl and share
many of the same tastes; some nobles are wealthy beyond
the dreams of Midas, others are paupers.

Of course I did not neglect the women, mentally sorting
them into ladies, respectable housewives, and courtesans.
Other cities are ashamed of prostitutes and try to hide
them; Venice brags of its courtesans, flaunting them even in
the highest levels of society. They are not confined to specific areas or required to wear some shameful badge; most of
them dress better than senators' wives.

A man barged past me, then spoke my name: "Saints preserve us! Alfeo Zeno!"

I knew the voice even before I turned, the most memorable male voice I had ever heard, rich and resonant as a pipe
organ. I could even recall the summer it had appeared, basso
profundo hatching from boyish treble in a matter of weeks.
I had turned bright malachite with jealousy.

"Danese Dolfin, as I hope for salvation!"

"How long has it been?"

"Years!"

Danese and I had been children together in San Barnaba
parish, but never close. He was a little older than me and
would disappear for a year or so at a time, whenever his father
was elected to some minor office on the mainland, helping

to rule some fragment of the Venetian empire. His father cannot have been very impressive in his work and obviously had no influential patron to back him, because he suffered long gaps between the postings, when he and his brood sank back in among the *barnabotti*, the impoverished nobility. Danese had still been a lot better off than those of us who did not have fathers.

Squashed together almost nose to nose—more specifically my nose, his chin—we inspected each other.

"You are doing well," I said.

He had always been tall and good-looking, with blue eyes, almost-blond hair, and a fair complexion. When a nobleman reaches twenty-five or so, he lets his beard grow in and switches to floor-length robes, unless he is a soldier or follows some unusual profession, but *sier* Danese was clearly not there yet. Nay, he was a strutting peacock in bright silk doublet and knee britches, all embroidered and padded. His ruff was crisply starched, his puffed bonnet bigger than any pumpkin. He wore a sword, too, and clearly did not belong among the *barnabotti* now.

"Moderately well," he said smugly. "And how is the world treating you?"

"I have no complaints."

His expression implied that I should have. His outfit had cost more than I would earn in several years. How had he done it? A nobleman can join a profession or engage in trade, but if he sinks to manual labor, his name will be struck from the Golden Book. Whatever Danese was up to was certainly not carpentry or canal dredging, but there are few honest ways for a man to shoot from poverty to wealth so quickly. The most obvious was marriage, because a nobleman's children are noble even if his wife is not. If Danese had found a rich merchant of the citizen class with a daughter and a craving for noble grandchildren, then his sudden prosperity had sprung from her dowry.

He had also had four sisters. Possibly one of them had married into money and towed him in on her bridal train.

"And your family?" I asked. "Your parents, sisters? Married yet?"

"My mother is still alive. My sisters all married *down*, alas. No, I'm not married." He smirked, knowing exactly what I was wondering. "And you?"

"No." I would not discuss careers if he wouldn't. I glanced around to make sure Violetta was not looking for me. "We must get together one day. Where are you living now?"

"Over in Cannaregio," he said vaguely. That told me nothing except that he did not want to get together. Palaces stand alongside tenements in Cannaregio, just as they do in the other five wards of the city. "And you?"

I laughed. "Not in San Barnaba, anyway."

"Lord, no!" He smiled as if he had reached a decision. "You know what's best about the sweet life, Alfeo? It's not silk sheets or fancy clothes. It's not fine wines or parties or roaring fires in winter. It's not even escaping to the mainland in summer. No, it's the food! Remember living on polenta and watermelon? My most sincere prayers are grace at table."

Suddenly I remembered why Danese and I had never been close—he had always been an insufferable pustule. Now red-hot pincers would not force me to mention that I lived in a palazzo, slept on silk sheets, and ate the finest cooking in all Venice.

"You are making my mouth water. I am still waiting to taste *gelado*." Mama Angeli's cooking is unsurpassed, but *gelado* requires boatloads of snow from the Dolomite Mountains, an extravagance the Maestro would not tolerate.

"You haven't lived, Alfeo."

"Ah, there you are!" Violetta appeared at my side in a blaze of silver brocade, auburn hair, a carapace of diamonds, and a scent of roses. With her breasts fully visible through a net bodice, the most prized courtesan in Venice has a body to drive any man mad. I puckered, so she kissed. Yes, right there in public.

"Wonderful talking to you again, Danese," I said.

His face was an open book. The first page said, *Good God, he's a pimp!* The second page said, *Then why doesn't she dress him better?*

There were no other pages.

Violetta is a people expert and read the situation at a glance. She fanned me with her lashes, breathed, "Come along, lover," so he would hear, and pulled me close as we eased into the throng. "A friend of yours?"

"One of the horrors of childhood. Meet anyone interesting?"

She smiled understandingly. "Not a soul." She meant that I was more interesting than men with money, nice of her. "There's an interesting couple, though."

I looked as directed. The man wore the floor-length gown and round, flat-topped bonnet of the nobility, with the strip of cloth called a tippet draped over his left shoulder, but in his case these were all colored violet, to show that he was a member of the *Collegio*, the steering committee of the Senate. I do not know all of the twelve hundred or so noblemen of Venice, those eligible to sit in the Great Council, but I try to keep up with the inner circle, the sixty or seventy who actually run the Republic. He was new to me.

The woman wore a full-length gown of sky-blue silk brocade with a square-cut neck and slightly puffed shoulders. It was expensively embroidered with seed pearls, but the oyster cemetery around her neck would have bought a small galleon. She carried a fan of white osprey plumes.

When they had gone by, I shook my head.

Violetta is a whole constellation of different women as circumstances require, and then she was in her political persona, the one I call Aspasia. Aspasia knows everyone who matters, meaning any man with money or power. "*Sier* Giro-lamo Sanudo. Recently elected to navy. A surprise."

There are five ministers for navy in the *Collegio*. The post is regarded as training for youngsters on the way up, but Girolamo had looked unusually young for a senior post, probably not yet forty.

"Son of *sier* Zuanbattista Sanudo?" I said. "Ambassador to somewhere."

Aspasia's blue-gray eyes twinkled. "Well done! Except his daddy is back home now and was elected a ducal coun-selor last week."

August and September are the peak of the political sea-son in Venice, when the Great Council elects the Senators and the Council of Ten and other senior magistrates. That is why the nobility had all returned from their country estates on the mainland. In October they would go back again for the bird hunting.

"And the lady?" Aspasia asked.

"Respectable, not a courtesan. About thirty, natural blonde, blue eyes, comfortably rounded, real pearls, richly but discreetly dressed, good teeth, developing pout lines around her mouth. I didn't notice her at all. His wife?"

"His mother, madonna Eva Morosini."

"Truly? I know they say Venetian nobles are born old, but *sier* Girolamo must have taken that to extremes. Step-mother, I assume?"

Aspasia laughed. "A big step—he's older than she is. She was Nicolò Morosini's sister—came with a fat dowry and lots of political pull."

"Dimples, too, back then. What is so special about the Sanudos, apart from the extreme age difference?" And the obvious fact that father and son together wielded much political heft.

She smiled with the innocence of a well-fed tiger. "Zuan-battista distinguished himself when he was in Constantinople;

he won major concessions from the Sultan. He has climbed very fast up the political bell tower."

As a ducal counselor, he was close to the top already. The doge is head of state, but we Venetians have always lived in fear of tyranny, so we keep him shackled with six counselors, one from each ward of the city. He cannot open his mail or meet with a foreigner except in their presence; he can do nothing without the approval of four of them. That meant that Counselor Zuanbattista Sanudo could block any government action he did not like with the support of only two others; for the next eight months he would be one of the most powerful men in the Republic.

"So when our present doge is called to a higher realm, the glamorous madonna Eva Morosini will become our *dogaressa*?

Violetta-Aspasia chuckled, "She dreams of it every night."

"She would certainly brighten up the stodgy old palace. Exactly how do you know what she dreams of?"

Even my darling's laugh is beautiful. "A friend told me."

I saw that I had missed something subtle, but I did not press her on the matter, as I had other ideas more pressing. We had reached the watersteps where my gondola waited— not truly mine, of course, but a public boat rowed by my friend, Vettor Angeli, Giorgio's eldest. He had agreed to transport me and my love to and from the theater that afternoon so I could play out my fantasy of being a rich noble. In return I had cast the horoscope of a girl he was thinking of marrying. It showed that she would be submissive, obedient, and faithful—not all qualities I would look for, but the news had pleased him, so we were both happy.

Violetta and I went back to her apartment and the rest of the day is irrelevant to my story.

Now you see why I did not notice the prologue. Think of it as the start of rehearsals for a play, or a bunch of friends planning a masque for Carnival, or even one of the *scuole grande* organizing a tableau for some great civic celebration. All of these begin with confusion as people mill around and someone hands out the scripts and assigns the roles. *You over there—you can play the traitor; you'll be the inquisitor. And for the murderer . . .*

That was Sunday.

1

All week the Maestro indulged himself in alchemical experiments on the sublimation of sulfur, stinking up the entire Ca' Barbolano and neglecting his correspondence. When his folly caught up with me, I had to spend all Saturday morning in the atelier, writing letters at his dictation, he at one side of the big double desk, me at the other. Progress was slow, because I kept correcting his Latin—he has a nasty tendency to confuse ablatives with datives and is too stubborn to admit it. Some of the letters would have to be enciphered, which would ruin my plans for the afternoon.

By noon he had questioned Walter Raleigh and Francis Bacon in England on geography and philosophy respectively, advised Michael Maestlin in Tübingen on the Copernican system and Christoph Clau at Collegio Romano on astrology. Now he was in the process of reassuring Galileo Galilei that his usual room would be available the next time he came over from Padua. I was hungry for dinner; he rarely remembers to eat at all. Mercifully, we were interrupted by a thump of our door knocker.

He scowled so horribly that he actually showed his

derelict teeth, which he does very rarely. "Did you forget to tell me of someone's appointment?"

"No, master. Your next appointment is on Monday at—"

"Tell them I'm busy."

"Who knows, it may be the doge," I said flippantly, heading for the door.

It wasn't, but not far off.

I went out into the *salone*, which runs the full length of the building and is furnished with huge mirrors, enormous paintings, gigantic statues, spreading chandeliers of Murano glass, and myriad other treasures, all of which belong to *sier* Alvise Barbolano. He lets the Maestro and his staff live on the top floor of his palace in return for the occasional horoscope, medical consultation, and financial clairvoyance. Visitors are frequently struck dumb by their first sight of such opulence. The moment I opened the door I saw that these callers would not be easily impressed.

The man was tall and gaunt, elderly but well preserved, with a face like the Dolomite Mountains that stand guard along our northern skyline—hard white stone above a spreading forest of silver-streaked beard. He wore the bonnet, long robes, and tippet of the nobility, but in his case they were cut from the rich scarlet brocade of a ducal counselor. To have such a man come calling was startling; to have him arrive without warning was epochal.

The woman beside him seemed more likely to be his granddaughter than daughter. Her face was plump and her dark silk gown well filled. Genuine blond hair is notable, but not truly rare in Venice. I knew who this couple was and so must you, if you were paying attention earlier. The surprising thing was not that I remembered his face from my childhood, because he must have marched in scores of feast-day processions, and the spectators vie to identify important magistrates; what was rare was that I knew his wife's name at first glance.

Bad luck, the Maestro says, *is misfortune; good luck may be treated as a reward for something.*

I bowed very low and kissed the man's sleeve. "Your Excellency is indeed welcome. Madonna Eva Morosini, you honor this house. The Maestro is expecting you and if you will—"

She gasped. *"Expecting us?* Who told him we were coming?"

Zuanbattista raised one shaggy eyebrow two hairs higher on his forehead. The reason Venetian nobles are said to be born old is because they never drop their dignity. They speak in grave tones after due consideration. A ducal counselor, especially, stands at the heart of the labyrinth of interlocking committees that run the Republic, being a member of the *Signoria*, the *Collegio*, the Senate, and the Council of Ten. One week in every six he presides over the Great Council. No one in the least bit gullible would ever be allowed anywhere near any of that.

I spread my hands in bewilderment. "Maestro Nostradamus is the finest clairvoyant in Europe, madonna. He foresaw the honor of your visit this morning. If you would be so gracious . . ."

"We just decided! We didn't tell anyone!" Madonna Morosini was much too much of a lady to dig an elbow in her gangling husband's ribs, but her tone told him that she had told him so. He remained inscrutable, suspending judgment.

And she? *A man rarely sees more than he looks for,* the Maestro says, and I had already learned far more from her than I ever would from staring at her companion. I decided she was very slightly disheveled, although it was hard to pick out any one feature that implied this. Were her eyelids slightly pink from weeping, or was her face powder patchy, as if applied in a hurry? Her hair was not as carefully dressed as it should have been. She wore no jewelry at all, and normally a great lady shows some.

The Maestro is old and very frail, but his hearing is as sharp as a scalpel. I had left the door half-open. I led the way to it, pushed it wide. "The Sanudos are here, master."

Unless newcomers know what to expect, they must be disappointed by their first sight of the celebrated pedant, prophet, polymath, physician, and philosopher. He is bent and wizened, and his black physician's gown and hat make him look even smaller than he really is. Badly lamed by an excess of rheum in his hips, he should walk with two canes, but prefers a single long staff inlaid with silver sigils. His hair hangs in untidy silver rat-tails, but he dyes his wispy goatee brown, for no reason I have ever been able to discover.

Visitors are always impressed by the atelier, though—the double desk, the examination couch, the great armillary spheres, globes both terrestrial and celestial. Sanudo was too dignified to stare at the alchemical bench or the wall of books, but he certainly noticed them in passing and would know that this room was the Maestro's own, not just borrowed for the morning.

The Maestro had left the desk and was standing by his favorite red velvet chair beside the carved marble fireplace—not that the fireplace was in use on a sweltering September noon, but that is where he sits to interview visitors. "You are a little earlier than I expected, Your Excellency . . . madonna Eva . . . but of course most welcome. My home is honored . . ." His flattery became a mumble as he bowed. He would have hobbled forward to kiss *sier* Zuanbattista's sleeve, but Sanudo stopped him with a gracious gesture.

"Do be seated, Doctor."

I led the way to the green chairs, and the nobility floated behind me with the grace of galleons crossing the lagoon. There are always two chairs opposite the red one and if the Sanudos assumed that they had been arranged especially for them, that was their own mistake, not misinformation from me. As soon as all three principals were settled, I returned to the desk by the windows to watch faces and take notes if needed. The Maestro had his back to the light, not by accident.

Madonna Eva was trying to appear as calm as her husband, but her lips were compressed and her seething hands struggled to destroy a wadded lace hankie.

Zuanbattista said, "If you foresaw our coming, *lustrissimo*, no doubt you already know the nature of our problem?" His tone contained no irony whatsoever, but it was there in his eyes.

I hate skeptics. I love watching the Maestro deal with them.

"Only in a general way, *clarissimo*. Family trouble, of course. Quite sudden . . . and just this morning? When did you discover her absence?"

Madonna Eva lost color under her paint and even *messer* Zuanbattista deigned to look startled, but it is simple enough if you work it out. *Family trouble* because Sanudo had brought his wife or, more likely, she had insisted he bring her to consult the famous clairvoyant. *Sudden* because of the woman's swollen eyelids. *Just this morning* because he knew they had not told anyone they were coming, and also to win another minuscule nod without committing himself to anything. And *her absence* because by then he could be nine-tenths sure that the problem was a missing daughter. Eva Sanudo was of an age to have nubile daughters, if only just. Even if it wasn't a daughter, half the things that can be lost take a feminine pronoun in *Veneziano*.

"You impress us, Doctor," Sanudo admitted.

"Now it is your turn." The Maestro smiled by stretching his mouth sideways and bunching his cheeks. "The details if you please."

"This is confidential." Sanudo glanced suspiciously across at me.

"Certainly. *Sier* Alfeo has my complete confidence in all matters."

He almost never uses my title in front of a client or patient. When he does, his instinct is infallible. Many nobles bristle when they hear that one of their own is demeaning his class by earning an honest living, but *sier* Zuanbattista glanced across at me with interest.

"Family?"

"Zeno, *clarissimo*," I said.

"A descendant of Doge Renier Zen?"

"Twelve-greats grandson. My father was Marco Zeno."

"The Marco Zeno who fought so well at Lepanto?"

"That one," I said proudly. "He died in the plague of 1576."

"Ah, as did so many! I saw your father at Don Giovanni's council the day before the battle, but there were many officers there and I had no chance to speak with him." That was nicely done—he had implied that he would have spoken to my father without actually lying about it. Nodding to show approval of my existence and presence, Sanudo looked back to the Maestro. "My daughter was taken in the night."

Was taken? The words saddened me. I would already have bet some of my dearest body parts that the correct term was *ran away*. Venice, on its hundred man-made islands, is a tight pack of tiny communities, an almost impossible place to stage a holding-for-ransom. Many people, especially women, never leave the parish of their birth and know the comings and goings of every other inhabitant. Start buying more groceries than usual and the fact will be noted and discussed; the Council of Ten's army of informers will overhear. No one keeps secrets in Venice! But the Sanudos were not ready to admit that their child had eloped.

I reached for my quill as the lady began to speak. She declaimed, as if she had memorized an address to the Senate: "My maid found her gone in the morning. She helps Grazia as well as me and there was no answer to her knock. The door was locked on the inside. She came straight to tell me, of course. We looked out the window and there was a ladder lying right there, on the grass under her room!"

I had heard similar stories before, and the way they were told mattered more than the words. Madonna Eva was neither terrified nor distraught. Madonna Eva was shocked, yes, but mostly she was *furious*.

Curious.

"We wakened Giro," she went on, "and sent him to look. He climbed in through Grazia's window. Her bed had not been slept in."

That, she seemed to think, was that, but then the Maestro began asking questions. No ransom note had been found or delivered. Nothing had been stolen and there seemed to be no clothes missing, or perhaps just a few minor garments. Her jewels had gone, but "only the trinkets she kept in her room; her pearls were still in the usual safe place." Even in its wild distress, the family had thought to check that.

And Giro?

"My son Girolamo," Zuanbattista explained, "minister for the navy."

"And who else lives in the house?"

Sanudo's pause was not quite long enough to be called a snub, but enough to imply nicely that he had not come to Ca' Barbolano to be interrogated by a foreign-born mountebank physician. "Her aunt, Madonna Fortunata Morosini, and three servants—Fabricio our gondolier, Pignate my valet, and the ladies' maid Noelia, mentioned earlier."

That was a small household for a man of Sanudo's high station, even in Venice, where land is at a premium and the nobility have a long tradition of thrift. Even today it is not uncommon to see senators buying their own vegetables in the Erberia. Possibly the Sanudos had other servants coming in during the day, or the ladies' maid might also clean silver, the gondolier just love gardening, and the valet like to dress up as a footman. Aunt Fortunata might even adore cooking.

"And they are all accounted for?" the Maestro asked. "No one else in the household is missing?"

"No one," Sanudo said firmly. "I fail to see the need for all these questions, *lustrissimo*. We came to consult you because you have a reputation as a seer. Can you tell us where our daughter is?"

"No, Your Excellency." The Maestro stretched his face in a close-lipped smile. "I may or may not be able to see where she will be at some point in the very near future. The questions are necessary if I am to have some idea of what I am looking for. Now, a strange thing to ask a man in your distinguished position, but have you informed the *sbirri*?"

"We don't want any scandal," the lady said firmly, with a glare to scare Medusa. Her reaction was reasonable in one who dreamed every night of becoming *dogaressa*.

Her husband's expression was cryptic. "I have little faith in the local constabulary. Nor do we want to put our daughter in danger."

That a ducal counselor would hesitate to involve the ineffective *sbirri* I could understand, for they are less use than wheels on a seagull, but what of the Council of Ten? The abduction of a ducal counselor's child was an obvious threat to the security of the Republic, a crime it both could and should investigate. Sanudo must be seriously at fault in not reporting his problem immediately. True, the full Ten would not meet until late in the day, but the three chiefs are always on duty in the Doges' Palace. They could order *Missier Grande* to start wheels turning—setting a watch on the ferries, and so on. Why not?

"That is good," the Maestro said, nodding so the wattles of his neck flapped. "An official investigation would make my seeing much harder."

"Why? How?"

"Please trust me on that, *clarissimo*. Clairvoyance is very hard to describe. Does your daughter have any romantic attachments?"

"Certainly not!" her mother said indignantly. "She never leaves the house except to take Communion, at Easter and Christmas. Even at Celeseo she did not walk in the grounds without madonna Morosini or I in attendance."

I could not see the Maestro's expression, but his tone expressed mild surprise. "She was not convent educated?"

"My husband's duties for the Republic have involved him in much traveling for the last few years. I chose to live in our house in Celeseo, near Padua, and keep Grazia with me for company. The country is healthier for a growing child. Grazia is extremely well versed in the classics and arts. Fortunata has tutored her."

"So when did you return from the mainland?"

"Is this relevant?" *sier* Zuanbattista demanded.

"Perhaps not," the Maestro admitted, but it would be very relevant if the young lady had run off with a lover she had met on the mainland. "Suffer me that one question, madonna?"

"At the end of July."

"No wedding plans?"

"We—"

"Nothing decided," Sanudo said quickly. "We have had some discussions."

"Of course," the Maestro said with a dry chuckle, "it takes two to elope, and if you suspected she had an accomplice, you would have investigated him before coming to see me." He waited for a confession, but none appeared. "So you want me to find and recover your missing child?"

"Can you?" they said together.

The Maestro gestured with one hand. He has very small hands. I could guess at his expression of unruffled confidence. "I have succeeded in similar cases in the past."

And men had been exiled as a result. I was confident that he was playing with his visitors out of plain nosiness, because he had promised me he would never again meddle in elopements. I was confident by then that Grazia had eloped and her parents knew who had been holding the ladder. Nostradamus also knew that, so in a moment or two he would tire of the game and demand a fee of three hundred ducats; I would show the visitors out, and that would be that.

"Just tell us where she is and we will fetch her," her father said.

The old man sighed. "If possible I would certainly do that, but prediction is not so predictable, paradoxical as that seems. I would do my best and my fee would be contingent on results."

"We must have no gossip or scandal," madonna Eva repeated.

"That objective is secondary to your daughter's safety, surely? I mean, the paramount aim is to return her, safe and sound, to the bosom of her family?"

"Of course." She sounded neither convinced nor convincing.

"Her date of birth, if you please, with the exact hour and minute if you know them?"

They did. I wrote it down. Grazia was fifteen, and thus in the pride of desirable maidenhood, as nubile as they get.

"Have you a recently painted portrait or miniature of her?"

The Sanudos exchanged glances. He said, "We have a family group, painted three years ago. It is too big to transport easily and she was only a child then."

The Maestro shrugged. "Describe her, please."

The woman said, "Grazia is vivacious, nimble. She sings and dances and is remarkably intelligent. She has a marvelous complexion and her eyes are just amazing. She looks even younger than her years, because she is so petite."

Her father smiled ruefully, as if amused by his wife's equivocation. "She is small and skinny—quite pretty, but her nose is too large for classical beauty. She does have wonderful eyes, I agree, and an endearing smile, but Titian would not have painted her."

His wife pouted but did not protest this vapid praise.

The Maestro sighed. "Thank you. A frank and helpful answer. What fee are you offering?"

His Excellency's angular, stony face seemed to petrify even further. "What is your usual charge?"

"You want me to put a price on your daughter?"

"A fee to do what?" *Sier* Zuanbattista's tone had chilled considerably. "To tell us stories of how she has been spirited away to the Sultan's harem?"

"If I produced proof, Your Excellency, even that would be an improvement on your present uncertainty. I expect no payment for my unsupported word."

"To help us get her back, safe and unharmed!" madonna Eva said, "a thousand ducats!"

I swore under my breath. The lady had sensed the Maestro's reluctance. The old miser would never resist such a bribe. A thousand ducats is a fortune; it is almost fifty times the legal annual wage of a married journeyman laborer.

In a notable breach of tradition, Sanudo raised both eyebrows. "I think we had better define the terms of this contract very carefully."

His wife glared at him. "You think I would grudge it to have my child back? If you will not pay it, *messer*, I will sell my mother's jewels."

"It is acceptable," the Maestro said. "I have charged more, but you did well to consult me so promptly." He had never earned a fraction of that on a missing person case since I had known him. "Returned safe and in good health, one thousand ducats."

There was a significant difference in wording there, depending on how one defined "unharmed," but *sier* Zuanbattista nodded. "Failing which, for proof of her whereabouts, one hundred."

"Very fair. *Clarissimo*, madonna, the sooner I get started, the sooner I should be able to tell you something." The Maestro gripped the arm of his chair and I rose to fetch his staff.

"How soon?" the woman demanded, rising.

"An hour, maybe two. I will send *sier* Alfeo with news as soon as I have some."

2

The Maestro's infirmity excuses him from excessive formalities. Normally I show his visitors out and am tipped a *soldo* or two for my pains. I rely on those tips. At the end of my seven-year apprenticeship Nostradamus will pay me my accumulated salary of seventeen ducats, but until then he provides only food, shelter, and a minuscule clothing allowance. In this case he had revealed my rank, so I had to behave like a noble, bowing low to Sanudo at the top of the stairs, waiting to exchange bows again when he reached the first landing, then going out on the balcony to bow farewell as they departed in their gondola. And no tip.

And only one gondolier? Most rich folk employ two boatmen, one fore and one aft. Of course good servants are hard to find and if the Sanudos had only recently opened their home in Venice, they might still be building up their household.

I went back into the atelier, where Nostradamus had disappeared into his chair again. He was thinking, tugging his beard, but not so lost in thought that he was unaware of my return.

"How did you happen to know the woman's name?"

I explained. He frowned when I mentioned Eva's brother, Nicolò, the publisher.

"The girl . . . You cavort with girls of that age. What do you think?"

I folded my arms, not presuming to sit unless told to. "Master, I am much too old to interest girls of that age and have been for at least a month, but I'll bet your thousand ducats to a *soldo* that she went down that ladder of her own free will and they know it."

He scowled, well aware that I was right. "Why do you say that?"

"Because they waited until noon to come and consult you. Because they did not bring clever brother Giro with them. Because Zuanbattista did not run straightway to the Council of Ten. He doesn't want the other geriatrics laughing at him, but surely that means that he believes his daughter is in no real physical danger. You noticed he accepted your definition of 'unharmed'? You are not required to restore her maidenhead by magic."

"Do not be salacious!" Filippo Nostradamus is a prude.

"It's what he meant, though. They had a splendid marriage in view and Grazia prefers someone half the bridegroom's age." That seemed certain as holy writ. "The matter is urgent financially. The rich fiancé will call it off if he learns she has wallowed in another man's bed."

"You spend too much time at the theater watching hackneyed plays."

"Hackneyed because they are based on life, and life keeps singing the same old songs."

Few masters permit such back talk from their apprentices. Nostradamus enjoys it because it gives him an excuse to snarl and snap at me, although he would never admit that. "And in this romantic drama of yours, whose side is her mother on?"

What had he seen that I hadn't? "She wants no scandal, doesn't she? And her daughter back?"

"So she says." He smiled wickedly. "Her own husband must be twice her age, even now, and was three times as old when they were married. Suppose she doesn't want to see her daughter put through what she was put through? Who did you say was holding the ladder?"

I humbly admitted I had not seen that possibility. "And she aided her daughter's escape by talking her husband into coming to you instead of initiating a proper pursuit?"

That suggestion made him scowl. "Then she may be surprised."

"I've heard you say that you'll never take another elopement case."

Scowl became snarl. "Nicolò Morosini was a friend of mine."

No. Tiny Venice is the greatest book publishing city in Europe, and two men especially made it so—Aldus Manutius and Nicolò Morosini the elder. Both are long dead, but Nicolò's family maintained his interests and a younger Nicolò had seemed likely to surpass his great-grandfather. On the very first day of my apprenticeship, a man with a nose like the ram on a war galley had come calling on the Maestro to show him some books. Needless to say, I have not forgotten a moment of that day, and I well remember how the two men argued over the value of some manuscripts while I stood in a corner, supposedly grinding rock salt in a mortar, but mostly listening openmouthed as they so casually batted incredible prices at each other over crumbling wads of paper.

They had behaved far more like rivals than friends, so the Maestro was rearranging his memories to suit his present needs. The thousand ducats must have been irrelevant, because he did not mention it. Instead he said, "What is your logic on the missing Girolamo?"

"That he is still hunting for the unknown lover. They know who he is and they wasted half the morning trying to find him. I expect Giro is over in Cannaregio watching the gondolas leaving for Mestre. Aunt Fortunata is no doubt pacing the Molo, keeping her beady eye on ferries to Chioggia."

The Maestro nodded. "Not bad thinking, Alfeo." From him that was ardent praise. "Give me an hour. But no more! I know the minute my back is turned you will be plunging into lechery with that harlot of yours."

"In a whole hour I should be able to plunge several times," I said, making him pout at my continuing salacity. What he was really doing was giving me permission and orders to find out what more Violetta knew about the Sanudo family. He would deny that, of course, although he knows that she will never betray my confidence.

"She's been away, may not be back yet," I said wistfully. Sunday's negotiations at the theater had borne fruit in the form of a new patron, a wealthy commoner named Agostino Buranello, who had whisked her off to Padua on Wednesday so he could flaunt her at a wedding. I had been trying not to think about how she must be suffering.

Nostradamus rose and hobbled over to the slate-topped table that holds the big globe of rock crystal. I saw him settled on the stool, lit the lamp, closed the shutters, and left him staring into the crystal. I locked the atelier door behind me. The *salone* was filled with mouth-watering odors, but a thousand ducats carries a lot of weight. I headed for my room.

Mama Angeli rolled out of the kitchen to accost me. Mama is too good to be true and works hard to remain so. She is also larger than life, always seeming as if about to give birth to twins or triplets, which she does at frequent intervals, and she is a magnificent cook, a rarity in the Republic. The Maestro tolerates the cost of feeding her enormous family because he thereby retains the services of her husband Giorgio, our gondolier, plus a whole army of odd-jobbers. Six or seven young Angeli were leaking out of the kitchen behind her, curious to know who the fancy guy had been and what their employer was up to this time.

"You haven't eaten dinner yet!" she said in tones normally reserved for pronouncing death sentences.

My stomach responded in the same key. "I know," I added. "I am fasting for the good of my soul."

"*You?* You could starve to death a hundred times on your sins."

"I need to make room for a few more. The matter is urgent, Mama." I did not move away, because I sensed she had some problem to discuss.

She pouted. "Vettor was here. He is going to marry that girl!"

"Giacomina? A wonderful choice! She's a Virgo, which means purity and service."

Mama added more grooves to her pout. "Her dowry is only twenty-seven ducats!"

"But the children she will give him!"

That was better, yet Mama's eyes still gleamed suspiciously. "Children?"

"Many, many children. But he must marry her soon, while Venus is in the house of Leo. I'll work out the best possible day for the wedding so she will bear sons. If they wait until the moon reaches conjunction with the Pleiades, then it will be daughter, daughter, daughter . . ."

"You swear this?"

"The stars never lie. Now, please, I must go. See the master is not disturbed." I made my escape, knowing from Mama's rapturous smile that the news of many future grandsons would be down at the wellhead in the *campo* in no time and all over the parish by evening—all over Venice, very likely, for the Angeli clan forms a substantial part of the population.

The reason the Maestro had not ordered me to try the crystal with him is that it never shows me anything other than my next encounter with Violetta. This is a problem of youth, he says, but youth has its compensations. Furthermore, tarot works well for me, although it lacks the detail of clairvoyance. My deck's great age makes it extremely sensitive. The cards are shabby and dog-eared, the inks of the drawings almost rubbed away in places. I retrieved it from under my pillow and laid the spread out on my dressing table, a quick five-card cross.

The face-up card in the center defines the subject or question, and this time it amply confirmed my suspicions, for it showed Love, number VI of the major arcana, a couple holding hands with Eros aiming his arrows. I dealt the other four facedown and turned them over in sequence. The one below, representing the problem, was the king of coins. On my left, which is the subject's right, the helper or path was the Pope, Trump V. The objective or solution, at the top, was another trump, the World, number XXI. And, finally, the danger to be avoided was the knave of swords. With the possible and worrisome exception of that one, the reading was as straightforward as any I had ever seen. The presence of three of the major arcana made it powerful, but it could not tell me where Grazia Sanudo was at the moment.

Having tucked my deck away, I went to peek out at Number 96, the smaller house next-door. The leaded panes of my windows bear colored or prismatic glass so no one can see in, but I can peer out through a few clear gaps, and much pleasure I have of them. Number 96 is a bawdy house and on sunny afternoons the inhabitants gather on the rooftop deck, the *altana*, to bleach their hair. They are fully dressed, you understand, even to hats with no crowns, only wide brims to shade their faces and spread out their hair. The view is admirable all the same, and that day there were fifteen shapely nymphs gathered there. To my joy, fourteen of them were outshone by the radiant beauty of Violetta.

The *calle* dividing the buildings is very narrow, so my preferred way of visiting her is to remove a couple of loose window bars, squeeze through, and just jump. That saves me having to walk down forty-eight steps and back up sixteen to her apartment. I haven't died yet, although a couple of times the results have been in doubt for a freezing fraction of a second. I would not try it before witnesses.

I opened the casement. "Damsels!" I cried. "I am available to the highest bidder."

Were I to record their replies, the Vatican would add this book to the *Index Librorum Prohibitorum*.

"Your ribaldry fails to conceal your lust for my incredible virility," I said. "Just ask Violetta!"

"We did," they replied in chorus, as if they had been rehearsing.

Abandoning the unequal struggle, I quit the field and went down the conventional way to the watergate, where a lighter was tied up, either half-loaded or half-unloaded, but deserted during the midday break by all save a youthful Marciana watch-boy. There is no pedestrian *fondamenta* flanking the Via San Remo on our side, only a narrow ledge, along which an agile young man can work his way crabwise as far as the watersteps at the end of the *calle*. Another ledge beyond that took me to the watergate of 96, where I was admitted by Milana, Violetta's maid. Milana is tiny and has a twisted back, but she is ever cheerful and devoted to her mistress.

"My, you must have moved fast," I told her.

"The thought of seeing you inspired me, *messer*. Hurry, she is waiting for you."

That remark inspired me, so I took the sixteen treads at a run. Violetta Vitale is the most esteemed courtesan of Venice, and men squander fortunes for a single night with her. Her apartment is opulent, the bedroom most of all. With a silken bed standing on gold columns, walls adorned

with splendid art and crystal mirrors, it would not disgrace
a king's palace and she has entertained royalty there. Violetta works by night and I by day, but when she is at home
we often manage to meet around noon. Sometimes we just
talk. Not often, I admit, and that day she rushed to greet
me barefoot, with her hair still flowing loose. She had discarded the high-necked sleeved robe she wears to keep sunlight from darkening her creamy skin, and her silken
undergarments hid no secrets. She eclipsed even the three
naked goddesses looking down at us from Titian's magnificent *Judgment of Paris*.

"I came on a business matter," I protested. "I cannot
stay."

"It has been three days! I am insanely desperate for you,
Alfeo Zeno, and if you do not feel the same about me, then
you have some explaining to do."

She was right, of course, and actions speak louder than
words. Our embrace was fervent, almost frenzied, and no one
can arouse a man faster than Violetta when she is in her Helen of Troy mode. By the time her chemise slid down to join
my cap and doublet on the floor, I was ready to sweep her up
and carry her to the bed. Then she pulled back to stare at me.

Gazing into furious green eyes, I realized with dismay
that now I was holding Medea, who is dangerous, capable of
anything. I tried to pull her close again and she resisted.

"Business? Three days without me and you come here for
business?"

"I was teasing!" I protested. "Joking."

"Joking? Teasing? I will teach you to tease." Hands
clawed at my face.

In my reflex move to avoid damage, I released her. She
ran nimbly to the door. I followed without trying to make
myself respectable, because the only other person around
would be Milana, who must have seen many men wearing
much less than I was.

Violetta's dining room is small and intimate, of course, sized for two, and there she was already seated at the tiny table, pouring wine. Two steaming dishes of ravioli awaited us, so obviously she had set this up with Milana, who is a good cook, although not in Mama Angeli's class. Yielding to the inevitable, I finished removing my shirt to help even the odds and sat down beside her.

Medea was amused by my pretense of calm, knowing perfectly well how ignited I was. She picked up a savory morsel and leaned even closer to put it to my mouth. I accepted it, licked her fingertips, and reciprocated. Most wealthy Venetians have taken to eating with silver forks instead of fingers, a procedure that greatly amuses foreign visitors. Not my courtesan. She can make anything, even feeding, into foreplay.

We ate in silence for a few minutes. The ravioli was excellent. But when Violetta offered wine and I refused, she realized that I was serious. I was thinking of the knave of swords, of course, when I could think of anything other than those incredible breasts so close. Fencing and drinking do not mix.

"What sort of business?"

"Zuanbattista Sanudo."

Try saying that with your mouth full of shrimp ravioli.

Violetta popped another treat in my mouth. "Easy. The Sanudos are one of the oldest noble clans, claiming descent from doges of the ninth century. Zuanbattista has served on all the big councils—the *Collegio*, the Senate, the Forty, the Ten. Fought at Lepanto. Now he's had three years as ambassador to Constantinople and before that he led a special mission to Paris, triumph upon triumph. He's in the innermost of the inner circles. His first wife was a Marcello and his second a Morosini, meaning he married into two of the biggest families in Venice. He did well financially out of the second marriage, I believe. She was the sister—"

"Madonna Eva?"

"Correct. She or Zuanbattista inherited the publishing business. Likely they're planning to marry their daughter into another of the big clans."

"So he's a possible future doge, then?"

"When he's old enough. Even now, with his diplomatic record and strong connections in the Great Council, he's almost a shoo-in to be elected a procurator of San Marco as soon as there's a vacancy." She fed me again.

"Rich enough?" I mumbled.

She shrugged, a magnificent sight. "He owns huge estates on the mainland."

Our thighs and shoulders were touching. I was going mad.

"And how do you know that his wife dreams of being *dogaressa*?"

Medea laughed harshly, but the laugh ended as something much gentler. Diamond features softened to pearl and emerald eyes to the dark of a moonlit night. Helen was back.

"An entertaining young noble I met on the mainland. He made a bid for my affections. He was mad at Eva—a beautiful young wife abandoned by an ancient husband in pastoral tedium, and he *so-o-o* handsome."

"She was not responsive either?" I could guess that the young man's bid for Violetta had not been high enough, or she would not be discussing him.

"He never saw even the outside of her bedroom door, so he told me. She claimed she dared not risk her husband's political future with a scandal. As if anyone would care!"

"I care," I said, rising from the table. "And now I really must leave."

Medea flickered into view for a moment. "Don't you dare!"

I shrugged and turned for the door. I felt the terrazzo

floor shiver as she moved. Two soft arms went around me. Hands groped. I moaned and leaned back.

And so on. Fill in the details for yourself.

No, it was much better than that. Violetta is the finest courtesan in Europe.

Later, while we floated together in what the major poets refer to as postcoital euphoria, she inquired sleepily what else I needed to know. Violetta as Helen is the sexiest woman in the world, but that was not her voice. I peeked at her, nose to nose, and confirmed that her eyes had changed from dark to blue, from night to day. She was Aspasia again, ready to share political gossip.

"And Giro, the son?"

Violetta, you will recall, had pointed out that gentleman to me at the theater for no apparent reason, so I expected her to clam up at that point, because she will never discuss her patrons. She didn't.

"A lawyer." She sounded oddly uninterested. "Attended university at Padua, served on the *Quarantia*, elected to some minor post on the mainland." She paused, reflecting. "He never seemed to care much about politics and they stopped electing him, until last month when they suddenly made him a minister. There were rumors that he wanted to refuse."

"He couldn't!"

"Not without the Great Council slapping a huge fine on him. They were really honoring his daddy, I heard."

It may seem odd that Venice would honor a man by electing his son to an office he did not want, but it does happen. The Great Council can be even more perverse than that, as for example, when it is angry at the doge and keeps on nominating his relatives to posts just for the satisfaction of voting them down.

"Giro himself's a nonentity," Aspasia said dismissively. "I'll ask around. Tell me why you need to know."

Fair's fair, although I knew that the reaction was bound to be stormy.

"Zuanbattista's daughter may have been kidnapped."

Violetta lurched upright, rocking the bed like a minor earthquake. "Or may have run away?" Claws flashed.

"That's certainly possible."

"You let her be, Alfeo Zeno, or I'll never speak to you again!"

Medea was back and I was in imminent danger of losing my eyeballs or worse.

"Even if she's been trapped by some predator?"

"And you will decide which, of course? You won't let her opinion count at all! Just a stupid, lust-ridden flibbertigibbet, you think, whose life has to be organized by men?"

I had no answer to that, because an apprentice must obey his master and madonna Eva had bought mine for one thousand ducats.

3

Dinnertime was over and a dozen men and boys of the Marciana family were back at Ca' Barbolano's water-gate, busily unloading the lighter, but not so busy that they failed to notice my emergence from 96. I worked my way along the ledge and fled upstairs pursued by much jealous ribaldry. A man cannot smile at a girl in San Remo without the entire parish discussing what he is up to—usually in intimate detail.

Armed with a glass of water from the kitchen, I returned to the atelier. The Maestro had made his way back to his favorite chair, but he was hunched over and shrunken, obviously in pain. Clairvoyance is an ordeal for him, leaving him drained and incapacitated, sometimes for days. He sipped the water, passed it back to me, then again bent over and held his throbbing head in both hands.

"What did I see?" he mumbled.

I went over to inspect the results, the scrawl chalked on the slate table. His writing is atrocious at the best of times; when he is foreseeing it can become totally illegible, even to me, and he never recalls what he has written.

"Impressive," I said. "Almost legible and the words make

so much sense I fear I must be missing something." Clarity normally means short-range prophecy, as this one seemed to be.

> *Where the fish stands on a shore of wine and no flags fly,*
> *Why does a black swan wear a white collar?*
> *Amid a hundred bronze mouths the great one is silent.*
> *Steel will ring louder and tears must flow.*

He grunted. "Tomorrow."

"That's how I read it, master."

The news would sound a bitter note in Ca' Sanudo. Give the girl a night away from home with her accomplice and "unharmed" would mean less than her mother was hoping. For my part, I disliked the mention of steel ringing. At least the quatrain mentioned tears flowing, not blood, but drawn swords automatically increase uncertainty and thus blur foresight.

The Maestro was aware of that also, of course, since he had taught me. "You need not do this, Alfeo," he mumbled. "Unless you want to."

"Good! It sounds far too dangerous. I won't."

He looked up in dismay, visualizing a thousand ducats subliming away like his sulfur crystals.

I laughed to put him out of his misery. "If you had thought there was one chance in a million I was going to say that, you wouldn't have made the offer, right? Of course I'll go. I am the knave of swords who stands between the lovers and the world."

"What?"

"Tarot."

He grunted again and heaved himself upright. I handed him his staff. He seemed steady enough, so I left him to thump his way across to the door while I headed for the desk.

"We need a contract," he said as he left. "And her father's authority."

"Italic, roman, or gothic?"

He slammed the door without answering, so I trimmed a quill to write italic.

Giorgio and I trotted downstairs to sea level and stepped out into the gondola. "That way," I said, making myself comfortable on the cushions in the *felze*. "Ca' Sanudo."

"Which one?" Giorgio Angeli is a wiry little man with the strength of a horse. He adjusted his feathered gondolier's cap and set his oar in the rowlock.

"Zuanbattista."

"Don't know it."

I turned to peer up at him in amazement. "I thought you knew every building in the city."

He shrugged, pleased but rueful. "Venice has more Sanudos than seagulls. I can ask."

A stroke of his oar sent us off along the Rio San Remo. It is a quiet little backwater canal, but on a Saturday afternoon it had traffic enough, and it had the timeless beauty of Venice, where every building is different, shining in dancing, ethereal reflected light, never the same from one moment to the next. Voices shout greetings or ribaldry, others sing. People going by in boats call to people in windows or on bridges, but there is never the clatter of hooves or rattle of carts that mar other cities.

Giorgio pulled up close behind a gondola going in our direction and shouted, "Giro?"

The gondolier looked around and said, "Ey? Giorgio!"

Obviously this was not the same Giro—noblemen elected to the *Collegio* do not row gondolas on Saturday afternoons, nor any other time. This Girolamo did not know the Ca' Zuanbattista Sanudo either, so he shouted to another

boat going the other way. I hastily closed the curtains on the
felze, but I could not disguise my gondolier and it would
soon be all over the parish, if not the city, that Master Nostradamus's henchman Alfeo was looking for Zuanbattista
Sanudo.

The third man asked advised us that the palazzo we
needed was the old Ca' Alvise Donato in Santa Maria Maddalena parish, over in Cannaregio. There are even more Do-
natos than Sanudos in the Golden Book, but Giorgio knew
the house and shouted thanks. If *sier* Zuanbattista had just
bought himself a grand new mansion, he must have done
well in Constantinople.

"I'll need you tomorrow morning," I said. "Early. Bruno,
too."

"Good cause?" Giorgio paused from eyeing the canal
ahead to give me a shrewd, appraising look. He has seen the
murky labyrinths into which my work for the Maestro can
lead me.

"A very good cause," I said firmly. But was it? I was going to make at least one person utterly miserable. The man
might be a seducer and predator but more likely was just a
crazy young lover like me. I would return Grazia to the unwelcome attentions of the king of coins, whoever he was, or
condemn her to lifelong imprisonment in a convent, but her
swain faced even more terrible consequences.

Nowhere is far from anywhere in Venice. I recognized the
Sanudo arms of anchor and swan on a gondola tied up at
some public watersteps, and Giorgio pointed out the house
about three doors along. The arcades of rounded arches in
white Istrian stone marking the ground floor and *piano nobile*
were in Byzantine style, so it was probably at least three hundred years old. It was also much smaller than I expected and
squeezed between two larger buildings, an odd contradiction

of Violetta's judgment that Sanudo might possess enough wealth to serve as doge. Some junior government posts pay a stipend but the senior ones do not. Some bring a severe financial burden, which reserves them for the rich. Perhaps Zuanbattista was merely observing the old republican tradition of frugality.

I banged a big brass knocker in the shape of an anchor. The door swung open almost at once, as if someone had been waiting for me, and the opener was no mere servant, but Minister Girolamo himself, the man Violetta had pointed out to me at the theater. Nobles shed their formal robes at home, and he was dressed like any other rich man, in breeches and hose, doublet and cape, with a fashionable white ruff, although the outfit was less colorful than most and of humbler stuff than the silk I should have expected. It seemed odd for a man of his age and station.

Hand on heart, I bowed, but he spoke before I could.

"*Sier* Alfeo?"

"*Sier* Girolamo, Maestro Nostradamus sends me with good news, *messer*." Goodness always depends on one's point of view. I would rather have delivered bad.

"Then you are doubly welcome to our house. Come and comfort my parents. My mother is anxious for word." I heard a hint that the Sanudo menfolk were humoring the foolish woman. "You know where Grazia is?" He bowed me in and almost rushed me along the hallway to the stairs.

There were no heaped bales and kegs of merchandise in Ca' Sanudo, as there were in Ca' Barbolano, but the walls were lined with bookcases all the way to the end and the floor was cluttered with crates, a few of which stood open, revealing that they contained books. The air was sickly with the odor of wood, varnish, and leather. This was a major library, many times larger than the Maestro's, but of course Zuanbattista had inherited the estate of his publisher brother-in-law.

"My master has foreseen her," I said, reluctant to have to tell the story twice. In fact, of course, the quatrain had given me a fair idea of where Grazia had gone and certainly the Maestro had seen that also, but the prophecy said to wait for her tomorrow on the Riva del Vin, so that was our best chance of apprehending her.

Giro mumbled something about not being properly settled in yet as we reached the midpoint of the hall and turned to climb the stairs. The treads were dished by centuries of feet, and slightly tilted. That is typical of Venice, built on the mud of the lagoon; everything sags after a century or two.

"It is astonishing," he said, probably meaning clairvoyance.

Of course lawyers are trained not to be too human or too trusting. What could be more alien to them than clairvoyance? If we all had it, they would all be out of work. If Giro himself was at all surprising, it was that he seemed surprisingly nondescript for a *nobile homo*. His hose covered spindly calves; his shoulders were narrow, his face, voice, and manner equally uninspired. Violetta had called him a nonentity.

We turned at the mezzanine level and a second flight brought us to the *piano nobile*. More crates stood around there, several of them too large and flat to contain anything other than paintings. Among them stood pedestals and busts, and a couple of freestanding statues, awkwardly placed. The Sanudos were still in the process of moving into their new city home.

Amid this transient clutter stood our host, smiling through his forest of beard. He, too, had discarded his formal robes, and he greeted me as an equal, which was an astonishing concession to my humble station. No aristocratic reserve there—*Sier* Zuanbattista was probably even more of a skeptic about clairvoyance than his son, but I was a guest and he had a politician's slant on life. By the time he was ready to make his play for doge, I might be a voting member of the Great Council.

"My wife is lying down," he explained. "She is very distressed, as you would expect."

Distressed enough to throw away a thousand ducats; distressed enough for him to keep her well away so she couldn't increase her offer.

A house clamped between its neighbors could have no windows along the sides. He led me to the rear and ushered me into a fine *salotto*, where several fine bronzes looked happily at home and seven paintings screamed at me to come and admire them. I also wanted to gawk at the ceiling decorations and the terrazzo floor design and even the furniture, which I rarely notice. The full-length windows stood open on a small balcony, providing welcome air on a sweltering day and a fine view of a surprisingly spacious and well-tended garden. I already knew the Ca' Sanudo had a garden, of course, but the sight of it raised my appreciation of the house. It was old and small, but exquisite as a reliquary.

"*Sier* Alfeo Zeno," my host proclaimed loudly, presenting me to a heap of laundry in a large chair, "Maestro Nostradamus's assistant. Madonna Fortunata Morosini."

The laundry nodded without taking her eyes off the crucifix she clutched in both hands on her lap. She was old and her all-black garb was normal widows' wear, but her face was swarthy, slashed and corroded by a million sour wrinkles, as if her life had been an endless series of disappointments, like the devil's mother's. Had I been a girl of fifteen summers with this Fortunata hag as my chaperone, I would have thrown her out the window instead of myself.

"Pray be seated, *sier* Alfeo," Zuanbattista said. "Now what news?"

Giro remained standing. Fortunata just stared at her crucifix. I would be the highlight of her next confession.

I said, "The Maestro has foreseen your daughter, Excellency. He is confident that we can intercept her."

"Go on! Where?"

"'When?' is more to the point," I said. "The Maestro foresaw me accosting her in a certain public place early tomorrow morning."

The two men exchanged pouts.

"But where is she now?" Giro demanded.

"That was not revealed to him."

"Go back and tell him to try again!"

"He could not, not today. He is exhausted. Believe me, Your Excellencies, I have tried many times to see visions in the crystal as he does. I rarely succeed, and when I do I expect my head to explode with the pain."

My admission made them squirm. The Church might burn me for it. Old Fortunata crossed herself, an unexpected movement proving that she was still with us in this vale of tears.

"That is illogical!" Giro complained. "Why can he foresee tomorrow and not today?"

Nostradamus may risk brushing off a patrician's questions, but I do not have an international reputation to protect me. "The way he has explained it to me, Excellency, is that there are many possible futures. The Lord gives all His children free will. There is a future where you decide to go to early Mass on Sunday, and a future where you go later, yes? There may be others, but only one of them will come to pass. The ideal situation would be that whoever has taken your sister has firm plans to remain in one place for a while, or be in some place at a certain time—a rendezvous, say. You see? Then one future is much more likely than the others and my master can foresee it and advise on appropriate action. If anything interferes to upset their plans, then the image blurs and disappears, like a canal reflection when a gondola goes by. Does that make sense?"

"No. Where is she now? She must be somewhere."

"Certainly, but the Maestro has to discover where that is. She and her, um, captors may be drifting aimlessly in a boat on the lagoon. Or she may be tied up in a dark attic—" My listeners hastily crossed themselves. "Either way my master might see her in his trance and still be unable to tell where she is. Whereas it is also possible that they have made an appointment to meet someone tomorrow at a certain time and place. Is that still illogical?"

"No," Giro admitted. "That makes sense." He meant that it was a plausible excuse, not that he believed it.

I noted that no one had asked me to define *they*. He might be thinking *kidnappers*. More likely we were all agreed on *lovers*.

"I will tell my wife the good news." Zuanbattista departed.

"Of course I will come with you tomorrow," Giro announced.

"That would be inadvisable," I countered. "Suppose, for instance, that the malefactors recognized you before Grazia arrived?"

Cold winds of suspicion blew while the lawyer considered this objection. I wished he would sit down and not loom over me. I pressed on.

"I have brought this letter of agreement. If I do not bring your sister home safely within three days, or at least supply proof of her whereabouts, your parents owe the Maestro nothing." Just in case he might think that we had been in on the plot from the beginning, I added, "Your sister will explain what happened and who abducted her."

I had a momentary nightmare of a spiteful and unwilling rescuee declaiming, *And after Zeno had done his worst, Maestro Nostradamus carried me down the ladder on his shoulder . . .* For now, though, the Sanudos had to trust us or dismiss us. Giro knew that and had nothing left to lose, for the terms were more than fair, even if the price was not. I passed over the two copies of the contract, emblazoned with the Maestro's seal and a signature more beautiful and imposing than any he could have done himself.

"And you will be able to identify the man with her?"

Man, not *men*, I noticed. A man Giro already knew, I strongly suspected. Had Grazia done something utterly appalling like running off with a tiler or a gardener? The family's reputation would be ruined for evermore.

"I do not expect to," I said. Did he think I hobnobbed with members of the kidnappers' guild? "My efforts will be entirely directed to rescuing your sister. I have also brought this letter for your father to sign, giving me authority to bring her here, because I do not wish to be arrested in place of the genuine kidnappers."

His father swept back into the room, a vastly more dynamic presence than his colorless son. "My wife is much relieved and sends her thanks. Your master inquired about a likeness." He indicated the wall behind me.

I rose and inspected the family portrait, but it told me nothing useful. Zuanbattista, Eva, and even Giro looked much as they still did. Grazia was only a wide-eyed child, as her father had said, impossible to imagine as a temptress inspiring a lover to insanity. It was an insipid piece of work, and a more skilled artist would have concealed Grazia's excess of nose better.

I would much rather have spent half an hour examining the *Madonna and Child* next to it, which I thought might be a genuine Jacopo Palma Vecchio. The model had certainly been Palma's daughter, Violante, but as I dragged my eyes away from it, on the adjoining wall I spotted both a face and a style I knew.

"Andrea Michelli!" I exclaimed. "Commonly known as Vicentino?"

"Indeed, you are correct, *sier* Alfeo." Zuanbattista sounded impressed, as he should be.

I could do even better. "I have never seen a wedding portrait by him, *messer*, but surely the bridegroom is Nicolò
Morosini?"

"You knew Nicolò?" This time his surprise meant I was
too young.

Time rolled back, and again I was looking at Nicolò, exactly as he had been that first morning of my apprenticeship, epic nose and all—that was where Grazia's curse had
come from. At his side a glorious beautiful, succulent young
bride. I tore my eyes away.

"I saw him once, *clarissimo*. It was six years ago, only
weeks before his sad death."

"The book was cursed!" This unexpected croak from Aunt
Fortunata made me jump—she was still not dead? Nicolò
died of a rotting finger, and popular superstition at the time
attributed that to a paper cut he had received when han-
dling a forbidden book, one of the titles on the *Index*.

"So it is said, madonna," I replied.

I caught *sier* Zuanbattista studying me. Assuming that
he was wondering whether I believed such twaddle, I looked
noncommittal. Before either of us could comment, the hard-
headed family lawyer brought us back to cold reality.

"I think you may safely sign both these documents,
Father. I admire the penmanship. Who is the Maestro's
scrivener?"

I bowed.

Giro bowed back. As his father headed to a desk in the
corner, he added, "Is there anything else?"

"The garden. I should like to see how the abductors
gained access to the house." I also wanted to search Grazia's
bedroom for signs of forced locks or love letters under the
mattress, but I knew I would never be allowed in there. The
grounds I might manage.

"Why?" Giro snapped, in his first sign of human emotion.
"What has that to do with Nostradamus and his crystal ball?"

"Nothing," I said as blandly as I could, "but it might limit the damage to my skin tomorrow. I hope I can find footprints to tell me how many men I may find myself up against. Will I need to enlist companions? And the ladder," I continued before he could interrupt. "I assume that they brought the ladder with them? It normally takes two men to carry a ladder long enough to reach a Venetian bedroom. Unless your sister slept on the ground floor?"

He frowned at my jibe, for only servants and the very poor live in sea level dampness. "I have already looked. The grass is dry after the heat. There are no footprints."

"I will show *sier* Alfeo the garden," Zuanbattista said as he brought back the letters, shaking sand off his signature. "Go and reassure your mother."

Giro and I bowed our farewells. I expressed gracious wishes for future good fortune to Fortunata, who did not react in the slightest, and was escorted out by Zuanbattista. He escorted me down to the *androne*, for Ca' Sanudo evidently lacked an exterior staircase, a feature of most Venetian courtyards. It did have a well in the center, for courtyards overlie cisterns, lined with clay and filled with sand to filter rainwater, although nowadays everyone except the poor drinks imported water from the Brenta River. The Sanudo yard was a garden, small but well planned. A century ago, it might have grown vegetables and held chickens, but now it was given over to flowers and fruit trees. The adjoining houses overlooked it on either side, the far end was closed off by a wall with a gate, and I could hear voices going by along the *calle* beyond.

The ladder had been laid against the house wall. It looked brand new and was short enough that one man could carry it, although the *Signori di Notte* would certainly stop and question anyone lugging a ladder around the city by night. It was also short enough to fit in a standard-sized gondola.

"The watersteps three houses along in that direction, *messer*," I said, "they can be reached from the gate?"

He nodded.

"And your daughter's window?"

The ducal counselor pointed to a window at the mezzanine level, under the twin balconies. The ladder would probably reach that far, but the casement was protected by an iron grille. Madonna Eva had testified that her son had climbed through it, and her husband not only knew that, he knew I knew that. Clearly the ladder was useless for gaining entry to the house itself.

I carried it to the far end and confirmed that it was a good fit for the garden wall. There were marks in the flower bed to show that someone had entered that way, bringing the ladder over with him. Only one man, so far as I could tell, with feet larger than mine. The intruder had carried the ladder to the house so he could climb up and tap on the window. Grazia had gone down, either to let him in or join him in the yard, and they had left by the front door or the gate. In the morning Giro had certainly not entered by the window, so either his sister had not locked her bedroom door behind her or her mother had possessed a duplicate key. I returned with my burden and laid it where I had found it. Then I inspected the door.

"If the bolts were properly closed for the night, *clarissimo*," I said, dusting off my hands, "then either the villains had help within your household, or your daughter may have been deceived into admitting them."

"Young girls without knowledge of the world may be very gullible," Sanudo admitted.

And some noble mothers are not above telling lies to tidy up a story.

Zuanbattista seemed to be studying the fruit trees. I waited, guessing that something important might be coming.

"It is strange to come home after three years abroad and find the child you once knew has become a young woman you do not."

"Without doubt it must be so, *clarissimo*."

"There are few names older and more honored in Venice than Zeno."

"I am aware of my burden."

Still he counted caterpillars. "I should hate to think that the son of the Marco Zeno who displayed such heroism at Lepanto had sunk to peddling nostrums to the gullible or fleecing distraught mothers."

"It would be unthinkable!" I snapped.

Now he did turn his gaze on me, the eyes of a man of overarching power. "You really believe you can find my daughter tomorrow, Alfeo Zeno?"

"By my ancestors I do, *messer*!"

"Then may our Lord and His Holy Mother be with you. And if you achieve nothing else, I beg you to tell Grazia that we love her and wish her to be happy."

Did madonna Fortunata think that way? Or madonna Eva? But *sier* Zuanbattista rose abruptly in my estimation. He might have wished to choose his son-in-law, but apparently he was not one of those moneygrubbing noblemen who condemn daughters to life imprisonment in convents just to preserve the family fortune for their brothers.

"I shall tell her if it takes my dying breath, *messer*," I promised.

4

I am not the greatest swordsman in the world. I rank third or fourth among the dozen in Captain Colleoni's Monday evening fencing class for young gentlemen. Most of the others are mere dilettantes, though, and there is a world of difference between recreational fencing and red-blood fighting. The great advantage I have over the playboys is that I have been in real sword fights and survived. I have bled, on occasion, but now I know I will not panic, and keeping your head is nine-tenths of a real battle. This knowledge was surprisingly little comfort when I was standing in a shadowy doorway on a misty, clammy dawn, and the world's greatest clairvoyant had warned me I was going to need my rapier. I shivered.

It was Sunday, so the great *marangona* bell in the Piazza San Marco had not rung to announce the start of the working day, but already the seventy or so parish bell towers were sounding for early Mass. This day, of all days, no laundry flapped from balconies and roof terraces. We had done everything we could to fulfill the prophecy and now it was up to Destiny to finish the job. I hoped she would do so soon, for the devout were setting out to church. Soon there would be crowds into which our quarry might disappear, and far too many witnesses.

I wore my rapier and dagger.

The henchman at my side was Bruno, our porter. Calling Bruno big would be like saying the sea is moist, but he is the gentlest of men, refusing to carry even a cudgel. He is a deaf-mute, so I had explained in the sign language that the Maestro invented for him: *Bad man—steal—woman. Alfeo and Bruno—find—woman—woman happy.* He has enough wits to recognize a good cause and had agreed to bring along the only weapon he will tolerate, Mama Angeli's largest flatiron in a canvas sack.

A path alongside a canal is a *fondamenta*, but make it wide enough for off-loading cargo and it becomes a *riva*. We stood in a doorway on the Riva del Vin, just seaward of the great Rialto bridge, the place the quatrain had named. On any other day this quay would be a buzzing hive of barges and lighters and gondolas, loud with abuse, banter, and complaint, but today it was deserted. The forest of striped mooring posts stood abandoned in the water, serving only as perches for yellow-eyed gulls, who stared suspiciously at us obvious intruders.

On the far side of the Grand Canal, the city's main street, lay the Riva del Ferro, backed by a wall of buildings, four, five, or even six stories high. The *traghetto* there was almost deserted, although one of the few boats lingering by it was the Maestro's, with Giorgio standing ready to hasten to our aid.

More gondolas plied the Grand Canal before us, standing well out to clear the marble arch of the Rialto. In my boyhood gondolas had been bright hued and flamboyant, vibrant with color and gilt, every *felze* sporting rich curtains and every hull proclaiming its owner's garish escutcheon. Alas, the Senate took offense at such blatant competition and decreed that gondolas should be plainer and plainer,

until now they are all black, with black curtains and black
leather cushions. Only a few trim items escaped the clammy
grip of uniformity, especially the rowlock and the post near
the bow that bears a lantern by night and a flower by day—
those posts are often gilded still—and private owners are allowed to display their arms on the left side of the boat.
Gondolas for hire show the Virgin or a saint.

Then came a gondola moving fast and bearing neither
flower nor lantern, but a white cloth tied around its bow
post so it could be identified at a distance. Black swan,
white collar, it glided in toward the watersteps in front of
us. Two people emerged from the calle del Sturion to my
left and walked swiftly across to meet it. They had not come
from the doorway of the Sturgeon Inn as I had expected, but
the Sturgeon is only the oldest and most famous of many
inns patronized by foreigners near the Rialto, and they
might have spent the night in a private house anyway. He
was tall, wearing a short blue cloak over an indigo doublet
and knee britches, and white silk stockings. He carried a
leather portmanteau. She did not come up to his shoulder,
but she was certainly not resisting him. In fact they were
holding hands and swinging arms in the sort of childish display that lovers use to warn other people away. I hoped
Bruno would do nothing reckless, but sign language cannot
convey such subtleties as, "The bad man may be only bad in
the eyes of the law and the girl may not be unhappy."

I ran forward. "Madonna Grazia Sanudo!"

The girl screamed. The man dropped his bag, flashed out
his rapier, and slashed at me like a madman. Rapiers are not
intended for slashing, but he was aiming at my face. I parried with my arm, then drew. Despite being forewarned, I
barely had time to go to guard before I was fighting for my
life. He was fast and had a significant advantage in reach,
but his technique was erratic and reckless. He had either
never taken lessons or, if he had, had forgotten them all in

the horror of being in a real fight. Captain Colleoni would have blistered him with derision.

"Stop it, you fool!" I said, more or less. I parried, parried, and parried, not riposting. "There are people watching!"

Then I recognized him, yelled, "Saints! *Danese?*" and narrowly escaped taking three feet of metal in my right eye. That did it. "Idiot!" I grabbed his rapier with my left hand and slammed mine down across his wrist. I used the false edge, but a steel rod can hurt without cutting.

He yelled and let go of his sword; his gondolier friend tried to smash my head in with his oar. Fortunately Bruno had seen the threat coming and arrived in the fight like a middling-sized earthquake. He snatched up the gondolier, oar and all, and without breaking stride bore him to the edge and threw him well out into the canal.

Grazia Sanudo screamed in fury and sprang at me, clawing for my eyes. I was forced to drop Danese's sword and grab her by the neck with my left hand to hold her off.

I shouted over her yells, "I intend no harm to Danese! Your father told me to tell you that he loves you and wants you to be happy."

She froze, glaring up at me with two of the largest, darkest eyes I had ever seen. They startled me. A man could drown in those eyes, had they not been so filled with rage and hatred. "You swear that?"

"I swear by all the saints. Danese has known me all his life, haven't you, old friend?"

Our ogreish abductor was clutching his right arm and trying to curl up without falling over. I released his wretched prisoner, who rushed to wrap herself around him with many cries of, "My darling, my lover, are you all right, my heart, my . . . whatever . . ." And so on.

Sickening.

"He broke my wrist!"

"You damned nearly killed me!" I retorted. I sheathed

my sword and retrieved his. Seeing that the fight was safely over, men were running in from both ends of the *riva* and also emerging from the *calle*. "Danese, old friend!" I detached the girl so I could embrace him myself. That, being a proper greeting in Venice, would hopefully discourage the busybodies starting to wander in around us.

I told his ear, "Let's get out of here before someone calls the *sbirri*. We can talk it over somewhere quieter." Releasing him, I said loudly, "I regret I frightened you, madonna. Your parents are very worried about you. I do have your father's written permission to take you home."

"I don't want to go home!" Her voice was larger than she was. "My father has no authority over me now. This man is my husband!"

"Yes," I sighed. "I know. Do you want to argue that to a magistrate? Now let's go before the *sbirri* get here." Taking him along was not part of the plan and would complicate matters considerably, but I knew him and had hurt him. Call me a softie, but I could not just abandon him.

Venetians are good Venetians first and good Catholics next, but most priests will marry a couple who threaten to embrace adultery—or embrace adulterously—no matter what the law says about parental permission. My tarot had told me what was brewing.

Giorgio had already brought the Maestro's gondola across and I urged everybody aboard. Danese was in too much pain to argue and the girl clung to him like tree bark. Their would-be gondolier had emerged from his bath. Had I thought that he was just a gondolier, I might have tipped him a lira for his trouble, but he had tried to brain me and I need all the brains the good Lord gave me. The fight had gone out of him; he did not try to block our departure.

A grinning bystander handed me the portmanteau Danese had dropped. I thanked him politely.

The girl went in the *felze*, of course, but when her evil

kidnapper tried to follow her I told him to sit on the thwart and trail his hand in the water to keep it from swelling.

"You think you're a doctor?" he snarled.

"Not quite, but that's the best way to ease the pain and stop it swelling." I clambered in beside Grazia, being careful to leave visible space between us. A grinning Bruno settled in behind the *felze*, raising our prow significantly, and of course Giorgio stood at the stern, wielding his oar.

I told him, "Ca' Barbolano please." The original plan had been straight to the Ca' Sanudo. He turned our stern to the Rialto and headed home.

Grazia was small, as I said, and seemed little older than she had in the family portrait. Her nose . . . Either Maestro Michelli had flattered his subject, or her nose had grown more than the rest of her since he painted her likeness. Truly she had her uncle Nicolò's nose and on a woman it was a disfigurement. Her body might just qualify for "sylphlike" instead of "skinny" but her complexion was unremarkable and there was an unwelcome trace of hardness about her mouth. Her dress looked childish and somewhat crumpled. But oh, her eyes! They almost atoned for everything else. Without her excess of nose they would have made her a beauty.

Danese I have already described. Normally he always seemed a little too conscious of his good looks, but just then he was more like a lemon, pale and bitter.

"Damn you, Alfeo Zeno!" he whimpered. "Why are you meddling in my life? And how did you find us?"

The first answer was, "One thousand ducats," and better not said.

"You have heard of the celebrated Maestro Nostradamus? Grazia's parents hired him to find her. I am his apprentice. I will take you to his home so he can treat your hand. And maybe we can talk this out. You do have a piece of paper with a priest's signature on it?"

"Of course we do!" the girl shouted at me, although we

were side by side. "What sort of a woman do you think I am?"

Young and incredibly gullible to fall for a fast-talking snake like Danese Dolfin, despite his luminous sapphire eyes and subterranean voice. "But you did not have your father's permission to marry, so you are married only in the eyes of the church, not under the laws of Venice."

Danese said, "But we are married." His sneer implied that he had made sure the Church would allow no annulment.

"Do you have the Great Council's approval?"

He went back to sulking without answering my question. His name would be struck from the Golden Book, but that would be the least of his worries if Zuanbattista Sanudo chose to lay charges. Then he would face exile, or three years in the galleys, or worse. The galleys are a slow death sentence, each year counted equal to two years in jail. Grazia would still be married and likely doomed to end her days in a convent.

Grazia sobbed at my side, her hands covering her face. She was hoping, no doubt that a lovable, romantic young man like me could never resist such an appeal, but she was miscalculating. I felt no impulse to clasp her in my arms and beg forgiveness. She was too young to light my touchpaper, and her fake tears merely made her seem more childish.

"Madonna," I said, "now that you are married, will not your family accept your husband and forgive? Your father did tell me that he loves you."

She muffled a couple of quite realistic gasps. "He should have thought of that before he ordered me to marry Zaccaria Contarini."

"What is wrong with Zaccaria Contarini?"

"He's old and ugly."

Now I knew the name of the king of coins. The Contarini

clan is one of the largest in the Republic, with scores of votes on the Great Council. That might account for Zuanbattista Sanudo's election to ducal counselor. With his own Sanudo clan, and marriage connections to the Marcellos, the Morosinis, and potentially the Contarinis, Zuanbattista would have about a hundred votes for the asking.

Grazia lowered her hands and fixed me with her lustrous eyes. They did not look as if they had been weeping much lately. "Who are you? I mean really?"

"I told you."

"An apprentice?" She glanced over my apparel and it did not impress her. "Look!" She pulled back a sleeve to reveal a bracelet of gold and amber. "This is very old. Byzantine work, from Constantinople. My grandmother left it to me. I'll let you have it if you'll let us go. It's worth two hundred ducats."

I thought maybe thirty or forty. They make them by the score on Murano. "It looks much prettier on you than it would on me, madonna. It probably wouldn't close around my wrist."

"You could sell it, you stupid boy!"

Danese curled his lip at me. "Don't try to bribe him, Grazia. You're wasting your breath. He's an idiot and always was."

Whereas Danese had always had an aye for a good offer.

Whether or not Grazia had been foolish to turn down a Contarini, I thought she had been utterly daft in her choice of alternative. A week before, at the theater, Danese had been dressed like a wealthy young patrician. That had not been a one-time extravagance or rags borrowed for the occasion, because his present outfit was even grander. Somehow he had come into real money. Not by marriage, unless he was a secret bigamist, and not from his sisters if they had all married artisans or laborers, as he had told me. Looks, birth, and money together work miracles for a man's eligibility.

Just because I had always found him insufferable did not mean that Grazia Sanudo was not entitled to worship his footprints. Nor did it mean that I wanted to see him chained to an oar for years on end.

My head and my heart were locked in battle. We could still report that the fugitives had escaped and hope that no details of the fight ever got back to the Council of Ten. The decision would be up to Maestro Nostradamus, but I could not imagine him passing up a thousand ducats.

5

As we disembarked, I signed Bruno, *Go quick—tell—Mama—lady—here.* He grinned and went charging up the stairs as if shot from a bombard. Grazia and Danese were entangled again and she was sobbing on his chest. I carried the bag and his sword.

The *androne*, where the business is done, was silent that holy day. We started up the stairs, passing the mezzanine apartments where the Marciana families live—Jacopo and Angelo are citizen-class partners of *sier* Alvise Barbolano. He contributes housing and certain trading rights restricted to the nobility; they and their sons do the work. We carried on up.

As we passed the *piano nobile*, where Barbolano himself dwells, Danese muttered, "You *live* here, Zeno?"

"I do." I did not mention cuisine or silk sheets.

He said, "Oh!" His eyes and mouth were round.

As we reached the top floor, Mama Angeli came scurrying along the great *salone* to meet us. I presented Grazia formally as "madonna Gracia Sanudo Dolfin," which produced a gasp of joy from her, followed instantly by a wail of despair. But Mama is not mother of half the world for nothing, and easily whisked her away for some feminine consolation.

I directed our other visitor to the left and marched him into the atelier. The Maestro was perched on his high stool at the alchemy bench, heating a brown fluid in an alembic over a brazier. He looked around in annoyance at the interruption. I closed the door behind us.

"Doctor Filippo Nostradamus," I said. "*Nobile homo* Danese Dolfin. *Sier* Danese and I used to fight over crusts from the garbage when we were cutie putti together in San Barnaba. Recently he has risen in the world, talked a priest into marrying him to madonna Grazia, and probably fractured his radial styloid process."

The Maestro said, "Tut! Careless of him. Show me your hand, *clarissimo*."

"I was trying to break your bravo's sword," Danese said as we approached the alchemy bench. "And how can a man be apprenticed to a doctor?"

"He can't," I said. "I am apprenticed to a sage, clairvoyant, alchemist, astrologer, and all-round philosopher, who also happens to be personal physician to the doge. If I ever need a degree in medicine, I shall go over to Padua and foresee all the answers in the finals before the professors have thought of the questions." I stalked across to the medical cupboard. "Plaster, master?"

"Just a bandage and a sling," the Maestro said. "At worst he has cracked the radius. It may need a cast in a day or two, when the swelling has gone down. You will live to fight again, *sier* Danese."

"He had better take more lessons first," I said. "Start talking, *messer*. How did you get rich?"

Danese glared stubbornly, but he was tense with fear. "What business is that of yours?"

"None. It is the Maestro's business, for he must decide what to do with you. We were not told your name, so our plan was to return Grazia to her parents and let you slither back into your hole, whoever you were. Now we have the alternative of sending them word that they can come and get her and you, too. Even if you still had your sword, which you don't, I could lock you up until Sanudo arrived with the *sbirri*. Yet another possibility, although a highly unlikely one, would be for the Maestro to let the two of you go free and lose his fee. So be persuasive."

The Maestro stared at me in outrage, wondering what I was dreaming of. Danese tried to fold his arms in defiance and yelped when he jostled his hand. I returned with the bandages.

"I'm not rich," he said sulkily. "If you're hoping to extort money from me, you're on the rocks. I had a well-paying job, is all. I gave it up for Grazia. We are madly in love. I love her more than life itself. We were heading over to, ah, a place on the mainland where I have friends."

"To starve?" I persisted.

"I can read and write. I'll find a job as a teacher, or a musician." He winced again as the Maestro started wrapping his wrist.

"What sort of job did you give up?" I demanded. "Teaching and writing didn't pay for those drapes."

"Mind your own . . ." He gave me a baleful look and the Maestro another, then remembered the power we had over him and shrank into a pathetic sulk. "I was a *cavaliere servente*."

I said, "Oh, my god! *For her mother?*" Even Nostradamus looked startled.

Danese flushed crimson. "No! Well, yes. But it wasn't like that! I fetched her fan and brushed her hair and fed her canary. I played the lute and sang to her, read her poetry, told her how beautiful she looked, squired her to recitals and viewings because her husband was away, and told her how beautiful she looked. That night you and I met at the theater I was hunting for her to tell her where her gondola was tied up. A *lapdog*, that's all—not what you're thinking."

Half the wealthy women of Venice employ handsome young men to dance attendance on them, but the duties normally extend to more intimate matters than any so far mentioned. Their husbands hire courtesans; why should they not employ gigolos? This is Venice. I could imagine Danese singing very well, with that deep rich voice of his. He would be very effective at whispering endearments into shell-like ears.

As he adjusted his patient's sling, the Maestro said softly, "I am somewhat amazed to hear that madonna Eva was stupid enough to keep her innocent, unmarried daughter sequestered in the same house as an exceptionally good-looking young man. That she would do so and also expect both of them to remain chaste I find incredible."

Danese grimaced. "Well, what if I was her mother's paid lover? Does it make you happy to hear me admit that, Alfeo? Most of the last three years she's been living at Celeseo and there's totally nothing else to do there except count ducks. A common gigolo, tumbling a fat old woman on demand? I worked hard for my pay, but I swear I did not prey on Grazia. I did not sink to that. We spoke of love, but we never as much as touched fingertips. Not until I found her weeping in a corner a week ago and she told me of the wedding plans. I kissed her—that's all, I swear! One kiss and I told her I loved her. Our first kiss. And right then her mother came around the corner and caught us."

I sighed at this romantic cliché. "Paolo and Francesca?"

"Who?"

"A literary allusion," I muttered, exchanging meaningful looks with the Maestro. The Sanudos had assured us that no household members were missing, but had not mentioned that one had been thrown out on his ear a few days earlier. Now we knew why the Sanudos were so insistent that there be no scandal. Grazia running off with a gardener would be a trivial misdemeanor compared to eloping with her mother's pretty boy. If Sanudo had promised his daughter to a Contarini and the daughter had preferred the gigolo, then the Great Council would roll in the aisles for weeks. It would be the scandal of the decade.

"What do you want me to do, master?" I asked.

The alembic had begun to bubble. Nostradamus's attention was wandering. He sighed angrily. "Is that the whole truth, *messer*? Did you purloin the lady's jewels when you left? Help yourself to silverware?"

"Nothing," Danese muttered, squirming in the nethermost pit of humiliation. "I give you my solemn oath. Grazia brought some jewels, but they're her own. I have a few trinkets Eva gave me. She let me take them and my clothes. That was good of her, but I had done my best for her until then. *Gesù*, had I ever! Grazia was a virgin until last night— *after* the wedding! She isn't now. What other prurient details entice you?"

I said, "The question is whether the Sanudos will accept you as her husband. Is that what you want? Or would you rather they just paid you to disappear?"

He flushed even redder. "If I had my sword—"

"You don't. I do. You got yourself into this," I said. "But I promise we won't turn you in. For old times' sake, I will not send you to the galleys."

He muttered, "Thank you, Alfeo," as if the words hurt. "I want Grazia to be happy. I love her, damn you! Have you never been in love? I want whatever she wants."

The Maestro was peering into the alembic. "Alfeo, take her home. I want my fee. I earned it."

Funny that I hadn't noticed him rushing to my defense on the Riva del Vin. "Yes, master."

"Negotiate anything else you like as long as it's legal. And hurry back because I have notes for you to transcribe."

That was ominous news. He probably meant he couldn't read his own scrawl and wanted the rest of my Sunday. I led the way out into the *salone* and closed the atelier door.

"Well, *clarissimo*?" I said. "*Sier* Zuanbattista really did tell me he wants his daughter to be happy. I don't know if that means he will accept her choice of sleeping partner, but it's up to you. You can trust him and come to Ca' Sanudo with us. Or you can head for the Mestre ferry and vanish into the sunset. You decide."

Danese dithered, looking everywhere but at me. "I want whatever Grazia wants," he muttered to the floor.

Looking tiny as a doll beside the great statues, Grazia was running toward us from the kitchen.

"You wait here," I told her husband. "I want to hear it from her own lips."

I strode forward to intercept her; she tried to dodge; I sidestepped to block her. We studied each other appraisingly. I had not veered from my first impression, that Grazia Sanudo was cast from the same hard metal as her mother. She was wondering how to play me, which should not be a difficult decision, given our respective ages and genders.

"Madonna, I must take you home. My master's orders. Do you want Danese to accompany us?"

She blinked several times, but no tears welled up in her magnificent eyes. "*Sier* Alfeo, how could you? You think I would marry a man yesterday and cast him off today?" She dropped her gaze and smothered a dramatic sob. Better, but she needed practice. She had never learned how to speak to men other than relatives or servants.

"No. But he may be taken from you. I told you the message your father sent. Do you trust his word? Will your parents accept Danese now?"

Another dry little sob . . . "You realize what they may do to him? You condemn me to a life sentence in a convent? You will send your childhood friend to jail or exile?"

"No. If you think that, he is free to go." Good riddance, mustn't say so.

She hesitated, chewing her lip. The tragic heroine role is hard for fifteen-year-olds. We both knew that if Danese walked out of her life now she would never see him again.

I was confident that whatever choice she made would be the wrong one. The previous day, just for my own amusement, I had cast Grazia's horoscope, using the date and time her parents had given the Maestro. The stars were very bad for her at the moment and had been for several days, with Mercury in the house of Virgo. Next weekend her fortunes should improve dramatically. Curiously, my own horoscope showed the reverse—good now, bad later.

"Your father said—"

"Yes, I know!" she snapped furiously. "I heard you. I always knew he would say that. Of course he will take me back! I never doubted it. But did my mother say the same? She's mad because Danese loves me and she thought he loved her!"

Both ladies had relied on information from the same source. Love makes fools of us all.

"Won't your father have final say? Why do you doubt?" I asked patiently.

"Because it's too soon!"

Ah! The Sanudos were supposed to suffer. "Would it help if I asked them for you?"

She melted. "Oh, would you? Please, *sier* Alfeo?"

Back down to the gondola we went. Grazia naturally took the place of honor, the left side of the *felze*, and this time I did not stop Danese from joining her. He wrapped his good arm around her and the two of them sat there like birds in a cage, scowling at me. Giorgio pushed off. Nobody said a word until we emerged from the narrow ways onto the Grand Canal.

Grazia had not given up on me yet. "How did you find us?"

"The Maestro foresaw you."

"That's witchcraft!" She appealed to her husband. "Isn't it, dearest?"

"Probably."

She tried her best tigress stare on me. "We shall report you to the Council of Ten!"

"Don't waste ink," I said. "Every year Nostradamus publishes his almanac and includes a dozen or so prophecies. Every year I deliver a copy for the doge and another for the cardinal-patriarch." I did not suggest that those esteemed gentlemen ever actually read the books, but they did not lay charges either.

"And can you foresee what my parents are going to decide about Danese?"

"The Maestro probably could, but he charges a lot of money for private predictions. I don't have the knack. I can cast horoscopes, though, and I drew yours."

She hesitated, but a desire to know the future stands very high in human wants. "And what did you foresee?"

"I saw your present trouble—which wasn't difficult, of course," I added quickly, foreseeing her sneer from the way her lip had started to curl. "But I also predict a dramatic improvement in your affairs about a week from now."

She turned and beamed at Danese. Danese was quick; he saw the ambiguity right away, but he turned his snarl at me into a smile at his wife.

"Then we may just have to be patient a little longer, beloved," he said.

I leaned forward and closed the curtains on them.

So we returned to the Ca' Zuanbattista Sanudo. Giorgio tied up alongside the family gondola and I left the lovers hidden in the *felze* while I set off to face the music for them. A footman opened the door, but he was young and broad

shouldered, and I recognized yesterday's gondolier . . .
Fabricio.

I gave my name and was escorted upstairs and to the
same *salotto* as the previous day. Zuanbattista stood with his
arm around his wife. Her antediluvian aunt had been moved
to another seat, but did not as much as twitch at my entrance, or indeed during my stay. Girolamo hovered in the
background.

I bowed. "*Messere*, madonna—Grazia is safe and I can go
and fetch her directly. I must inform you that yesterday she
performed the sacrament of holy matrimony with *sier*
Danese Dolfin."

Eva's mouth hardened like cement.

Zuanbattista sighed. "Your news is welcome. I hope no
daughter of mine would sleep with a man without the blessing of Holy Mother Church."

At their back, Giro merely shrugged, which for him was
a wild display of emotion. I gathered that the decision had
already been made.

"I confess," I said, "that I exceeded my instructions. By
coincidence, Danese and I knew each other as children. He
drew on me and I had to disarm him. I gave him my word
that I would not turn him in to the authorities. If you will
give me your word likewise, *messer*, then I can bring him
here also."

Eva showed her teeth and looked up at her husband as if
daring him to do any such thing. She had been made the
laughingstock of the Republic, the woman who lost her
daughter to her *cavaliere servente*. Dreams of being dogaressa
clad in cloth of gold had been dashed by a child's romantic
delusion.

"We do not want a galley slave in the family," Sanudo
told me. "You have my word as a Venetian nobleman, *messer*.
Go and fetch them both."

Good for him! I resisted the temptation to slap him on

the back, and bowed instead. "I brought them both with me."

The old man had guessed I would say that. I returned to the watergate with the Sanudos trailing at my heels. To my surprise, they even followed me out to the *fondamenta*, which was conveniently deserted. The *felze* blinds were still down, but as I approached I heard a girlish snigger, followed by a deep male chuckle. For the moment, at least, Grazia was happy.

"You can come out," I said. "The pasta is ready and the fatted calf won't be long."

Danese handed her ashore and watched her tumble into her mother's arms in an orgy of mutual hypocrisy. He followed and bowed warily to his father-in-law.

Feeling unwanted, I stepped aboard. "Home, Giorgio, please."

"Wait!" Zuanbattista's command knelled in the manner of one that must be obeyed.

"Clarissimo?"

He parted his jungle of beard long enough to display a smile. "I shall make arrangements to pay Maestro Nostradamus his fee. Meanwhile, this is for you, *messer*, for a job well done." He tossed me a purse, whose weight astonished me.

Noble is as noble does. I bowed so low I almost fell out of the gondola. He had my vote for doge.

6

And that, I thought, was that. The Sanudo affair was closed. When I got home I noted it in the casebook and entered one thousand ducats in the ledger under accounts receivable. Many members of the nobility, even the richest, are notoriously reluctant to pay their bills, and this fee was so outrageous that I could imagine myself haunting the Ca' Sanudo for months trying to collect it. I asked the Maestro if he thought he would ever see a *soldo* of it.

He scoffed. "Certainly! You think they want a lawsuit? It would cause the very scandal they tried to prevent. Besides, if word gets around that daughters in Venice are so valuable, half of them will disappear in the next month." So would he, if the Council of Ten decided he had extorted money from emotionally vulnerable parents, but I did not tell him so.

Although I feel I have risen a long way in the world, San Remo is not far from San Barnaba, and my encounter with Danese had reminded me of old friends I had not seen in too long. On impulse I walked over to attend Mass in the old church. I met numerous acquaintances, and in particular Father Equiano, who baptized me—many years ago by my count, just yesterday by his. He is elderly now, getting a little forgetful. Most of the parish work is done by younger men, but he is still well loved—and not least by those former youngsters, whether commoner or noble, in whom he recognized a spark. A priest has little time to call his own, but Father Equiano cheerfully sacrificed his leisure to introduce us to letters and start us on the long climb out of the pit of ignorance. For many he found promising apprenticeships, too.

I invited him back to Ca' Barbolano for dinner, as he is one of the few people whose company the Maestro enjoys and Mama's cooking is a great treat for him. While we walked I told him what I had been doing, without mentioning names. He smiled tactfully at the happy ending to the story. He did not state that it was he who had performed the marriage. There are many priests in Venice and I would have been astonished if Danese had even approached this one. They knew each other of old, and Equiano would not have been taken in by a slick smile and a mellifluous voice.

The thousand ducats had put the Maestro in a remarkably good mood. All through the meal he and Father Equiano discussed astrology, in which they are both expert, and in particular the strange heliocentric theories of Niclas Kopernik. I do not know if the earth turns, but those two soon had my head spinning. I left them still hard at it, and the Maestro did not mention the work notes I had to transcribe.

I went to visit Violetta. She was so pleased to hear how Grazia's wishes had carried the day that her demonstrations of gratitude lost me whatever divine credit I might have earned at church.

My euphoria was short-lived.

At supper that evening the Maestro kept peppering me with questions about the Sanudos, so I could barely get a bite to eat. When I mentioned that I had recognized Nicolò Morosini in the portrait, he looked startled and demanded an explanation. I reminded him about my unforgettable first day as his apprentice.

He shook his head sadly. "It seems only yesterday that he died."

It seemed like a very long time ago to me, but I didn't say so, and he was distracted enough to start reminiscing about the publisher as a book collector, which gave me a chance to eat. From there he wandered to the subject of art. He rarely shows any interest in either painting or sculpture, but he can talk knowledgeably on both of them when he wants to, which is quite typical of the man. Geniuses can be very wearing.

Then he took it into his head to instruct me, as he does sometimes, and in this case he chose an excessively obscure tract by Albertus Magnus. I would struggle to translate it, sentence by sentence, and then we would discuss what it actually meant, he quoting centuries of commentaries and analyses by half the sages of Europe. As an evening's entertainment it did not compare for excitement with watching the tide come in. It also gave me a raging headache, but I knew that I was receiving the finest education in the occult that the world could offer. Who knows when I may need to exorcize a kobold from a silver mine?

Nevertheless, I have seldom been happier to hear the downstairs door knocker. Three hours after sunset, when the curfew rings, the Barbolanos' antiquated watchman, Luigi, shoots the night bolts on the watergate. About the same time I do the same for our front door, but that night I had not yet done so, and Giorgio would be up in the garret, helping Mama stack children in beds. I excused myself and went out to peer down the stairwell while Luigi spoke through the hatch. If the caller wanted *sier* Alvise or one of the Marcianas, Luigi would go and tell them, but most late visitors want the Maestro, in which case the old man looks hopefully upward and waves if I am there. He waved. I waved back.

Trouble came plodding up the four flights of stairs, carrying his bag in his left hand. My face must have shown him just how pleased I was to see him, because his smile was uncertain.

"I brought a first instalment on your master's fee," he said hastily. "*Sier* Zuanbattista asked me to explain that he does not keep enough bullion around the house to pay it all at once."

"Very reasonable," I said, impressed to see any money so soon. "I can congratulate you on being welcomed into the family?"

Even his efforts to look modest turned out smug. "They're making the best of a bad job. The old man's being a little stingier than I had hoped on the dowry. That's Giro's doing, of course, but Grazia is working on them. I won't be going back to watermelon and polenta! There will be an intimate wedding, just a few dozen guests. October seventh. That's as soon as they can reasonably arrange it."

Even that was indecently short notice, socially speaking, but after the previous night there might be good reason to move things speedily along.

"Congratulations." Since his hand was in a sling I did not have to shake it. Danese had every excuse to be satisfied. Life stretched out before him as an unbroken paradise of silk sheets and *gelado*—San Barnaba boy makes good. From boy toy to wealth and influence; his future was assured.

"They'll get me into the Great Council right away and organize a political career for me—I've no talent for commerce. Rhetoric and elocution lessons."

"You certainly have the voice for it," I said, stalling for time. "You've seen the Hall of the Great Council?"

"Giro said the same thing. I've been told about it."

"About seventy paces long." Many good men have failed in Venetian politics because they could not make themselves heard in such a vastness. My mind shied away from an image of a thousand or more nobles sitting there listening to Danese Dolfin pontificate.

"I'll see you and the Maestro are invited to the wedding."

"He won't come, but I certainly will." I would take Violetta and bask in the massed jealousy of all the other male guests.

Having given the Maestro enough time to disappear, I led the way into the atelier. The second door, the one through to the dining room, is not exactly secret, but it needs a sharp eye to see it. Danese counted out ten gold sequins and I fetched the scales. The coins were full weight, so I made out a receipt for twenty-seven ducats, four lire. I wrote it in my finest *Cancellaresca Formata* hand, just for a change, and sealed it with the Maestro's signet.

"Very pretty!" he said. "You ever need a job as a scribe, just let me know."

"Thank you." I would rather jump off a bell tower. "Anything else?"

"Well . . . Yes, there is." Danese turned on his most unctuous smile, cute as a shampooed puppy.

My heart sank like the doge's wedding ring. As far as society knew, Danese and Grazia were not yet married, so propriety would not allow them to live under the same roof before the wedding. It was late on a Sunday evening, although that was his fault, not mine. I put on my stupid face and waited attentively, so he would have to ask. Ask he did. Shyness had never been one of his faults.

I shuddered to think what the Maestro would say, but the request was not unreasonable. I admitted we had a spare bedroom. It is a luxurious twenty-foot cube and, like everywhere else in the Ca' Barbolano, is opulently endowed with art and treasures. I refrained from mentioning that I kept a detailed inventory of its contents. Nor did I tuck him in and hear his prayers.

I always wake at dawn, just moments before the *marangona* rings. By the time I had dressed and reached the kitchen in search of hot water, Mama Angeli was already baking bread and feeding six or seven offspring gathered around the big table. I warned her that we had a houseguest.

Any apprentice is expected to keep his master's work area clean, and early morning is almost the only time the Maestro is not anchored in the atelier. Monday is my day to wash the floor, a job I rarely manage to finish before he appears; then I have to postpone the rest until after he goes to bed. That day I completed it, though, and had fetched a tray with my usual breakfast of cheese, hot rolls, and a steaming cup of *kahve*. I was hard at work deciphering the illegible work notes when he came hobbling in, but he disappeared into the red chair with a book, saying nothing. Obviously he had not yet learned about Danese.

I rarely speak before he does in the morning. It is not his best time. About an hour went by before he suddenly said, "Forget about those notes. Throw them out. I was wrong. I need more sulfur."

"The Lord be with you this fine day, master."

"And with you. I need it right away."

I rose. "Swift as the stooping eagle."

He grunted. "I meant send Giorgio. The Donà horoscope is urgent."

I took some money from the cash cache and went in search of Giorgio. Giorgio, I learned, was presently delivering *sier* Danese to the Ca' Sanudo. Before leaving, *sier* Danese had eaten a large breakfast, so Mama informed me in unusually cool tones.

"Did he take his bag when he left?" I asked hopefully.

Like any first-class servant, Mama can make her feelings known without a word or expression that could possibly cause offence, but the way she shook her chins clearly indicated that she shared my opinion of Danese. Fortunately Giorgio walked in just then, saving me from having to break the bad news to the Maestro so early in the day.

I explained about the sulfur. I walked him to the top of the stairs, so we would be alone when I asked, "Did he tip you for the ride?"

Since Mama has all the spare flesh in the family, Giorgio has only one chin. He wears a neatly trimmed beard on it. The beard bristled. "No."

"You amaze me," I said. Danese had not rewarded Mama for his breakfast, either, although guests are expected to tip their hosts' servants liberally. Perhaps he really was broke, if he had not yet gotten his talons into Grazia's dowry, but I suspected that the new Danese Dolfin was the same old scrounger I had known back in San Barnaba. I went back to start wrestling with aspects, ascendants, conjunctions, and ephemerides—casting a horoscope, that is.

Near to dinnertime, I explained the situation. The Maestro's reaction was as negative as I had expected, although he stopped short of turning me into a toad. There are very few people in the world whose company he enjoys, and freeloading guests belong in the nether circles of hell.

"Get rid of him!"

"Yes, master. If I know Danese, though, he will turn up after dark and pull his lost-waif act again. He cannot defend himself with his arm in a sling, so turning him out in the streets at night would be unfair. I can tell him that tonight is the last night."

"Pack his bag and put it outside the door."

"He may bring another sack of sequins with him."

Grunt. Scowl. "Take the money and then throw him out."

"Yes, master." Giving him the benefit of the doubt, I assumed he did not mean that.

I copied out the horoscope in fair. The Maestro approved it with barely a glance, and I went out on foot to deliver it, wanting the exercise. The lady whose future I had foretold did not thank me in person, being less than a month old.

Supper came and went with no sign of Danese, but if he turned up late again he would have to be given a second night's shelter.

Monday being my fencing night, I retrieved my rapier and dagger from the top of the wardrobe, made sure Giorgio knew exactly what to tell Danese, and trotted happily down the stairs. As I neared the *piano nobile*, I heard voices. There, just inside the doorway, stood our landlord, *sier* Alvise Barbolano, chattering happily to *sier* Danese Dolfin. Danese had a lute slung on his back and a very large leather portmanteau at his feet.

Sier Alvise is older than San Marco, gaunt and stooped and toothless. He moves in a senile fog much of the time, with disconcerting flashes of shrewd cunning, and he can throw the entire Nostradamus household out on its collective ear at any time without a moment's notice. We are all, even the Maestro, very nice to *sier* Alvise. I cast horoscopes for his ships, mix rat poison for his rats, and audit the Marcianas' ledgers for him so they do not cheat him unreasonably.

He beamed his gums at me. "Ah, er . . . Zeno! You didn't warn me you would be entertaining *sier*, er . . ."

"Dolfin," murmured Danese.

"Dolfin. I knew his father, er, Domenico, when I was wha'ch'm'call'it at Padua! Or was it Verona?"

"Both, *clarissimo*. My grandfather."

"Quite. And, um, Danese has promised to play his lute for us as soon as his arm heals. Wonderful young fellow, his father, er, Domenico! Wonderful singing voice . . ." And so on.

Eventually I managed to make my excuses and creep back upstairs to warn everyone that Danese had arrived to stay.

My fencing that night was terrible. I learned nothing except some spectacular invective, which Captain Colleoni must have picked up in his campaigning days during an especially nasty siege. Even my friend Fulgentio Trau hammered bruises all over my chest and shoulders. I can usually give him as good as he gives me, which is reasonable, as we are exactly the same size and weight and were born only a few days apart.

Fulgentio lives in San Remo also, so we strolled home together through the hot and moonless darkness, our way lit by two Trau servants walking ahead with torches. That saved me from having to light my own torch, but it was a sad reminder that the Traus, although commoners, are richer than Croesus ever was. Fulgentio's only fault is that he tries too hard to share his good fortune and cannot see how humiliating that can be to us deserving poor. In bad weather he arrives by private boat and gives rides home to three or four of us. That night the air was so unbearably steamy that I wondered why he had chosen to come on foot and why he had not invited others to walk with us. I am suspicious by nature; Fulgentio is not.

The doge's equerries are always chosen from the citizen class, but usually from those in humble circumstances, so Fulgentio's appointment had been a surprise. Some members of the Senate had grumbled that they normally worried about the equerries accepting gifts, but now they had to worry about this one offering them. The doge himself had risen to point out that equerries are appointed for life, or until they reach sixty, and most of his were holdovers from previous reigns. One of the equerries' duties, he had added pointedly, was to guard the ducal bedchamber at night and he had chosen Trau because he was an excellent swordsman—an exaggeration, but one I could take as a personal compliment when I heard about it.

Like the senators, I could not see why Fulgentio should want such a tedious job, playing servant, showing visitors around the palace, and so on. He just said it would be less boring than banking and he would mingle with the great. Why should he want to do that, though? Most of them are too dull to be admirable and not evil enough to be interesting. I am convinced that Fulgentio is completely honest and honorable, but his brothers are quite rich enough to have won him the job by bribing even the doge. More likely the family has some sinister purpose in mind for him that he hasn't realized yet.

So we walked along *calli*, over bridges, and across *campi*, grumbling about the endless summer overstaying its welcome. I admit I was glad of the company, although I never walk the streets at night without making sure I do not look worth robbing, which is not difficult for me. Suddenly my companion changed the subject.

"I hear you were displaying your pathetic swordsmanship on the Rio del Vin yesterday."

I made some brief remarks.

"Well? Were you?"

"My lips are sealed. What else did you hear?"

He laughed because I had not denied the story. "That *sier* Zuanbattista's daughter eloped with his wife's gigolo. It's all over the city, Alfeo! There wasn't a single Contarini to be seen in the Great Council today and usually there's at least a score of them clucking around there. Hilarious!"

I groaned. "I suppose this means the end of Sanudo's ducal ambitions?"

"His what?" Fulgentio said sharply. "Him? Doge? He's a fine man, one of the best, but he could never afford to be doge, my lad! Not before the Second Coming, anyway. Have you any idea of the gold it takes to buy the votes of the forty-one? Or the running expenses in office? Many a doge is worth millions of ducats when he is elected and dies bankrupt. That printing business of Sanudo's earns him maybe one thousand ducats a year, and the rest of his interests have gone downhill while he's been gone. He's been neglecting them! The best fertilizer is the shadow of the farmer on the field, remember."

"He may have made a lira or two on the side in Constantinople?"

"Not as I hear it. The Senate always expects a ducat's worth of display for every *soldo* it votes for its ambassadors' expenses. A diplomatic posting can bankrupt a man, no matter how rich he was beforehand, and the general view is that Sanudo was unusually honest while he was there."

"He owns large estates on the mainland."

Fulgentio snorted. "What if he does? Land is a safe investment but it doesn't produce great revenues. The only way Sanudo could finance a run at the dogeship would be to sell everything he owns, and that would leave his son penniless. No Venetian patrician ever breaks up the family fortune. He hoards it to pass on to his sons. Nobles think in terms of centuries."

This was a startling contradiction of what Violetta had told me. Her source must be mostly pillow talk, either direct or secondhand. Fulgentio was in a unique position, surrounded by money at home and political power at work. She knew what people wanted. He might be a better judge of what they could get.

Poor Eva! Her dreams had been vain even before Danese Dolfin sank her ship. And poor Danese, who would never be the doge's son-in-law!

7

Life was strained around Ca' Barbolano for the next few days. To be honest, Danese troubled no one but the servants. He rose early, ate breakfast, and disappeared until nightfall. Twice more he brought instalments of the Sanudo fee back with him, but he was curt with Mama and Giorgio, never tipped them, and snapped at their children. He cultivated old *sier* Alvise and his wife, even singing for them—a lute is fingered with the left hand, and he could still strum with the right. As long as he kept the Barbolanos happy, we dared not evict him.

The Maestro never saw him, but he resented the interloper's presence unreasonably and considered the intrusion to be all my fault. Never easy to live with, he became steadily more pettifogging, punctilious, and persnickety than ever. I retaliated with an odious servility, creeping around on tiptoe and inserting "master" into every phrase. That made him even madder, as I intended.

Thursday evening brought unwelcome relief. He and I were supping in our usual silver and crystal splendor, seated under priceless Murano chandeliers at a damask-draped table that can hold fifty. I was savoring seconds of Mama's exquisite *Cape Longhe in Padella*. He was picking at his plate with his fork as if looking for pearls; I did not have the heart to tell him that pearls come from oysters, not clams. I had arranged to go carousing with Fulgentio, just to get out of the house.

"You should eat more, master," I said. "You have told me more than once, *lustrissimo*, that fasting is very bad for the brain, as evidenced, I believe you instanced, master, by the hallucinatory disquisitions of certain holy—"

"And you should eat more because it is the only useful purpose to which you put your mouth."

Before I could frame a suitably unctuous apology, there was a rap on the door and Marco Martini strode in without waiting for a response. Martini is one of the *fanti* who guard the door when the Council of Ten meets and generally run its errands. They seem innocuous enough in their blue cloaks, but look at them closely enough and you will see that each one carries a rapier hidden in the folds, hanging vertically under his left arm. Martini is short and trim, aged around forty, with a no-nonsense expression stressed by a pointed beard that juts forward. He has the reputation of being handy with a sword, but I can't vouch for that.

Giorgio hovered behind him, looking alarmed. I sprang up and bowed, prepared to leave if told to do so and hoping it was not me he wanted.

"Maestro Filippo Nostradamus?"

If the doge had been taken ill, one of his equerries would have come, and would have addressed Nostradamus as "Doctor."

The Maestro snorted. "By the saints, Marco, if you've forgotten my name, it is time you retired."

"The Most Excellent Council of Ten," the *fante* continued without taking offense, "requests and requires that you attend Their Excellencies this evening at your imminent convenience."

Some people would have fainted out cold on the floor. The Maestro calmly dabbed at his wizened lips with a finely starched napkin. "It is always an honor to wait upon the noble lords. I may follow you in my own boat?"

"That will be permitted. I shall report that you are on your way." Marco nodded at me. "Don't forget." With a hint of a trace of a shadow of a bow, he departed.

We did not have to answer the summons. We could flee into exile.

"If Sanudo has let slip the fee you charged him," I said, "you will surely find yourself jailed for extortion."

The Maestro actually laughed . . . well, chortled. For the moment his ill humor was forgotten. "Rubbish! It was his wife who offered it. They would have sent *Missier Grande* and a squad of *sbirri* if they wanted me arrested. They probably seek my advice on the doge's health. I have warned him he is overdoing it."

I was less optimistic. As I told you, the Republic is ruled by a pyramid of interlocking committees, so that every man has another man looking over his shoulder. The system is deliberately inefficient, but that inefficiency has let the Republic retain its freedom for nine hundred years. Nevertheless, some matters must be handled swiftly and in secret, and this is where the Council of Ten comes in. It cuts all the knots. If dawn reveals conspirators dangling from gibbets in the Piazza or floating facedown in the Orfano Canal, then that is the Ten's doing. Men drop dead in distant lands by the hand of the Ten. It runs the finest intelligence service in Europe, both inside the Republic and out, interprets its duties as widely as it pleases, and answers to no one. It handles all major crimes, such as rape, murder, and blasphemy, and there is no appeal against its decisions.

Nevertheless, I would assume I was included in the invitation until a door slammed in my face. "Do I have time to change?"

The Maestro was already wearing his physician's black hat and gown and therefore had no such need. "Certainly. They will keep us waiting for hours."

Giorgio, having seen our visitor out, reappeared in the doorway.

"Bruno?" I said. "And a twin?"

I hastened to my room. Christoforo and Corrado, the dreaded Angeli twins, arrived there before I did and tried to wrestle each other out of the way. Chris won, being the larger, and I stepped between them before Corrado could charge back in and turn shove into mayhem. I flipped a *soldo* and told Chris to call it. He guessed "Doge!" which was wrong. I gave it to his brother and sent him to tell Fulgentio I had to break my date, forbidding him to say why. Chris went with him to make sure he did it right and in the hope of sharing in the reward Fulgentio would certainly supply. Arguing furiously, they disappeared down the stairs.

Armed or unarmed? I should not be allowed to wear a sword in the palace and we should be traveling by gondola all the way, so I decided to go unarmed.

Bruno always becomes excited when told that the Maestro needs him, and rushes away to find the carrying chair. By the time I had donned the better of my two cloaks, he was striding around with the chair on his back. Giorgio had appeared in his best gondolier's garb of baggy trousers, short belted tunic, and feathered bonnet, and was giving Mama strict orders to admit nobody, other than the twins when they returned. Did that apply to *sier* Danese? Regretfully I decided that Danese would have to be let in, lest he complain to *sier* Alvise. Soon we set off down the great staircase, the Maestro riding high and smirking childishly, me at the rear carrying his long staff.

It was another hot night, with a full moon peering through the chimneypot forest to daub silver on the canals. There was singing in the distance, as there always is, and the warbles of gondoliers as they warn which side they intend to pass. And cat fights. I was not happy. Nothing frightens me more than the Council of Ten—except the Council of Three, of course.

Foreigners are always amazed at how easily anyone may enter the Doges' Palace by day, but at night even Venice posts armed guards on the doors. We disembarked at the watergate on the Rio di Palazzo, where Martini was waiting for us among pikes, muskets, helmets, and pages holding lanterns. The door to the Wells, the worst of the dungeons, is right there, but no one rattled any keys at us. Giorgio rowed away to wait at the Molo; Bruno and I followed our guide along the passage to the central courtyard, and then up the great Censors' staircase, with gold and tinctures flashing overhead in the lights borne by our link boys. It is spectacular in daylight, overwhelming by night.

The Doges' Palace is where the reigning doge lives, where the criminal courts, Great Council, and all other councils meet, where records are kept, laws enforced, criminals imprisoned, tortured, and sometimes executed. It is the greatest treasure house of art in the Republic. Parts of it are centuries old. We came at last to the top floor and through into the magnificent Salle della Bussola with its Sansovino fireplace and stunning Veronese ceiling.

There it seemed that the Maestro's prediction of having to wait for hours would be fulfilled. About two dozen men were standing around in small groups, most in the black robes of the nobility, several looking seriously worried. I saw no women, of course. The few benches in sight being occupied, the Maestro remained in his chair on Bruno's back. The weight did not bother Bruno in the slightest; he was happy to be of use. He liked to visit the palace and look at the pictures. I usually like to look at the pictures, too, but didn't just then.

Our *fante* went to report to another guarding the door to

the Ten's chamber. Near them stood two men I knew well. Gasparo Quazza, *Missier Grande*, has the impassive solidity of a Sansovino statue. He did not acknowledge me when we made eye contact, but that is just his way. Although I do not like him, I respect his honesty—he would arrest his own mother if the Ten ordered him to. A glimpse of his red and blue robe would strike terror into the hearts of the toughest gang of bravos.

Beside him was his assistant, *Vizio* Filiberto Vasco. Vasco and I have three things in common: we are about the same age, we both attend Captain Colleoni's Monday fencing class, and we detest each other. I am a better swordsman than he is, but that is the only good thing I can tell you about him. He is too immature for his job, liking to pester women and bully men. He scowled in my direction. I licked my lips, although a careful observer might have thought I had stuck my tongue out at someone.

The Ten's door opened and words were passed to and fro. Martini disengaged and strode through the crowd, every eye on him, coming straight to the Maestro.

"Their Excellencies summon you, *lustrissimo*." The rest of the room rustled with outrage. Nobles do not willingly yield precedence to physicians or nostrum-peddling charlatans.

I took Bruno's arm and we marched over to the door together. The giant knelt. I helped the Maestro dismount and gave him back his staff. His lameness varies depending on circumstances, usually being much worse in public. Wanting me with him, he leaned a hand on my shoulder.

"Is Zeno allowed in?" the *vizio* asked disbelievingly. His displeasure was encouraging, for if I were on my way to the galleys, he would be wearing a sneer wider than the Grand Canal.

Missier Grande shrugged. "For now."

I said, "Of course," and almost succeeded in treading on Vasco's toe as I went by.

The chamber of the Council of Ten is large and very impressive, with paintings by Veronese and Zelloti adorning its walls and ceiling. A dais at one end bears a long bench curving across the full width of the hall, with the doge's throne in the center. Despite its name, the Council comprises seventeen men, and when we entered they were quietly chatting among themselves, discussing their last item of business or the next, ignoring us.

The doge, Pietro Moro, wears robes of cloth-of-gold and white ermine, although that night the room still held the heat of the day and the many lamps did not help. His hat, of course, was the golden ducal *corno* with its distinctive peak at the back. It is a cause for ribaldry that the bulge bears no small resemblance to His Serenity's most distinctive feature, because all his life he has been known as *Nasone*, "Big Nose." Moro is a good man. He tips me generously whenever I deliver his medications, but I would approve of him even without that.

He was flanked by his six ducal counselors in scarlet, three on either side. I was impressed to see that the patriarchal Sanudo beard was borne by the man at the doge's right hand, the place of honor. Flanking the counselors, in turn, sat the ten elected members in their black robes, seven to the left and three to the right. Of the seventeen, three were patients of the Maestro, and I counted five others who had consulted him on occult matters. Secretaries and clerks were clustered at desks at either side of the hall.

As we approached this sinister tribunal, a minion brought forward a chair and placed it alongside the lectern that stands before the doge's throne. This was a remarkable tribute to Nostradamus, for Venice rarely makes concessions to age. Moro himself is in his late seventies and many men there were older.

I helped the Maestro to the chair, saw him settled, and then stepped behind it and waited to be ordered out. A secretary brought forward a jeweled crystal reliquary and guided the Maestro through an oath that he would speak the truth and not discuss the questions, his answers, or just about anything. Having done that, the flunky looked uncertainly at me. Before he could appeal for instructions, I laid my hand on the sacred vessel and rattled off the same oath, word for word, inserting for my own name and station. Much to my astonishment and his, no one objected.

The doge looked tired and displeased. This was probably his third or fourth meeting of the day, and all those other men still waited outside. He nodded to the Maestro—and even to me, which was a signal honor—and then glanced to his right and said, "Chiefs?"

That one word brought the meeting to order.

The doge serves for life, although most doges are very old men when they are elected. The Ten's four secretaries are of the citizen-by-birth class and appointed for life. Everyone else is temporary. Members serve for one year, counselors for eight months, and neither can be re-elected to the same position until they have sat out at least one term. There is nothing to prevent them from being elected to the other position, though, and many of the nobles on the dais would have served as both in the past. The three black robes to the doge's right wore red tippets and were therefore the three "chiefs of the Ten," that month's steering committee. It would be they who had decided to summon the Maestro.

"Doctor Nostradamus," said the middle chief. He was a gaunt, silvery man of considerable age, *sier* Tegaliano Trevisan, and the Maestro had cast his horoscope a few years earlier. Offhand I did not recall its predictions, although I knew I could if I had to. His elongated face reminded me of driftwood, eroded and bleached by long turmoil in the breakers. "The Council understands that you have many times displayed great skill at finding missing persons."

I wished that I had left while I had the chance and kept on running. Trevisan *might* mean that the Council was seeking advice from the greatest clairvoyant in Europe, but he might equally mean that the Maestro had been accused of black magic. I would be interrogated as a witness, very likely tortured, and probably burned at the same stake. I glanced at Zuanbattista Sanudo in his huge black cloud of beard and wondered why he had reported the story, for it made him seem a fool who could not even control his own daughter. So far he had paid about a third of his fee. A heap of cinders cannot sue to collect a debt.

The doge pulled a face. His Serenity is a total skeptic where the supernatural is concerned. He is not alone in that folly, but most of those present probably knew better.

"I have," the Maestro said calmly. "How may I assist Their Excellencies?"

"Could you locate a spy?"

The other sixteen had all known what was to be asked, and showed no surprise.

"I assume that Your Excellency refers to a specific spy?"

Every state in Europe employs spies. If you include the Ten's own army of informers, you could fire a musket across the Piazza and pick up one or two any day.

"A specific spy," the chief agreed in his dusty, wormwood voice. "We have good reason to believe that a particular spy is doing great damage to the Republic and we are anxious to identify him."

The Maestro waited, but when nothing more was said, he cleared his throat. "Your Serenity, Your Excellencies . . . This noble Council is renowned and envied everywhere for its expertise and resources. If your normal methods have failed, you are obviously asking whether I can employ spiritual methods? If I speculate on this, it will be understood that I speak of what I have read in my studies and not from first-hand experimentation?"

"You are not on trial, Doctor," Trevisan said. "Your testimony is privileged and will not be held against you."

I started breathing again.

"My almanac for this year," the Maestro said, "showed no great calamities in store for *La Serenissima*, so I am optimistic that someone will catch your scoundrel soon. Indeed, the imminent conjunction of Venus and Mercury provides strong support for that surmise."

I knew that he was merely letting his mouth run while he rummaged through his brain, but Moro was scowling ferociously along at the three chiefs. Even with only one vote among the seventeen, the doge has enormous power to bear grudges and reward friends. None of the three chiefs looked at him, but they all began to fidget.

"I will certainly provide whatever assistance I can," the Maestro said. "But I can do nothing without more information about the person I am to locate. Normally I have at least a name to go on. Can you give me a sample of handwriting? A description? Even the nation or cause he serves?"

Trevisan nodded. "We anticipated such a request. If you present yourself tomorrow morning at the Chancellor's office, the learned Secretary Sciara will show you what we have. We can provide a desk . . ."

The Maestro was shaking his head and I knew what was coming. Very few people defy the Council of Ten, but he was not going to come trotting to the palace every day like some whistled dog. "No," he said. He was adamant. He would work at home with his library, or he could do nothing.

"Oh, saints preserve us!" the doge shouted. "I told you he would say that. Give him what we agreed."

Trevisan nodded nervously. "We can provide you with the little information we have, but we shall set restrictions on its use and send a guard to watch over it. May Heaven bless your work."

That was that, we had been dismissed.

8

The man who rose from the secretaries' table to lead us out was the chief secretary himself, Raffaino Sciara, widely known as *Circospetto*. Noble politicians come and go; like the doge, citizen Sciara goes on forever and he hoards more secrets than the Vatican. He and I have tangled in the past. He has a face like a skull and a sense of humor to match, but that evening I looked forward to fireworks, for the Maestro dislikes him even more than I do.

Out in the anteroom, Bruno had been standing within a wide clearing, glowering ferociously at the door. Seeing us safe, he spread an enormous grin and swept forward like a galleon, nobility hastily clearing a path. He was not needed yet, though, because Sciara led us across to the corner screen, which conceals two doors, one leading to the jails and torture chamber, and the other to the room of the chiefs of the Ten. That was our destination and I beckoned for Bruno to follow us through.

It is a rich room, although small, but that evening it was dim and haunted by shadows, lit by only two small lamps on the grand table behind which the three chiefs sit while interrogating witnesses, and two more on the recording secretaries' desk at the side. Beside that stood *Vizio* Filiberto Vasco in his red cloak, looking as if he had just been sentenced to twenty years in the galleys. For once his distress did not make me happy, because I could guess what was going to happen. He appeared to be guarding a leather satchel, and it was to the secretarial desk that Sciara went.

I helped the Maestro to a chair, Sciara took another, and I plonked myself down on the third. Vasco just stood, scowl firmly in place, arms folded. Very few chairs fit Bruno and he knelt to grin at the tiled floor, whose pattern of black and white reverses perspective while you look at it. Sciara proceeded to open the satchel.

"We refer to the unknown as Algol," he said. "We know of his existence from reports by our own intelligence."

"Venice's spies in the Porte," the Maestro said.

The Sublime Porte is the Turkish government. Algol is the name of a star, but it means The Ghoul.

"Possibly." Sciara extracted a sheaf of papers. "These are copies—"

"I need originals," the Maestro said.

"You can't have them. Our agent risked his life to supply even this much."

I saw at a glance that the text was enciphered, the letters grouped in fives.

The Maestro looked disgusted. "You expect me to decipher this for you?"

The worst thing about *Circospetto* is his smile. I always expect maggots to fall out of it. "When you do you may instruct us."

The Maestro is a genius in steganography, or hidden writing, as he is in just about everything, but the Council of Ten has been renowned throughout Europe for its expertise with codes and ciphers ever since it employed the great Giovanni Soro. The Vatican itself would send Soro intercepted dispatches to be deciphered and he would send them back in plaintext—keeping a copy, of course. They say that the only time he was stumped was when Rome sent him a message in its own cipher and asked if he could read it; he sent it back, saying that he could not. It must be a terrible sin to lie to the Pope.

The Ten are reputed to keep three cryptographers toiling away somewhere in the palace behind locked doors. If they could not break Algol's cipher, no one in Europe could.

"What language?" the Maestro demanded.

"We don't know."

I lost interest at that point, knowing of no way to decipher an unknown language. The Maestro did not seem deterred, though. He held a sheet closer to the lamp.

"Roman alphabet. How many letters?"

"Twenty-three."

In Venice we mostly use the old twenty-three-letter Roman alphabet, dropping *K* and *Y* and adding *V* and *J*. Tuscan spurns *J* and *H*, but a cryptographer may double up rarely used letters or add some, at his whim.

"Not a nomenclator, then," Nostradamus said, "unless the characters are represented by letter pairs. Have you checked couplet frequency?"

"Minor deviations," Sciara said. "Probably just happenstance. The same with single letter frequency. It is not truly random, but certainly neither a Caesar nor a transliteration of Arabic letters into Roman."

"Nor a transposition, then. Curious."

It is a rare treat to watch the Maestro fencing wits on equal terms with someone. I had a fair idea of what they were gabbling about because I have to encipher and decipher much of his correspondence, but a glance at the *vizio* told me that he was utterly at sea. Bruno had gone to smile at the pictures.

"I put a summary of our experts' work notes in here," Sciara said, tapping the satchel, "to save you from wasting time attempting to decipher the code. I know it is the sort of puzzle that distracts you. Their Excellencies accept that it is unbreakable." The skull sneered. "They hope your occult methods will identify Algol where our cryptography has failed, and this is the only lead they can offer."

Nostradamus snorted. "But if I break the cipher, the plaintext would lead you back to Algol, almost certainly, and would also be admissible evidence. I shall do both. What else can you tell me? How long has this Algol been operating? What departments of government has he pene-trated? How does he communicate with the Porte that you are able to intercept his mail?"

"Their Excellencies have not authorized me to release such information."

"Have they asked for a *zonta*?"

The secretary twitched as if jabbed by a needle. "I do not discuss Their Excellencies' deliberations!"

The Maestro smiled foxily. "And to whom do I report my findings?"

Sciara actually hesitated before replying. "If you have ev-idence pertaining to the safety of the Republic, report it to the chiefs of the Ten—*messere* Tegaliano Trevisan, Tommaso Soranzo, and Marino Venier. If you find nothing of interest, just return these papers to me. Me personally."

"Why bother, if they contain nothing of interest? Have they been debated in the Council, *lustrissimo*?"

Even Vasco had caught the drift of the Maestro's ques-tions now and looked horrified.

Circospetto said, "I told you, Doctor, I do not discuss Their Excellencies' discussions."

The Maestro chuckled and handed the papers back to Sciara. "On what terms may I take these?"

"They stay in the possession of *Vizio* Vasco. He will watch while you study them, collect them when you are fin-ished, also any copies or extracts you have made of them and all your work notes. When you are done, he will bring the material back to me." The old man handed the satchel to Vasco.

"Then I shall see what I can do," the Maestro said.

"You really expect to succeed?" Sciara said scornfully.

Nostradamus stared at him with an expression of bemused innocence. "Why not? I have already narrowed the field, haven't I?"

I rose and went across to tap Bruno's arm and gain his attention.

As we trooped down the great dim staircase—the link boys first, then Bruno and the Maestro, with Vasco and me in the rear—Vasco caught my arm to hold me back.

"What did Nostradamus mean by narrowing the field?" he whispered.

"It's not too difficult to guess, *Vizio.* Even you—"

His nose twitched. "He thinks there's a traitor in the Council of Ten? That's outrageous!"

"Sciara damn near confirmed it," I said cheerfully. "He made sure we knew the names of the chiefs! They haven't told the whole council what evidence they have, because that would betray the Republic's agents in Constantinople. And why not? Remember 1355?" No Venetian forgets that date, the year the doge himself, Doge Marino Falier, was beheaded for conspiring against the state. If a doge could be a traitor, anyone could. "You need me to spell it out for you?"

"Oh, please do, *sier* Alfeo. In large type. Very large!"

Vasco attempts wit only when he thinks he is on top and ahead, so that sarcasm should have alerted me, but I missed it.

"Well, the procedure was wrong to start with. Normally the chiefs would have summoned the Maestro and questioned

him themselves, then either just authorized him to proceed
on their own authority, or asked the Ten's approval at the evening meeting. They would not drag him out before the whole
council.

"This elliptical procedure suggests," I continued,
amused to hear echoes of the Maestro's lecturing manner in
my own voice, "that the chiefs are very scared indeed, and
whoever else is in the know is scared also." I meant the
doge, most likely, and probably Zuanbattista Sanudo, because it must have been he who suggested bringing in
Maestro Nostradamus. "The fox is so well disguised as a
hound that they don't know which one he is. The Ten's normal reaction to a sticky problem is to ask for a *zonta*,
right?" A *zonta* is an addition, usually of fifteen men,
elected by the Great Council. The advantage of the Ten being thirty-two instead of just seventeen is that all the great
clans can be represented. This spreads the guilt and dilutes
grudges.

"Sciara did not deny that they were thinking about it," I
concluded. "No, 'no' means 'yes' in that world. Would you
like the lecture on cryptography now?"

"Later," Vasco said. "Much later. Tell me again why the
Maestro was paraded before the entire Ten, if the spy may
be a member?"

I used a phrase I would have to remember for my next
confession. Why had I not seen that for myself?

"Blasphemy!" the *vizio* said smugly. "But I think you've
got it this time."

"And are you being sent along to guard—what?" I asked
furiously.

"Maestro Nostradamus, of course." Vasco smiled beatifi-
cally at having caught me out.

"*Bait?*"

"Exactly. There's a remote chance that Algol will be su-
perstitious enough to believe in the old fraud's posturing.

In that case he must seem to be a danger, so Algol may try to dispose of him—and then he will run into me. *Missier Grande* mentioned that I should keep a protective eye on you at the same time, but I'm sure he was just joking there."

9

Vasco took his absurd mission seriously and proceeded to demonstrate how efficient he was, requisitioning a couple of night guards to escort us out to the Molo and see us safely aboard the gondola. He was the last to board and the first off at Ca' Barbolano, where he would not let the rest of us disembark until Luigi had opened the door and confirmed that all was well within. Nor would he let Bruno carry the Maestro upstairs before Giorgio and I had finished bringing in the oar and cushions for overnight storage in the *androne* and the door had been locked and bolted. Then he shepherded us up the stairs, made sure the apartment was properly secured after we entered, and ordered Giorgio to inspect his family's quarters in the attic and report any intruders. I smirked and he sneered.

The Maestro had endured this exhibition with astonishing self-control. Now back on his own feet, he wanted to get to work. "The bag, please."

"Not until I am finished securing the house, Doctor."

"If you are looking for ghouls, Filiberto," I said, "then you should begin over here. This is our only guest room, so you must either share the bed with the resident ghoul or sleep out here on a couch."

The *vizio* bared his teeth like a dog. "Who's in there?"

"*Sier* Danese Dolfin, about to become son-in-law to *messer* Counselor Sanudo. Evict him if you wish. We have had very little success."

Vasco faced a tricky decision, whether or not to intrude on a nobleman and near relation to a ducal counselor in a nobleman's house, but he rose to the challenge. After a brief glance at the Maestro, who remained studiously blank, he took up a lamp and marched into the spare room. Unfortunately I did not witness the expression on our guest's face when the dreaded *Missier Grande*'s deputy appeared like an apocalyptic nightmare and demanded to know who he was and what he was doing there. Vasco was smirking a little when he came out. He locked the door behind him and I would really have enjoyed seeing Danese's reaction to that, too.

The *vizio* inspected the bedrooms with special care— mine, the Maestro's, Bruno's—peering in wardrobes and under beds. He went over the kitchen, the dining room, and started in on the *salone*, confirming that no assassins or demons crouched behind the statues. By then the Maestro and I were in the atelier, I lighting lamps for an all-night session, and he at his desk with a great leather-bound manuscript of Johannes Trithemius's *Steganographia*.

He looked up angrily as Vasco entered and began snooping around, peering at everything: terrestrial globe, celestial globe, armillary sphere, alchemy bench, reagent shelves, wall of books. The alcove in the center of the books contains a huge oval mirror framed by overweight cherubs. Vasco studied it for a moment, took another moment to locate the hidden catch, then slid the bolt and pushed on the frame. The whole back of the alcove turned on its pivot. There was enough light on the far side for him to recognize the dining room he had seen earlier. He nodded as if satisfied, closed the door again, and bolted it.

Only then did he deign to deliver the precious satchel to the Maestro, who opened it without a word and began going through its contents like a child at Christmas. Vasco settled himself in one of the green chairs, where he could watch. I took the red one facing him, confident I would not be left in peace for long.

"You really think those papers are of any true value?" I inquired. I knew that the entire Turkish army could march through the room without distracting the Maestro from whatever he was doing.

Vasco glanced at him, came to the same conclusion, and answered, "Worth killing for, easily."

I shook my head. "*Circospetto* would never have parted with them without keeping a copy. What he would love to do, of course, is catch Algol and then use his cipher to send false information to Constantinople."

"How do you know that Algol is spying for the Porte?"

"I don't," I admitted. "He could be working for the Vatican, the Louvre, the Escorial, or even Whitehall. All states play the same sort of game. I just happen to have a grudge against the Turks. Perhaps the reason Venice can't break the cipher is that its man in the Porte has been taken or turned and the writing on those papers is pure canal mud, meant to tantalize the Ten into insanity."

Vasco shrugged. "You'll go mad thinking that way."

"Or *Circospetto* made it all up by himself to bait his trap for Algol."

"I wouldn't put that past him. You're an expert in code breaking as well as everything else, I suppose?"

"Not *everything* else."

He scowled at the fireplace for a moment, then asked in a bored tone, "So what's a Caesar, that you mentioned earlier?"

"The cipher Julius used. You shift every letter a known number of places along the alphabet. Instead of A you write, say, C, and instead of D you write F. It's easy to break, because in any language some letters are used much more often than others. In *Veneziano*, for instance, E and A are about the busiest and they're close together in the alphabet, so if your ciphertext shows a lot of, say, M's and Q's, you assume those are A and E. Also R, S, and T are used a lot and fall next to each other, so they'll stand out as a group. It would be easier if everybody spelled words the same way, and it depends a little on whether your spy has ignored accents or not, but that's the principle. Once you have pinned down a few letters, the rest follow automatically, as was shown by Leon Battista Alberti of Florence in—"

"But shown much earlier," said the Maestro, "by Abu Yusuf Ya'qub ibn Is-haq ibn as-Sabbah ibn 'omran ibn Ismail al-Kindi. Ninth century, in fact. Come over here and make yourself useful. You, too, *Vizio*."

We rose and went like good little schoolboys.

"Every one of the sheets," the Maestro said, "has ten five-letter words in a row, and no more than thirty-two rows on a page. This may be steganography, where the text is hidden in full view. You may have to take the first letter of the fourth word and the third of the one below and so on, or it may even require a Cardan grille to identify the meaningful letters. Let us hope that the original was copied exactly. But it wouldn't be, of course. The spacing between lines varies, see? And we can't tell whether it did in the original or not. I want you each to take a pen and a sheet of paper and invent a page just like these, 320 nonsense words in 10 columns. Go to it."

Vasco was frowning, but I suppose it seemed a better alternative than total boredom, so he accepted a pen and an inkwell, and went over to work on the slate-topped table with the crystal ball. I sat at my side of the desk and rapidly discovered that the job was not as easy as it seemed. When we turned in our assignments, the Maestro studied them while we peered over his shoulders.

Then he chuckled. "You have disproved your own hypothesis, Alfeo! You see where you both went wrong?"

Fortunately I did. "We weren't repeating ourselves," I said. "I never wrote a double letter, but the originals have lots of them. There's even three *K*'s in a row there. I never began a word with the same letter I'd used to start the one before. And we never wrote a real word. Algol has a *MOLO* and even *PASTA* if you ignore the space in the middle."

"And so on," the Maestro said sourly, annoyed that I had spoiled his revelation. "You were too random! Your lack of order is a sort of order in itself. That means that these originals were not made by someone just writing random letters. There is meaning in them. Now all we have to do is pull it out."

"How can you do that if you don't know what language it is?" Vasco demanded.

"Not many languages are likely—Tuscan, Latin, Spanish, *Veneziano*, Arabic, Turkish, French. They use Old Persian in the Porte sometimes. I can read most of those and recognize the rest. But perhaps I can find another way. Take this trash away, *Vizio*." The old man heaved himself to his feet, I handed him his staff, and he hobbled over to the crystal. "You can both get some sleep. I'll lock up, Alfeo."

I doused the other lamps and shooed Vasco out of the atelier ahead of me.

I did not offer to share my bed with him, but I did find him a blanket and a pillow. He stretched out on a couch in the *salone*.

The last thing I did before going to bed was to consult my tarot. It gave me an assortment of the minor arcana, all low numbers without a single court card or trump. I had not seen such a disgusting heap since before I was toilet trained. Deciding I must be overtired, I fell into bed.

10

I awoke at dawn as always. Remembering the work I had to do, I growled myself upright, groaned myself into my clothes, and grouched out into the *salone* in my stocking soles. The *vizio*'s blanket lay unoccupied beside the couch, so he had presumably gone to recharge the canal, and I had a chance to reach the atelier without attracting his unwelcome attention.

The atelier door is both locked and warded at night. The Maestro might have omitted setting the wards if he was exhausted after his clairvoyance, but I played safe and cast the counter-spell before using my key. As soon as I had let daylight in, I went to inspect the slate-topped table.

What I found was ominous. It began in the usual barely legible scrawl:

When the cat is in the trap, the mouse . . .

But that was followed by mere chalk scribbles, snail tracks bearing no resemblance to writing at all. I have known the Maestro to prophecy in such appalling cacography that neither of us could read half of it, but I could recall no occasion when he had failed to produce a reasonable attempt at a quatrain.

And my tarot had failed me.

The door closed behind me and I spun around angrily. It was not, as I had expected, Filiberto Vasco snooping. It was Danese Dolfin, obviously released from his kennel and apparently not snooping, because he came striding straight over to me, his manner all but shooting lightning bolts. He had given up wearing his sling.

"Why is the *vizio* here?" he demanded.

"I can't tell you."

"You don't know?"

"I know, but I can't tell you."

That stopped him. I was tempted to suggest he ask around his new family, but even that hint would violate my oath.

"Does *sier* Alvise Barbolano know he's here?"

"No," I said, "and I strongly advise you not to tell him." Then I remembered old Luigi, whose mouth is larger than the Adriatic. The news would be out the moment Luigi could find a listener.

More wary now, Danese said, "Is he going to stay long?"

There were witty retorts I could have made to that, but I wasn't feeling witty. "Several days."

"It's intolerable!" Danese shouted, turning on his heel.

"Yes," I said softly as he disappeared. Life holds many trials we can do nothing about, but with luck Vasco would rid us of one of them.

I followed Danese out, locked the atelier, and went in search of shaving water. Halfway along my trek to the kitchen stood Vasco, folding his blanket with the satchel strap over his shoulder like a tippet, as if he had worn it all night. We greeted each other with cold nods, acknowledging that our enforced cooperation was only temporary and battle would resume at the first opportunity.

The kitchen was redolent with ambrosial scents of fresh

bread and the *khave* Mama Angeli was just preparing. Giorgio and four sons sat gobbling at the big table—the older girls would still be dressing small fry. We exchanged blessings and they waited hopefully for me to explain the additional houseguest. I just asked them to keep down the noise outside the Maestro's room.

In stalked the *vizio* wearing sword and satchel, closely followed by Danese wearing his lute. They both looked rumpled and unshaven—Danese less so, because he was blond and had not had to sleep in his clothes—and their joint arrival seemed so staged that I half expected them to burst into song.

Vasco asked me, "When will Nostradamus want to see these papers again?"

"Probably not for a couple of hours."

"May I ask your gondolier to take me home to fetch some clothes? I won't be long." He couldn't resist adding, "Just promise me you'll keep the door locked while I'm gone."

"Should I wear my sword?"

"You're probably safer without it."

"Very true," I said, "I hate inquests." I glanced inquiringly at Giorgio and he nodded, of course. "He will be happy to oblige you, *lustrissimo*." I was sorely tempted to add, "But don't tip him too generously; he isn't used to it." I didn't say that, though, and the self-restraint required must have made all the angels in Heaven cheer.

Danese said nothing, but when gondolier and *vizio* departed, he went with them. I looked across the table at the amused stare of a descending line of dark eyes—Christoforo, Corrado, Archangelo, and little Piero.

"It's a good job I like your father," I said. "Or I'd be praying for sharks to sink his gondola. Chris, go and bolt the front door behind them."

Eight eyes widened. "Why?" chorused one bass, one baritone, one tenor, and one alto.

"You know the doge is a great book collector and the Maestro is an expert on old books? He's examining some very rare documents for the doge, so valuable that the doge sent the *vizio* along to guard them." That was as close to the truth as I could come and it satisfied the youngsters, although probably not Mama, who never missed a word of any conversation, spoken or unspoken. Hating myself for even that much deception, I beat a fast retreat with a mug of hot water and another of *khave*.

I checked that *both* doors were bolted as well as locked.

As soon as I had shaved, I took my tarot deck from under my pillow and tried another reading. It was no more informative than the last one and I tucked the deck away again, fearing that any more attempts to force it might desensitize it. My tarot skill had apparently become as useless as the Maestro's clairvoyance, which confirmed what I already suspected—that whatever we were up against would not be deterred by bolted doors or Filiberto Vasco's sword.

When Vasco returned, he found me at my side of the big desk behind a pile of every book on cryptography in the Maestro's library—Roger Bacon, Johannes Trithemius, Girolamo Cardano, Leon Battista Alberti, Giovani Porta, Blaise de Vigenère. Al-Kindi was there, too, but I can't read Arabic. Needless to say, I had made small progress with those I could read.

"No sign of the Maestro," I said. "May I have a look at the evidence?" You cannot conceive how much it hurt me to sound humble.

The *vizio* could, though, and smirked. "What for?"

"Not the ciphertext, just *Circospetto*'s notes."

He had the effrontery to make himself comfortable in the Maestro's chair and beam across at me. "Why?"

"I have an idea and I wanted to see if the Ten's gnomes thought to check for it."

"What sort of idea?"

"About nomenclators."

"What's a nomenclator?"

"This frantic impulse to exercise your brain after so many years of disuse may do serious damage."

He just smiled.

"I taught you last night," I said with saintly patience, while silently vowing epochal revenge, "that a simple Caesar alphabet cipher is too easy to break. The most popular way to improve it is to add more symbols, usually numbers. So you have, say, *32* standing for *D*, *14* for *N*, and a dozen or so different codes for a very common letter like *E*—and so on. Then you start adding symbols for common words, perhaps *42* for *the* and *51* for *and*. That sort of list is called a *nomenclator*. It makes the cipher harder to break, but not much. Carry it too far and you're writing a whole codebook, with numbers for *King of Denmark*, *Venice*, *Janissary regiment*, and Lord knows what. That's more secure, but then your spy can't carry the cipher in his head anymore and has to lug a book around with him. If the enemy captures it, a codebook is enough evidence to hang him and reveal all your coded correspondence, past, present, and future. If a Caesar alphabet is compromised, you only have to change the key, which is a single number, whereas replacing a codebook is a huge task. But codebooks are how most states encipher their dispatches."

Vasco nodded as if he understood. He does have a certain low animal cunning. "Algol doesn't use numbers."

"No, he uses twenty-three letters, and if he is pairing them up he has hundreds of couplets available. So the first thing the Maestro asked was if Sciara's gnomes had checked for couplet frequency. Perhaps *GX* stands for *A*, *NT* for *B*, *EO* for *King of France*, understand? Now you pass me the notes and I'll tell you what to look for in the ciphertext and if we're quick about it we may have this thing broken before the Maestro comes."

"And if we're really lucky, angels may appear to transport you to Paradise."

I thought that was the end and the pleasure of refusing me had overridden his duty, but then he shrugged and opened the satchel. He held out the work notes, making me stand up to reach them.

"So what do I look for?" he asked.

"My initials. *LAZ*, for Luca Alfeo Zeno. How many times can you see those letters together? I know they appear more often than they should." I set to work reading what Sciara's team had tried, ignoring more scoffing from Vasco.

Sciara's notes were thorough and detailed. I learned that the ciphertext comprised four Algol dispatches, varying in length from three pages to nine, twenty-four pages in all. The Ten's cryptologists had tested for letter frequency and couplet frequency and even "word" frequency, although the five-letter groups could not be real words. Their conclusion was that the distribution of letters was not truly random, but not skewed enough for a substitution cipher, such as a Caesar, or a transposition cipher, which is a gigantic anagram. They suspected that all four dispatches had been written using the same code, so very likely it was a nomenclator.

They had not tested for triplets, though. Of course my own initials in a page of meaningless text will always jump out at me, and the previous evening I had seen them twice on one page when I was looking over the Maestro's shoulder. After a few minutes of angry muttering, Vasco announced that he had found my initials seven times, and at least once in each of the four dispatches. We had grasped a thread in the labyrinth! That ought to lead somewhere.

But where? There were thousands of other three-letter

combinations to look for, and the only sensible next move I
could think of was to hand the problem back to Sciara and
tell him to put his legions to work on triplet frequencies.
I suggested we each try to find another repeating triplet.

Eventually the thump of the Maestro's staff on the terrazzo outside announced his approach and Vasco hastily
vacated his chair. The old man came hobbling in, looking
murderous.

"Make any sense of it?" he growled at me, with a wave at
the slate table.

"Nine words," I said. "That's all."

He grunted, meaning that he had reached the same conclusion.

"And my tarot doesn't work either."

He seemed unsurprised. "Why do you think he's called
Algol? *Vizio*, who named the unknown that and why?"

"I have no idea, Doctor."

More grunt.

I doubted that Algol would turn out to be a true ghoul, a
monster that haunts graveyards and eats corpses, but he might
well be a demonologist, and the laws of demonology dictate
that anyone who employs demons will soon find that the shoe
is on the other hoof and the demons are employing him.

Vasco was looking puzzled. I thought it kinder to leave
him that way.

"Can you break a nomenclator in an unknown language?" I asked.

The Maestro's scowl darkened. "Given time and enough
text to work on, yes. But there are far more good ciphers
than good people using them. When a cipher is broken, it is
almost always because the operator was careless. Human error damns us all! If we look hard enough and long enough,
we will find that he has made a mistake somewhere."

That was my cue. "He likes my initials. He used them
seven times."

The effect on the Maestro was dramatic. He sat up straight and his eyes blazed with excitement. "Where? Show me!"

Two minutes later he snapped, "Bring me the pastels!"

I fetched our box of pastels.

We marked every *LAZ* in red. After another ten minutes or so we had located and highlighted four more triplets that were repeated at least once. Nostradamus told me to round up the three oldest Angeli children currently available. Reading and writing are uncommon skills among the citizen class, but I taught Mama and she teaches all her children.

Archangelo was on a ladder, dusting the tops of high pictures in the *salone*, and so was happy to be recruited. Corrado and Christoforo happened to come running up the stairs as I emerged from the atelier and were not, but they brightened when I chivied them into the dining room and they saw the pile of shiny *soldi* in front of the Maestro. Most of the time he is as tight as a coffin lid where money is concerned, but he has little idea of how much it means to adolescents and often tips them extravagantly.

He handed out a pastel crayon and four or five pages of ciphertext to each of us. He explained the rules. The boys received a *soldo* for each new repetition they found. Vasco and I did not. The *vizio* was clearly torn between the excitement of the chase and regarding this labor as far beneath the dignity of a major officer of the Republic—which he is not, but likes to think he is.

The pile of coins shrank rapidly. We found ten different triplets that were repeated. None of the others repeated as often as my initials did, and most only once. My initials were always in the middle of the five-letter groupings, and the others usually had their own places also, with a couple of exceptions that could easily be due to chance. Archangelo found a four-letter repeat and was rewarded with two *soldi*.

Whatever we were discovering was a clue to analyzing the cipher and might even lead us to breaking it, so I grew quite excited. The Maestro became crabbier and crabbier until he slapped his hand on the table and said, "Stop!"

Surprised, we all stopped.

"This is a waste of time. Off you go, boys, thank you. *Vizio*, please gather up the papers. Alfeo, has that freeloading friend of yours removed his belongings yet?"

"He was never a friend of mine," I protested. "He had no baggage with him when he left this morning."

"Then pack up his things and take them to Ca' Sanudo and tell him to find someone else to sponge off!"

It was almost noon. I had hoped to call on Violetta, but I was lacking several hours' sleep and might well have settled for a siesta instead.

"After dinner?"

"No, now! The *vizio* is our guest and that simpering pretty boy is not. I want him out of here."

"I don't mind sleeping on the couch," Vasco said, with the martyrdom of a triptych saint. "I can guard the house better there."

The Maestro ignored him. "You heard me," he snapped.

I sighed. "Your wish is my command, Oh Most Illustrious Master!"

Although Nostradamus has uncommonly small hands, they have always packed a lot of sleight, and when Vasco tucked his papers back in his satchel, he didn't think to count them.

11

I laid Danese's admirable, expensive leather portmanteau on the spare room bed and began to pack it with Danese's admirable, expensive silken garments. Eva had been generous to her hired lover. He owned luxuries I had never seen before—scented soap and a pearl-handled razor. He had no less than three spare pairs of shoes. One shoe was perceptibly heavier than the other five, though, a phenomenon I soon tracked down to a roll of gold coins tucked in the toe. Faced with a large sum of money and only my own honesty to defend me against later charges of pilfering, I decided to count it, and made it 60 sequins, equal to 165 silver ducats. That is a *lot* of money. Either Eva had been insanely generous to her hired lover or Danese had been working something on the side. Even I, in my boyish innocence, could think of several possibilities. I put the coins back in the shoe and the shoe in the case.

I let Bruno carry it downstairs for me, because he would have been hurt had I not. Giorgio rowed me to Ca' Sanudo and did not offer to lift the case ashore because he knew I would refuse if he did. I wielded the big brass anchor and the summons was answered by Fabricio, the footman. This time he was dressed as a gondolier.

I was dressed as an apprentice and carried luggage, but he knew me and knew I was recorded in the Golden Book, so he bowed. I inquired after Danese and was assured that he would be informed directly of the honor of my visit if I would be so gracious as to wait in the *androne* . . .

There were fewer crates and fewer empty shelves than before, but a forest had sprouted on the floor, trees of books both high and low, indicating that the huge collection was still being sorted. Let loose in such a feast, the Maestro would starve to death before he remembered to eat. Lucky, perhaps, that he was no longer mobile enough to indulge himself in such bibliophilic orgies.

Fabricio returned, scooped up the portmanteau, and led me upstairs. Since my last visit the landing at the mezzanine level had been furnished with three marble busts and the fair madonna Grazia, she of the divine eyes and devilish nose. Her gown was a glittering mist of silver taffeta and pearls, her hair had been set in a much less childish style than before, and only time would ever make her look like an adult.

She beamed, extending both hands to me. *"Dear sier* Alfeo! I am so ashamed of my cruel words to you on Sunday! Such ingratitude for all your help! Can you ever forgive me?"

Forgiveness, it is well known, requires repentance. I kissed her knuckles. "Think nothing of it, madonna! You were understandably upset. Your frowns are forgotten and your smiles compensate a thousand times for any trifling service I may have been privileged to offer."

"My husband and I are so grateful to you. If the foolish man had just told me that you were a *nobile homo* I should not have spoken so ungraciously. *Sier* Danese says you are his oldest friend and he will ask you to be his witness at the formal wedding ceremony." And so on. Her life had been transformed thanks to me, et cetera.

I was more than happy, et more cetera. If I was Danese's best friend, that said a lot about Danese.

"Fabricio!" the sylph commanded. "Go down and tell *sier* Alfeo's gondolier that he can go. *Sier* Alfeo will dine with us today."

There were two doors opening off that landing and Fabricio, interestingly, was just closing the one on the garden side—wrestling with it, for Venice is built on wooden piles sunk in the mud and sand of the lagoon; doors develop minds of their own as they age. I knew that must be Grazia's chamber. Fabricio no longer carried Danese's portmanteau. Had Grazia ordered this arrangement and did her parents know of it? That was no business of mine.

As a matter of form, I had to protest the dinner invitation, but the idea appealed to my gastrointestinal apparatus, which had been complaining noisily all the way from Ca' Barbolano. Quite apart from the prospect of food, I always enjoy snooping in the homes of the rich, especially if I can win a chance to admire their paintings. With my customary grace I let myself be persuaded.

I offered the lady my arm to steady her on her platform soles as we proceeded up the second flight, while she continued to chatter. Awaiting us in the *salone* were Danese, clad in a smug golden glow, and madonna Eva with a smile of welcome carefully chiseled in place. She was decked out in a dark blue gown to set off her golden hair and a treasure of golden ornaments speckled with diamonds. The wonderfully feminine roundness of her chin and bosom were offset by the sapphire hardness of her blue eyes, two jewels on velvet.

"*Sier* Alfeo! What a pleasant surprise! You are most welcome. You must join us for dinner."

I accepted again.

She forced the smile a notch or two wider. "*Sier* Zuanbattista and I never properly thanked you for all you did. Truly you were the white knight to the rescue! So romantic! So poetic!" *So nice that you hit my son-in-law with a sword.*

"Come!" Grazia snapped, unwilling to be upstaged. She detached me and dragged me in the direction of the *salotto* I had visited on Sunday. Mother and daughter were still on speaking terms, but only barely. I could not believe that women would seriously quarrel over Danese Dolfin himself, but they were playing for points that men could not appreciate.

Great-aunt Fortunata had not been tidied away during my absence, perhaps not even moved for dusting. Crabbed, wizened, lipless, toothless, and malevolent, forked tongued and hairy chinned, she appraised me with two bleary eyes like agate chips in milk and then, to my astonishment, spoke. "The Good Lord told us to judge the tree by the fruit it bears!" I had forgotten how discordant her voice was, the sound of a granite lid being pushed off a crypt.

"Blessed be the name of the Lord."

"Father Varutti says that even your use of demonic forces to rescue Grazia may not have damned you to Hell because it was in a good cause."

"I hope so and believe so," I agreed, "trusting in the salvation that—"

"But he is sure that you are damned anyway."

If contemplation of homicide was cause enough, then I certainly was. I did not bother to explain that I had used no demonic forces and that clairvoyance is no more a black art than astrology is. Even the Pope employs astrologers.

A strikingly pretty maidservant brought us wine. I overheard her being addressed as Noelia, so she was the ladies' maid who had discovered the empty coop. She could not be a day older than twelve.

Trying to edge closer to the Palma Vecchio portrait, I got

cornered by the leering Danese, who thanked me for returning his baggage. The cause of his good cheer was too good
to keep secret. "You saved me a journey, old friend," he
whispered triumphantly. "Grazia has finally made her
mother see reason. We are man and wife in the eyes of the
church. There can be no sin in admitting it." Or admitting
him, in other words. Bedtime, all.

"Congratulations."

So it went. We were obviously waiting for someone, and
my next attempt to stalk a painting brought me within
range of madonna Eva again.

"I am so happy that you can stay to dine, *sier* Alfeo" she
declaimed. "I know my husband will be devastated at having missed this opportunity to thank you again, but he will
be unable to join us."

Danese and Grazia were locked in eye-to-eye adoration,
out of the conversation. I rose to the occasion.

"I don't imagine you see very much of him just now,
madonna."

She pouted, obviously not for the first time. Despite her
comparative youth, her mouth was settling into mean lines.
"Not much more than I saw of him when he was ambassador
in Constantinople! The *Signoria*'s schedule is *brutal*! At least
sier Zuanbattista only has to put up with it for eight
months; I cannot imagine how the poor doge stands it as a
lifetime ordeal. The *Collegio* in the morning, the Senate
most afternoons, and the Council of Ten in the evenings, not
to mention all the purely ceremonial functions, the Great
Council on Sundays, and many diplomatic meetings."

Then she glanced past me and brightened like fireworks
over the Grand Canal. I turned, expecting to see her husband striding through the doorway in his scarlet counselor
robe, but it was merely the nondescript Girolamo in his
ministerial violet.

There were many emotional crosscurrents in Ca' Sanudo

just then, and that new one sent a shiver down my backbone, followed by several other shivers in tandem. I remembered Violetta drawing my attention to Giro and Eva at the theater, not two weeks ago yet, although it felt like a lifetime. Why? She had never explained her real interest in them. I responded automatically to Giro's greetings, apologies for not being there to greet me, and protestations of gratitude for services rendered, while part of my brain spun like a windmill trying to work out relationships. If Giro was his stepmother's lover, as Violetta had hinted . . . That would hardly be surprising, when he was older than she was and she was thirty or forty years younger than her husband, who had been away for years anyway. These things can happen anywhere, not only in Venice. But if Giro and Eva were lovers, why had Danese lied to me about being her lover as well as her *cavaliere servente*? Could the lady have *two* lovers? At the same time? Day shift and night shift?

And what went on at night in the house now that Zuanbattista was back?

Giro had returned from the regular morning meeting of the *Collegio* with the rest of his day free, likely. He hurried off to shed his formal robes and we went into dinner as soon as he returned. Madonna Eva smiled like Medusa as she saddled me with the job of squiring her aunt, who gripped my arm in one claw and a silver-topped cane in the other, and moved like a glacier.

The dining room was adequate, but far from Ca' Barbolano's palatial grandeur. The food was better than Venetian average, but not a patch on Mama Angeli's—the *Risotto di Gò e Bevarasse* was overcooked and the *Branzino al Vapore in Salsa di Vongole* practically raw. It was served by the child Noelia and a fresh-faced youth addressed as Pignate.

I like risotto. The Maestro denounces rice as a newfangled foreign fad and forbids Mama to serve it. She does, quite frequently, which doesn't matter because he never notices what he is eating. He often eats more than usual when there is rice in the dish.

Ca' Sanudo conversation was infinitely duller than any of the Maestro's table monologues. Politics was a forbidden topic, of course, as was anything to do with sex. Madonna Eva discoursed at length about the wedding plans, lamenting the haste required and the limits this imposed on the scale of the celebration. I hung on every word—with the rope cutting into my neck. Old Fortunata mercifully remained silent, poking listlessly at the tiny portions put in front of her but rarely eating anything. Danese and Grazia stayed in their locked-eyeball trance, smiling inanely. Giro was as colorless as always, rarely speaking, watching his stepmother's lips move, but with so little expression or interest that I rejected my earlier suspicions. No one could love a snowbank like Giro. Or perhaps one could and the snowbank could not respond?

Mother and daughter ignored each other throughout the meal. There could be no question which of the two had the better face or finer figure or greater experience, yet youth could trump all of those. Madonna Eva's lover had been stolen by her own daughter, and a certain amount of acrimony was understandable. If she had cherished secret hopes of one day wearing cloth-of-gold as dogaressa, they had been trampled in the dust of dead ambitions. One might even permit a small amount of rub-your-nose-in-it jubilation from Grazia. But where was Girolamo in all this? Whose side was he on? I could not hazard a guess.

Then Danese flashed his perfect teeth at me and asked how I had enjoyed the play. *What play?* of course, and I had to explain how he and I had met outside the theater the previous week.

"I understand that some of the dialogue was on the racy side?" he said blandly.

That was an understatement, because Violetta, always

unpredictable, had chosen a bawdy Rabelaisian farce performed by a traveling company from the mainland, a rehash of the adventures of Captain Fear. No woman in Europe is better educated than Violetta, able to quote Ovid or Dante or Sappho at the flicker of an eyelash. She can sing, play the lute, and dance well enough to dazzle men who have known the courts of Paris or Milan. She might have made her selection to spare the strain on my threadbare purse, but she is a woman of unbounded variety and had enjoyed the vulgarity, laughing as loud as any of the groundlings.

"We do not need to discuss that," Giro said. "Did Father tell you, Mother, that the tallies of the grape harvest are in?"

Eva smiled blissfully and I saw that one of Giro's virtues in her eyes was that he could squelch his new brother-in-law. That did not mean that he had no others, of course, but evidently the lady needed his support against the triumphant Dolfin duo. I could easily imagine Danese throwing off three years' humility and the rags of obsequious *cavaliere servente* to swagger in the finery of son-in-law and heir. Every smile must rub salt in the wounds of Eva's humiliation.

Giro expounded on the grape harvest from the mainland estates; Danese went back to glowing at his bride in wordless rapture. He held all the cards now.

Eventually I asked about the Tintoretto on the wall opposite me, although even at that distance I was sure that it was a *School of Tintoretto* Tintoretto.

"Oh, my father is the collector," Giro told me. "He has a great eye for art."

He glanced at his stepmother as if this was one of those in-jokes that all families share, and for once there was a hint of a smile in his eyes. It was instantly reflected in hers. That was far from proof of guilt—of course a woman and her stepson are allowed to share a joke about her husband's foibles! But by then my imagination was running riot and seeing double meanings in everything.

The meal ended at last. I thanked my host and hostess, congratulated the happy couple again, and was assigned to Fabricio to be rowed home to the Ca' Barbolano and my afternoon's labors, whatever they might turn out to be.

I had more immediate plans, though. I had sensed something far wrong at Ca' Sanudo and if anyone could re-assure me about that noble house, it was Violetta. I asked Fabricio to let me off at the watersteps between Ca' Bar-bolano and Number 96, as if I intended to go along the *calle* to the *campo*. I tipped him more generously than usual, proving to myself that I was not Danese Dolfin. He flashed me an angelic smile as he thanked me. Not *another*, surely? My conscience roared at me for being an evil-minded prude.

I went into the alley, then retraced and emerged. I watched Fabricio row away as I walked along the ledge to the door of 96 and knocked, not having brought my key. If someone in the Sanudo family fancied handsome youngsters on principle—or lack of principles—then Fabricio was a logical choice. The serving girl, the gondolier, the *cavaliere servente* . . . madonna Eva herself. *Saints!* Even the cherubic footman, Pignate! *Messer* Zuanbattista Sanudo had a great eye for art, his son said. Had he meant beauty?

Draped in a gown of silver and violet silk, Violetta was seated at her dressing table while Milana brushed out her hair, but she twisted around to offer me a hand. She was Niobe, whose eyes are a gentle hazel, brimming over with pity.

"Alas! Alfeo, my poor darling! I do wish you'd come sooner, but I cannot dally with you now, or I'll be hopelessly late. Late even for me, I mean."

Seized with guilt for causing such distress, I knelt so I could continue to hold her hand without standing over her.

"I'm already late and I have all the time in the world for you. I need to ask you some questions."

No matter what persona she happens to be wearing, Violetta can read me like a public inscription. A trick of the light, perhaps, but it was the shrewd gray eyes of Minerva that then appraised me. "Still on about the Sanudos? Ask your questions, *clarissimo*."

"Why the Sanudos?"

"Because it is not like you to miss a hint, Alfeo." Minerva's eyes twinkled with deadly humor. "I've been waiting for this."

"Why did you point out Giro and Eva to me at the theater two weeks ago?"

"Because I had found you talking with Danese Dolfin and wondered if you knew who or what he was. You didn't."

"Do you?"

"I don't like to gossip," she announced with a coquettish toss of her head that Milana did not appreciate. "Is it important?"

"Of course it's important! Zuanbattista is one of the senior men in the government. Is he not vulnerable to blackmail?" I could not mention Algol, of course, but I was starting to wonder if there was a connection.

Violetta made a moue, considering. "I don't think so. The whole city is laughing at his wife but Zuanbattista himself is well liked and the seduction, if it happened, occurred while he was away on government business, so he gets a lot of sympathy. Girolamo doesn't seem to care about politics."

"He is not one of your clients, is he? Or any other lady's?"

She chuckled. "His preferences do seem to lie elsewhere. He keeps his emotions under tight control, from what I've heard."

"A cold fish," I agreed. Sodomy may be punished by burning at the stake, but in practice is usually ignored or awarded lesser penalties, such as exile. "So, about three years ago, Zuanbattista goes off to Constantinople, leaving wife, daughter, and son behind in Venice, or at the country house at Celeseo."

"Both. Mostly the mainland, but they came and went."

"Both, then. Knowing his son's inclinations, he was probably not worried about Eva, and at his age he may not worry much anyway, as long as there is no scandal. Giro is in charge of the household. To discredit rumors of his illegal tendencies, he pretends to be having an affair with his beautiful young stepmother, who is younger than he is."

"You're putting it too crudely, dear. Come around to the other side and hold this hand instead. He was seen squiring a beautiful woman. As long as proprieties are observed, nobody really cares."

"But then he instals his catamite, Danese Dolfin, as his stepmother's *cavaliere servente*?"

Minerva regarded me under lowered lashes. "Or Eva hires Danese and Danese takes on additional responsibilities? It would be dangerous to make either statement in public." Sarcasm dripped slow as syrup. "Or Giro stole his stepmother's gigolo for other uses?"

"Then who was Eva's lover? Danese or Giro? Or," I added with a gulp, "did she have two?" This was Venice, where almost anything is tolerated, but even the canals seldom get as murky as that.

Violetta laughed. "Oh, my, darling Alfeo! Who are you to judge them? You claim you love me, yet you know how I earn my crusts. Forget Eva and wonder about young Danese. In whose bed did morning find him—Eva's or Giro's?" Her lashes fanned my fevered brow. "In my profession, one sees everything conceivable, or otherwise, but I am inclined to guess that Dolfin was the busy one of the three. Remember what Cato said about Julius Caesar?—'Every woman's husband and every man's wife'?"

And now Dolfin had Grazia also. I could see why Eva had regarded him as an unsuitable match for her daughter. Poor Grazia! When would her gorgeous eyes be opened to the lecher she had married?

"I must go," I said, rising. "Tomorrow?"

"Tonight," Violetta said. "My evening is free. You can come any time after sunset and stay until dawn—unless you believe that overindulgence will be injurious to your health?"

"Madonna," I said, kissing her ear, "I won't care if it kills me. Until tonight, then!"

12

"Get him to tell you the one about the sea monster," I said as I went past.

The *vizio* was sitting in the *salone* telling stories to a pack of Angeli youngsters—Piero, Noemi, Ambra, and Archangelo. No prize for guessing who would be the hero of all of the tales. His eyes measured me for a gibbet.

The Maestro was at the desk, studying a manuscript folio of *Sun of Suns and Moon of Moons* by Abu Bakr Ahmad Ibn Wahshiyah, his favorite ninth-century alchemist, known to me as Abu the Confusing. There were no other papers in sight, other than the pile of cryptography books on my side of the desk. Since they had not been disturbed, I concluded that the Maestro was no longer working on the Algol cipher. He might still be working on Algol himself, though. Demons live a long time; Abu might have met him.

The room was suffocatingly hot. All the windows were open, but not a breath of wind came or went. I could hear the cries of the gondoliers on the canal below as clearly as if I were a passenger.

"You're late," the Maestro said without looking up.

"I was following up a juicy piece of scandal. It seems that the Sanudo family is vulnerable to blackmail."

That got his attention. "Blackmailing a member of the Ten would be a dangerous career. Are you suggesting that Zuanbattista is the traitor, Algol?"

That was what I was trying not to worry about. I liked Zuanbattista! He had been more than generous to me and unusually kind to his daughter. But it was possible. He had just returned from the Sultan's court, and a really suspicious mind, like mine, might wonder if his trumpeted success there had been contrived by the Porte to foster his political career here.

"I hope not," I said. "He seems to be the injured party. His wife employed Danese, but everyone knows that already. His son probably has uncommon tastes, so he might be vulnerable."

My master pouted, took a sheet of paper from under his book, and passed it over. "A fair copy, quickly." *Fair* means *legible*.

I sat down, opened my inkwell, and then froze. The writing was even worse than his usual scrabbled hand, all badly spaced capital letters, but it was the meaning that stopped me cold:

> *. . . GRAVE SCARS ITADI CORDE ETAST ENUOV EDALL IADAL MAZIA RISOL TAINE STATE MACER COREM ATORI . . .*

I made that: ". . . grave scarsità di corde et aste nuove dallia Dalmazia risolta in estate ma cerco rematori . . ."*

It went on to discuss powder and shot, caulking, and raw linen for sails.

I gulped. "Master, is this a report on the Arsenale?"

---

* . . . serious shortage of cordage and fresh spars from Dalmatia overcome by summer, but finding rowers . . .

He was back in his book again. Still not looking up, he said, "Quite a detailed survey, it seems. The Ten will know whether or not it is accurate and how much damage such knowledge of our navy yard will do in the hands of our foes. Regrettably, that page does not identify the writer. 'Quickly,' I said."

I opened my pen box and chose a quill. I so often see the old rascal work wonders that I have come to expect them of him, but if he had broken the Algol cipher from the evidence of a single sheet, after the Ten's renowned experts had failed to crack twenty-four pages in God-alone-knew how many weeks or months, then that miracle would top them all. I passed over the fair copy.

As he read it, he held out a tiny hand for the original. "Now bring your friend in."

His crabby tone suggested that he was pleased with himself. I went to poke my head around the door and whistle for Vasco, then went back to my chair.

The Maestro laid a ribbon at his page and closed the book. He puckered his thin cheeks in a close-lipped smile. "Ah, *Vizio*! I have a problem. Sciara dropped a broad hint that the spy known as Algol may have agents within the Ten. He instructed me to report progress to the chiefs, but even they must be to some degree suspect until we know otherwise, right?"

"I am not privy to such information, Doctor," Vasco said stuffily.

"No, you wouldn't . . . I have some progress to report already and no further need of those papers you guard so diligently. Which reminds me." The Maestro opened a drawer and took out a sheet of paper. "This was on the floor in the dining room. It is yours, I think. Now, where was I?"

Vasco angrily restored the lost sheet to the others in his satchel. He did not look at my smile, which was a masterpiece worthy of extended admiration.

"When you take the documents back to the palace," the Maestro continued, "to whom will you deliver them?"

Smelling traps now, Vasco was wary. "I shall report to *Missier Grande*, of course. He will probably send me to return the documents to *Circospetto*, but that will be his decision."

Nostradamus nodded. "But Sciara reports to the Grand Chancellor. I must be confident that my information will not disappear in some unfortunate accident. Take a chair. No, on second thought take Alfeo's, where I can see you more easily. My neck, you know . . ."

I never heard him complain of his neck before, but he was certainly up to something. Suppressing outrage at being evicted from my rightful place, I yielded it to Vasco and then stood over him to watch.

"Alfeo, give the *vizio* a sheet of paper and a pen. Good. Now, if you please, *lustrissimo*, write the alphabet along the top. Capitals are easier."

"May I help him?" I murmured, but Vasco managed to win through on his own:

$$A\ B\ C\ D\ E\ F\ G\ H\ I\ J\ L\ M\ N\ O\ P\ Q\ R\ S\ T\ U\ V\ X\ Z$$

The Maestro had even worse torment in store for him. "Now, write *B* under *A* and the rest of the alphabet until you reach *Z* again, and complete the row with an *A*."

I was already flipping through Giovan Batista Belaso's *La cifra del Sig* to find the illustration.

"You see where you are going?" the Maestro said. "The next row would begin with *C*, yes? You would end by listing all Caesar alphabets possible with an alphabet of twenty-three letters. If you were to include some of the barbaric runes that northern tribes like the English and Germans use, you would have more."

Vasco nodded uncertainly.

"Alfeo told you how easy it is to break a Caesar cipher. But if you use several Caesars by turn, then the cipher becomes unbreakable! Or so the sagacious Belaso believed and later authorities have agreed. The only thing you need to establish in advance with your correspondent is the order in which you will use the alphabets. No? Well, let us attempt an example. A little farther down the page write the sentence, 'Sciara, who is furtive.' In uppercase letters, if you please."

Vasco wrote, *SCIARA, CHE È CIRCOSPETTO*.

"And then put it in five-letter groups, as Algol does."

SCIAR ACHEÈ CIRCO SPETT O

The Maestro pressed his fingertips together, enjoying his lecture. "Now we shall apply the key, and in this case the word will be *VIRTÙ*, as that was Algol's choice. The man has a sense of irony, if not humor. Pray write that under each of the groups."

SCIAR ACHEÈ CIRCO SPETT O
VIRTÙ VIRTÙ VIRTÙ VIRTÙ V

"Excellent. Now leave a line and write out the normal alphabet again. Good. Under it write the Caesars you will use to encipher your plaintext." He frowned at Vasco's blank stare—he is accustomed to dealing with my less-circumscribed intelligence. "The first row, you begin with a *V . . . VXZAB . . .* and end with *U*. The next begins *IJLMN . . .*"

It took a while and Vasco's rows and columns were not as straight as might be desired, but he got there. The Maestro was beaming.

"Excellent! We'll make a scribe out of you yet. Now to begin the encipherment! Under the first letter of the plaintext, *S*, you see the *V* of *VIRTÙ*, yes? So you find *S* in the normal alphabet, the one that begins with *A*, and go down to the alphabet that begins with *V* and what letter do you find?"

Thoroughly bewildered, Vasco did not find any, so I directed him to *P*, and he wrote it underneath the *S*, as instructed. The next letter, *C*, on the *I* alphabet, came out as *B*, and so on. By the time he reached the middle of the second group, he was managing by himself and I was making admiring noises.

> SCIAR ACHEÈ CIRCO SPETT O
> VIRTÙ VIRTÙ VIRTÙ VIRTÙ V
> PBLTN VLAZ . . .

"This is absolutely brilliant!" I said. "How in the world did you do it?"

The Maestro made no effort to appear modest. "The pattern you noticed indicated that a letter's position within each group was important, so I tried a frequency analysis on the initial letter of each group. It showed too many *B*'s, so I hypothesized that *B* stood for either *E* or *A*, in which case the Caesar alphabet began with either *V* or *B*. Then I tried the second letter of each group, and so on. A rigorous analysis would require more plaintext than just one page, but I found enough clues to work out that the key must be *VIRTÙ*. It was not so difficult once I recalled the theories of Trithemius, Cardano, Porta, and so on. I'm astonished Sciara and his rabble did not see it. I admit, though," he added, being hypocritically gracious, "that I have never heard of polyalphabetic substitution ever being used in practice."

He had been lucky. *Che* is not merely a common word in itself; that combination of letters appears in many words in both Tuscan and *Veneziano*. Whenever it fell in the middle of a five-letter group, it had enciphered as my initials, which had caught my eye. In any other position it was represented by some other triplet, and with another key word it might always be. Then we would not have noticed the repetition. The best ciphers are broken because of human error, Nostradamus had told us, and Algol should never have left the ciphertext in five-letter groupings. That was incredible carelessness.

Vasco, meanwhile had completed the enciphering and was staring in bewilderment at the result:

PBLTN VLAZA ZRJVJ L

He had not even noticed my *LAZ* in there.

"So there you are, *Vizio*," the Maestro said. "That is how it is enciphered. Now let us try some deciphering. We need to know if the same keyword will work for all four intercepted messages. Page one of one, if you please."

With surprisingly little help from me, Vasco managed to reverse the process and start recovering the original plaintext:

XIAGO ILCON SIGLI ODEID E . . .

He stopped. "This is gibberish!"

The Maestro sighed. "Perhaps the key word is not the same, then." He was carefully not looking at me, who could read over Vasco's shoulder. Unlike Vasco, though, I was reading: *11 Agosto. Il Consiglio dei Deci* . . . *

"Let us try the final dispatch then. Page one of four, please."

Again Vasco balked after a few groups, but this time a ray broke through the clouds. "Wait a moment! They begin with dates!"

XVSET TILPR ESDI . . .

*Aug. 11 The Council of Ten . . .

15 Settembre. Il presidio . . . *

"Why, so they do!" I cried.

The game was over. Vasco hastily covered his work with his hands.

"You don't need to see this!"

"Of course not," the Maestro agreed. "You can let *Missier Grande* into the secret and he can decipher the rest."

But I was confident that the Maestro himself would break the news to *Circospetto*, so he could watch Sciara gnash his fangs in mortification. Vasco looked at him as if suspecting the sort of elaborate hoax that I love to play on him every time I get the chance, but which the Maestro considers beneath his dignity.

"This nonsense will translate everything?"

Nostradamus sighed and opened a drawer. "Here is a deciphered version of the page you left in the dining room."

It was his own version, and Vasco needed some time to decipher the scrawl and artificial letter groups. As he did, he grew paler and paler.

"The interesting thing," the Maestro remarked, and now he was looking at me, although his expression gave away nothing, "was that *Circospetto* lied to us."

"Yes, he did," I agreed. Today was September 23. If Algol's fourth dispatch reported news of events on September 15, there had not been time for it to reach Constantinople and the Republic's spy there to copy it and report back to Venice. Of all the states Algol might be working for, even Rome, the closest, would require almost impossible timing. If the Ten were opening Algol's mail right here in the city, why did they not know the sender?

Vasco would never work that out, but before he rose to the bait, the door swung wide and in marched Bruno, carrying a bundle of firewood that would have flattened me. We

*Sept. 15 The garrison . . .

have taught him to knock on doors, but he does not understand "audibly," so it does no good. Beaming at us, he delivered his burden to the hearth, then strode out again, leaving
the door open.

"Chilled?" Vasco inquired icily.

"Important business," the Maestro said. "I must report to
the chiefs. You are welcome to accompany us, *Vizio*. Go and
pack up your things. You can be of no further use here."

Almost no other commoner in Venice would have dared
speak to Vasco like that, but he took it from the Ten's con-
sultant. Glowering at me to indicate that our temporary
truce was now ended, he stuffed the latest paper in his
satchel and departed.

The Maestro detests having to go out, and I could not recall him ever doing so two days in a row. He must be expecting a handsome reward, in satisfaction, if not in coin. I
hurried to my room to don my best. This time I decided to
sacrifice good manners on the altar of security, for I knew we
were on dangerous business and would be lacking Filiberto's
dubious protection on the way home. I retrieved my rapier
and dagger from the top of the wardrobe.

As Giorgio's strong oar sped us along the Grand Canal
toward the Doges' Palace, I heard the bells of San Giacomo
di Rialto tolling sunset.

13

So we returned to the palace and the same chamber we had left not twenty-four hours earlier, the *Sala dei Tre Capi*. The three chiefs themselves must have been rounded up especially to hear our report, for we were kept waiting only a few minutes and Marino Venier still had crumbs in his beard. The Pope himself could not have asked for greater deference than that. Obviously the government was still extremely worried; *La Serenissima* was anything but serene.

The heat of the day had left the room stifling. The lamps were lit, but their glimmer hardly showed against the remains of daylight. As the Maestro shuffled in, leaning on my shoulder, the chiefs were just settling behind their raised table, and the only aide in sight was Raffaino Sciara, the Grim Reaper in blue. Vasco had left us, gone to report to *Missier Grande*, no doubt. Sciara placed a chair for the Maestro and retreated to the secretaries' desk. I saw my master seated, then took my place behind him.

Three old men peered anxiously down at Nostradamus.

Trevisan was in the center. "Well, Doctor? You wasted no time. What news?"

I had never seen the Maestro's pussycat smile better displayed.

"I have not yet identified your Algol, *messere*, although I have my suspicions. To confirm or disprove those will take a little longer, but I am satisfied that he exists and I have broken his cipher. I deemed this sufficient cause to interrupt your supper."

Six eyes turned toward Raffaino Sciara. I looked at him also, because I had never seen a skull look humiliated before.

"You will show Their Excellencies the restored plaintext?" *Circospetto* demanded acidly.

"I did not venture to pry into it all," the Maestro said with false humility. I could tell he was enjoying himself hugely, although the others might not be reading the signals. "I have no need to know the Republic's secrets. I deciphered one page, just to be sure, and most of it seemed to be street gossip with a few nuggets of intelligence. I can confirm that the key is the same in all the four documents. Alfeo?" He handed me the fair copy I had made for him, and I stepped forward to hand it up to Trevisan. Three heads almost banged together as the chiefs all tried to read it at once.

"So what is the cipher?" Sciara demanded, quite as furious now as he was supposed to be.

"A simple polyalphabetic," the Maestro said mildly.

"I am impressed, Doctor." Sciara had to admit that, however sourly, after his minions had failed to crack it. "I have always understood that there was no way of breaking a polyalphabetic cipher."

The three chiefs were still muttering together, jabbing fingers at the plaintext.

"The simple Cardano form used by this Algol person is vulnerable," the Maestro said, rubbing salt in the wound. "Had he followed the subtler recommendations of the sagacious Monsieur Vigenère and used the plaintext to encode itself, then even I might have failed to break it. As it is, I showed it all to Filiberto Vasco. He will explain the technique to you." He stretched his lips in a helpful smile.

I came very close to exploding. The thought of Sciara taking lessons from dear Filiberto was exquisite.

"We are deeply impressed, Doctor," Marino Venier growled. "This document appears to be genuine. As you saw, it does include some covert information." The chiefs were all smiling, though. Their decision to consult Nostradamus had borne fruit and the skeptics within the Ten would have to eat their doubts. "You said you had other evidence for us?"

"Nothing that you can put before a court, *messere*. May I inquire who named this spy 'Algol'?"

The heads exchanged glances. The outer two nodded. Trevisan said, "We have reason to believe that his employers refer to him by that name. A codeword or a joke, perhaps."

"I fear it may be more," the Maestro said. "I may speak in confidence, *messere?*"

"You have certainly earned that right."

I certainly did not expect him to mention that his foresight had been blurred or my tarot confused, for that would be tantamount to a confession of practicing witchcraft, but he came close.

"I have detected occult interference with my work. I have even had a premonition that Algol will seek to entrap me, planning to destroy my usefulness to the Republic."

"We shall provide additional guards!" Soranzo barked as the other two spluttered in alarm.

That was the last thing Nostradamus wanted. "No, *messere*! I do not expect the entrapment to take the form of physical violence, for that would be too easily traced back to him. The attack will be of a supernatural essence. I can take steps to defend myself and *sier* Alfeo from it, but others would be more vulnerable. Even the admirable *vizio*—and I assure you that I have absolute faith in Filiberto Vasco's loyalty and dedication—even the *vizio* could be corrupted by black art. I ask that you remove him from my premises. His sword cannot defend against the powers of darkness, and he may merely get in the way of what I propose to do."

Neatly done, I thought. He had used Vasco to rid himself of Danese and now was getting rid of Vasco also. That would be convenient, as long as he did not find Algol taking their place.

"May we inquire exactly what that is?" Soranzo asked narrowly. "Just what are you proposing to do?" Although far from being an outright skeptic like the doge, he was ranking doubter among the three chiefs.

"I propose to unmask Algol," the Maestro said testily. "Quite apart from menacing the beloved Republic of which I have the honor of being an adopted citizen, he has used demonic powers against me and my apprentice, an intrusion I shall not tolerate. Doubtless he was originally a loyal subject of his ruler, who believed that he was serving a noble cause when he began to dabble in black arts, but the laws of demonology are infrangible, and he has undoubtedly fallen into the power of the Powers he sought to control. I shall identify him and report him to—"

I thought for a moment that he was going to continue, "—Holy Mother Church for exorcism." That would have been disastrous. The last thing Venice ever wants is the Vatican trying to meddle in its affairs of state. He caught himself in time. "—your honored selves."

The chiefs had sensed the hesitation and were frowning.

"Just how do you propose to identify this demon-wielder you describe?" Trevisan demanded, perhaps imagining holy water being splattered in all directions in the name of the Council of Ten. That would not do, either.

"No demon-wielder, *clarissimo*. A damned soul, fallen into the clutches of the Evil One. There is a procedure . . . I do not contemplate black magic, Your Excellencies, but of invoking certain elementals, spirits that are morally neutral, neither good nor evil. Fire elementals are particularly attuned to demons, understandably, but are not in themselves damned, because fire is one of God's boons to mankind. Fire can purify or it can destroy. Certain ancient authorities list some obscure procedures to elicit the aid of these spirits. I believe it would be possible to call on them to identify the possessed person or persons."

Soranzo rolled his eyes. The other two chiefs crossed themselves.

"You can do this?" Trevisan demanded.

I suspected the Maestro could smell another thousand-ducat fee, maybe ten thousand. On the other hand, I did not think he would ever descend to witch hunting.

He sighed. "Alas, no. In my youth I might have essayed the effort, for it is a skill of the young. Now it would kill me. Fortunately my apprentice, *sier* Alfeo Zeno, here, is extraordinarily well attuned to pyrogenic forces. He has an astonishing natural talent for pyromancy. I believe I can guide him to . . . Of course the risks are bloodcurdling, so the final decision must be his alone."

Every eye in the room fixed on me. As I had never heard of my natural talent in pyromancy before, I attempted to look modest and calmly courageous. What in Hades was the old rascal up to this time?

What exactly were these "bloodcurdling" risks?

"Let us get this straight," Soranzo said. "You realize that you are still bound by your oath to give true witness in this inquiry, and you are stating that your apprentice has the power to identify any demons that may be wandering around the city?"

The Maestro waved a hand dismissively.

"Of course not! There are minor demons everywhere. Would you expect him to stand on the bell tower of San

Marco and locate every cooking fire in the city? But if there happened to be a great building ablaze, then he should be able to locate that, surely? A major demon is a furnace of evil and this one has dared to meddle in my affairs. Alfeo is a brave and resourceful lad, and with my guidance . . . I am merely saying that there are methods he may be able to use to identify a *major* demon within the city, and I do not know any man with greater skills in this field."

I made a mental note to demand a substantial raise before it was too late. Meanwhile the chiefs had realized that they were on the point of contracting Maestro Nostradamus to perform magic for them.

"Then we urge you to continue your investigations," Trevisan said hastily. "The Republic will be generous if you are successful. Remember how confidential this matter is."

What he meant was, *Go away and do it, but don't tell us.*

14

Having seen the Maestro securely loaded on Bruno's great shoulders, and retrieved my rapier from the *fante* who had confiscated it, I led the way out of the palace by the Frumento gate with no small sense of relief. Dusk was settling over the basin, where a dozen galleys lately returned from distant lands had been unloading cargo all day and now were falling silent. Giorgio was chatting with a dozen other gondoliers on the Molo, and waved when he saw us. In moments we were skimming over the waters of the Grand Canal, homeward bound and rid of both our uninvited guests.

The long day was over, I hoped—I had a date with Violetta. Yet I had not forgotten all the firewood that Bruno had taken into the atelier. Pyromancy? I knew nothing about pyromancy and would happily wait until tomorrow to learn. It was too hot for pyromancy, although sunset was painting blood on great clouds to the east, the first clouds I had seen in weeks. The heat might be going to break at last.

Mama had supper ready, of course. Dismissing mention of it, the Maestro went straight to the atelier. Eating he considers a waste of time. I unlocked the door for him and detoured around him to get ahead and light the lamps, hoping we could have a discussion about those bloodcurdling risks he had mentioned and the decision that I was to be allowed to make.

He hobbled over to the red chair. "Bring me *Sun of Suns*, then go and eat."

I was pleasantly surprised. "Thank you, master."

"You need to keep your strength up." Since he did not know about my date with Violetta, that last remark was not encouraging.

Restored by two helpings of Mama's excellent *granceole all ricca*, I returned to find him as I had left him, nose deep in Abu the Confusing. Without even looking up, he said, "Warn Giorgio that we are not to be disturbed on any account. First you must set the *Aegia Salomonis*. Let me hear the incantation."

I sat down, regretting my second helping of spider crabs. "It is still early, master. Not all the Marcianas will be home yet."

He dismissed my objection with a *Pshaw!* noise. "Residents returning will not harm the wards as long as they come with peaceful intent. The incantation!"

The Armor of Solomon was easily the longest and most complicated spell he had taught me, and I took a few moments to rehearse my memory. One slip during the actual ritual and I would have to start all over from the beginning. Then I drew a deep breath and repeated the incantation from start to finish.

"Not bad," he admitted, which is effusive praise from him. "Proceed. Just remember it is your neck you are saving." He went back to his book.

Inspired by this admonition, I fetched a fresh beeswax candle, our jar of balm of Gilead, and a twig of olive wood. The roof was the obvious place to begin, because that was where the candle was most likely to be blown out, another

fault that would require me to start over. As I climbed the
attic stair, I heard the youngest Angeli children being put
to bed, but I managed to slip out the hatch to the *altana*
without being detected. Absolutely the last thing I needed
was a band of chattery witnesses asking what sort of devil
worship I was engaged in now, or—even worse—trying to
help. The clouds were ominously closer although there was
no wind; it was the calm before the storm. I knelt, opened
the jar of oil, and glanced around to see if I was being
watched. I wasn't, so I lit the candle and began.

The ritual required me to draw the tree of life on the
deck with the olive stick while holding the candle in my left
hand and reciting the incantation. The tree of life schema
comprises twenty-two paths connecting the *sephiroth*, the
ten attributes of God, and again no errors are allowed, although the balm is so close to invisible that you have to locate each node as you go along pretty much by memory.
This is not the sort of exercise you would want to try while
calculating solar eclipses or dancing the *moresca*. I reached
the end without a stumble, corked the jar, and set off back
down the stairs, still clutching the lighted candle and wondering why I had not enrolled as an archer on a war galley
instead of apprenticing to a philosopher.

Luck was with me, and I managed to descend all the way
to the *androne* without encountering anyone. There I found a
secluded nook behind a stack of wine barrels and repeated
the ritual undisturbed. In the still, enclosed space, the balm
suffused the air with its distinctive sweetness. When I finished this second station, the worst of my ordeal was over,
because the aegis would already be powerful enough to protect me from casual interruption. Back up in the Maestro's
apartment, I performed the ritual four more times—in my
bedroom, the dining room, the kitchen, and finally in the
atelier, each time writing the tree on the floor under the
windows. The last time, the Maestro heaved himself off his

chair to hobble over and watch. As I completed the drawing and the recitation, the candle went out of its own accord, signifying that the *Aegia Salomonis* was now in place. By warding Ca' Barbolano at zenith, nadir, and the four cardinal points, I had made it proof against satanic influences.

"Whew!" I sat down on the floor with a thud, feeling as if I had just swum the length of the Grand Canal in plate armor.

"Good," the Maestro said, with heartwarming indifference for my exertions. "Now go and fetch the Guise of Night."

With a sigh almost inaudible, if not quite, I rose to do as I was bidden. Of course no occult defense can withstand the evils of the world for long, and even the *Aegia Salomonis* could not deflect an armed intrusion. The moment a physical enemy gained entry, the spiritual barriers would fail also.

I store the Guise of Night in a bag at the bottom of my clothes chest, accompanied by some aromatic herbs, yet it still smells old and fusty, with an ominous overtone of singed. I returned to the atelier, locking the door behind me.

Without looking up, the Maestro said, "Lay the fire."

I obeyed, although I was still decked out in my palace best. Nostradamus continued to frown over the book, comparing text on two or three different pages. Obviously he was not completely familiar with whatever procedure he was planning to inflict on me, which was not especially comforting. I finished placing the smallest sticks over the tinder and stood up, dusting my hands. Building a fire is something I have always been good at; my mother would always have me strike the flint for her.

"You want me to light it, master?"

He still did not look up. "Put on the Guise of Night."

"I don't need to."

Now he did look up. "Mm? What?"

"I can perform pyrokinesis without wearing the Guise. I never use it unless I am alone, as you warned me, but I don't need to get dressed up for it."

He chuckled. "Of course you don't! You heard what I told the chiefs about your natural talent for pyromancy. Did you think I was making all that up? I remind you that I was under oath."

"Oh," I said. "Then do let's discuss the bloodcurdling risks."

He shrugged his narrow shoulders. "I may have exaggerated just a trifle. What do you remember about the first spell I ever taught you?"

"About a month after you took me on. You made me dress up in that ridiculous *stuff*"—I pointed at the Guise of Night bundle—"and then you showed me how to ignite a scrap of tinder."

"And you did it. Right off."

"Well you told me it was an easy spell and it was." That was how I had lit the candle for the *Aegis* spell.

He stretched his mouth in a close-lipped smile. "I told you it was easy just to give you confidence. It turned out to be child's play for you, amazingly so. You did it in a few minutes. It took me a month to master it when my uncle taught me. You know you have skill at calcining and vesication. Boy, you seethe with so much phlogiston it's a wonder you don't self-combust!"

I distrust the old rascal when he flatters. On the other hand, Violetta sometimes expresses similar opinions, couched in less-technical terminology. "Thank you, master."

"I've never bothered to teach you any more pyromancy because I know you'll swallow it whole." The fact that he expected me to be much better at it than he was would be quite irrelevant, of course. "Now put on the costume."

"I don't need it," I repeated. "I don't even need the ring." There was an unlit candle on the mantel. I pointed my left thumb at it, turning my palm outward so that my fingers stood up like flames. I moved them gently, spoke the Word, and a wisp of smoke rose from the wick, followed by a tiny yellow flame. "See?" I probably smirked.

He sighed. "Your elemental balance is hopelessly skewed! No wonder you can't foresee in the crystal. No matter. We must follow the directions of the sagacious Abu Ibn Wahshiyah, so stop arguing and put on the Guise."

Grumpily I picked up the bundle and went over to the examination couch in the corner. Feeling ridiculous, I stripped to the skin. The Guise is made of some rough cotton, dyed black. I don't know where it came from, or how old it is; it is big on me and would swallow the Maestro completely. I began with a waistband; then loose stockings that extended from toes to crotch and laced up to the waistband; then a thigh-length smock and gloves. Leaving the hood for later, I returned to the fireplace, feeling utterly absurd.

"The crystal shows the future," he said, laying the book facedown on his lap. "As you know, glass won't work. It must be rock crystal, which is eternal. Fire both purifies and destroys; it shows spirits, both sacred and demonic. According to Ibn Wahshiyah, you must use a fire you ignited yourself with the Word and you must be wearing the Guise of Night. Here."

He held out a gold ring bearing a ruby, which tradition requires but I do not need, at least for simple fire lighting. I slid it on my left thumb and donned the hood, so that only my eyes were visible.

"Early for Carnival," I said, in a voice that sounded muffled even to me.

"Don't be flippant. How much frankincense do we have?"

"Half a jar." I fetched it from the reagent shelves, being careful not to trip over the floppy ends of my hose.

"Scatter it over the pyre and then ignite it."

With the ring to symbolize sunlight and fire, pyrokinesis was as easy as snapping fingers. I pointed my thumb at the tinder . . . the gesture . . . the Word . . . smoke curled. Then flames. I made the twigs and chips around it blaze up also.

The Maestro muttered something flattering. "Now you must extinguish all other lights and close the shutters."

I admit that I was feeling skeptical. Perhaps my endless efforts to foresee in the crystal had made me give up hope of ever developing prophetic skills of my own. I should have remembered that I was skilled with the tarot and had been making progress in oneiromancy. I extinguished all the lamps and candles and returned to sit cross-legged on the hearthrug.

"Build up the pyre," the Maestro said. "Use lots of wood, because this may take a while. Then just watch. Let your thoughts wander. We have all night."

"I'll be well cooked in five minutes in this heat," I grumbled.

Sitting staring into a fire by night is the most soothing experience I know. As a child I had sat for hours like that, in the tiny single room I shared with my mother, whiling away the tedium of winter nights. As predictor of my future the fire had served me poorly, for I had never foreseen the Maestro or my hands massaging away an ache in the doge's back. To a bored—and often hungry—boy, the glowing embers had illustrated great ships venturing out over the seas, bound for wonderful places. I had seen myself aboard them, strong and handsome, swaggering with a sword, massacring pirates, bowing before great ladies—although ladies had not interested me much back then. Now, I thought, I should be able to find Violetta fairly easily, but I searched the blaze in vain for her.

At first the flames were too unsteady but as the fire

burned hotter, coals began to glow and images grew crisper. Unburned wood became stone and the brightnesses between morphed into caves and crypts and passages, leading deeper into labyrinths of infinite mystery. It seemed that my fancy should be able to penetrate inside those fiery voids, exploring around corners and onward, deeper into the fire; that I, shielded and made invisible by the Guise of Night, could wander unharmed within those vast caverns of heat. Stalactites of fire hung on every side, draperies of flame enclosed me in a world of red and black, but I strode freely on, seeing wonders all around. Glowing basilisks and demons on guard could not see me or challenge my right to pass into a truly magical world.

In my dreaming progress I saw sphinxes and cherry trees, galleons and gladiators, but I did not linger until I arrived at a dark alcove, a hallway on my left, vast and cryptical, where stood two men I could not identify, for they were men of flame that wavered as flames will. One was gold and the other red. Nor could I make out their voices through the busy crackling of the fire all about me, but I could tell that they were quarreling. Their dispute grew ever more agitated until Red suddenly charged, raising a weapon—a cudgel, I thought, from the way he held it. Gold leaped back and drew a sword. He tried to lunge, but Red struck his blade aside and closed with him. Two flames joined, Red and Gold striving for possession of the sword. Gold evidently lost, for he broke loose and tried to flee, but Red stabbed at his legs with the sword; he dropped to his hands and knees, and Red plunged the blade into his back. He collapsed, understandably. I caught a brief glimpse of Gold lying prone and the victorious Red standing over him before the tragedy vanished in a blizzard of sparks.

Somewhere far off I could hear my own voice angrily describing what I was seeing, responding to the Maestro's questions as if they were intolerable distractions. The part of me that wandered through the inferno was unaware of him, preferring to admire the twisted columns of flame that supported the roof, unseen far above. This was not the Inferno of which Dante sang, but a metaphorical playground of the fire elementals. Faces watching me were not damned souls, for many smiled. Some I knew, but they were all unimportant for my quest, so I pushed on through them without response.

Now the floor tilted downward until I walked thigh-deep in a sea of flame. Waves ran through it, and at times ran through me also, so that I walked underwater, except that the water was fire. In the troughs, when my head was above the fiery sea, I saw a figure in the breakers, two figures contesting together, so I headed in their direction.

One was undoubtedly Neptune, the old man of the sea, easily recognizable by his flowing beard as the model for the statue in the courtyard of the Doges' Palace. The other was a mighty horse—a seahorse, obviously—plunging and bucking amid the fiery foam. This was important and I watched until I was certain that Neptune was going to win the tussle before I resumed my journey.

Clear of the ocean again, I walked down a long canyon lined with an infinity of alcoves holding infinities of shelves, each bearing infinite fires. "This," I declared, "must be the storehouse of all wisdom," for some shelves burned with clear, pure golden light, and others with dark red evil. Clothed in flames and whirling sparks, many people moved to and fro along the central hall, veering off to explore alcoves, ever seeking whatever it was their hearts desired. One couple I followed, although they did not seem to notice me trailing them. The woman was of rare beauty and they walked together bravely, hand in hand.

The man cried out and fell; in that moment I recognized him as Nicolò Morosini, Eva's dead brother. The woman reeled back from whatever it was that had struck him down and turned to flee. I stepped aside as she approached, but after her came a small but fearsome thing of evil, perhaps a spider, moving too fast for her. Like a cat it leaped upon her. I rushed to help, brandishing flame, but she succumbed before I reached her and then the thing, whatever it was, darted toward me. Now it was my turn to fly in terror. I ran as hard and fast as I could but it pursued, racing over the ground, a fiery scorpion on many tiny legs. It was gaining, gaining . . .

I cried out and the Maestro battered the pyre with the poker to shatter the visions and bring me back.

15

The last relict logs collapsed in heaps of ash. Jumping awake, I squealed and almost fell over backward. I must have been sitting there for hours, for the wood had sunk to a bed of glowing coals. The real world seemed dark, cold, and unpleasantly solid. My eyes ached.

"Oh, well done, Alfeo! Well, well done!"

I could not recall the last time he had given me such praise, but I hardly registered it at the time. "What'd I say?"

"You don't remember?"

I did, or at least I would when I had time to separate all the confused images, but I just shook my head. My throat hurt too much to speak.

"Wonderful things. Are you all right?"

I nodded, but thirst tormented me as if I had been eating salt. My legs were numb, my throat burned. I staggered to my feet, cotton hose slipping on the terrazzo. "Need a drink!"

"Of course. You go to bed. I'll close up here."

That was an unparalleled concession! I really must have done well. I had discovered a whole new talent.

"Yes." I skidded and staggered across the room. The air out in the *salone* was probably as hot as ever, but felt like a welcome caress of cold after the atelier. Sweaty cloth clung to my skin. The big hall was dim, for only two lamps were lit, so it was the sound of a sword scraping from its sheath that stopped me, before I even saw the flash of the blade in front of me.

"*Gesù!*" Vasco's startled face came into focus.

"*Saints!*" I croaked. "You back again?" I hauled off my hood.

"You?" He sheathed his sword. "What in Heaven's name are you doing?"

"Rehearsing for Carnival. Why are you here?"

"The Council of Ten sent me back to guard you."

Disgusted, I said, "That's a wonderful step up for you. Now get out of my way." I headed for the water barrel.

In the kitchen, I found Giorgio in the near darkness, asleep with his top half sprawled on the table, and the bench taking his weight. I made enough noise with the ladle to waken him. He sat up, showing no surprise at seeing me clad in black from the neck down.

"I'm sorry, Alfeo! The *vizio* bullied his way in past Luigi and insisted the Ten had sent him. I made him promise not to disturb—"

I paused for air. "You did right." Another long, long drink . . . "You couldn't refuse him. No harm done." Except, of course, that Vasco was an armed man and he had entered uninvited, so he had broken the *Aegia Salomonis*. He might have done no direct harm himself, but what else had he let in that might? Sensing our barrier, had Algol used the *vizio* to break through and perhaps been able to pervert and falsify all my pyromancy? Damn!

"But before that—"

"Never mind!" I insisted. "Tell us in the morning. Go to bed."

So Giorgio slunk off up to the attic, furious at having failed in his duty. I, having drunk enough to fill the Grand Canal, stalked back into the *salone*. I could hear the Maestro and Vasco arguing, so I left them to it and went into my room, locking the door behind me.

Here the air was even cooler, for all three windows stood wide and the heat had broken at last. As I hurried over to close the casements, I heard rain and distant rumbles of thunder. I had drunk so much water that I ought to have been breathing steam, yet I burned as if I were still infested with fire elementals. The effect they had on me then was that I needed—desperately needed—Violetta. Fortunately, she seldom goes to sleep before dawn. My clothes were still in the atelier and I could not waste time in changing. Although I rarely attempt the jump across to the *altana* of Number 96 when there is a wind blowing, that night I was ready to dare anything.

Having tied my keys around my neck with a lace, I opened the central casement again and lifted out the three loose bars, setting them on the floor with their tops leaning on the sill. Then I scrambled out and stood with my heels on the extremely narrow ledge just below, clinging to the fourth bar for support and already soaked. I heard the *marangona* bell in the Piazza toll midnight as I replaced the other bars and pulled the heavy casement ajar. Then I turned, leaped into the dark, hit the tiles with my foot, caught the rail of the *altana*, and was across.

The higher rooms at Number 96 were still jubilant with laughter and music and even a few angry voices, but the corridor and the stairs were dark and empty, so no one saw the bizarre apparition running down from the roof. Probably no one would have cared anyway, except to ask what special service I was getting and what it cost. The topmost floor houses the gentlemen's brothel and the ground floor provides speedy service for those who cannot afford better, while between them lies the floor where the four owners have their personal apartments; visitors there are admitted by appointment only and are few, because two of the owners are now retired. I let myself into Violetta's suite and went straight to her bedroom. She always keeps a light burning, and that night she had two, for Aspasia was reading a book.

But instantly Helen was there in her place, hurling the book away, casting off the sheet, and extending the world's loveliest arms in welcome. "Darling! I had almost given up hope! What in the world is that you are . . . were . . . wearing. Oh, you're all . . ." Wet, perhaps, but she had no time to get the last word out before I was all over her, kissing her frantically.

"Saints preserve me," she muttered when I gave her a chance. "I've never known you quite so . . . *ardent!*"

"Burning." I kissed her lips again in passing.

"Combusting?"

"Deflagrating."

"Cheat! No such word."

"Is so. Ebullient, too."

"Fervent."

I thought, "Glowing," but had no opportunity to say it and by then it didn't matter. We never got to "Hot" or "Incandescent." I do not recommend pyromancy to anyone, but it does have interesting side effects. It was almost dawn before I was completely burned out.

An hour before dawn the city's churches ring for matins but I never hear them. Roosters scream and I respond with snores. Only at sunrise, a few minutes before the *marangona* rings, do I crack an eyelid—but that morning I suffered a sharp poke in the ribs.

"You must go."

I grunted negatively and tried to cuddle closer.

"Listen to it!" she said. "You'll have to go by the front door."

The unpleasant noise in the background was a rattling casement and rain pounding the glass, which meant very high wind. In such a storm the high road would be close to suicide, so I would have to risk the watergate. Big storms are rare so early in the winter. Venice rules the seas but the weather pleases itself.

I persisted. "Luigi doesn't open up until sunrise."

"It will be sunrise in a few minutes. So stop that and go!"

I stole a last kiss, disengaged, and left her bed.

I shivered my way into my Guise of Night hose and smock, which were still damp, but were going to be a lot wetter before I reached home. I left Violetta's apartment, locking it behind me, and trotted downstairs to sea level. Her timing had been perfect, because I heard the *marangona*— loud and clear, carried by the wind—as I let myself out the front door. Now workers would start emerging all over the city, a rising flow of men hurrying to their workshops, foundries, markets, and so on, hailing one another, stopping at churches and shrines for a hasty prayer. So far my luck was holding, for there were neither boats on the Rio San Remo, nor pedestrians on the *fondamenta* along the far side.

Getting into Ca' Barbolano unseen would be the problem. Old Luigi unbolts the front door at daybreak and usually takes a look outside, just from habit. After that the Marcianas are supposed to post a boy to keep watch on it, except when the men are working in the *androne*, which is most of the time. But the old night watchman often interprets dawn a little earlier than the sun does, and adolescents have contrary instincts, so there can be a brief interval between man and boy. If I could slip in then, I should be able to run upstairs unseen. Of course I would leave a trail of wet footprints, but clean water does not show up on white Istrian marble.

So I crossed to the narrow *calle* and continued on to the Barbolano watergate, working my way along the ledge with my back hard against the wall, my toes over the lip, rain needling my face, and a howling gale trying to throw me off. No one saw me, or at least no one started a hue and cry about burglars, and with a sigh of relief I peered around the corner, saw that the great door was closed, and slipped into the loggia. Danese lay sprawled in a corner with the blade of a rapier protruding from the middle of his chest; the hilt under his back explaining his awkward, arched position. His doublet and the front of his breeches were brown with dried blood. His jaw hung open, his blue eyes stared in amazement at the ceiling, and he was very obviously dead.

This was an unexpected complication.

16

Enough rain had blown in to soak the loggia floor, so my wet feet should leave no traces. I went over to him and said a hasty prayer for his soul. This must be the murder I had seen in the fire, but I swear that this prompt proof of my talent for pyromancy gave me no pleasure. Although I had not liked Danese, I never thought he deserved such a sordid and untimely end. With his fishy stare and idiot mouth agape, he was no longer handsome.

I could not close his eyes, but rigor mortis begins with the face and there was still some play in his fingers, so the Maestro would be able to estimate the time of his death. His knees were scuffed and dirty, as were his hands and cheeks, which confirmed that he had scrabbled on the ground, as I had seen in the fire. There was blood on his right shin and calf. His head lay in the corner farthest from the arches; his legs and lower torso were wet, his hair and shoulders dry. I decided that the bloodstains had dried before the rain started blowing in, so he might have been lying there while I was speaking to Vasco upstairs. Would the judges of the *Quarantia* accept that argument? The case would never go before the *Quarantia*. Even without a possible link to the

Algol investigation, the murder of a nobleman in another nobleman's house would be taken over by the Council of Ten as a matter of state security.

What I needed least just then was Luigi coming out and finding me there in my bizarre burglar costume. There was still a chance that he had unbolted the door already and omitted his normal look outside, so I went to check that it was still bolted, which it was. Definitely I was not going to be sneaking in unseen through that door that morning. And now I saw that, while the floor of the loggia was cleaned frequently, the *calle* and the ledge never were, and my cotton hose had left a trail of muddy smears.

Think!

Cadavers in corners or face down in canals are not rarities, for Venice has its share of bravos and thugs. I dared not take time to search the body for Danese's purse, but the killer had left a gold ring on his hand and a valuable rapier in his back. It had struck him almost horizontally from behind, missing his heart, for a heart wound would not have bled so profusely. Why leave him there to be found and not drop him tidily in the canal? Why had he returned to Ca' Barbolano anyway, when he was supposed to be enjoying the connubial bed, back home in Ca' Sanudo?

Grazia's horoscope I must not think about. It had shown a dramatic upturn in her fortunes just about now.

Then the first bolt clattered and I was gone. The wind caught me as I swung around the corner, very nearly blowing me into the water, but I squiggled my way along the ledge and was almost at the *calle* when I heard Luigi scream. He would run inside for help, I knew, but my luck still held, for there was no traffic on either the water or the *fondamenta* opposite. Unseen, I reached the door of 96 and let myself back in.

While I ran upstairs, my mind flew even faster. Even if Luigi in his distress forgot that the *vizio* must still be upstairs, someone would think to summon the resident doctor. I must get back to my room soon, and if I could do so without being seen, Vasco himself would give me a perfect alibi. If I couldn't, then I would have a lot of explaining to do. My backdoor highway would be exposed and then even Violetta could not give me an alibi, for a courtesan's word is given little credence. In any case, I could have killed Dolfin on my way to visit her. I would do myself no good by going back to her then and might do her much harm. I went on up to the *altana*.

The wind on the roof was terrifying, eddying erratically off the higher Ca' Barbolano. Had I waited to plan my jump I should have frozen in terror, so I just scrambled over the rail, took a last deep breath and a long stride down the tiles, then leaped into the gale. Obviously I did not fall fifty feet and break my neck, but I came unpleasantly close. My right hand caught one bar; my left slammed into another so hard that I twisted my wrist and failed to get a grip. My left heel found the ledge, my right missed it. As my fingers slid down the wet metal, I dropped, cracking my right shin on the ledge hard enough to bring even more tears to my eyes than the wind and rain had already put there. Forcing my left hand and wrist to do their duty, I managed to get a second hold and haul myself upright, getting first a knee and then both feet on the ledge. I clung like a spider for a couple of moments while my heart calmed down a little, then I pushed on the casement, but it was latched.

This was another unexpected complication.

That *calle* is very little used, for there is a much better one on the far side of 96, but I was visible from too many windows. To jump back or even hold on much longer in that storm were equally impossible. I lifted out one of the loose bars and used it as a battering ram against the pane nearest the window catch. On the second attempt I managed to break it, the thick bottle glass in the center falling out as a unit, and the thinner edges shattering. With some difficulty, I freed a hand to reach in and open the casement. Then it was only a matter of lifting another bar loose and squirming in through the gap.

Who was it who said that the best thing about travel is coming home again?

I cut a toe on a sliver of glass.

Ca' Barbolano must be in turmoil by now, but no sounds were leaking through my door, which I confirmed was now unlocked, although I was certain I had locked it to keep prying Vasco out. I stripped and assessed my injuries. My hand would turn purple in a day or so, but my leg was much more serious—bleeding and in need of bandaging before I could put my hose on. The medical supplies were all in the atelier, as were my palace clothes. Had the *vizio* rushed downstairs to view the corpse, or was he still lurking outside in the *salone*?

Discretion seemed advisable. I tore up an old shirt to wrap my shin, dressed quickly—shaving would have to wait—and swept the fragments of glass against the wall with the Guise of Night rags, which were wet, dirty, and in places bloody. What to do with them then was another problem. Throwing them out the window would have been the solution had my room overlooked the canal, which it doesn't, so in the end I just tossed them in the bottom of my wardrobe. Vasco had seen me wearing them; he had almost certainly been the intruder who closed the casement. I took a few deep breaths and quietly opened the door. The way out was blocked by a faceless mass that I identified easily as Nino Marciana, an amiable fellow with more muscle than a Michelangelo model.

"The Lord be with you, Nino."

He spun his bulk around. "And with you, *messer* Alfeo."

"What are you doing here?"

The kid pondered, looking troubled. "*Vizio* said I was to stand here and not let anyone in."

"Did he say I was not to come out?"

"Um . . . Don't think so."

I waited, then said, "Then may I pass, please?"

He shifted, and at that moment a procession came trooping in through our front door. It was led by Bruno, with the Maestro on his back and tears running down his face, for any form of death or violence upsets our gentle giant horribly. He had known Danese, which would make it worse, and would never understand what had happened, for sign language cannot explain such complicated matters.

Right after them came four more hefty Marcianas carrying the mortal remains of Danese Dolfin on a blanket—to leave a good Christian corpse lying around would be disrespect to the dead. Behind them came Father Farsetti, and I caught a glimpse of Filiberto Vasco in back of him, but by then the pallbearers were going into the atelier. Since the Maestro was occupied in dismounting, I hurried over to see that the corpse was properly delivered to the examination couch.

The priest had already done that and was dismissing his helpers with a blessing. Rigor mortis was well progressed, for the body still lay awkwardly twisted although it was no longer supported by the hilt of the rapier, which had been removed. My palace clothes were nowhere in sight, so the Maestro must have hidden them when he tidied up.

"Who did this?" I asked.

"That has still to be established, Alfeo." Father Farsetti was covering the corpse with a sheet, the one that always lies on the examination couch. He is a tall, spare man, soft-spoken, witty, and understanding. His flock adores him, especially the women, although I have never heard a word of scandal about him.

"He was run through from behind," the *vizio* said at my

back. "A dastardly murder by some bravo too cowardly even to look his victim in the eye."

Turning to make suitable response, I closed my mouth with a click as I recognized the rapier Vasco was holding. It had bloody smears on the blade. He raised it as if to admire the hilt.

"*Omnia vincit amor et nos cedamus amori,*" he said, reading out the inscription on the guard. "My Latin is not as good as it should be, Father. 'Love conquers all,' of course . . ."

" 'Love conquers all and we yield to love,' " Farsetti said. "It is a quotation from Virgil, quite appropriate for a weapon. It should be possible to trace the original owner, although I expect it was stolen."

"Not necessarily," Vasco said, leering at me so widely that he almost drooled. "The other side reads, *From VV to LAZ*, and a date. Remind me who *VV* is, *Luca.*"

Danese had been killed with my rapier. The day just kept getting worse.

17

When Luigi saw the body, he rushed upstairs as fast as he could totter, and thundered on the door of Angelo Marciana's mezzanine apartment. More than just a fiendishly cunning bookkeeper, Angelo is a man of steady nerve and many sons. He told Nino, Renzo, and Ciro to follow him and the women to stay home with the children, then ran down to see for himself. At once he ordered Nino to fetch Doctor Nostradamus, Renzo to inform Father Farsetti, and Ciro to stand vigil over the body and make sure nobody looted it. Renzo probably ran right underneath me as I clung like moss to the side of the building. Meanwhile Luigi had informed the Jacopo Marcianas also, so several of them arrived. By the time the *vizio* appeared and saw that he had serious work to do, the loggia must have been as crowded as the Piazza in Carnival. He ordered whoever was the best boatman to go and fetch *Missier Grande*—no nonsense about informing the local *sbirri* when the Council of Ten was already involved, although I am sure he did not say that. He also ordered everyone else back upstairs, but by then whatever marks I had left on the floor had been scuffed out of existence.

Father Farsetti would have been in San Remo's at that time on a Saturday. He is a young man and not too puffed up with ecclesiastic dignity to run in an emergency, but he found Danese well past the need for last rites. Giorgio arrived, accompanied by the twins—they being uninvited but irresistibly eager to view a real corpse—followed closely by the Maestro on Bruno's back. He at once dispatched all three Angelis to the Ghetto Nuovo to fetch Isaia Modestus, whom he freely acknowledges to be the second-best doctor in the Republic.

The body could not be left where it lay and the Maestro wanted to inspect it, so Father Farsetti agreed that it should be moved upstairs and that was arranged. The *vizio* extracted the rapier and took charge of it. I can barely imagine the intensity of his joy when he read the inscription and saw whose it was. No doubt he fantasized juicy visions of watching my beheading between the columns on the Piazzetta.

Pessimists, on the other hand, are rarely disappointed.

A very few minutes later, when Vasco confronted me with it in the atelier, Father Farsetti shot me a horrified look. He is well aware of my full name. As my confessor he certainly knows of Violetta Vitale.

My head was spinning, but I believe I concealed my bewilderment fairly well. "I must have a talk with you soon, Father," I said cheerfully, "but the problem is no more urgent than usual." He nodded, looking relieved.

Vasco smiled happily. "You acknowledge that this is your rapier, *messer*?"

"It was until it was stolen," I said, "and I know who took it."

He scoffed.

"If not you," I said, "then who? You were on watch in the *salone* all night, weren't you?"

"What is this?" the Maestro screeched in the doorway. "Carnival? The Giudecca Festival? The *marangona* has rung, has it not? Out of here, all of you!" He hates strangers in his atelier. About a dozen Marcianas shamefacedly withdrew, leaving four of us and the corpse.

Vasco was still tying my bonds, as he thought. "You were in bed and asleep from the time we met last night until the alarm was raised this morning, is that correct?" he said.

My wiggle room there was thinner than a razor, as we had all removed our hats out of respect for the dead and my hair was still damp. "I do not have to answer your questions, citizen."

His smile spread over his face like a cancer. "But you will answer the inquisitors when they put those same questions, *clarissimo*."

"This is an unseemly conversation in the presence of mortality," Father Farsetti said heavily. "Filippo, do you really believe you can learn something that may help the authorities catch the murderer?

The Maestro came forward, thumping his staff. "If you will evict these two yapping puppies, Father . . . Thank you." He moved into the space Vasco had vacated and handed me his staff. "Bring my instruments."

He poked and prodded while I fetched his medical bag. The best way to determine time of death is to estimate internal temperature, but Farsetti might not permit that indignity to a corpse, and he would certainly forbid any sort of dissection. The Maestro thrust two fingers into the corpse's mouth, but did not suggest any worse intrusion. I gave him one of the scalpels I keep razor sharp for him and he slit open the blood-encrusted doublet to examine the exit wound. The dying man had lost so much blood that his clothes were stiff with it, yet still tacky near his skin.

The Maestro demanded that the corpse be turned over, so Vasco and I obliged. Face down, it seemed even more widely contorted, and I held one of its ankles lest it roll off the couch. The Maestro examined the entry wound, which was

surrounded by a circle of subcutaneous hemorrhage where
the hilt had impacted or pressed against the flesh, but the
deceased had bled much less on that side. The blood on his
leg had come from a stab wound in his calf, which confirmed my vision in the fire. There was a separate patch of
blood on the back of his ruff, which was badly crushed, and
his right wrist showed faint subcutaneous bleeding, too recent to date from my blow on it a week ago.

"Well, apprentice?" Nostradamus said. "What do you
conclude?"

"He was stabbed in the back, master."

Vasco crowed, as if I had just initialed my own death
warrant. "How do you know that, since you weren't downstairs to see?"

An easy one. "You told me so a moment ago, but the condition of the corpse proves it." I returned my attention to
my master. "The stroke missed his heart and likely pene-
trated the aorta, accounting for the massive hemorrhage in
the dorsal area. A heart wound would not have bled so
much. He died of exsanguination and asphyxiation. I mean
he bled to death, but he may have suffocated first, as his tho-
racic cavity filled with blood. The punctures are so tiny it
would not be possible to remove the sword and replace it
from the opposite direction without leaving evidence. I estimate that he died about nine o'clock last night, but you can
undoubtedly judge that more closely than I can, master."

I thought that I had done quite well so far. There was
another conclusion to be drawn, a very obvious one, except
that I was not supposed to know about the absence of significant bloodstains in the loggia. Since nobody had yet mentioned that, I yielded to temptation and dangled a lure to
see who would bite.

"He must have known his assailant," I said, "and trusted
him enough to turn his back on him, because no man will
stand still to be impaled when he can leap into a canal.

Dolfin was never much of a swimmer as a child, but the Rio San Remo is barely deep enough to drown in, even at high tide." No one commented and I pushed on. "So he was standing in the loggia, looking outward—perhaps hoping a gondola would come by, although the hour must have been late. His companion was farther back, possibly on the pretext of seeking better shelter from the rain. Or possibly he came from the door."

Vasco's eyes gleamed, and I realized that I had given myself away in earnest this time.

"Or else," I continued, "Danese was waiting for Luigi to open the door for him, and the murderer came from the watersteps, perhaps disembarking from the very same boat. When Dolfin was struck, he fell back on the hilt of the sword, driving the blade in as far as it could go. It would have snapped if he had fallen forward on it. Which way was he facing?"

For a moment no one spoke, although the Maestro's lips were pursed hard enough to hurt.

Then Father Farsetti said, "His head was almost in the corner of the house wall, which means he had been facing outward." The priest is the finest player of simultaneous mental chess I have ever met—I have watched him play six games at once—so either visualizing violent crime was not another of his skills, or he was playing along with me just as the Maestro was.

A clatter of feet announced the arrival of Corrado and Christoforo, jostling their way through the door, competing to be first with the news and shouting over each other: "Dr. Modestus says—" "The Jew says he—" "—he is sorry but he—" "—will visit a sick person—" "—cannot come to view a corpse—" "—but not come—" "—on the Sabbath." "—to see a dead one."

"*Damnātio!*" the Maestro snapped. "Very well, then! Away with you! That is unfortunate," he confided to the priest. "I would value his opinion on the time of death, for Their Excellencies will certainly want to know that." He was more annoyed at himself for having forgotten that today was Saturday.

The boys slunk out, angry at not being paid.

"I arrived here about ten o'clock," Vasco announced confidently. "It took me much hammering to fetch that oaf of a doorman, and some minutes to argue my way in. There was certainly no carcase cluttering up the loggia then."

"You are sure of the time?" the Maestro demanded, cutting off Father Farsetti's protest about disrespect for the dead.

"Reasonably. It was about an hour after the curfew rang. The doorman says he locked up at curfew. For what the old fool's testimony is worth, this morning he agrees that my knock came about then."

"Luigi does not always interpret curfew the way the sun does," I said, "is it possible that *sier* Danese was killed later than ten o'clock, master?"

He frowned, but did not look at me. "I estimate time of death as being within an hour of curfew, either before or after."

My sword had killed Danese, so only a total blockhead would not see that I was in very grave trouble. But Vasco himself was now testifying that I had been in Ca' Barbolano until after ten, so the earlier Danese had died, the less my peril. Ironically, Vasco had not yet seen this.

"I assure you," he said, "that I did not overlook a corpse at my feet while I was waiting for that wreck of a doorman."

"I did not say you did, *Vizio*. Turn him over again, please." The Maestro slit Danese's doublet and shirt and pulled free the bloodstained cloth. "Water and a cloth, please Alfeo."

I assumed he wanted to look for postmortem bruising, evidence of the way blood had settled after death.

As I turned toward the doorway, it was suddenly occupied. The big man in the red and blue robe was Gasparo Quazza, *Missier Grande*. Behind him came a nobleman in black robes and then Sergeant Torre, chief of our local *sbirri*. Out in the *salone* were several more constables and a very worried Giorgio. Without a word, *Missier Grande* nodded to the priest and Nostradamus, made the sign of the cross in respect to the corpse, and then turned to his *vizio*.

"The deceased," Vasco said, "is *nobile homo* Danese Dolfin, recently married to Grazia Sanudo, daughter of the ducal counselor, Zuanbattista Sanudo. His body was found in the loggia this morning by the night watchman when he opened the watergate at sunrise. It was not there when I arrived here, as per instructions, at approximately ten o'clock last night, although Doctor Nostradamus judges that the time of death was between eight and ten. I assume the murder was committed just after I arrived, but I have not yet asked the watchman if there were any other callers. The weapon was this rapier, which had been thrust through the deceased from behind and has been identified by Alfeo Zeno as being his."

Missier Grande looked to me for confirmation. So far not a single muscle in his face had moved.

"It is my rapier," I said. "I wore it to the palace last night, and the *fante* who took charge of it will confirm that he returned it to me. When we came home, about seven o'clock, I put it back in its place on top of my wardrobe, out of reach of children. I did not touch it after that. It was stolen."

"By whom?"

"Filiberto Vasco."

Vasco chuckled. Nobody else did.

Quazza studied me in silence for a few moments. I studied him right back. Soon after I was apprenticed to the Maestro, Quazza's daughter was abducted, literally snatched out of her nurse's arms. The Maestro foresaw her and I recovered her, much as I recovered Grazia Sanudo, except that on that earlier escapade, in excess of juvenile rashness, I veered much closer to collecting my eternal reward. Quazza owes me a debt, therefore, but that will never divert him from doing his duty.

"Why do you say that?" he asked.

"Because he was the only other person I know of to enter my bedchamber during the night."

The deadly gaze returned to Vasco.

Vasco, regrettably, maintained his confident smirk. "I was keeping watch for intruders in the *salone*, as instructed. When the storm struck, the casement in Zeno's room began to bang. After a few serious crashes, I decided he was either dead or absent. To prevent damage to the building, I made my way in and—"

"You picked the lock," I said.

"—obtained entrance and latched the casement. The bed had not been slept in. I did not look underneath it, nor in the wardrobe. Nor on top of it. I went out and closed the door behind me. I did not see his sword and did not take it."

My bruised and abraded shin was hurting. The other was undamaged, but in fact I did not have a single leg to stand on. If I denied leaving Ca' Barbolano during the night, I would easily be proved a liar by the evidence of the broken glass, removable window bars, and wet clothing. Calling Violetta as a witness would merely make everything worse, because the distinction between an "honest" courtesan and a common harlot is easily blurred. The court would assume I was her bravo protector, that Danese had hurt her or failed to pay her, and I had run him through. Off with my head.

"You deny this story?" *Missier Grande* inquired.

"I cannot answer your questions, *lustrissimo*." I did not have to, for *Missier Grande* is not an inquisitor; he carries out the orders of the Ten.

"But you will answer mine." The patrician stepped forward. Andrea Zancani was serving a term as one of the Lords of the Night Watch, the *Signori di Notte*, and thus was Sergeant Torre's current boss. That is a starter position for the nobility, and I would have put him around the tender age of thirty. He is a resident of San Remo, so I often see him in church.

I bowed to him. "Alas, *clarissimo*, I was about to explain that this is a matter of state, in which I can answer only to the noble Council of Ten."

Vasco did not make a sound, but was obviously enjoying himself hugely.

Zancani pouted and turned to *Missier Grande*. "You are taking this man into custody, *lustrissimo*?"

"I have no instructions regarding *sier* Alfeo," Quazza said. "I should point out, though, that he is in fact of noble birth, *sier* Alfeo Zeno. Consequently he can only be tried by the Council of Ten itself."

Zancani pulled a face. "He doesn't look it. But let us make sure we know where he is when Their Excellencies want him. Sergeant, arrest *sier* Alfeo."

"Bah! That is absurd!" the Maestro said. *"Missier Grande*, you know what work I am engaged in, or at least for whom I am working. You know why your *vizio* was sent here last night—to protect Alfeo. Now you will let him be dragged off to share a lockup with drunks and thugs? Who defends him there?"

Missier Grande looked thoughtfully at Vasco, who flinched. Yes, truly, his happiness was quite cast down. If he were sent to the local dungeon with me in order to continue guarding me, he would be in considerable danger from the other inhabitants.

"I should welcome his company," I said, "but Sergeant Torre may resent the damage to the reputation of his establishment."

"I shall put Zeno under house arrest," *Missier Grande* said, "and leave—"

"Absurd!" the Maestro repeated furiously. "Enough of this nonsense." He grabbed his staff from me and elbowed me aside. "Come and sit down, *clarissimo*, and you also, Father. Alfeo, bring a chair for *Missier Grande*, and you, Sergeant, kindly send one of your men to fetch Giorgio, my gondolier."

The invitation to be seated obviously excluded Vasco and Torre, so I brought one more chair to the fireplace and then stationed myself behind the Maestro. Zancani, Quazza, and the priest sat opposite us, seeming wary, inscrutable, and mildly amused respectively.

"Now, Alfeo," the Maestro said without trying to look around at me. "Why were you talking such rubbish just now?"

"Rubbish, master?" Mainly I had been trying to muddy the waters and pin Vasco down so he could not change his evidence to suit the case he wanted to make.

"You know what I mean! What did you really learn from looking at the body?"

"I may have been a little hasty in jumping to conclusions," I admitted. "Now I realize that I see no gory footsteps on our floor here, so the watergate loggia is not drenched in a mixture of rain and blood, as it would be if Danese bled to death there. So he could not have been murdered downstairs. He died somewhere else and was brought here later. In fact, he was almost certainly dead before the *vizio* claims he arrived at Ca' Barbolano."

"With your rapier in him?" Vasco demanded.

"That is a curious detail, isn't it?" In fact that detail was almost driving me crazy. Fortunately I do know something about ghouls, so I could blame Algol, even if I had no hope of convincing a court. "Dolfin died facedown, but he could not have been run through from behind and fallen forward, as one would expect of a man stabbed in the upper back. Does the point of that sword show damage, Filiberto?"

Vasco looked and said, "It's blunted," with a poor grace.

"A good lunge with a rapier will go right through a skull," I continued. "A lung would offer almost no resistance, nor would a rib, and yet the sword did not break, so Danese did not fall with it sticking out of his chest. Yet it must have protruded from his breast because that was where his ruptured aorta hemorrhaged most. The wound in his right leg also came from behind, and we must explain the separate bloodstains on the back of his neck, where the ruff has been crushed. There is no mud on his dorsal side, as there is on the ventral."

"And your conclusion?" the Maestro asked impatiently.

My conclusion was what I had seen in the fire and had described to him at the time. "Danese was in a fight, master. The murderer wrestled his sword away from him and stabbed him with it."

"You base that assumption on the fact that his right thumb is broken?"

I had missed that. "Of course, and his wrist shows damage also. These things may have happened when he fell, but more likely when the killer wrenched the sword out of his grip. The leg wound must have come next, when he was trying to run away. He would have fallen. Having disabled him, his assailant then callously stabbed him in the back as he was trying to rise. Danese probably still tried to get up, and the murderer put a bloody shoe on the back of his neck to hold him down while he bled to death."

Even *Missier Grande* winced at that image. Father Farsetti covered his face with his hands. My sympathy was quite genuine. It had been a fairly quick death, but not a pleasant one, if there can ever be such a thing.

"After he died," I said, "the rapier was pushed all the way through him, perhaps just to make him easier to move. The killer brought him here. Thanks to the *vizio*'s acute observation we know now that the point did hit something hard, so we must look for a place with hard footing—brick or stone—and extensive bloodstains."

"Thank you," the Maestro said. "Now you are making sense." He looked around to where our gondolier was waiting. "Ah, Giorgio. Last night, what time was it when Alfeo told you that he and I were not to be disturbed?"

Giorgio looked thunderous at having been fetched by a *sbirro*—such a thing never happened to respectable citizens—but he took a moment to think, "It must have been a little after eight o'clock, Doctor. We were putting the children to bed."

"And what happened then?"

"*Sier* Danese Dolfin came and asked to see *sier* Alfeo."

For a moment we were all silent, as we digested this information. Vasco scowled.

The Maestro nodded, as if he had expected something like that. "When?"

"About half past eight, roughly."

"Go on."

"I explained that you and he were not to be disturbed. He said the matter was urgent and he would wait."

"How did he seem?"

"He seemed distressed, Doctor, agitated." Giorgio himself was starting to look distressed, and also apologetic. "He did not say why he was worried, or what he wanted. But he was very jumpy. He had stayed here as—"

"As a guest, yes. So you let him wait in the *salone* unattended?"

Giorgio nodded glumly. "I was helping Mama . . . I heard the front door close. He had gone. I ran to the stair and saw him going down. I did watch him leave the building."

"Did you get a good look at him?" the Maestro persisted.

Giorgio shook his head. "Mostly just his shadow, *lustris-simo*."

There are times when one has to throw in one's cards and hope that the next deal will work better. "I apologize, *Vizio*. You were not the only one who could have stolen my sword last night."

The Maestro was ahead of me, of course. "Where is it?" he asked.

Danese had come to reclaim his own sword, which I had forgotten to return to him with his portmanteau. Either he had snooped around Ca' Barbolano at some time during his stay here or—more likely—he had taken the risk of search-ing my room for it while Giorgio was bedding his brood. The top of a wardrobe is not an unlikely place to keep weapons when there are small children around. He had found mine and taken it. Had he also taken the matching dagger? Probably not, because he had been disarmed in a hand-to-hand tussle; with a dagger he could have stabbed his opponent when they closed. Men who sport swords should know how to use them, and he had not. In a real fight, as opposed to a formal duel, a rapier needs a parrying partner, either a dagger or another rapier.

A *sbirro* moved out of my way. I walked around our seated audience and headed to the medicine supply cup-board, taking my time while I worked out the least incrim-inating way of explaining why we had what I was about to produce. To confess that I had crossed swords with Danese on the Riva del Vin less than a week ago would not clear me of suspicion—far from it.

Danese's rapier had no fancy inscription on the guard, just his initials. I handed it to *Signore di Notte* Zancani.

"Yesterday my master instructed me to pack the clothes Dolfin had left here and deliver them to him at Ca' Sanudo. In doing so, I forgot to include his sword."

That was entirely true, but as an explanation it was lame,

practically paraplegic. How had the aforementioned sword found its way into the medicine cupboard? *NH* Zancani's eyes narrowed like air slits in a dungeon. He got as far as, "And just how did—" when we were interrupted and the case was removed from his jurisdiction.

18

S *ier* Ottone Gritti is a short and portly man who has seen many winters. The years have softened his features, weathered his face to a sienna red, faded his eyes to a milky blue, and frosted his close-trimmed beard; wisps of silver show under the edge of his flat bonnet. Stooped and flat-footed, he looks like an archetypical grandfather. Although he is rarely seen without a sleepy, benevolent smile, his nose is a bony hook that a raven might admire. That is a warning. He wore, of course, the black robes of the patriciate, marked in his case by the dangling sleeves of a member of the Council of Ten. A couple of *fanti* followed him in.

The sight of an inquisitor at the door would rank high in most people's list of Ten Worst Nightmares, especially if the inquisitor in question happened to be Ottone Gritti.

The three state inquisitors are not the three chiefs of the Ten. They are a permanent sub-committee of the Ten, always two of the elected members and one ducal counselor, two black robes and one red. Both positions carry a *contuma-cia*, meaning that a man must sit out one full term before being re-elected, but an easy way around that restriction is to alternate the two posts. I remember few times when

Gritti was not one of the Three. As soon as his term in one office lapses, Gritti is elected to the other. Even that wriggle should leave him off the Council of Ten for four months in every twenty-four, but at least once I recall the Great Council enlarging the Ten with a *zonta* of fifteen and including him in it. It is as if the nobility cannot sleep well unless Gritti is keeping an eye on things for them, probably because he is reputed to be the most skilled and merciless interrogator in the Republic. The Council of Ten never reveals secrets about its methods or its members, of course, but rumors persist that Gritti is quite happy to sit on the rostrum in the torture chamber and direct the torment, a task most sane men shun. They say that he can break a stubborn witness faster than anyone else can—which is a sort of mercy, I suppose.

So far so good. Gritti is staunch in the defense of the Republic against her enemies and we all support him in that.

He has a darker side. Where Doge Pietro Moro is a profound skeptic concerning the supernatural, Gritti is a fervent believer, which is much worse. If I pulled a silver ducat out of a child's ear, the doge would not believe I had pulled a silver ducat out of a child's ear and might have me charged with fraud. Gritti would believe. He would call it black magic and me a witch. He is reputed to be more assiduous at torturing confessions out of suspected witches than even the King of Scotland is. Sometimes his colleagues manage to restrain him, but sometimes they do not, and in the present instance we had hints of demonic forces involved with an issue of national security. No one would try to hold Gritti back in that. The Maestro has repeatedly warned me that he is the most dangerous man in Venice.

The room had fallen silent.

"Well, well!" the newcomer murmured, beaming around. "I hear we have a problem here." He acknowledged those present with nods: *"Clarissimo?"*—to Zancani—"Father?

Doctor? *Missier Grande? Vizio?* Sergeant Torre, I trust your wife is on the mend now? And Alfeo Zeno, of course! Are you in trouble again, Alfeo?"

I bowed low. "It seemed so for a few moments, Your Excellency, but I believe the crisis is over."

Vasco's face said it had barely begun. Vasco will die happy if he can just see me hauled off to the galleys, but burning at the stake would be much nicer.

Without going close, Gritti frowned at the corpse in the corner. "Nostradamus, is this misfortune connected with the matter you were asked to investigate two nights ago?"

The Maestro said, "I am certain it is, *messer*."

That was enough. A state inquisitor outranks just about anybody. In seconds, Father Farsetti had gone, Zancani had gone, taking Sergeant Torre and his *sbirri*, and Giorgio had been sent off to attend to his duties. *Missier Grande* was dismissed with a terse, "I know you are urgently needed elsewhere, *lustrissimo*." The two *fanti* were last to leave, ordered to guard the door.

Gritti settled himself on one of the green chairs, while Vasco and I took up positions behind out respective superiors to sneer at each other over their heads. The bizarrely contorted remains of Danese Dolfin remained under a sheet in the corner.

The inquisitor folded his hands over his round little paunch, and said, "Proceed, Doctor." After that he almost seemed to doze, eyes half-shut, as he listened to the story. Once in a while he would nod thoughtfully, or even smile. I suspect that at the end he could have recited the entire report word for word.

The Maestro recounted the events of the last week. He left out the size of his fee for finding Grazia and did not mention pyromancy or the *Aegia Salomonis*, but he did admit he had used clairvoyance. His celebrated uncle, Michel de Nostredame, made clairvoyance as respectable as astrology.

Even Gritti would have trouble declaring that to be black magic. Fortune telling with tarot, on the other hand, remains a criminal offense.

I listened with half an ear while I worked out the tide of events in the Doges' Palace after we had left. The Maestro's *VIRTÙ* bombshell would have launched a frantic hour of deciphering. At the end of it, the chiefs must have known a lot more about Algol's activities than previously, but they had not uncovered his identity. If they had, then Gritti would never have bothered to come to Ca' Barbolano; a mere murder would be beneath his notice. Contrariwise, if Algol's dispatches had turned out to be gossip and fraud, the case would have been closed presto. Therefore, by elimination, the chiefs had concluded that Algol had knowledgeable sources high in the government, perhaps even in the Council of Ten itself. Rather than reveal this new development to the spy, they had turned the case over to the Three. Overruling the chiefs' decision to withdraw Vasco, the Three had sent the *vizio* back to Ca' Barbolano. The fact that he had arrived not long after ten o'clock showed that *La Serenissima* can move fast when she wants to.

"Fascinating," Gritti murmured at the end. He sat in silence for a while.

I realized I had stopped breathing, and started again.

"The doctor failed to mention," Vasco said, "that his apprentice left the building clandestinely during the night."

"He climbed out the window and jumped across the *calle?*" Gritti said. "He does that all the time. Whose lust is aroused by the danger, Zeno? Yours or the harlot's?"

"Hers, Excellency," I said. "Just the thought of her is all I need."

He chuckled. "I don't blame you. I'm jealous."

Of course the Ten keep a dossier on me and Gritti knew my mistress's name. My midnight excursion was no longer

relevant as long as Gritti accepted that Danese had stolen
my sword.

"Fascinating," the inquisitor repeated. "I am familiar
with the Sanudo story, of course. The tale has been the talk
of the *broglio* for days—the Contarini betrothed who ran off
with *barnabotto* trash."

Vasco shook his head pityingly at the other *barnabotto*
trash. I ignored him.

"Zuanbattista's political career may never recover," the
inquisitor mused. "He is due to chair the Great Council tomorrow and so far he has not backed out. This murder may
finish him, though. Now you say that Dolfin's death is 'certainly' connected to the Algol espionage case. I do not see
that as self-evident. Justify your allegation, Doctor."

The Maestro put on his bewildered senility expression. "I
am certain that it is correct, Your Excellency, but I am not
yet in a position to back it up with evidence."

Gritti smiled fondly, as at a stubborn child. "I do understand the difference between a proof and a working hypothesis."

"Yet I must decline to reveal conjectures I cannot yet
substantiate."

Vasco raised two eyebrows; nobody defies the Three and
gets away with it.

Gritti settled back in his chair and dropped the comedy
mask in favor of the tragic. "Your work in breaking the Algol
cipher was brilliant, Doctor, and the Republic will reward
you handsomely for it, but now you are implying that one
of the most senior men in the government is a traitor and I
demand to hear your reasons. I will not rush out and arrest
people on mere suspicion. Let us hear it, Nostradamus."

A grunt from the Maestro made my heart plunge. His
stubbornness approaches suicidal insanity.

"I cannot accept these conditions," he said. "I regretfully
decline to work further on this case."

"You think you can withhold evidence vital to the security of the state?"

"I specified that it is mere opinion, not evidence."

I could not see the Maestro's face, but his voice seemed amazingly calm. Gritti, opposite, was starting to show signs of annoyance. His already ruddy face was redder than ever.

"Alfeo, will you answer my question?"

I hope that my start of alarm concealed my simultaneous cold shiver. "I cannot, Your Excellency! I have no idea why my master believes the two crimes are connected. On the face of it, that would be a very strange coincidence."

"No it wouldn't," Gritti said impatiently. "Dolfin is . . . was, I mean—a notorious lecher. The Ten opened a file on him when he was fifteen. Yesterday, you tell me, he was restored to the delights of his new bride's bed after a week's enforced celibacy. Yet instead he leaves Ca' Sanudo and rushes back here to Ca' Barbolano to consult the Maestro in an 'agitated' condition. Did he know of the Algol case?"

"I do not believe . . ." I said. "No, he couldn't possibly. The Angelis never gossip about the Maestro's affairs and even they know only that he went twice to the palace. The Marcianas downstairs jabber like starlings, but they knew nothing of importance. Danese . . . he saw the *vizio* here that morning and would have guessed that he had come on state business. Danese was clever."

"Sly, you mean," the inquisitor said with distaste. "So he went looking for his sword and found yours instead? That was enough, apparently. That was what he had come for. Any sword would do. So he ran off. Does it not make sense that he had stumbled on evidence of treason at Ca' Sanudo and that was why he wanted his sword? Do you swear that this idea has not even occurred to you, Zeno?"

My mouth was very dry, my bladder unbearably full. "I thought of it and discarded it, Your Excellency."

"Why?"

"Because Danese was no hero. He was an inept, untrained swordsman, a playboy who wore a sword for swagger. Had he found the evidence you suggest, he would have run straight to the palace and informed the chiefs in the hope of gaining a reward. He cuckolded *sier* Zuanbattista, then betrayed his mistress so he could seduce her daughter, all in the quest for money. I remember when he was a child . . . If you look at the first entries in that dossier you mentioned, Excellency, I think you will find reports that his greed exceeded his scruples even then. He would have betrayed his wife's father or brother for gold, but he would never have faced them down himself."

"It remains a valid hypothesis. Doesn't it, Doctor?"

"Not to me," the Maestro said. "I agree with Alfeo. If Dolfin had been able to inculpate the Sanudos, father and son, then their daughter would have inherited everything and he could have cleared the table. It would have all been his."

Gritti said. "So who killed him?"

"I suspect but cannot prove." We were back to the beginning.

"Are you gambling that I dare not use force on you because of your age, Nostradamus?"

The Maestro cackled. "Faugh! Tie me on the strappado and I would break in pieces at the first hoist. My heart would stop."

"Your apprentice is a strong young lad."

Vasco raised his eyes to Heaven, silently mouthing prayers of thanks.

"Alfeo doesn't know what I think," the Maestro said, less confidently. "His brain is not his best organ."

"You can stop his interrogation at any time."

"Bah! Has the Republic sunk to torturing the innocent?"

The inquisitor laughed. "Not yet! You always were a pig-headed old scoundrel, Doctor, and every year you get worse.

Keep your theories, then, but I shall cancel your reward for the code breaking."

That was different. The Maestro thumped a tiny fist on the arm of his chair. "It is blatantly obvious! I warned the chiefs last night that I expected attacks against us that the *vizio* could not repel, and by morning there was a corpse on our doorstep. Why here, at Ca' Barbolano? Surely Algol arranged that to ensnare my investigation in an irrelevant murder case?"

Gritti leaned forward eagerly. "You credit the spy with magical powers?"

"Who named him Algol?"

"That means nothing. He could as easily be called Hercules or Solomon. I want *you* to name him for me. *Now.* His real name. If all you have is a suspicion, I will still hear it. If you refuse, I shall be forced to take you and your apprentice into custody. *And* cancel your bonus."

I was holding my breath again. Gritti had the powers to issue any threat he liked and then carry it out.

Nostradamus knew that. Stubborn is stubborn, but this was ridiculous. He pouted. "Give me until tomorrow. Then I shall give you Algol, if not in person, at least his name and address and the evidence to hang him."

Gritti sat back to consider the offer. "When?"

"About this time. But here at Ca' Barbolano, if you please. I have done far too much traveling in the last few days, and my joints already feel as if I had spent all yesterday on your strappado. My staff please, Alfeo. Come and have *prima colazione* with us tomorrow, Your Excellency. I have an excellent cook, and I will serve up Algol to you for dessert."

"Mmm? And in the meantime, you do what?"

"Collect the evidence I require to confirm my hypothesis."

Gritti smiled angelically. "I am a patient man. As you

wish. But that will be your last chance." He laid his hands on the arms of his chair to rise. "Now I must go to Ca' Sanudo and see what that end of the story reveals. I shall, as you suggested, look out for a puddle of blood. *Vizio*, last night my colleagues and I ordered you to defend Zeno, so I suppose you had better continue to do so." He smiled a silver-framed, snaggle-toothed smile.

The old scoundrel was going to have Vasco dog my footsteps on whatever errands the Maestro had in mind for me. If I uncovered Algol, Vasco would be able to arrest him on the spot and claim the credit. He had not yet worked that out, though. All he could see was being my nursemaid for another day, and he looked disgusted at the prospect. "Certainly, Excellency. Do I defend him against the perils of foreign travel?"

"Meticulously."

That was better—he was to be my jailer. "And what should I do with his sword?" The answer he would really like was obvious.

Gritti heaved himself to his feet. "Clean the blood off it and give it back to him. I hope you never seriously believed, *Vizio*, that Alfeo Zeno would murder a man and forget to take his own monogrammed rapier out of the corpse?"

19

I went ahead to get the door, but it was opened before I reached it by one of the *fanti*. Behind him stood *sier* Zuan-battista. Very few people would have been allowed to interrupt Ottone Gritti, but ducal counselors are not just anyone. The week since I had last seen Sanudo had taken a toll. He seemed grayer and not quite so erect as before, but it would be hard for a man of his eminence to endure the mirth of his peers behind his back. He had to be aware of it and yet there was nothing he could do, no way he could strike back or deny allegations that had not been made to his face. He and Gritti greeted each other with the usual deep bows, but omitted the embrace. They ignored the rest of us.

"We were on our way to the palace," Sanudo explained. "We are already late, of course." He meant late for the daily meeting of the full *Collegio*, which the doge and his counselors attend, and therefore should include both him and Girolamo. "I came around this way to ask the good doctor if he had seen any sign of Danese Dolfin, who disappeared from our house last night." He stopped then and waited, but it was obvious that he had heard the news—possibly from the *fanti* or even the Marcianas downstairs—and his eyes kept flickering to the draped shape on the medical couch.

"He has been called to the Lord, *clarissimo*." Gritti led him over to the corner and uncovered Danese's face.

Zuanbattista's reaction seemed convincing, neither too much nor too little. You cannot tell, though. A man who has killed another in near darkness may faint at the first daylight view of his corpse, but I have seen mass murderers display complete indifference.

"He was found this morning, downstairs," the inquisitor explained. "He had been run through with a rapier. My wife will join me in extending our deepest sympathy to you and your family. Your poor daughter will be distraught."

Zuanbattista flashed him a searching look, as if he suspected mockery, or was tempted to say that his stupid daughter was the cause of all this trouble. "Downstairs? Here?"

"In the loggia. He was not killed there, though."

"And you have no idea who did this, or why?"

"Not yet. He may have been an innocent bystander caught up in the affair that Doctor Nostradamus has been investigating for us. That is the learned doctor's belief, at any rate—that Dolfin was unfortunate enough to be handy when the person we seek wished to confound the doctor's investigations by leaving a corpse on his doorstep. When did he leave Ca' Sanudo?"

Only now did Zuanbattista turn around as if to inspect his audience—Vasco, the Maestro, and me. We all bowed. He did not respond, so perhaps he did not even see us. "According to my daughter, they spent a quiet evening together, just talking. They have had very little time alone to get to know each other." Much too little, he meant. "About eight o'clock he informed her that he had a call to make. She was annoyed, of course, but he explained that he had promised to visit his mother in San Barnaba and would not be long. He assured Grazia that he had enough money to hire gondolas. About an hour later she retired and eventually went to sleep. Obviously, he had not returned by morning."

"Your gondolier says . . . ?"

"Nothing. Fabricio had already left to fetch my wife and me from a concert. Giro was also out."

Gritti turned his milky blue eyes on me. "How long would it take you to get here from Ca' Sanudo, youngster?"

The snag, of course was that Santa Maria Maddalena is in Cannaregio, north of the Grand Canal, and San Remo is south of it, in San Polo, so a pedestrian must go around by the Rialto bridge. "At night? No more than ten minutes if I managed to flag a gondola, Excellency. On foot, fifteen or twenty. If Danese was not armed, he might have taken longer to avoid the seedy areas."

In other words, we could not tell exactly, but the timing was reasonable. San Remo was not on his shortest route to San Barnaba, but not far off it. He had arrived here about half past eight, according to Giorgio, and left before the curfew rang at nine, when Luigi was supposed to lock up. And he had died, by the Maestro's estimate, before ten. At an unknown hour before the heavy rain started, his remains had been delivered like groceries back at the Ca' Barbolano. *Where* he had died was now much more important than *when*. There had been time for him to walk to anywhere in the city.

"You are telling me," Sanudo said, "that my son-in-law's death was just one of those random killings that so grievously blight our city?"

Silence.

He was tall and doubtless still quite strong, but he was old. Despite his age, if *messer* Zuanbattista Sanudo were a trained fencer, I could imagine him besting Danese with a sword. Not at wrestling, though. If the fire vision had given

me a true witness of events, Zuanbattista had not personally
murdered his son-in-law, but he did have a potent motive
and he certainly had enough money to hire bravos to do it
for him. Such alley rats usually work in gangs, while pyromancy had shown only one assailant. How literally should
I take those visions?

"That is one hypothesis," Gritti conceded at last.

"But you do not believe it." Despite his normal patrician
stolidity, Zuanbattista's craggy face flushed almost as red as
his counselor's robe. Street crime belongs to the *Signori di
Notte*, not the Three. Gritti was investigating treason.

They stared hard at each other, those two old men, one
red-robed and one black-, one tall and angular, one short
and grandfatherly—at the very least they must have worked
together for decades, on and off, on councils and boards and
committees. For all I knew they had been friends since boyhood, yet now one must consider the possibility of arresting
the other for treason. Zuanbattista had not said, *Et tu, Brute?*
aloud, but he was looking it.

Gritti sighed. "I did not mean that. I could believe that
the choice of victim was happenstance had he been found
floating in a canal, but the location where the corpse was left
was certainly chosen for some reason. I am honor bound to
distrust the coincidence, as Nostradamus does, of a murder
complicating his sensitive work for the Ten."

Zuanbattista seemed remarkably unimpressed by that.
"You will forgive me if I suggest that the choice of victim
might equally be intended as a distraction to turn suspicion
on my house and away from the real quarry?"

"That is another valid hypothesis, *clarissimo*," Gritti
agreed. "Why did you come here, though? Did you not inquire first whether he ever arrived at his mother's house?"

The pause grew into a silence before Sanudo said, "Grazia
seems to have made a mistake when she took note of
madonna Agnese Correr's address. It is somewhere in San

Barnaba, but when Giro and I inquired where she told us, the lady was not known there."

Other residents of the parish would know where she lived, but would not willingly disclose that information to strangers, especially two senior members of the government.

Gritti glanced at me. "If memory serves . . . ?"

I sighed. "The lady's name is Agnese Corner, not Correr."

"A handwriting slip," the inquisitor said soothingly. "It is not the first time those two noble patrician names have been confused. You have not met the lady?"

Zuanbattista was not deceived by the politeness. "No. The day we learned of the marriage we sent Danese off with an invitation to meet us, but she declined, pleading infirmity. Danese told us that in fact she was ashamed of her poverty and asked us to be patient while he found her some clothes worthy of his future station. And now she must be informed of her son's death, and asked her wishes about the funeral."

"The priest will know where she lives," Gritti said smoothly. The Ten's informers would know, too. "I will send word, so he can go and comfort her. It will be best if I come and make some inquiries of your household right away, *lustrissimo*, and get it over with. You will be returning home now, I imagine, to break the tragic news to your daughter?"

And the welcome news to your wife? Did he mean that also? Was he hinting that he could carry the entire Sanudo establishment off to the palace for interrogation? That would be how lesser folk would be treated.

Sanudo's shoulders sagged. "Yes, we must. Can you spare a man to carry a message to His Serenity, explaining our absence?"

"Certainly. Alfeo, some paper, if you please."

I swiftly produced pen, ink, sand, wax, and paper, laying them out on my side of the desk, because I knew Sanudo to be right-handed and he would prefer the window on his left. By the time he had settled into my chair and I had lit a candle so that he could seal his letter, the door was open again and Gritti was calling to the violet-robed Girolamo, who must have been waiting out in the *salone*.

Suspect number two.

Giro returned the inquisitor's bow perfunctorily, for his eyes had already located the ominous figure in the corner. Without a word, he strode across and lifted the sheet from the face. He stood in silent contemplation for a moment, then sank to his knees and prayed. I looked thoughtfully at the Maestro, but he was studying Gritti, who in turn was watching me, and seemed amused by something. Who could tell what might amuse such a man?

Suspect number two: Girolamo would certainly have a better chance in a brawl with Danese than his father would, but I would still have bet against him, especially if Danese had been armed with a sword and he only had a cudgel, as my pyromancy suggested. Like his father, Giro could afford to send hired help in his stead. Again, motive was easy enough to find. Not likely politics, I decided, nor even money. Zaccaria Contarini would have commanded a huge dowry to marry Grazia, but Danese Dolfin would undoubtedly have had to settle for much less. But passion? Had he in truth been Giro's lover? Jealousy and betrayal have triggered many a violent death.

Girolamo finished his prayer and rose. When he turned around, his expression was as impassive as ever, and yet there was a shine to his eyes that suggested he had been weeping, or very close to it. The man of ice was melting. "Who did it and why?"

Gritti explained again.

The Maestro still sat in his red chair, clutching his staff as if he were some evil, wizened little tree elf, eyes missing nothing. I was wondering what he had seen or worked out to make him so sure of Algol's identity. It sounded as if he needed more evidence and gathering evidence is my job, but how was I supposed to do that with Vasco on my heels all day? My stomach muttered something about breakfast. I had not even had a chance to shave.

Zuanbattista sealed his note with wax and his signet ring and rose to hand it to Gritti. Then he turned to Nostradamus. "I understand that he had no male kin, so it is up to us to organize the funeral. I will send for the body." He looked to me. "Zeno, do you know where madonna Corner Dolfin lives?"

"I know where she lived six years ago, *clarissimo*." It was longer than that since I had spoken with the lady, and the prospect of breaking such terrible news to her did not appeal at all. I could, of course, just find Father Equiano or another priest and drop the dread burden on his shoulders. On the other hand, I did want to know if Danese had gone there after he stole my sword.

"Grazia says you were his best friend. It would be a favor to her and all of us if you were to break the news to his family."

I rejected the temptation to tell him that his late son-in-law had been an egregious liar, but I did make a note to clarify that with the inquisitor.

"Alfeo can do you a much bigger favor than that, Your Excellency," the Maestro said with a smirk I had long since learned to distrust. "I mean no personal offense when I say this. Please believe that I have only your well-being at heart. I am now convinced that there is a curse upon your house and it is the cause of all of your troubles."

Ottone Gritti tensed like a hound scenting game. Everyone else just looked stunned and I am sure that included me.

"What sort of curse?" the inquisitor demanded. "You talk of witchcraft?"

I had a very uneasy feeling that Nostradamus was talking nonsense just to get his own back for Gritti's bullying. If so, he was playing a very dangerous game and I might be the first to suffer for it.

"No," he said solemnly. "Or rather, yes, but not witch-craft performed by any living witch, no one within your reach. I don't know where it came from. I suspect it is an-cient, dating back several centuries. Have you ever heard of a jinx, Your Excellencies?"

"There's a bird by that name," Zuanbattista said. "I saw a caged one in Constantinople."

"Interesting," the Maestro murmured, staring at him. "But probably irrelevant. Yes, too late. These misfortunes predate your visit there. The *jynx* is a type of woodpecker found in the Balkans, among other places. When disturbed, it will turn its head around to an extreme degree and hiss at the intruder. It has long been used in witchcraft as a means to lay misfortune on people. Indeed, it has given its name to such curses, so if I say that your current problems stem from a *jinx*, *clarissimo*, I do not imply that you have a dead bird hung around your neck."

"Just what do you imply, then?" the big man demanded angrily.

"That there is some cursed item in your house that is spreading evil as the miasma of a fetid marsh spreads fever. It is a talisman in reverse, a source of misfortune instead of good. Whatever it is, it should be hunted down and de-stroyed. Alfeo can at least identify the source of the evil for you."

Zuanbattista's beard writhed in disbelief. "And how does he do that?"

I raised my chin so I would look competent and fearless, instead of just bewildered.

"He knows what to look for," the Maestro said. "He will be guided by the man from Vicenza."

I still did not understand, but I could guess that he wanted a free hand without Filiberto Vasco underfoot, and the only way to get rid of him was to get rid of me. I just hoped the separation would not be too permanent.

Sanudo glared at me, dropping his patrician inscrutability. "When was Zeno consecrated bishop or elected state inquisitor? Have I not enough troubles that I have to put up with him again?"

"There is no harm in letting the lad try," Ottone Gritti said with a benevolent smile. "I shall be most interested to see how he goes about it."

Sanudo sighed. "Very well. If I must carry the camel, I will not count the fleas."

20

Down at the watergate, Ottone Gritti was still very much in charge. He bid farewell to the Sanudos, promising to follow them shortly. Had he written it in fire, the message could have been no plainer: *If you murdered Dolfin, fly for your lives.* A less-exalted family would not have been given such a chance, but some senior patricians guilty of major crimes have been allowed to go into voluntary exile and return when the fuss has died down, after having negotiated a massive fine. There were extenuating circumstances when the victim had been a gigolo and legally a rapist. There was a second message, too. Treason was much worse than murder, and Gritti would not extend such mercy to suspected traitors. He must be very sure that the Sanudos were not involved in espionage. What did he know that I did not? A GREAT deal.

After we had bowed the Sanudos away along the canal, he turned to me.

"*Sier* Alfeo, I should have asked the good doctor this, but he has obviously trained you well, so give me your expert opinion. You mentioned internal bleeding. How much external bleeding occurred, would you estimate?"

For a man in his position to flatter a youngster like me in this way was so out of character it was almost farce. It alarmed me greatly.

"I am no expert, Your Excellency! I am certainly not a doctor. Your own opinion on such matters would be worth far more than mine would. But since you honor me by asking, I note that the corpse's garments were drenched with blood, so whatever surface he was lying on must have been stained at the very least. The mud on the rest of his clothing indicates that he died outdoors, so the storm may have washed away the evidence by now."

He nodded gravely, as if my words were a promulgation from the University of Padua. "That is a danger, certainly, but the matter is important." He turned to one of his *fanti*, the same Marco Martini who had summoned the Maestro two days before. The other, a taller man of about the same middle years, I later learned was Amedeo Bolognetti.

"Marco," Gritti said, "I want you to scout the parish. Search the *calli* and *campi* for bloodstains. The dead man bled to death a few hours before the rain started. Amedeo, deliver this letter to the *Signoria* and then find out from the chiefs if any bloodstains have been reported in the city. Report to me at Ca' Donato Maddalena."

They boarded the government gondola and their boatmen pushed off, letting Marco disembark at the end of the *calle*. That left Gritti, Vasco, a surprised-looking Giorgio, and me.

The old man smiled fondly. "You will not mind company when you call on madonna Corner?"

Of course I bowed acquiescence. "Your support is welcome and an honor, Excellency. Campo San Barnaba, please," I told Giorgio.

Gritti boarded and placed himself in the *felze*. When I tried to join him he waved me forward. "You sit there. The *vizio* is too conspicuous."

That left me out in the drizzle, of course, facing Gritti
and a smug Vasco under the *felze*, but in truth the rain was a
relief after the long months of heat. Soon we were gliding
along, as Giorgio's oar stroked the rain-dappled waters. On
either hand the centuries flowed by—a fourteenth-century
building, a fifteenth, then a twelfth, a modern sixteenth.
Soon we should start on the seventeenth, which would seem
odd. Gondolas passed us and followed us. Even on such a
drab day, gondoliers sang on the water and canaries in high
windows.

"I should explain, *clarissimo*," I said, "that I never
counted Danese Dolfin among my friends. He certainly
never behaved like a friend to me. Why he told his wife otherwise I cannot imagine. He must have lied about his
mother's name and address, too."

"Some liars need no reason, alas," the inquisitor said.
"They seem to feel they have failed if they have to speak the
truth." Probably nobody knew more about the subject than
he, but he was still playing his jocular, grandfatherly role.
"Tell me how one goes about identifying a jinx. Should you
not have brought some equipment with you? A bible? A
trained cat?"

No scribes stood ready to write down my words. If I
asked him, he would assure me that they would not be
quoted against me, but that would not stop him from asking the same questions again in more stressful
circumstances—as, for example, when my wrists were tied
behind me and taking my weight as I dangled on the strappado.

Fortunately I had worked out by then what the Maestro
had hinted. I wanted to strangle him for not telling me
sooner, because he had known something I had not, but perhaps he was not as sure as he had pretended.

"If my master meant what I think he did, Your Excellency, then I can just point and you will understand. If I am

wrong, then I won't be able to identify anything. Nostradamus is often needlessly cryptic, as you know."

He chuckled. "I think you are picking up the habit. Tell me about the fire elementals."

Warning bells rang.

"According to theory, Your Excellency, one would identify the source of evil by invoking fire elementals, which are—"

"Morally neutral. I read your master's testimony. I am not certain Holy Mother Church agrees with his interpretation, but carry on. What is involved?"

"Much hocus-pocus, but basically it meant sitting in front of a fire and daydreaming."

"And what did you see?"

He sounded genuinely interested. I am sure he was, because almost anything I said could be taken as an admission of witchcraft. I reminded myself that I was dealing with a fanatic. "I saw many things. Shoes and olive trees, galleons and bell towers. Women. Just daydreams. No demons, no Algol." To confess that I had seen the murder before it happened would be fatal: Exodus 22:28, Deuteronomy 18:10.

"Who killed Dolfin?"

"I have no idea, *clarissimo*."

"But you have suspicions. Tell me."

I was flattered that he thought my opinion worth listening to, but a friendly chat with Ottone Gritti was a romp with a full-grown leopard. "Any man can be stabbed in the back. But the sword that killed Danese was his sword, legally mine of course; I mean he was wearing it. Only an agile and strong opponent could disarm him in a hand-to-hand struggle. When he stole my rapier, he should have taken my dagger as well!" I patted it, dangling at my right side. My sword was back in place on my left, and comforting. "The sword was left behind, so the motive was not theft, and a random killer would not have known to dump his body at Ca' Barbolano."

Gritti was listening with flattering attention. "So?"

"A hired bravo seems most likely, *clarissimo*, and there are many such ruffians to be had. So the question becomes, who hired him? Just about anyone in the Sanudo family had a motive. *Sier* Zuanbattista and his wife have been made laughingstocks, politically and socially. *Sier* Girolamo to a lesser extent, but there are rumors that his interest in Dolfin was less than honorable. Any of them may have wished to rescue Grazia from a potentially disastrous marriage. And she may have realized her mistake, although I see no practical means for a lady of her age and station to go out and hire a killer. As you said yourself, Your Excellency, Dolfin was a lecher, so even the servants might have had motives." I waited for comment, and when there was none continued, "I would like to know where Girolamo was at the time of the murder."

"Ask him."

Puzzled, I said, "Your Excellency?"

"Ask him. I mean it!" The inquisitor smiled with secret amusement. "He will tell you the truth. Your list of motives leaves out the one that interests me most. If either Zuanbattista or his son is Algol, then Danese may have stumbled on the secret and been killed to keep him from revealing it."

Gritti was playing games with me. He was very sure that neither Sanudo was the spy, and by then I had worked out why. It made sense and it complicated things. If the Sanudos were not traitors it was much harder to see them as murderers.

"It would have to have been done very quickly," I said, "because Danese was no hero, as I told you. *Sier* Zuanbattista grabbed him, *sier* Girolamo disarmed him and stabbed him? There should be traces of blood somewhere in their house. Why did he come for his sword? Why did he steal mine? Was the agitation that Giorgio reported just impatience because he was keeping a gondola waiting?"

I persisted, because murder was a safer topic than pyromancy. "I have read only one page of the Algol documents and that dealt with naval matters. I know another began by naming the Council of Ten, but I don't know what came after. Perhaps it went on to report nothing more earthshattering than last month's edict on men's clothing. Yet I must assume from your own interest in these events, Excellency, that the dispatches contained significant leaks of state intelligence."

The grandfather mask slipped slightly. "Assume anything you like, but be careful whom you tell it to."

"I do not make so terrible an allegation against such honored noblemen," I protested. "Indeed it is obvious that they are not guilty. No one would dream of suspecting them were it not that *sier* Zuanbattista is a ducal counselor and *sier* Girolamo a minister of navy. I don't suppose that combination occurs in any other family in the Republic at the moment."

Gritti sighed, but continued to watch me closely. "It doesn't. Why do you say that they are obviously not guilty?"

"Because you clearly do not believe they are or you would have used the murder as a pretext to arrest them and search their house. I wonder if perhaps the information in Algol's dispatches, although basically correct and damaging, also contained some errors that neither Sanudo would have made?"

The old villain could not be trapped so easily. "The inquisitor asks the questions, Alfeo."

I squirmed. "Yes, *clarissimo*."

"*Vizio*, are you quite certain that Nostradamus did not decipher more than one page and the opening words of two more?"

"Quite certain, Your Excellency."

The deceptively benevolent gaze came back to me again.

"Are you by any chance one of those tricksters who can memorize pages of text at a glance, Alfeo? Is Nostradamus?"

"He is much better at it than I am," I said. "But memorizing a page of text is easy compared to memorizing a page of random letters. Neither of us could have done that, not even one page. I know, because I tried."

Our boat turned into the Rio di San Barnaba and the old church loomed up on our left, with the *campo* beyond. The rain made it less busy than it would normally be and the gossip crowd around the wellhead smaller.

I said, "The *campo* watersteps please, Giorgio. Madonna Corner used to live over there, Excellency—the brown house, top floor."

The old man had already drawn the curtain. "It would have to be the top floor, of course. The *vizio* and I are too conspicuous. We shall remain under cover while you find out where she is now."

21

Had I needed to visit the group gathered around the wellhead, I might have been detained there all day, but I had the good fortune to cross the path of old Widow Calbo, who remembered me very well. She had never tolerated idle chatter and still did not, so I soon returned to the gondola to report that madonna Agnese Corner still lived where she had when I had left San Barnaba and she took in lodgers. I offered a hand to help Gritti disembark.

"You fetch a priest," he told Vasco. "But very slowly. Zeno, come with me."

No stranger in patrician robes and elongated Council of Ten sleeves could cross the *campo* without attracting attention, but the sight was not rare enough to attract a crowd. The *vizio* heading for the church drew more stares, distracting attention from Gritti and his apprentice companion.

I knew those stairs. A dozen years ago I had run errands up and down them and scores like them all over San Barnaba. I knew every worn and cracked step, every broken pane in the windows, every tilted landing. Long-forgotten smells still lingered; the cough on the second floor had not killed its owner yet. I could almost feel the handles of the ancient water buckets I had carried biting my hands. Gritti trod a slower pace than my young self had used, and he halted a few steps from the top, although he did not seem breathless.

"You go ahead, Zeno. I hate the sight of women's tears."

But not the sound of men's screams? I went on alone. From there he would be able to hear what was said.

There were four doors. I knocked on the one I remembered as hers. I could hear water dripping from a leaky roof and the air was still unpleasantly warm, despite the rain. This attic would have been an oven for the last six months.

After a while I began to feel hopeful that the lady was not at home and I could escape the terrible duty. I knocked again, louder. A door creaked behind me and I knew I was being watched, but that is normal and even commendable.

"Who's there?" asked a voice I recalled at once, a deep voice for a woman.

"Alfeo Zeno, madonna. Remember me?"

A bolt rattled and she opened the door. I remembered her as a tall and grand lady, flaunting the fine clothes she wore when her husband held office on the mainland, although in retrospect I suppose they had been remarkable only by the standards of the *barnabotti*. She was shorter than me now and the fine garments had no doubt long vanished into the pawnshops of the Ghetto Nuovo. She had the light at her back as she inspected me, but I could see the sagging flesh of her face and the hump of age only too well.

"Yes, I remember you. It won't be good news brought you, I vow."

"No, madonna. It is not." My conscience rebelled at the prospect of letting Gritti continue standing there, eavesdropping on her sorrow. "May I come in?" Let him reveal himself if he wanted to hear.

"No," she said. "I have work to do. Tell me and begone. What has he done now?"

I opened my mouth to ask *Who?* and the contempt in her

eye stopped me. "He . . . was in a fight, madonna. Danese was."

"He's dead you mean?"

I nodded. "God rest his soul, ma'am." I crossed myself; she did not.

Indeed she shrugged and I thought she was going to try to close the door in my face. Clearly she was not going to weep, certainly not where I could see her and perhaps not at all. She was a daughter of one of the great families, but of an impoverished branch. Life had long since wrung all the weeping out of Agnese Corner that it was ever going to get.

"How?"

"We don't know. He was stabbed with a rapier," I said. "It must have been very quick," I lied. "He . . . You do know that he was married?"

Finally I won a reaction from her—she laughed. "To a wealthy widow three times his age?"

"No, madonna. Wealthy, yes, but young. Grazia Sanudo, daughter of *sier* Zuanbattista and madonna Eva Morosini. You did not know this?"

She shook her head as if trying to rid her mouth of a bad taste. "I have not heard from my son since the day I found out where he was getting his money and how he earned it, and that was before he was shaving. I don't know if any of his sisters stayed in touch because I forbade them ever to mention him in my presence. So don't expect me to pay for his funeral. Nor mourn him, either."

She could not have known that Gritti was listening. She must have known that neighbors were; she wanted them to hear. Her words roused ten years' sorrows like ghosts in the dusty hallway.

"His wife's family will attend to the rites. Danese did tell them that he had told you of his marriage."

She laughed again.

"He did not come to see you last night?"

"He did not knock at my door and I would not have opened it if he had."

I was sweating. I had never had a worse conversation with anyone and the knowledge that a state inquisitor was lurking just around the corner was not making me feel better. "Madonna, do you know anyone who might have had reason to want your son dead?"

"Any husband, father, or brother in Venice. Any woman or mother. I've heard good things of you, Alfeo. Thank you for coming."

I removed my foot before she discovered it was there and the door closed.

The one behind me closed also. Bolts were shot simultaneously.

I went down three steps and found Gritti blocking my way.

"She already knew?" he demanded.

"I don't know," I admitted. "I just don't know."

"It's possible?"

"Yes," I said. "It's possible. Please let's go before the priest comes." I was in no state to face Father Equiano's reproaches.

22

Giorgio rowed us to the end of Rio di San Barnaba and turned north along that finest of all the great streets of Europe, the Grand Canal, a parade of splendid palaces on either hand. The huge waterway was only slightly less busy on a Saturday morning than most days, quite busy enough. North and east we went, under the crowded arch of the Rialto, swinging around to the northwest, skirting the bustling vegetable and fish markets on our left and Cannaregio on our right, until we turned into the narrower ways of the Rio di Noale.

As we glided in toward the watersteps on the Rio di Maddalena, I noted the Sanudo house gondola moored there among some others, including a government boat, but I saw no signs of the *fanti*. Women on the *fondamenta* stopped their chatter to watch Gritti disembark, although the *vizio*'s red cloak probably impressed them more, for his visit could not be social.

Vasco thumped the brass anchor knocker. The door was opened instantly by the young valet, Pignate. His face was fish-belly pale, so he had been told of the murder, probably also been warned that the visitor he was waiting for was an inquisitor. He bowed us in.

That was the fourth time I had seen the great book collection in the *androne*, and each time it had progressed farther along the road from packing cases to shelved library, yet I had never seen anyone working on it, as if the books rearranged themselves at night when people could not see. I concluded that ordinary porters could not sort books properly, so the work was being done by clerks from the family publishing business, brought in at odd hours. No one would ever find time to read such a collection, but libraries like that are not intended to be read, only envied. I fervently hoped that my duties would not require me to go through it volume by volume, looking for spiders.

We mounted the staircase to the *piano nobile*, where Giro awaited us. Having shed his official robes, he was again no more than a private gentleman wearing oddly drab garments. He made no offers of welcome or pretense that our visit was social.

"My parents are with Grazia," he said conducting us to the *salotto*. "This is a very painful time for us."

"Of course it is," Gritti said, "and your ordeal shall be as brief as I can manage. I will talk first with the servants, if you please."

Today the balcony doors were closed against the rain and the garden looked glum and dank. The inquisitor chose a chair that put his back to the light, such as it was, and I picked one nearby, from which I could study the Michelli wedding portrait. Andrea Michelli is also known as Andrea Vicentino, the Andrea from Vicenza. That must be what the Maestro's hint had meant, for I had told him of the unusual wedding portrait. Why had a dead man intruded on my pyromancy? I had seen his wife struck down also. My mind shied away from the implications.

Vasco chose a chair where he could watch me, but did not get a chance to sit on it.

"*Vizio*," Gritti said, "take a look around the neighborhood and the garden down there. Look for traces of blood-stains."

Vasco departed. Giro returned, remaining just inside the door.

"The servants have all been told of the tragedy?" Gritti asked.

"Certainly. Come in, girls."

Three young woman shuffled in, lined up, and then stared in horror at the demon inquisitor. To be accurate, they stared at his feet, avoiding his eyes. Giro presented them: ladies' maid Noelia Grappeggia, cook Marina Alfieri, and housemaid Mimi Zorzin, all uniformed in aprons and head cloths as if interrupted in cleaning chores.

I had watched Ottone Gritti in action before, so I was not surprised at the ease with which his benevolent smiles and cooing voice won them over. They did want Danese's murderer caught, didn't they? They would like to help, wouldn't they? All three nodded like drinking chickens. Two of them he eliminated very quickly, because neither Marina nor Mimi lived in. They had left for home at sunset, so they could contribute no information about Danese's movements. Noelia slept on the mezzanine level, but yesterday she had been given time off because her mother was sick. Her father had come for her at sunset and brought her back before curfew. Pignate had let her in and she had gone straight to bed. None of the three had any idea who might have killed poor *sier* Danese. There had been no quarrels or threats. Gritti did not ask them if they had liked Danese, because "yes" would make them seem flighty and "no" suspect.

First the oil and then the vinegar. "Tell me about the *blood*!"

They jumped at his sharp command, but none of them fainted or burst into tears. There had been no massive bloodstains that they knew of.

The angels were dismissed and flew away.

I had not expected much help from them, but I found them a puzzling trio. The cook was much younger than most cooks, who are typically mature widows. The cleaning maid was dainty, although she must have to move heavy furniture as part of her job. Noelia I knew already to be a beauty, which is not too uncommon for a ladies' maid—nobody wants to be primped by an ogre—but the other two were beauties also. Not a missing tooth or smallpox scar among them. Dress them well and they would attract men like sharks to blood. Combining that observation with the strapping gondolier, Fabricio, and the cherubic valet-page, Pignate, I felt I had established a pattern, although I could not see what significance it might have to murder or espionage. I wondered if the Sanudos paid extra to hire and keep especially decorative staff, and that was only a step away from wondering why. Were they assigned special duties?

"The menservants, if you please," the inquisitor said.

Now things should become more interesting. If anyone in Ca' Sanudo had wrestled Danese for possession of my rapier and won, it must have been either young Pignate or the gondolier, who could probably have done it with one hand. Moreover, only he could have delivered the corpse to the watergate at Ca' Barbolano. Rowing a gondola—with a single oar, standing upright on a narrow boat—is no job for an amateur. It takes long practice and many involuntary cold baths to acquire that skill. Fabricio was odds-on suspect for the accomplice paid to dispose of the body.

Giro had been conferring at the door. I detected Pignate's voice and he followed Giro in.

"Our valet, Pignate Calabrò, *clarissimo*."

The boy was even more nervous than before. He tucked

his hands behind him so we wouldn't see them shake, but he managed to hold his head up and meet the inquisitor's eye, although his chin quavered. If the torturers were going to be involved, they would start with the servants.

Gritti chuckled. "I am not going to eat you, Pignate! I just want to find out when *sier* Danese went out last night, and why. How long have you been in service here?"

Just two months, was the answer, since the Sanudos returned from Celeseo and moved in. He was seventeen. Yes, he could read and write. Told to describe his actions the previous evening, he answered clearly and without hesitation. He had polished shoes, starched ruffs, sorted laundry. He had taken charge of the door while Fabricio was ferrying the master and mistress to their engagement, and later when the gondolier went to fetch them home. He had let Danese out and locked up behind him. There had been no visitors, and no notes handed in for Danese or anyone else. He was eager to help, and when Gritti doubled back or fired unexpected questions, he did not hesitate or contradict himself. In only one respect was his testimony lacking—he had no idea of time as measured by a clock. His life was run by waking and sleeping, by meals and the city bells, but he could not measure a day into twenty-four hours. After all, why should he?

"You are a very good witness, Pignate," the inquisitor said. "I wish there were more like you." Without turning his head, he added, "Alfeo, have you any questions?"

To be treated as a colleague by an inquisitor was a scary experience. Why should he so flatter me? Was he just putting me at ease, planning to catch me off guard later?

"Just one, if I may, Excellency. Yesterday I brought back the dead man's portmanteau. Did you unpack it for him?"

The boy glanced uneasily at Giro. "No, er, *sier* Alfeo. I was not told . . . I have not attended *sier* Danese in the past." A *cavaliere servente* might be better rewarded for his services than a valet, but he was still only a servant to the other servants.

"I just wondered," I said. "That is all. Thank you."

Pignate was dismissed.

Giro closed the door behind him and turned to the inquisitor. "I am embarrassed to report, *clarissimo*, that Fabricio Muranese, our gondolier, appears to—"

"Does he have any money?" said Gritti, that patient, understanding grandfather.

"He probably has some," Giro admitted, face frozen into inscrutability. "He has been in my employ for six or seven years."

The inquisitor nodded. "And did he tell you anything before he left?"

That was a leading question, but Giro ignored the implications. "He repeated what he told us earlier, when we learned that Dolfin was missing. He brought my parents home, carried in his oar and the cushions from the gondola, bolted the front door, checked the rear door, went to bed. About two hours after curfew, roughly, I came home and he let me in. The men sleep at the front, so they can hear the knocker, and I have a special knock—I am often late." He glanced at me and showed a rare trace of a smile. "I tip whoever comes, so they almost fight over the honor."

By now Fabricio would be on the Mestre ferry, or even already on the mainland. As a suspect, he was too obvious. Whether or not the Sanudos had suggested it to him, his flight was a sign of prudence more than of guilt; better exile than interrogation. If the real culprit could not be found, Fabricio could be labeled a murderer and the case closed.

At that moment Vasco slipped in, nodded meaningfully to Gritti, and sat on the chair he had chosen earlier. The nod meant that he had found blood.

Gritti did not criticize Girolamo for letting the gondolier

flee. "Before we meet with the ladies, *sier* Alfeo has a question to ask you."

Giro turned an inquiring gaze on me. Again my hair follicles twitched in alarm. More and more the inquisitor was making me think of cats and mice, with me in the supporting role. I swallowed hard.

"*Clarissimo*, since you mention that you were late coming home, may I inquire where you went last night?"

The navy minister stared at me in silence for a long moment, letting me stew in my impertinence, before saying, "It is no secret. I spend most afternoons and evenings helping out at the *scuola*. Last night I was cutting elderly toenails."

Charity work. If true, that would be a better alibi than just about anything. I evicted Girolamo Sanudo from my mental parade of suspects.

"And who hired the servants here?"

"I did. While my father was closing the house at Celeseo, I was opening this one. You approve of my taste?" Giro's cold stare said that he could guess what I was thinking and nothing in the world mattered less than my opinion.

"So none of them has been in your service more than a couple of months?"

"Fabricio. And Danese, but he was no longer a servant at the time of his death." Giro did not express any hypocritical regrets. "I hired him about five years ago. Before my duties for the Republic interfered, I provided legal advice for the poor at nominal fees, and he came to me with a problem. I was able to help him with that and he revealed that he was in the service—unwillingly, he assured me—of a man of high standing who is also a notorious pervert. I offered the lad a job as a clerk, which he accepted eagerly, and eventually he graduated to being my mother's companion."

But he had not won his way back into his own mother's favor. Had he even tried? Giro waited to see what else I wanted, but I understood that I had been thoroughly put down and just thanked him politely.

"If the ladies are ready for a few questions?" Gritti prompted. Girolamo nodded and went to see.

The inquisitor said, *"Vizio?"*

Vasco drew a deep breath. "Excellency, I have the honor to report that I found no bloodstains in the yard here, but a large amount of blood had been spilled in the *calle* three houses east of here, near the watersteps. *Fante* Bolognetti was there, calming a trio of *sbirri*, who were supervising a worker cleaning it up. Much of it had already been washed away by the rain, but traces ran all the way to the watersteps." Vasco looked smug at having completed so difficult a mission successfully. "We informed the *sbirri* that Their Excellencies know who died there and I took their names in case they are needed as witnesses."

So Danese had left Ca' Sanudo, gone south to Ca' Barbolano to get his sword, returned north to Ca' Sanudo to die, and then been transported back to Ca' Barbolano again. In the names of all the martyrs, *why?* He had probably never gone near his mother in San Barnaba.

Gritti nodded. "Very good." The shrewd old eyes stabbed at me. "Why did you ask the page about Dolfin's portmanteau, Alfeo?"

Prevarication time. I wanted to locate Danese's gold and find out where it had come from, but if I mentioned the gold itself, I might have to reveal that he had been ferrying sequins from Ca' Sanudo to Ca' Barbolano, and out would come the Maestro's extortionate fee. I must find an alternative explanation. The Maestro insists I cannot tell lies with a straight face, but I can. I did.

"I wondered after I brought it here whether I should have gone through it to check for migrating silverware. You noticed that *sier* Girolamo admitted Danese had been in some sort of trouble when—"

"Your master said he sent you to pack the portmanteau. Did you or didn't you pack it yourself?"

"It had never been unpacked. I just threw in a few loose clothes he had left lying around. Hosts shouldn't rummage through their guests' luggage."

Gritti gave me the sort of silent stare that is intended to make a witness keep babbling. I took the chance to change the subject.

"I admit I misjudged *sier* Girolamo. I am impressed by a member of the *Collegio* cutting old folks' toenails."

He shrugged and allowed the diversion, although he had noticed it. "Be more impressed by a man who does the Lord's work being elected to office. That was mostly a compliment to his father and I am sure that *sier* Girolamo will be glad to see his term end. Young Sanudo took a vow of celibacy when he was sixteen, you see. His father talked him out of entering a monastery, but I think there is a time limit on that promise." The old rascal was flaunting the Ten's intimate knowledge of the nobility's secrets. "A few years later Zuanbattista married again to try for an heir, but madonna Eva has given him only one daughter and a stillborn son."

No doubt Girolamo's religious zeal explained his drab clothes and frigid self-control. I had never known Violetta to be so wrong about a man before, but he was not a potential patron and had only just come into the public eye, so her error could be excused. "He likes to keep pretty boys and girls around just to torture himself?" I asked.

"Or to test his resolve. For all I know he wears a hair shirt, too." The inquisitor rearranged his jowls in a pout to indicate that the subject was closed.

But for me a new door had opened. "So madonna Eva's hopes of one day being dogaressa were not so unreasonable after all! If Girolamo takes holy orders and turns his back on the world, and Grazia is married off to a wealthy Contarini, then the family fortune need not be saved for the next generation. The mainland estates can be cashed in to finance *sier* Zuanbattista's continuing career?"

Gritti's answer was a stony stare. I ignored it as I recalculated motives. I had not given enough thought to the matter of dowry, which in Grazia's case could be several tens of thousands of ducats, enough to make the lapdog Danese into a very rich man by normal standards. Surely the murder on top of the elopement scandal would destroy whatever was left of Zuanbattista's reputation? Would he banish Grazia to a convent now, or find her another husband? How much dowry would she bring the second time around? For that matter, how much had Danese been promised? Now my personal list of suspects had acquired some new names—the rejected suitor, Zaccaria Contarini, who had been cheated out of a large fortune in dowry, and even Danese's sisters, who had all married commoners. If Danese had left a will . . .

"What's squirming around inside your agile young brain now?" the inquisitor demanded.

I jumped. "I hadn't realized, Excellency, that if the marriage contract was signed before last night"—which might explain why Danese had been allowed to move back in as Grazia's acknowledged husband—"then he may have died a comparatively rich man."

Gritti snorted. "And perhaps the young scoundrel had debts that had suddenly become worth collecting? Have you gotten that far, Alfeo Zeno?"

23

Zuanbattista ushered in his womenfolk. Madonna Eva was magnificent in full mourning, swathed in black lace and taffeta. She had experience of mortality and funerals, of course, and would keep a complete outfit ready in her closet. Black flattered her fair coloring. To Grazia a brush with death must be a new experience, and even to my untutored eye her gown looked as if it had been assembled in haste and fastened on her with pins. We visitors rose and bowed, remaining standing until the ladies were seated, side by side on a divan.

Eva lifted back her veil. After a moment's hesitation Grazia copied her, revealing the red eyes and pink nose of recent weeping. Her mother had not wept, but any joy she felt at being rid of an unwanted son-in-law was well hidden behind maternal concern for her bereaved child. Even if the romance had been a flash in the pan or puppy love contrived by an experienced seducer, Grazia's shock and loss must be genuine. I felt truly sorry for her, and perversely happy that at least one woman mourned Danese Dolfin.

"I realize that this is very painful for you," Gritti said, "and I will be as quick as I can. When your husband announced that he had to go out last night, madonna, where did he say he was going?"

Grazia sniffled. "To visit his mother in San Barnaba."

"He did not mention anyone else he might see on the way?"

Another sniffle, a head shake.

"She says he did not arrive, and we have reason to believe that he was killed on his way back here, not far from this house, about two hours after he left you. So what was he doing in the meantime?"

She whispered, "I do not know, Your Excellency."

There was a long pause, while the inquisitor sat as if half-asleep. I wondered if he was about to spring some dramatic catch-them-napping question, as he had with the maids, but all he said was, "Alfeo, have you anything to ask?"

"No, Excellency."

He smiled without looking at me. "Then why don't you reveal to us the terrible curse that your master thinks has been laid upon this house?"

If I blurted out my suspicions without confirming them first, I would be dismissed as a lunatic. "We are still one short, Excellency. Madonna Fortunata Morosini is not here."

Gritti frowned as if annoyed that he had forgotten her.

Still standing by the door, Giro said, "She is having one of her bad days," as his father was saying, "She could not contribute anything, Your Excellency."

Nothing could have aroused an inquisitor's suspicions faster than those simultaneous refusals. Gritti ruffled up his feathers. "Nevertheless, if my precocious young friend wants to try interrogating her, let us humor him."

He could have been more tactful. Zuanbattista glared at me as if he were about to choke, and Giro marched angrily out of the room, which was his version of a screaming tantrum.

The icy silence remained behind.

"That portrait of your honored brother, madonna," I asked Eva. "When was it painted?"

Although she had no choice but to put up with the state inquisitor, she was no more in favor of the upstart, busy-body apprentice than her husband was. The clefts framing her mouth deepened into canyons. "When they were married, of course."

"And how long ago was that?"

"Fifteen years ago, just a month before Grazia was born."

Assuming that the painter had not flattered his subjects too extremely, the woman ought to be in her thirties by now, if she still lived. I was about to ask her name when a cane *tap-tap-tapped* outside.

Giro entered, walking slowly and supporting Fortunata on his arm. The men rose while he guided her to a chair. Once she was settled, he presented the inquisitor, speaking loudly. She peered at us as if the room was filled with dense fog and perhaps it was, for her. I could imagine nothing in the world less likely than the decrepit Fortunata Morosini wrestling a rapier away from a ruthless young ne'er-do-well like Danese Dolfin. Nor did I expect her to be much help to the inquisitor in the investigation. But the Maestro had been right—her resemblance to the bride in the portrait was undeniable now that I knew to look for it. My scalp prickled.

"Ottone Gritti?" she muttered. "I knew a Marino Gritti."

The inquisitor sat down again and stretched his legs as if his left hip hurt. "My son, madonna. You have heard of the sad death of *sier* Danese?"

"Eh?"

Louder: "You have heard of the sad death of *sier* Danese?"

"Not sad!" She bared a few yellow fangs. "Pretty-boy thief, that's what he was. Good riddance."

"Why do you call him thief, madonna? What did he steal?"

In the background Giro was shaking his head.

"Stole my pearls!" she said. "Stole my ring."

"You mislaid them, Auntie," Giro said softly. "We found them for you." She was not expected to hear that and did not seem to.

"When was the last time you saw him?" the inquisitor asked.

"Who?"

"Danese Dolfin."

She mumbled and mouthed a while, then pointed her cane at me. "When he was here."

"Yesterday at midday," I offered.

"Fortunata suffers from terrible headaches," Giro said. "She retired to her room soon after Zeno left and would not have seen Danese after that."

Gritti said, "Then I do not see . . ." He looked at me.

"May I ask first," I said, "how long the jewels were mislaid?"

Zuanbattista frowned at me, but this time there was calculation mixed in with the resentment. "About a week, I think. Old people get confused. She had hidden them inside one of her shoes."

"Or somebody else did? I mean someone stole the originals, had them copied, and then hid the replicas there to be found?"

He nodded. "I see what you mean. I will have them appraised."

That, I thought, had been the source of Danese's gold, which I could not mention but might manage to discover later if I got the chance to explore his room. I turned to the inquisitor and pointed at the painting.

"Your Excellency, did you ever meet *sier* Nicolò?"

"Several times. Very tragic. Why do you . . ." Gritti's reaction was everything I could have hoped for. He lost his normal high color, his eyes bulged. Then he stared at the wizened crone on the chair.

"How old is madonna Fortunata?" I demanded.

"She has aged a lot recently," Eva said defensively.

"But how many years?" I persisted. The family frowned at my insolence.

"What possible business is that of yours, apprentice?" Zuanbattista barked.

Fortunata Morosini wore widow's weeds, but most Venetian women continue to use their maiden names after marriage. She was not a sister of Eva's father, but of her brother, Nicolò. Not Eva's aunt but Grazia's. Zuanbattista had said so on the day he and his wife came to Ca' Barbolano, but after meeting the old woman I had made the natural mistake, or the jinx had deceived me also. I had skipped a generation in my thinking. She had done worse than that, something unthinkable.

"Call it my business," Gritti said grimly. "How old is this woman?"

Zuanbattista shrugged. "Thirty-four? No, thirty-three. As my wife said, she has gone down a lot in the last few years. I admit I was shocked when I returned from Constantinople."

"She looks at least seventy!"

I would have said eighty, but I was engrossed in watching the reactions: Giro's horror, Vasco's disbelief, and the overall confusion of the Sanudos as they fought free of the web the jinx had spun over them. Giro muttered, "Seventy?" to himself and dismay crept over his face. Eva, also, and Zuanbattista . . . and Grazia? Too late! I had missed it, but there had been something wrong with her reaction. Had Grazia approved of her tutor's misfortune?

Ancient Fortunata herself had caught up with the conversation. Her face had crumpled into a wad of creases and she was trying to clench her knurled fists. "Old!" she mumbled. "Old! Don't want to be old, old, old."

Giro crossed himself. "She is younger than I am," he said,

almost inaudibly. "She has failed a lot these last few years. Every time I went across to Celeseo I was . . . shocked . . ."

"The curse blighted her and blinded the rest of you," I said.

"Foul witchcraft!" the inquisitor growled. "Whom do you accuse, Zeno?"

My scalp prickled again. Even in Venice, where the law is fairer than anywhere else, there is really no defense against an accusation of witchcraft. You can be tortured until you confess and then you are put to death. Just by exposing the curse I might have revealed too much knowledge of the Devil's works. I was saved from having to answer by Fortunata herself, who suddenly exploded, hammering her cane on the floor and shrilling, *The book was cursed! The book was cursed!*" After a dozen repetitions she broke off into coughing and weeping.

"Nicolò's death?" Gritti demanded of nobody in particular. "Is that what she means? Was there such a book?"

Eva was looking much more distressed by this discussion than she had been by Danese's death. "My brother died of a poisoned finger and he always said it started with a paper cut, but he could not remember which book did it. My brother handled a hundred books a day, maybe several hundred."

"And what happened to his collection after his death?"

"Most of it is downstairs," Zuanbattista said, looking much more skeptical, "still being unpacked and sorted. We have added to it, but I don't believe we ever sold off anything."

"You accuse a book, Alfeo?" Gritti inquired sourly. "Which book? How do you tell an accursed book from all the rest?" To him an accursed book would be much less satisfying than an accused witch. Venice disapproves of burning books. He would be laughed at if he burned a mountain of books.

Two of my three visions had now been vindicated—
Danese had been murdered exactly as I foresaw, and the
woman in the painting had been cursed by the same evil influence that had felled her husband. That left Neptune and
his seahorse. I would trust the pyromancy and hunt for
Neptune, but if I said that I would be asked why.

"An object can be touched by Satan, Your Excellency,
just as a person can. There are talismans of good fortune,
like blessed rosaries or San Christoforo medallions, and
there are evil talismans also. In the days before printing,
when books were treasures in themselves, they were often
protected by a curse written on the first page, threatening
misfortune on anyone who stole the book from its rightful
owner. The curse might be worded so that it fell on anyone
who possessed the book thereafter. I certainly do not accuse
the late *sier* Nicolò of theft. He might in all innocence have
purchased a jinxed book, though, and then the curse would
transfer to him and his house." I fell silent, realizing that I
was talking too much.

If I had only one believer in that room, it was *sier* Ottone
Gritti. "And how does one detect such an abomination?" he
demanded eagerly.

"I would be inclined to send for a priest, perhaps even the
cardinal-patriarch himself. My master has never taught me
a specific procedure." What he had told me often enough,
though, was that, *Truth must sometimes hide behind a curtain of
lies.* My Christian duty was to locate and destroy the jinx before it did any more damage. It had killed Nicolò Morosini,
blighted his wife, perhaps turned one of the Sanudos into a
traitor. It might have brought about Danese's death. I must
do whatever I could to track it down and destroy it, even at
risk to myself. I had a brain wave. "Except possibly dowsing," I added thoughtfully.

All around the room eyebrows rose like pigeons in the
Piazza.

"Dowsing?" Giro said.

Even Gritti would have trouble classifying dowsing as witchcraft. Even our skeptical doge might admit that there could be something to dowsing. Dowsing is not practiced in Venice, sitting in the middle of a saltwater lagoon, but everyone knows of and believes in dowsing—except the Maestro. Dig a hole deep enough almost anywhere and you will find some water, he says, so dowsing is a fraud almost without risk. I hoped it would be for me.

"Apple wood would be best, I think," I mused, looking profound. "The tree of knowledge, of course. The tree of the serpent."

"We have an apple tree!" Grazia said brightly. "I will show *sier* Alfeo." She rose to her feet.

"That is good of you, madonna," Gritti said with a benevolent smile. "By all means let him try his dowsing for evil." He nodded to Vasco, who stood up also. I would have my jailer in attendance and a reliable witness, while Gritti could have a private talk with the Sanudos, in the absence of the kiddies.

24

We trooped downstairs, Grazia and I, with our macabre shadow treading close behind. Grazia had abandoned any pretense of liking me. I was a *barnabotto*, I worked for a living, and I was continuing to meddle in her affairs. So why her sudden desire for a private tête-à-tête? I had a strong suspicion that we would shortly be discussing horoscopes.

"Danese," she murmured. "He did die quickly, didn't he?"

No. "Yes," I said. "It must have been instantaneous. He would have known nothing."

"I am glad. He is with the Lord. He never reached his mother's house?"

"So the lady says."

"Was she lying to you?"

"I do not know, madonna."

By this time we were parading along the *androne* amid all the books, and Grazia stopped suddenly, as if to add import to her next question. "Or are you saying that *sier* Danese lied to me?" She was back to using her speaking-to-servants voice to me, but clearly the unwelcome truth was starting to sink in.

"I do not know, madonna."

She bit her pretty lip. "He must have been killed on his way to see her?"

Even as a child I had despised Danese's mendacity and I felt that Grazia deserved the truth from somebody. "He first went back to Ca' Barbolano to fetch his sword. The Maestro and I were busy, so he could not find it, and he borrowed mine instead. We don't know why he needed a weapon. Do you?"

In the gloom of the *androne*, her memorable eyes seemed even more huge than usual. "No! You have no idea who did this terrible thing?"

"Not yet, but we will catch him, I am sure."

"And I suppose my husband's death was the upturn in my fortunes you read in my horoscope?"

There are times when lies are necessary. "No, I do not believe that at all, madonna. I am hoping that what your horoscope predicted was the removal of the jinx. Let us proceed with that, please. We are dealing with a very potent evil."

Now, that was the truth. What I was about to try might be dangerous. Not dowsing—I was deliberately cozening with that—and not much in arousing Gritti's suspicions of witchcraft, but in looking for Neptune. Two of my fire visions had proven to be true predictions, so I could hope that the Neptune one would lead me straight to Algol, and I had developed a deep respect for Algol's demonic powers.

We continued our trek to the back door and out into the garden and a misty rain. My guide pointed her dainty finger at an apple tree, which was not the one I had had in mind and would be harder to climb. No matter, we hot-blooded young gallants can always be trusted to show off in front of a fair damsel. I jumped high to catch a branch. The result was an instant deluge, drenching me. Ignoring Vasco's hoots, I hauled myself up and into the tree. There I chose a twig as long as my leg, with good side-branches, and cut it off with my dagger. I followed it down and we all retreated under the shelter of the upper-floor balconies where I stripped leaves and unwanted growth off it, leaving only the traditional *Y* shape.

"This is exciting!" Grazia informed Vasco. "Have you ever watched anyone dowsing for evil before, *Vizio?*"

"No, madonna. I don't suppose I ever shall again."

"You should let me teach you," I said. "Except that we must concentrate on your fencing lessons first." I opened the door and bowed Grazia ahead of me, letting Vasco follow us. "Now, madonna . . ."

I surveyed the long hall lined with ten-foot high bookshelves along either side, fitted with wheeled ladders for access to the upper layers. There were still two or three thousand volumes on the floor, in stacks and boxes. My heart failed me. Even to fake a survey of all this would take hours, and Gritti might decide to leave at any moment. Either he would take me with him or the Sanudos would evict me as soon as he had left; my chance to find Neptune would have gone.

The wall of bookshelves along the right side of the *androne*—which was currently on my left since we were at the rear of the house—was broken by three doors, opposing two doors and the staircase on the other side. The nearer door on my right was open and led to the kitchen, directly under Grazia's chamber. Marina and Pignate were bustling around in there, preparing dinner. I told my mouth to stop watering.

"I think I will leave the main collection until I have surveyed the rest of the house, madonna. That will help me get the wand attuned. And I will leave the kitchen until the end, so I do not interrupt the cooks' important labors. Now, what are those other rooms? Not more books, I hope?"

I had spoken in hope and jest, but Grazia said, "Yes!"

She crossed to the right side and threw open the rearmost

door. The room beyond was packed with crates of books, piles of lumber, and half-completed bookshelves. I believe I groaned.

"Tiring work, is it, dowsing?" Vasco murmured behind me.

"And that's still not all!" our guide proclaimed, heading to the front of the house. The room there was in much the same condition, except that the construction was further along. "This will be for the most valuable volumes."

Now I had the plan clear in my mind. The right side held two rooms of books, and the other side had the kitchen at the back and a front room that I could guess.

"This," I said, heading for it, "must be Fabricio and Pignate's?" Girolamo had said they slept close to the door. "Let us start there."

The chamber was spacious. A bed apiece and a chest for clothes and a couple of chairs, all of them quality pieces. The Sanudos were generous to their servants, even if they worked them hard, for I have seen dormitories half its size with a dozen flunkies packed in like salted fish. Holding the branches of the wand, I raised it so the stalk pointed straight forward.

"Please do not speak for a few moments," I said, concentrating. I mouthed a prayer, which was perfectly sincere, an appeal for forgiveness for mendacity in a good cause. Then I began to walk slowly forward gently swinging the wand from side to side to point at this or that. When I had gone all the way around, I shook my head.

"Nothing, I'm afraid." Following Grazia out, I pointed across to the central door on the right side, between the two rooms of books and opposite the staircase. Whatever lay behind it could have no windows. "What's in there?"

"The way to the mezzanine." She was enjoying herself, managing to forget her grief. She swept across in her mourning gown and opened the door to reveal narrow stairs, dimly illuminated by the two open doors at the top. Up we went.

The female servants' dormitory was at the front. It was a very fine bedroom, and at the moment Noelia had it to herself, except that it was also being used to store furniture. I dowsed my way around and found nothing suspicious. What sort of a Neptune was I supposed to look for? A book about Roman gods? A statue? A painting? Fiery spiders?

The other mezzanine room had been Danese's before his eviction. It had a fine view of the garden and the iron grille over the window matched Grazia's on the other side. The furnishings were superb, and the paintings on the walls cried out for study and appreciation. The only criticism I could have leveled at it as a room was that its ceiling was no more than about nine feet high, which I found oppressive after Ca' Barbolano. Even in Ca' Sanudo, the *altana* and *piano nobile* ceilings were at least twice that. But Danese had indeed done well for himself, and I wondered what quarters he had enjoyed at Celeseo, for the mainland palaces of the rich sprawl far larger than those in cramped Venice.

"You had better dowse this room well, *messer*," Grazia proclaimed, with an attempt at aristocratic hauteur. "Who knows what missing jewels it may contain?"

I portrayed wronged virtue. "Madonna, it was your aunt who accused your late husband of theft. I never did. Remember that no one here observed how your aunt had been cursed. She looks twice as old as she should, and yet none of you noticed. When valuables disappear for a day or two and then turn up again, it is only common sense to inspect them carefully, and apparently nobody had thought to do that. It was my duty to suggest that precaution, but any servant could have made the switch. I did not hint at Danese."

She ignored me, deaf as Odysseus to the sirens.

I persisted. "The jewel incident was recent? It happened after you moved back from Celeseo?"

Reluctantly she nodded.

"Then I should certainly suspect the new servants more than Danese, who had been employed by your family for years." I did not point out that Danese would have found it easier to have stolen jewelry counterfeited here in Venice than he would have done in Padua, or that he might have been worried about his tenure as *cavaliere servente* since his employer's husband returned from foreign lands.

There was no obvious Neptune in sight, but I dowsed my way around the room. No demons emerged. Vasco kept yawning behind Grazia's back.

We went downstairs, crossed the hall, and started up the main staircase. At the mezzanine level, Grazia swept right by the two doors and continued on up toward the *piano nobile* without a hint that the rooms there ought to be inspected also. I caught Vasco's eye and for once we shared smiles of real amusement.

Martini and Bolognetti, the two *fanti*, were sitting patiently on a divan, and Madonna Eva was just emerging from the *salotto*, assisting the blighted Fortunata.

"Let us begin with your aunt's room," I said. "After all, that is the most likely place to find the source of the evil that cursed her."

Fortunata would have to be billeted on that level, being unable to manage stairs, and Grazia led us across to the right-front corner, overlooking the canal. The room itself was magnificent. The ceiling paintings alone made me want to hurl myself down on the bed and spend half an hour admiring. There were several fine oils hung on the walls, also, although they were poorly arranged and matched. The furniture was of fine quality, but scanty, and some pieces obviously old, perhaps heirlooms. The bed was gracious, standing upon golden pillars in the center of the room. I was able to dowse all the way around it. No Neptune, no jinx, no demon.

We were safely back out in the *salone* before the owner arrived at her tortoise creep. I crossed to the open door opposite and found myself in the dining room. Little Noelia was laying out silverware and crystal. She stared with octopus eyes at me and my twig as I solemnly paced my way around the room and her, but neither of us spoke.

Now I had the *piano nobile* worked out also: on the right, Madonna Fortunata's room and the *salotto*; on the left, the dining room and what must surely be the Sanudos' own bedchamber at the rear. With Eva attending her aunt and Zuanbattista closeted with his son and Gritti in the *salotto*, now was my chance to pry there also. Grazia started to protest, but I rapped on the door and entered.

It was different. Here the former ambassador displayed his souvenirs—rich silk rugs on the floor and walls, ornate silver urns, carved ivory tables, and other oddities. The ceiling painting seemed old and faded by comparison and, with the big doors out to the balcony closed, the air held a peculiar, foreign scent that I disliked. I did my dowsing as fast as I could without breaking out of my role and returned to the doorway, where Vasco watched me with amused contempt and Grazia with extreme displeasure.

She twitched her nose at me, "Are you ready to start on the library now, *sier* Alfeo?"

I was not going to be browbeaten by a sulky child when I was engaged in a war with Ottone Gritti. "Not quite, madonna. We still have to investigate your own room and that of your honored brother."

25

Girolamo's room I could have predicted. The furniture was minimal and Spartan: a bed, a chair, a lamp, and one small cupboard to hold his clothes, with or without hair shirts. The only art was a magnificent triptych on the wall opposite the window, which I had to stop and examine. It was old, certainly pre-Giotto, and not Venetian work. I could not guess at the artist's name and perhaps nobody could, but in its way it was the finest thing I had seen in Ca' Sanudo. I played out my act with the dowsing rod and was not surprised by the lack of results.

Vasco closed the door behind me as I crossed the little landing to the lady's chamber. Scowling at this invasion of her privacy, Grazia wrestled the door open for me, so I walked right through.

"I shall be as quick as I can, madonna," I said, but my eye had spotted Danese's portmanteau in the far corner. That was why I missed Neptune. My rod did not; it twisted in my hands like a snake, wrenching me around to face my objective and causing me to gasp out an *Ooof!* of alarm.

"I didn't know you practiced Dalmatian dancing," Vasco

remarked with childish sarcasm. "That doesn't look much like a book to me."

But it did look like my vision, Neptune taming a sea-horse. The bronze itself was about three feet high, standing on a pedestal of green-veined marble of roughly the same height. It was magnificent, so I wondered why it was hidden away in a girl's bedroom where only she and her maid would ever see it. Had even Danese ever been in this room?

"Where did it come from?" I asked, examining it carefully without touching it. I threw the apple-wood wand away.

"How should I know?" Grazia snapped. "It's been around as long as I can remember. I asked for it when we moved back to town. Why does it matter?"

"Who made it?"

"I don't know and I don't care!" Grazia was trying to be imperious again.

It had to be hollow, I decided, or it would weigh as much as a cannon and the floor beams would collapse. I took out my dagger and rapped the hilt on the god's chest. Yes, it was hollow. Bronze castings always are.

"Stop that!" Grazia squealed. "Now finish what you came to do and go down and start dowsing the books."

I peered closely at the top of the pedestal and thought I could see faint scratches in front of the bronze. Vasco was watching warily. He knows I play tricks, but he also knows I have knowledge he does not. I was going to make an almighty fool of myself unless there was something significant about that statue. So be it! I had never tried dowsing before and never believed in dowsing, and yet my rod had gone for the bronze before I had even seen it myself. Now I believed. I sheathed my dagger and drew my rapier.

"What are you doing?" the lady screamed.

"I want to see if there's something hidden inside that thing," I said. "Stand well back, so I don't hit you by mistake. *Vizio*, can you lift it?" I very rarely give Vasco his title.

Giving me an even odder look, he embraced the figure and tried. "No."

"The horse part is smaller than the god, so it should be lighter on that side. Can you push it forward until the horse overlaps the edge of the pedestal? Shout if it starts to over-balance and I'll help you push it back."

"Crazy!" Grazia shouted, having retreated to a safe place by the door. "You have gone crazy! That statue is worth thousands of ducats." Her outrage was convincing. If there was any evidence of witchcraft inside it, she ought to have been quaking with terror and much shriller.

"We won't damage it," I said. "Go ahead, *Vizio*."

He shrugged and decided to humor me, since he might get me in trouble with little risk to himself. I stepped well clear and watched carefully as he began to push. At first he was reluctant to apply his full strength in case he toppled the statue to the floor, but he soon found that there was lit-tle chance of that. Still nothing happened and his face grew red with effort, but then the figure nudged forward, a finger-width at a time. The horse's flailing front feet moved clear of the base and then its belly began to move over the edge also.

"Wait!" I said and went close enough to prod the point of my rapier underneath. "Yes, it is hollow, see?"

"It doesn't feel it," he muttered.

"Keep trying and one day you'll grow up big and strong." I stepped back again.

The overlap grew until I began to worry about balance. As Grazia had said, that figure might be worth more money than I would earn in a lifetime, and dropping it on the ter-razzo would not improve either of them. I was just about to tell Vasco to stop when something showed underneath the base, a dusty gray something. It wriggled free, dropped on the floor, and then came straight for me, fast as an arrow. No human reflexes could have impaled it with a rapier, but I flailed sideways at it, which was an easier stroke, and swatted it six feet away.

"Look out!" Sacrificing any pretense of dignity, I scrambled up on a dainty little marble table. "Don't let it bite you."

Grazia screamed and jumped up on a chair. Faster than a striking snake, Vasco took a flying leap onto the bed. He drew his sword.

"What is it?" Grazia shrieked.

That was a very pertinent question. When I looked straight at it, I saw a primitive book, eighty or ninety pages of ancient, tattered paper sewn between soft kidskin covers, lying facedown as if some reader had just set it there for a moment, open at his place. If I looked at it out of the corner of my eye—a technique the Maestro taught me—it was much more like a huge gray spider, watching me, waiting for me to leave my perch. It certainly moved like a spider. They run so fast that the eye cannot see how their legs move, and the jinx was even faster. It must move its pages like legs.

"It is one of Zeno's stupid tricks!" Vasco said, realizing how undignified he looked standing on the bed. He jumped down.

The jinx ran at him. Fortunately he had not sheathed his sword and he struck at it as I had, flipping it away. He was back on the bed by the time it hit the floor. A loose page fluttering free.

This time the jinx was not content to lie in wait. It darted over to the bed and tried to climb a golden pillar to get at him. He swiped at it again, only this time he missed, as if it was learning to avoid rapier strokes. The jinx rushed to try another pillar. He floundered and staggered across the soft down bedding to defend that corner.

"What is this thing?" he yelled.

"It's the jinx," I said. "Ancient, vintage evil, a curse that has grown and matured for centuries. Madonna, no!" I was just in time, for Grazia had filled her lungs and opened her mouth to scream. "If you summon help, the jinx will attack them."

"Why don't you exorcize it?" Vasco yelled. "You're the one who summoned it." I wish I had a good painting of him as he looked then; I would hang it in some conspicuous place.

"No, I just found it for you. Why don't you apply the law? Arrest it."

"Oh, this is ridiculous!" The *vizio* bounded off the bed and headed for the door as if all the demons of Hell were after him, instead of one tattered manuscript. Alas, Venetian doors dislike being bullied and that one chose that moment to stick. He swung around at bay, with the jinx already almost at his feet.

I jumped down also. It dodged Vasco's sword stroke, but did not follow up its attack on him; instead it reversed course and came again for me, as if I were its preferred prey.

I extended my left arm and used the Word. Normally my pyrokinetic skills need a few seconds to obtain results, but that paper was centuries old and the horror exploded in a ball of fire. Smoke billowed upward. Grazia screamed. And so did the jinx, or at least I heard an impossibly shrill noise in my head, a sound that a tortured bat might emit in its death throes. I sheathed my sword. The floor was terrazzo, with no rugs or exposed wood to burn.

Vasco yelled, "Look out!"

The sheet of paper his sword had detached was fluttering across the floor in my direction, blown by a wind that disturbed nothing else in the room. I ignited it also and it vanished in a flash of sparks and ash.

The emergency was over. The jinx was gone, the house was not going to burn down, and all that remained were clouds of bitter-smelling smoke. Coughing and choking,

Vasco and I threw open the casements. Grazia had her hands over her face, but I could see that she was pale as milk and gasping for breath. I lifted her down.

Vasco tried the door again and this time it opened sweetly, on its best behavior. We heard screaming coming from the *piano nobile*.

26

Aunt Fortunata was having hysterics in her bedroom. The family had just run to see what was wrong when Grazia came tearing in and threw herself into her mother's arms. There was much shouting and alarm as the stench of smoke wafted up from the mezzanine floor. The two *fanti* ran down to see. Vasco and I, following Grazia up, were accosted in the *salone* by Inquisitor Gritti demanding an explanation.

"Witchcraft!" Vasco said. "Zeno conjured some sort of paper animal out of a statue and it attacked us. Then he used more witchcraft to set it on fire." The *vizio* had suffered a severe fright and showed it, but he also wore a savage grin of triumph. This time he truly had me, he thought; this time I would not escape.

I was inclined to agree with him. So was Gritti, for I had never seen a man so resemble a cat that can feel a mouse's tail under its paw.

"Your Excellency, I located the jinx," I said. "My dowsing rod found it for me. It was hiding in madonna Grazia's room, although she did not know it was there. It did attack us, as Filiberto says. He took refuge on the bed, I climbed on a table, and the lady on a chair. Fortunately it burst into flames and—"

"Zeno burned it!" Vasco cried. "He pointed his hand at it like this and made gestures and spoke in a strange language and it went on fire instantly. And then a loose page attacked him and he did it again!"

"A loose piece of paper *attacked* him?" Gritti licked his lips.

"The *vizio* is a little upset," I suggested. "His recollection of events is confused. I was, in fact, saying a prayer, and Our Lady took pity on us and saved us from the demon. Of course paper that old can be so dry that when it is exposed to the air . . ."

Then the Sanudos came flocking out of Aunt Fortunata's room, demanding to know what was going on, and the six-way conversation became more than a little confused.

An hour or so later, the situation had been somewhat clarified. The jinx had been accepted as a reality and its destruction as good fortune. From that point of view, I was being hailed as a hero. Vasco insisted that I had used witchcraft to locate it and destroy it, and possibly to create it in the first place, although even Gritti seemed unwilling to accept that suggestion—he was reserving judgment on the rest. He had lots of time. I wasn't going anywhere.

Aunt Fortunata looked and sounded several years younger and every few minutes would mumble how much better she was feeling.

Grazia was very quiet, staying close to her mother. I wanted to believe that her nose was less conspicuous than it had been, but perhaps that was just charitable thinking. Vasco and I had both testified that she had been as frightened of the jinx as either of us, had not known where it was hiding, and it had not been her familiar. She refused to discuss what had happened, neither confirming nor denying that I had used witchcraft.

Giro had disappeared into his room and shut the door on the world. *Sier* Zuanbattista had retreated behind the traditional gravitas of the Venetian aristocracy, watching everything and saying nothing. He certainly was not going to thank me for my actions until they had been cleared of the taint of sorcery, and he was too much a gentleman to denounce them when they had so obviously worked to his benefit.

About then we had all descended to Grazia's room to reenact the encounter with the jinx, inspect the scorch mark on the floor where it had died, and peer into the base of the Neptune statue. I spotted Danese's portmanteau again and decided that it might make a welcome diversion. I carried it over to the bed and prepared to tip out its contents.

"Stand back, Zeno!" Gritti barked. "I distrust those nimble hands of yours. Marco, Amedeo, search that bag and see if there is anything in there that should not be."

A few minutes later we were all standing around the bed admiring sixty gold sequins and a gold and amber bracelet. In fact we were admiring two bracelets—the brass-and-glass one that Grazia had fetched from her jewel box, and the genuine one that had emerged from Danese's underwear.

Grazia wept on her mother's bosom again. Madonna Eva's face was rock hard, but her emotions were no doubt disheveled by this exposure of the viper she had nourished so long. Even Vasco admitted that I had had no opportunity to plant the evidence, at least not that day.

"No Ca' Barbolano silverware," I admitted. "My suspicions were unfounded."

"I shall have every valuable in the house appraised," Zuanbattista declared, and even his studied impassivity could not completely conceal his fury. "I am very grateful to you for drawing this treachery to our attention, *sier* Alfeo."

I bowed. "I am saddened to have increased your sorrows. Meanwhile, Your Excellency, I beg leave to return to my master, who may have need of me."

Pause.

Then Gritti nodded. "I shall come calling tomorrow, as arranged, and when we have completed that business, we can pursue the question of just how you located the jinx and managed to set it on fire." He smiled. "In the meantime, the *vizio* will keep you safe from harm."

27

Giorgio was sitting in the government boat, trading gossip with Gritti's boatmen—waiting for me is a large part of his job. He knows me so well that one look at my face was enough to inform him that I was not my usual cheerful and witty self. He said, "Home?" and accepted my nod as sufficient reply.

Feeling understandably malicious, I spread myself on the *felze* cushions, forcing Vasco to sit on the thwart outside. Unfortunately the rain had stopped. Finding my contempt amusing, he beamed around benevolently at the scenery as Giorgio sped us along the Rio di Maddalena and Rio di S. Marcuola. When we emerged onto the Grand Canal, he honored me with the most sanctimonious smile I had ever seen.

"Alfeo, Alfeo! You cannot say you were not warned. I have told you many times not to meddle in matters that imperil your immortal soul. See where it has gotten you now? Do you not feel repentance?"

"I feel homicidal. It has gotten me to thinking that I would rather be beheaded than burned at the stake. I'm a better swordsman than you are. Giorgio won't notice a quick murder—will you Giorgio?"

Normally Giorgio pretends not to overhear what is said on his boat, but this time he answered. "Not if it is done in a good cause, *clarissimo*."

"Couldn't be better," I replied, but my threat failed to worry the *vizio*, who merely smirked more broadly than ever.

I truly thought that a day that began with my finding a corpse on the doorstep and continued through my being charged with homicide, menaced by a demon, and then accused of witchcraft could not possibly get any worse. I was wrong. Back at the Ca' Barbolano, I jumped ashore and trotted up the stairs without waiting for Vasco, who would be certain to stick to me tighter than my ears from now on. I heard his boots tapping close behind me as I reached the *piano nobile*. To my dismay, one flap of the great double doors stood open and on a stool outside it sat Renzo Marciana. His relief at seeing me suggested that he had been ready to expire from boredom. The Marcianas jump to our landlord's bidding also, just as high as the Maestro and I do.

"*Sier* Alvise wants to see you," he explained. With an uneasy glance at my keeper, he rose and went in to announce my return.

"No doubt the noble lord dislikes corpses cluttering up his watergate," Vasco opined at my shoulder. "So untidy!"

I suspected the crusty antediluvian patrician liked the recent living intruders even less than the dead ones and in a few moments Barbolano came dithering out to confirm my suspicions. I know from auditing the Marcianas' ledgers that he must have one of the largest incomes in Venice, yet he and his wife never employ more than a single servant; they wear old-fashioned garments, faded, threadbare, and often in need of a wash.

He peered at Vasco with extreme distaste and then literally wagged a finger in front of my nose. "I won't have it, you hear?"

"God bless you, *messer*," I said. "How have I displeased you?"

"How?" the old man barked, spraying me. "*Sbirri* all over the place? Inquisitors, *Missier Grande* himself, and"—he pointed—"*him*? You think I run a house of ill-repute? I won't have it! Get out, all of you! Go! Go and tell Nostradamus to take his rubbish and leave! Today! Now!"

He might have continued in the same vein for some time, but my display of horror stopped him. "Why're you pulling faces, boy?"

"Because of the date, *clarissimo*! The stars! This is a fearfully inauspicious day. The Maestro says he has never seen a day so ill-omened for making decisions."

The old man shied. "Stars?"

"And planets. Mars is in Libra in opposition to Mercury, *messer*! The moon in your own birth sign of Virgo makes you especially vulnerable. I beg you to wait at least until Tuesday before making any move that you might possibly regret later. Any decision you make before that will certainly be star-crossed."

Barbolano chewed his tongue for a few moments indecisively. Then he pointed again at Vasco. "Well, at least get rid of him! You write out a notice evicting Nostradamus and bring it to me to sign on Tuesday without fail!"

I bowed. "Very wise, *clarissimo*."

He disappeared in a thunderclap of the great door.

"A disastrous decision, I would say," said Vasco. "So that is how it is done? Bombast and stultiloquence!"

"You think this day is not disastrous?" I strode off up the stairs.

He followed. "So far it has proved highly auspicious, one of the best I can recall."

I marched into the atelier, closed the door in his face, and locked it.

"Greetings, noble master!" I proclaimed, detouring

around by the big mirror to make sure the spyhole from the dining room was closed. "I unmasked Algol for you. I foolishly saved Filiberto Vasco from the demon and out of gratitude he accuses me of witchcraft. *Messer* Ottone Gritti is much inclined to agree with him. Also *sier* Alvise has given us notice to vacate the premises by Tuesday and what's the matter?"

The Maestro was huddled in his favorite red chair, clutching a pottery jug in both hands and looking about a thousand years old. He grunted. I paused at the slate-topped table with the crystal ball, whose cover lay crumpled on the floor. He had been foreseeing and the resulting chalk scrawl was just one more horror to add to the day. I would need an hour to decipher it, if I ever could.

"It doesn't help," he muttered.

"What does it say?"

"I don't know. It's too far off to be relevant."

I noticed with relief that the late Danese Dolfin had been removed, although the medical equipment and a blood-stained sheet still lay under the couch. I headed in that direction to tidy up.

"Sit down here and talk." The Maestro raised the jug to his mouth and drank.

Obediently I settled on one of the green chairs—an unusual honor for me—and talked. I gave him everything that had happened since I left with Gritti to visit madonna Corner. I didn't mention eating, since I hadn't, but only barely managed not to mention that I wasn't mentioning it.

Although never predictable, Nostradamus is almost always bad tempered after a farseeing. But when I came to the end of my morning and told him how I had deterred Alvise Barbolano from evicting us on the spot, he actually swore, which he almost never does. We were in trouble.

"So that nuisance Vasco is still underfoot?"

"Like dirt."

"Bah! Well he mustn't find out what we're doing. I promised to deliver Algol to Gritti personally, and I shall."

I repeated that sentence to myself and decided I had heard it correctly. "You don't think the walking book was the ghoul?"

"Bah! No. Certainly not! You are confusing Algol with the jinx, and they're completely different. Oh, the jinx made the Sanudos prone to disaster. You notice that Sanudo himself did very well when he was in Constantinople, far out of its range, but plunged into trouble as soon as he returned? It cursed everyone who came in contact with it. As soon as we became involved in the family's affairs, it blurred my clairvoyance and blinded your tarot. But Algol is a person, one of the jinx's evil effects, no doubt, but not the jinx itself. The fact that Algol's employers, whoever they are, named him The Ghoul may be only a coincidence. I don't recall the Church ever informing us of a patron saint of coincidences, but a patron demon may be more appropriate. It's the human Algol that the Ten want. I could tell Gritti what he's overlooked and he would put all his spies to work and find the real Algol in a few days, but I promised to turn him in myself, so I must."

To call Maestro Nostradamus pigheaded is an insult to swine.

"Yes, I know. Tomorrow at breakfast. Can you think of a way to stop him burning me at the stake for witchcraft right after?"

"You were an idiot to use the Word in front of a witness, especially him."

"I didn't use it in front of Gritti himself, but I agree it was stupid. After all, how much worse could demonic possession make Vasco? And he might have bitten the jinx, instead of the other way around."

"I'll worry about you later," my master said impatiently. "Meanwhile the most important thing is to preserve my reputation by exposing Algol. I decided there were three ways to proceed—three strings to my bow."

"And the first one didn't work?" I jabbed a thumb over my shoulder at the crystal ball.

He pouted, which was agreement. "I overshot the mark by at least a century. You've eaten?"

Astonished, for food rarely enters his mind, I said, "Not this week, I think, master."

"Well, I am waiting for—"

Knuckles rapped.

I raised an eyebrow and, when he nodded, the rest of me also. I went and opened the door to find the twins, Corrado and Christoforo, beaming eagerly. They will never interrupt the Maestro without express orders to do so, so I stepped aside and let them enter. Then I closed and locked the door again, although there was no sign of Vasco out in the *salone*. The boys were sweaty and puffing as if they had been running, but they had taken time to rehearse, because they reported in counterpoint.

Corrado began, "Marco Piceno, cobbler . . ."

"Marco Gatti, attorney . . ."

"Matteo Tentolini, musician . . ."

"And Dario Rinaldo, carpenter," Chris concluded triumphantly.

The names meant nothing to me, but from the Maestro's demonic expression, I guessed that they were bad news, so the second of his three bowstrings had just proved as untuneful as the first. Two down, one to go.

"Very good!" he said. "Alfeo will give you two *soldi* apiece after he has dined. Meanwhile, I have another errand for you. Fetch Michelina if she is around. Go and eat, Alfeo."

Michelina is a year older than the twins and a splendid beauty, engaged to be married. The only reason the Maestro could possibly want her then was to dictate a letter, because she writes a fine secretary hand. I taught her my-self.

"I won't die of starvation in the next hour," I complained, resentful that anyone else would sit at my desk and do my work.

"No, no." He waved his hand in dismissal. "You must keep up your strength for tonight's ordeal."

When he gets in that mood, he keeps secrets even from me, because he is convinced my face always gives me away when I tell a lie. This is an absurd untruth, but that day we had that historically celebrated snoop Filiberto Vasco un-derfoot and peering underbed, so extreme caution might be justified.

"I dread the prospect," I said and marched off in search of nourishment, ignoring the twins' wide-eyed stares at this hint of dark deeds ahead.

28

It was long past our usual noon dinnertime, but nothing daunts Mama Angeli and I found Vasco in the kitchen cleaning up a plate of her magnificent Burano-style duckling, *Masorin a la Buranella*. I asked her to send mine to the dining room, where the company was more appealing, and on my way there I helped myself to one of the few remaining bottles of the Maestro's hoarded 1583 Villa Primavera. This might be the last decent meal I would ever eat.

I was not allowed long to enjoy my solitude, of course, before Vasco sauntered in to join me, bringing his raisin fritters *dolce* with him. He sniffed the wine bottle and pursed his lips.

"Nice! The condemned man ate a hearty last meal?"

"Not at all. Celebrating the coming exposure of the false witness."

He smiled and leaned back to admire the ceiling art and chandeliers. "Nice place you had here. A pity about your landlord's little fit of pique."

"He laughs best who laughs last."

"I entirely agree," Vasco said solemnly. "And I admit it feels very nice. I have warned you so often!"

"*Nil homine terra pejus ingrato creat.*" Violetta taught me that, but she was not applying it to me at the time.

"The ingrate is certainly the worst of men," Vasco agreed, "but what makes you think I have reason to be grateful to you? You have always been an upstart, conceited, interfering pest."

If I accused him of ingratitude for denouncing me after I had saved him from the jinx, he would claim I was confessing to performing magic, so I ate on in silence. I took comfort from reflecting that I had been in tight corners before and the Maestro had always jumped to the rescue.

Corrado peered in. "Old . . . The Maestro wants to know if we have . . . I mean if he has any henbane and, er, mandrake?"

"Henbane is the third jar on the second shelf down, labeled *Hyoscyamus*," I said. "Mandrake root is in the fourteenth jar, bottom shelf, *Mandragora*. Be careful with those!" I yelled after him as he ran off. The Maestro knew the answers quite as well as I did, so the purpose of his questions had been to misinform Vasco, who must know those two plants' reputation for magical powers. Misinform him of what, though? And why? Well, it was an encouraging sign that the old mountebank had something in mind. Or up sleeve, perhaps.

Later, as Mama was asking me if she should fry up a third plateful of fritters for me and I was regretfully deciding that I would not be able to do them justice, Christoforo appeared.

"Maestro says he is going to rest, but we must waken him when anything develops. And he says you should rest, too."

"Tell him my strength won't fail him."

"And he wants to see you, Mama."

His mother frowned and waddled out.

"Burning isn't so bad really," Vasco remarked. He took a

swig from the wine bottle. "They strangle you with a cord before the flames get to you. Usually, that is."

Could my position be any more desperate if I set his hat on fire right then?

A scream of mortal agony echoed along the *salone*, loud enough and long enough to bring Vasco off his chair and startle even me.

"Mama has a weakness for dramatics," I explained as my companion bolted out the door, hell-bent on rescue. "Nostradamus probably found a spider under his bed," I called after him. By the time I had polished off the last scraps of my *dolce*, drained my glass, and followed the *vizio*, I was just in time to see the Maestro disappearing into his bedroom and Mama Angeli shooing almost her entire clan out the front door—Giorgio, Corrado, Archangelo, Christoforo, Michelina, and even Noemi. The most junior members were apparently being left in the care of Piero, who is only eleven. Two of them thought they had been abandoned and were screaming in terror.

"What is going on?" Vasco demanded.

"Oh, it's often like this around here," I said. "Make yourself useful. Practice your babysitting skills."

I went back to the atelier, leaving the door open so I could keep an eye on the spy. I had the big room to myself, but some badly trimmed quills were evidence that Michelina had been working at my side of the desk. I tidied that and the medical corner, then set to work on the ugly scrawl beside the crystal globe.

Working for a clairvoyant is frustrating because you know you will never live to see half your work completed. In Nostradamus's case, the worse his writing and the more obscure his syntax, the further out the prophecy, and that was why he had told me that this one overshot the mark. At least it was in words, not doodles, so the jinx's evil influence was no longer evident, but I spent most of the rest of the afternoon trying to read the quatrain before I decided I had done all I could with it. I was still unsure of a few words.

> The {tide} has turned, the sands ebb
> Nine times the {greater} glass turns and only {twice} remain
> When the son of Ajaccio closes the volume
> The mainlander shall uncover.

I didn't know then what it meant, don't now, and likely never will. It did not look complete and the Maestro did not include it in his next book of predictions. Who was Ajaccio? Uncover *what*? Angry and frustrated, I copied the verse into the book of prophecies and cleaned the slate. I could see no sign that the jars of henbane or mandrake had been disturbed. I wished I could jump across the *calle* and visit with Violetta, but I knew Vasco would either stop me or follow. Besides, I had to stay at my post.

Vasco had stayed at his, draped on a couch in the *salone* equidistant from the front door, the atelier, and the Maestro's room opposite, a natural hunter's blind. One by one the Angelis returned, all carrying bundles, and none of them would tell him where they had been or what they had brought back. I did the best I could to conceal my mystification; I suppose Vasco was doing the same.

I was standing in front of the big mirror practicing finger exercises with a silver ducat when I heard the door knocker rap and went to answer it.

Understandably, Vasco beat me to it, but I knew the page standing there, recognized the livery of the Trau household, and almost lost my temper at the sight of the note he was clutching, because it was sealed with Fulgentio's signet. I do not grudge Fulgentio his wealth and good fortune, but I cannot forgive the way the Maestro shamelessly takes advantage of our friendship. He has hundreds of influential patients and clients, from the doge on down—why does he have to poach my friends?

Besides, if he was hoping to appeal to the doge for help against Inquisitor Gritti, he was wasting his time. Foreign born, Nostradamus often has trouble comprehending how powerless our head of state really is, hemmed in by his six counselors in the *Signoria* and by ten other men as well in the Council of Ten. He has no vote among the Three. There was a loud scandal a few years ago when Venice learned that in some cases the Council of Ten did not just delegate some of its powers to the Three but sometimes *all* of them. The Great Council failed to forbid that nasty practice, so it is still possible in certain instances for the three inquisitors to reach a verdict and have *Missier Grande* carry it out before the rest of the Ten even know. What good could Fulgentio do?

"I have to give this personally to Doctor Nostradamus," the boy said, "or," he added with a cheery smile, "to *sier* Alfeo Zeno." He handed it to me. "I was told that there would be no reply."

"But there will be a gratuity," I said. "Just a moment." I removed my silver ducat from Vasco's left ear and handed it to the page, who gasped and protested that all he had done was walk across the *campo*. I insisted he keep it and closed the door before he tried to kiss my shoes.

"Trickster!" Vasco said.

"Sneak," I retorted. Reminding myself to enter the ducat in the ledger as expenses, I rapped loudly on my master's door and marched in without waiting for a response. I locked it behind me.

The Maestro had changed into his nightgown and nightcap, but he was awake, leaning back on a pile of cushions, peering at a book. He took the letter, read it, and closed it up again without a word.

My attention had already gone to the manuscript he was

consulting. It was obviously old, written in an antique hand on many sheets of bound vellum. I had thought I knew every one of his books, even those hidden in secret compartments, but this one was unfamiliar. He noted my interest and smirked.

"The Depositions of Brother Raymbaud," he said. "I expect the Vatican has a copy but I doubt that anyone else does. How would you date it?" He handed it to me so I could examine the penmanship.

"It's French," I said, "written in a *littera psalterialis* hand. Late thirteenth century?"

"Close. It is dated 1308, but it was probably written by an elderly scribe, so your judgment is sustainable. Brother Raymbaud did not write it himself. He was testifying."

I glanced back to make certain I had closed the door. "Was he a witness or a defendant? I mean, was he Brother Raymbaud of Caron?"

The Maestro smirked. "Of course that Raymbaud. Preceptor of commanderies of the Knights Templar in Outremer. The *last* such preceptor, naturally. Outremer was the French name for the Holy Land."

"I know that," I said grimly. This was heading into territory so dark that it would make my use of the Word seem like a minor misdemeanor. In 1307 King Philip the Fair of France broke up the order of the Knights Templar and tortured the senior officers into confessing to every terrible crime the tormentors could think to suggest. "Was Raymbaud one of those burned at the stake?"

"Apparently not." The Maestro frowned at having to admit ignorance. "His fate is a mystery. There has been speculation that he bought his way out by revealing certain secrets that even Grand Master Jacques de Molay did not know."

"Such as the true nature of Baphomet, perhaps?"

Nostradamus pouted sourly. "That is a very astute guess! Sometimes you surprise me, Alfeo."

"Sometimes you scare me to death, master."

"Well, there are some obscure points," he admitted. "Take the book and prepare the schema. We must be ready to start at midnight."

And I had still thought that the day could not get any worse.

29

Nothing serious happened until after curfew. I went back to the atelier with the book and wasted the rest of the afternoon beating my brains to a pulp trying to make sense of three-hundred-year-old French. When I needed a break, I cleaned my rapier and filed the point sharp again, repairing the minor damage done when Danese was felled. If Vasco tried to arrest me, I would need it.

At sunset I also brought the Head down from the attic, well hidden in its leather bag from the *vizio*'s prying gaze. A box of human bones in the medical cupboard is permissible property for a physician, if only barely, but the Head dwells apart, among the Maestro's collection of curiosities. The Head's original owner died several thousand years ago, probably of chronic dental caries, and was undoubtedly a high-ranking native of Egypt, worthy of careful mummification. His eyes are closed, his mouth open, and he still sports wisps of white hair. He is quite light, because his brain was removed during the embalming process, but he does not seem to care about that now. The Maestro insisted that the Head would play the role of Baphomet very well, so I stood him on the slate table in place of the usual crystal globe.

Amid all the charges of heresy, blasphemy, and perversion hurled at the Knights Templar were some peculiar accusations that they had worshipped a detached head named Baphomet. No one had ever properly explained why they should have done so, and it is generally assumed that Baphomet was just a wild tale made up by some poor wretch to stop the pain after he had confessed to everything else he could think of. The tale has proved remarkably enduring, though. The name is said to be a corruption of Mohammed.

"Far from it," the Maestro said that evening as he and I settled down to attempt some major black magic. "Didn't you read the book?"

The spyhole was covered, the door locked, and Vasco outside. The shutters were closed and the Angelis engrossed in their long duty of bedding down children. Yet I still felt a nervous need to keep looking over my shoulder.

"I tried, but Old French is beyond me, and there's other script in there that I've never seen before."

The Maestro was huddled in his favorite chair with the Raymbaud manuscript in his lap, dimly lit by a lamp on the mantel. In his black robe, he was almost invisible. He was enjoying himself hugely. He had been evasive when I asked if he had ever tried this procedure before, but he obviously felt that he had a good excuse to try it now.

"Ah, well according to Raymbaud, the technique was very ancient, long predating Islam. The invocation is in Sahidic Coptic, the language of the Pharaohs, and he claimed that the ritual was devised by the embalmers to ask the dead's permission to prepare their corpses. That sounds unlikely, but a technique for interrogating the recently dead would have been very useful to the Templars when they were defending the Holy Land from desert marauders. If a patrol gets massacred and you can invoke their spirits soon enough, you can ask them who did it, or ask the dead brigands who sent them."

I shuddered. "Necromancy!"

He blinked with childish innocence. "Not if you define necromancy as the ancients did. The learned Strabo, for instance, relates necromancy to divination and the Chaldeans—"

"Tell me tomorrow, while we're waiting for the torturers to finish their dinner break." I was still fidgeting, unable to sit. "What else do we need?"

He peered at the manuscript again. "There are only six appurtenances named but there must be seven. What's missing?"

The list of ingredients was about the only thing I had managed to decipher. "Salt."

"Ah, of course! Go and bring some."

I went out and locked the door behind me, for the Head was in full view. Vasco was still draped like a discarded cloak on the couch. He knew we were up to something but were not about to let him find out what, and he just scowled when I told him we would be some time and he should curl up and catch some sleep. I purloined a nugget of salt from the kitchen and returned to the atelier. The Maestro had moved to one of the green chairs, which I had earlier arranged a safe distance back from the table, facing our elderly accomplice, the Head.

"Put it between the iron and the wood," he said. "Now read off the appurtenances."

I named the seven objects I had arranged around the Head: "Iron, salt, wood, amber, cinnabar, copper, and gold." All of those have been appreciated as having magical virtue since the most ancient times, of course.

"Now light the incense."

Seven sticks of incense stood in holders around the Head and the ring of appurtenances. I pointed at each in turn and it began to smoke.

He said, "Now I shall . . . Ah, the hair!"

"Hair?"

"Hair. You must relate the Baphomet to the spirit you wish to invoke, or you might call the wrong one. Fortunately in this case we have a lock of Dolfin's hair. I put it in the small implements drawer for safekeeping."

An attending physician stealing a lock of a cadaver's hair seemed perilously close to desecration of a body to me, but we were well outside moral law already, so I said nothing as I obediently fetched. Just the sight of that blond tress lying there, tied with a ribbon, appalled me. I said a silent prayer of apology to Danese as I followed the Maestro's directions and draped it over the Head.

"Now!" he said. "Hand me the bell. Sit. Not so close. Now, I shall read the invocation. When the seventh stick has gone out, you will have a few seconds to ask your questions."

"Me?"

"He knew you better. You should be allowed three and only three questions, but have a couple of extras ready just in case. Find out the murderer's name and where he lives. Do not pry into matters that do not concern you in this life."

"No." I expected to discover those for myself fairly soon.

"Ready?"

"Ready, master."

He began reciting the Coptic, taking it slowly but rarely stumbling. Repeatedly he mentioned Baphomet, although the way he said it made it sound more like a command than a proper name. After a few lines he rang the handbell once and the first incense stick I had lit stopped smoking. I shivered. A few more lines and he rang twice. The second stick . . .

The first time in my life that my hair ever genuinely stood on end was after the final, seventh, flame extinguished. There was an awful moment's pause and then the

Head spoke. Yes, a voice emerged from the gaping mouth, soft but unmistakably Danese Dolfin's sonorous, unforgettable bass scraping at my nerves.

"Who summons me back to this world of sin?"

I swallowed hard on a throat as dry as salt. "I, Alfeo Zeno, do."

"Alfeo Zeno, why do you dare disturb the passage of my soul?"

"To avenge your murder."

"Avenge? Or revenge? Would you have me sin even in death?"

How typical of Danese to argue from beyond the grave, even if he wasn't buried yet. I wiped my damp brow and put the first question. "Danese Dolfin, who killed you?"

The Head moaned as if in pain. *"Leave me, leave me!"*

"Answer, I command you! Who killed you?"

He sighed and whispered, *"Mirphak."*

"What is his real name?"

"Francesco Guarini."

I heard the Maestro sigh happily. His third bowstring had found the target.

I asked my third question. "Where does Francesco Guarini live?" For a long moment I thought I would receive no reply but then Danese's voice came again, very faint, as if from a great distance.

"Above the magazzen *in San Giorgio in Alga."*

Got him! With both a name and an address, even the *Signori di Notte* could catch him, let alone the Ten.

"And by what words is he commanded?"

Silence.

"Again I order you to answer! What words command Francesco Guarini?"

This time I heard a sound no louder than a passing mosquito. I said, "What?" several times and tried a few more questions, but nothing more happened. I whispered, *"Requiescat in pacem."* The séance was over.

The bell jangled as the Maestro laid it on the floor beside his chair.

"Very satisfactory!" he said. "Before dawn, you will go to San Giorgio in Alga and arrest Francesco Guarini. Bring him back here and I will serve him to Ottone Gritti for his *prima colazione*."

"I have no authority to arrest anyone." Especially not on that testimony.

"But you have the word to command him. Didn't you hear it?"

"Mirphak?" I said. "Mirphak and Algol? Should I bring in Sirius, Polaris, and Vega also?" *Sì* -

"Keep a look out for all sorts of trouble. You will have the *vizio* with you!" The Maestro chuckled as he heaved himself to his feet. "Be very careful. He is dangerous."

"Which is? Or do you mean both?"

"Guarini is. Vasco isn't, not now."

30

As the eastern sky began to brighten on a chilly Sunday morning, Giorgio was rowing me south across the wide Canale della Giudecca, which is the main shipping channel separating the city from the long string of islands called the Giudecca. Giudecca is known for great palaces and playgrounds of the very rich, so I am not as familiar with it as I should like to be. Cool or not, the morning was spectacular. Light danced on the ripples like fireflies and ever-hopeful seagulls floated by overhead, eyeing us for signs of imminent garbage ejection. The city seemed to stand on its protecting lagoon and the first rays of sunrise were giving the tops of the Alps a good-morning kiss

Beside me in the *felze* sat the *vizio*, huddled in his cloak, grumpy and sleep deprived. I was in no better shape, for we had had an epic row over sleeping arrangements. He had refused to let me sleep in my own room, because he knew about the other way out of it. I had refused to let him lock me in the spare bedroom. In the end we had both slept on couches in the *salone* with the lamps lit. Then I had wakened him at an iniquitous hour, saying I was going sightseeing in San Giorgio in Alga, did he want to come?

For once I was glad of his company, since I did not share the Maestro's cheerful confidence that I could persuade a murderer to accompany me back to Ca' Barbolano for a cozy breakfast with a state inquisitor. Just having Filiberto Vasco with me would give me many times the impact I would have by myself, although I could not see him providing any practical assistance unless I told him why I wanted this un-known Francesco Guarini, and that I was most certainly not about to do.

St. George in Seaweed is in the far west of the Giudecca, and is one of the smallest parishes in the city, so I had been surprised to learn that it even had a *magazzen*. A *magazzen* is an all-night wine shop, which, unlike a tavern, sells no food, although clients can usually send out to a nearby pork butcher for a snack. None of us admitted to knowing where San Giorgio's *magazzen* was located, but I did not expect it to be hard to find, and it wasn't. Giorgio let us off at the watersteps, we walked along a short *calle* to the *campo*, and there it was, with its signboard over the door and a light in-side still just barely visible in the brightening day. I could not imagine the rich patronizing such a slum, but where there are rich there are servants and artisans and tradesfolk to live off the crumbs they drop.

"Only two stories," Vasco remarked as we headed to it. "That simplifies your search."

I needed a moment to steady my voice. "What do you mean?"

He smiled with a saintly innocence worthy of San Francesco himself. "You don't expect the locals to help you, do you? I just meant that a two-story building is easier to search than a taller one would be."

"It is kind of you to share your professional expertise so willingly."

I told myself that Vasco was merely prying, trying to dis-cover how much information I had. He could not have spied on our séance, because I had closed the spyhole; the atelier door is absolutely soundproof. No, he was merely putting things together. The only possible explanation for my early morning dash across the Canale was to catch the spy that Nostradamus had promised to deliver.

San Giorgio in Alga's *magazzen* was just as smelly and seedy as all its brethren, but smaller than most. Into one small room it crammed four stools, two benches, a couple of tiny tables, three unsavory-looking male customers—one of them asleep on a bench—and one cat, asleep under the other bench. Another man, probably either the owner or a relative of his, sat beyond an open window at the back, ready to vend vile vintages. A door in the corner connected the customer area with his den.

Eyes turned when I walked in. They widened when Vasco followed me, and then all except the proprietor's quickly looked away. One of the customers kicked the sleeper to waken him.

I kept moving until I reached the window. "Francesco Guarini?"

The man was middle-aged, overweight, and unhealthy looking; the amelanotic nodule beside his right eye told me that he had only a few months to live. The tiny room behind him was packed with barrels, crates, buckets, gondola cushions, two oars, fishing rods, some rope, an ax, tattered baskets, broken crocks, and much else. He flinched, glanced at Vasco momentarily, and then jerked a thumb upward. An open staircase angled up the wall of his kennel from just beyond the door on my right.

"Up there? Which way at the top?"

"Only one door at the top, boy."

"Is there another way out?"

"No."

The *vizio* might not be actively helping me, but his mere presence had been enough to produce cooperation. Had I been alone, I would have been consigned to the Devil in vivid language and meaningful gestures.

"Coming?" I asked my assistant.

"No." Vasco leaned against the wall beside the hatch, where he could keep an eye on the clientele. "I prefer to watch your antics from a safe distance, *clarissimo*. You there, sit down!" The customer who had risen duly sat down. It was amazing what a red cloak and a silver badge could do. "Padrone, I'll try a glass of your best red." Vasco ostentatiously did not reach for his money pouch.

I opened the door, left it open, started to climb. It was narrow, with no handrail; the treads creaked. I turned a corner at the back of the shop and mounted more steps until I was facing another door. I rapped on it with the hilt of my dagger. Noting that it opened outward and the top tread was barely larger than any of the others, I hammered again, then backed down two steps. There was a chink of daylight under the door, and in a moment it was darkened by a shadow.

"This is appalling wine," Vasco complained from below. "Did you remember to wash your feet?"

"Who's there?" growled a man's voice behind the door.

I steadied my rapier with my left hand, ready to draw. "I want Francesco Guarini."

"Guarini's not here. Come back tonight."

"Let me speak to Mirphak, then."

"Don't know him. Go away."

So much for words of command.

"Come out, Guarini. I know you're in there. Danese Dolfin sent me."

"Who?" But this time the door opened a chink. With barely a pause, it flew wide and a chair came hurtling into my face. I went over backward and somersaulted down to the corner, unfolding against the wall with a crash that almost broke my neck. The man rushed down after me and

tried to kick me in the face as he went past, but by then my
dander was up. I caught his foot with both hands and
twisted. He toppled over the chair and it was his turn to
fall, pitching face-first down the lower flight and out through
the door into the *magazzen*. I went hot behind him, practically in free fall.

Vasco, to his credit, jumped forward to block Guarini as
he scrambled to his feet; Guarini head-butted him. I
slammed into both of them and we all went down. Guarini
was considerably heftier than me, but I was on top and I got
an arm around his neck. He was done for then, because I
grabbed my wrist to form a choke hold, which I tightened
until he went limp.

"Padrone!" I bellowed. "Bring me some of that rope you
have back there." I looked up at the three customers, all of
whom were on their feet, looking down. I have rarely been
grateful for the presence of Filiberto Vasco in this world,
but that was one of those precious moments. I was an out-
sider intruding and had he not been there to represent *La
Serenissima*, I would have been the bottom layer of a five-
man imbroglio, possibly ten-man by this time. Favoring
discretion over valor, the San Giorgio militia turned away
and strode out.

"Lemme ub!" Vasco yelled, who was still pinned under
my prisoner. "You crathy thon of a ditch-born . . ."

I ignored the rest of what he said until I had accepted
a dirty coil of cord from the barman and bound Guarini's
wrists. Then I eased back onto my knees and hobbled his
ankles for good measure. He was a bullnecked, youngish
man with a Borgia beard, taller than me and undoubtedly
powerful, and he was starting to demonstrate a very foul
mouth.

"Be silent!" I shouted. "Or I will gag you."

My head still rang from its encounter with the side of the
stairwell. I had twisted my ankle, and could count more

bruises than there were treads in the stairwell, but Vasco looked worse than I felt. He struggled to his feet, bleeding dramatically.

"Thanks for the help," I said. "What happened to your face?"

"Hith head hid my noath! An' he knifed me." He was clutching his left wrist with his right, so he had no way to deal with his nose, which was pouring blood. I was much more alarmed by the red jets spurting through his fingers.

"Sit down!" I snapped, leaping to my feet. "Bring towels!" I ordered the proprietor. "Run! I take it, *Vizio*, that citizen Guarini is officially under arrest?"

Vasco's reply was too lengthy to report verbatim, but the gist was in the affirmative.

"I'd better attend to that gash before you lose too much blood," I said, realizing that he might bleed to death before my eyes. "Hurry!" I bellowed to the patron, who had rushed off up the stairs, but I couldn't wait for the towels. I pulled out my dagger and slit Vasco's sleeve open, all the way to his shoulder, so that I could make a bandage out of it.

Guarini had awakened and was squirming, so I poked him with my toe, not especially gently. "Lie still, dog! If it makes you feel any happier, brother Filiberto, I testify that this scum is the man who killed Danese Dolfin."

"You know him?" Vasco demanded through his bloody mask.

"I do. And I know someone else who can identify him, too." It's amazing what one good, hard crack on the head can do to clear it. I was starting to catch up with the Maestro, who had seen the answer a whole day earlier.

The landlord came hurrying down with some dirty rags, but by then I was using the hilt of Guarini's knife to tighten the tourniquet. "Is there a barber-surgeon nearby?"

"No, *lustrissimo*. Not on Sunday."

"Go and fetch my gondolier. Tell him—"

"I cannot leave my premises."

"*Go!*" I roared. "You want *Missier Grande*'s deputy to bleed to death in your vermin pit? Tell my gondolier that Filiberto is hurt and Alfeo needs help. *Move!*"

I told Vasco to hold the tourniquet steady while I cut pieces of his shirt to pack his nose. He moaned a little at that, and I assured him that it wasn't broken, although it was already so swollen that I could not be sure. He looked like the aftermath of the Battle of Lepanto.

"We must get you to the convent," I said. "The sisters will care for you."

"No!"

"San Benedetto is very close."

"No!" Vasco must know he had lost a serious amount of blood, but he insisted that he would return to Ca' Barbolano with me and my prisoner.

"I missed a good party?" asked a familiar voice, and I turned with relief to Giorgio Angeli.

"It was brief but energetic," I admitted. "We need to get the *vizio* to a surgeon."

"I know the best doctor in Venice," Giorgio said, helping Vasco stand.

Vasco promptly fainted and Giorgio, who has learned many things from being Nostradamus's gondolier for so long, expertly hoisted him on his shoulders in a fireman's carry.

I prodded Guarini again and said, "Up, pig."

31

Giorgio won gondola races in his youth and that morning he spared no effort to speed us homeward. It was a long journey, though, and twice I released the pressure on Vasco's wrist to let the gash bleed. I knew that if I did not do that, his hand would die before we reached Ca' Barbolano. I grew steadily more worried that he might do so himself. By the time we arrived in the Rio San Remo, he was comatose, a study in red and snowy white.

Sunday bells were ringing. It was exactly a week since I had crossed swords with Danese on the Riva del Vin, and one day since I had found his corpse at our door. Now I was bringing his murderer in to face justice, and that felt good. Alongside the two Marciana boats at our watergate floated one bearing the winged-lion insignia of the Republic, so Inquisitor Gritti must be an early riser and I would have no chance to report to the Maestro in private. Nevertheless, I was very happy to see the two government boatmen, who jumped up in alarm when they saw Giorgio's three blood-soaked passengers.

Guarini had not spoken a word since I tied him up, but he must have known he would have ample opportunity and encouragement to talk in the near future. I poked him ashore at swordpoint, leaving the boatmen to bring Vasco. Giorgio had collapsed in a heap to recover from his exertions.

The front door was locked but not bolted. I let us in and we climbed the stairs. To my great relief, the doors to both the Marciana and Barbolano quarters were closed and we arrived unseen at the Maestro's apartment. Just inside the *salone* sat the two *fanti* who had accompanied Gritti the previous day, Marco Martini and Amedeo Bolognetti. They stared in understandable surprise at me and my prisoner, then rose and followed us into the atelier. The conquering hero had returned.

The Maestro was in the red chair with his back to the windows; Gritti nursed a glass of wine on one of the green chairs across the fireplace from him, and a small fire crackled on the hearth between. It was a touching scene, these two black-robed geriatrics at their ease, except that they held the power of life and death over others, including the power to terminate the lives of men who should long outlive them.

I took the Maestro's expression of extreme disgust as he surveyed us to imply heart-warming praise. "You're sure you have the right man, Alfeo?"

"Quite certain, master, although he is an incompetent killer. He tried to cut the *vizio*'s heart out and succeeded in severing a blood vessel in his wrist, which needs attention. He will be here in a moment." I looked to Gritti, who was wearing his smiley grandfather mask. His silver locks had been especially polished by a silversmith. "The prisoner can also be charged with deliberately head-butting an officer of the Republic."

"A serious offense," the inquisitor said mildly. "Whose blood is that on you, Zeno?"

"Vasco's."

The grandfatherly expression hardened as he turned to study the prisoner. "Your name and station?"

"Francesco Guarini, citizen by birth."

Expectant silence.

". . . Your Excellency."

Gritti nodded. "Take him to the palace, Marco. Put him in the Wells. Come right back."

Marco and the boatmen removed my prisoner, who went without protest; even the notorious Wells would be little worse than that slum in San Giorgio in Alga, except perhaps at high tide.

I headed over to the medical cupboard as the two boatmen carried in Vasco. He seemed to be aware of what was happening, but not truly conscious. If he died, the Ten would hunt down the witnesses in the *magazzen* to testify who had killed him, but would the locals lay the blame on Guarini or on me? I brought the Maestro's bag to the couch, where Vasco was being laid in the same place Danese had occupied the day before.

"Well," the Maestro said in his cheerful medical voice. "We shall see how Alfeo's first-aid skills are coming along. Any injuries other than your nose and arm?"

"My pride," Vasco mumbled. So he was conscious, which was what the Maestro needed to know.

"I can't treat that," the Maestro said. "But lots of people get wounded there when they try to keep up with Alfeo." It was extremely doubtful that his patient had meant it that way. "Alfeo, bring him—"

But I was already there at his elbow with a full glass of wine, raising Vasco enough to let him drink it. "Water and a bucket, master?" I said. "Honey? More wine?"

"Much more wine. You are learning. *Fante*, bring the scuttle!" As the startled Amedeo obeyed, the Maestro barked, "Without the logs, you fool!" He wanted it to catch the blood while he restored the flow to Vasco's hand to see if the color returned, but he is accustomed to having me around, able to interpret incomplete orders correctly.

By that time, I was already going out the door. I ran along the *salone* to the kitchen, which was a madhouse of confusion, with eight or nine Angelis all shouting at the same time and running in eccentric circles. None of them seemed to notice that I was covered in blood. Even allowing for the love of high drama that Mama has nurtured in all her children, a single breakfast guest should not justify such turmoil, but I was too worried to tarry. I snatched up the things I needed and beat a hasty withdrawal back to the at-elier.

I discovered that the Maestro had requisitioned Amedeo Bolognetti to assist him as he began stitching up Vasco's tendons and blood vessels.

"I don't need you," he told me when I delivered the honey and wine and replaced the bloody scuttle with the bucket. "Go and make yourself respectable for company."

More than happy to obey, I made a brief return visit to the riot in the kitchen for some water and then headed to my own room to clean up. As I stripped off, I realized that I was going to have some wonderfully colored bruises to impress Violetta. By tomorrow I would out-spot a leopard. I was still washing when Inquisitor Gritti walked in without knocking. He closed the door, seeming to ignore me as he strolled over to peer out the window.

"So this is the lover's leap! One forgets how wonderful is youth."

"All the more reason to enjoy it . . . Your Excellency." I was not in a mood to be courteous if he wasn't and walking in on a man when he has no clothes on is frowned upon in elevated circles.

He turned to look at me, his ruddy, weathered face expressionless. "Tell me what happened this morning."

To anyone else, I would have retorted that I must report to my master first, but to try that on a state inquisitor would be ridiculous, so I gave him the story from the time we arrived at the Giudecca, verbatim. Not liking the way he was looking at me, as if assessing me for the torture chamber, I threw down my towel and reached for my shirt, the only silk one I own.

"If you are lying about falling downstairs, you went to considerable lengths to obtain supporting evidence." He was not smiling, so I didn't.

I didn't deign to answer at all. I pulled on my white hose—like the shirt, the only silk ones I own. The Maestro's idea of an adequate clothing allowance for an apprentice is ludicrous. In a city where anyone who matters goes around in funereal black, young males are expected to preen and strut like peacocks, and that is not easy on a *soldo* here and a *soldo* there. I was lacing my hose to my shirt when my tormentor spoke again.

"The *vizio* confirms that his wounds were caused by Guarini, not you."

I could not let that one go past without comment. "I am distressed that you would even feel required to ask him, Your Excellency." I donned my best britches, voluminous scarlet brocade.

"I question everything. The *vizio* is a very courageous young man." Gritti stumped across to a chair and sat down.

"That's interesting." My best doublet is striped in blue and white, ornamented with acorn-shaped glass buttons, and cost me my entire clothing allowance for a year. I admired it in the mirror as I prepared to fasten my finely starched ruff around my neck.

"He accompanied you and your gondolier across the Canale della Giudecca early on a Sunday morning."

I turned from peering in my mirror to stare at my tormentor. "That takes courage? Giorgio is a very competent boatman."

The old scoundrel sneered. "But Angeli is devoted to Doctor Nostradamus and, no doubt, to the invaluable assistant without whom the old man would be virtually helpless. There would be almost no other traffic and you would be far enough from land that no spectator would be able to see what was happening in the gondola."

This was starting to feel like a nightmare. "What could happen? Are you suggesting that Giorgio and I might have presented a *danger* to Filiberto Vasco?" Of course he was. Anything one says or does can be distorted into evidence of evil intent.

The old man sighed. "The Grazia girl is young and inclined to hysteria, so the *vizio* is the key witness to your use of black magic yesterday at Ca' Sanudo. By silencing him, you could have overthrown the case against you."

I tucked my hair into my bonnet. "With respect, Your Excellency, I believe that your labors with evil persons have given you a very biased opinion of humanity. Far from attempting to harm Vasco this morning, Giorgio and I did everything in our power to save him. Giorgio is not a young man and I feared he would kill himself, the way he was rowing."

Gritti smiled, all snowy-bearded grandfather again. "A noble effort! Of course mere brawn is common enough. Brains are much rarer. I watched you in action, *sier* Alfeo. I admit I was impressed. Definitely it is time your services were placed at *La Serenissima*'s disposal."

So that was what yesterday's excursion had been all about! Nothing appealed to me less than being a spy for the Council of Ten. "I am enormously flattered, Your—"

"December," Gritti continued as if I had not spoken, "is the earliest we can get you into the Great Council." He rose and strolled back toward the window. "We shall see you get elected to some minor post with a stipend—the Salt Commission, perhaps. Just enough to explain how you can afford to eat, but the covert remuneration will be substantial and the prospects dazzling."

"Your Excellency, I am bound to the good doctor. He is too old to train another assistant. While your offer—"

The inquisitor grunted and turned to frown at me. "I suppose we can tolerate him for a year or so. He will have to retire soon, and I could tell you within fifty ducats how much gold he has stashed away in that secret drawer in the couch. Your work for him will give you a good excuse to—"

"Your Excellency, I thank you for—"

"You would, of course," the inquisitor said coldly, "first have to be cleared of suspicion of witchcraft and attempted murder."

"Attempted *what?*"

He smiled, but no child would want a grandfather who smiled like that. "Just this morning you bled Vasco several times, I understand. Barbers and doctors hesitate to bleed patients who have already lost significant amounts of blood, but you, having no medical qualifications at all, felt free to bleed this noble man who had been wounded while attempting to rescue you from an assailant."

He was goading me, trying to frighten me. He was doing very well.

"I was trying to save his hand. Ask any doctor—"

"You would save his hand at the cost of his life? Of course a hand on its own cannot testify before the tribunal. If you had felt genuine concern for the *vizio*'s welfare and survival, you would have found someone to treat him in Giudecca." The inquisitor's eyes shone with a cold, ophidian gleam.

"I offered to take him to the Convent of San Benedetto, *messer*. I urged him to go there, but he refused. It was he who insisted on returning to Ca' Barbolano."

"You would say that, of course. He cannot recall such a conversation. And yet, alas, he managed to survive your malicious abuse and lives to testify against you! A tough as well as a courageous young man!"

"But inclined to sycophantic prevarication."

"I have two witnesses to your sorcery yesterday. My colleagues were very distressed to hear of this outrage when
I reported to them last night. They were inclined to give
some credit to your youth and lay most of the blame on the
evil old man who has perverted you. These things would
come out at the trial."

He smiled again. Likely the job offer had come from his
two fellow inquisitors. He had delivered it and I had refused
it. Now I was fair game.

I had my shoes on, I was ready. "But you admit that one
witness is a hysterical juvenile. Shall we go and see if Doctor
Nostradamus has managed to silence the other one yet?"

32

Out in the *salone*, I detected mouth-watering odors from the kitchen. Noemi was hovering there anxiously. Noemi is so delicate she could almost hover literally, and I can never meet her eye without smiling.

"Ready?"

She nodded vigorously.

"I shall tell the Maestro," I said. "It seems our feast is ready, Your Excellency."

Gritti walked on without comment, ignoring the statuary and paintings. Back at the atelier we found Vasco sitting on a chair—not one of the best—and sipping a glass of wine. Loss of blood always imparts a strong thirst and the redness of wine makes it the best fluid to help the body replace the loss. He was huddled under a blanket, which at least hid his bandaged arm and blood-ruined garments. His pallor was less marked than before, but with a grotesquely swollen nose trailing wisps of packing and two rapidly developing black eyes, he looked as if he had fallen headfirst off a bell tower. I don't say he had earned all that. I don't say he hadn't, either.

Beside him stood *Missier Grande*, who was a surprise but

not much of one, for he would have heard from the *fante* about his deputy's injury. The look he gave me conveyed little appreciation of the work I had done to bring the man back alive.

The Maestro was wiping his hands on a damp cloth. He scowled approvingly at me. "If you must waste so much money on clothes, they deserve to be worn in good company. I was just telling *Missier Grande* that his *vizio* owes his life to you yet again, Alfeo."

"Again?" murmured the inquisitor. "You mean again after yesterday?"

"No." The Maestro's smirk told me that he had been dragging bait, although Gritti might not realize that. "I was thinking of the time when the gondola overturned and Alfeo had to tow the *vizio* to shore."

"Our *prima colazione* is ready, master," I said hopefully.

"Your Excellency," *Missier Grande* said, "I should see the *vizio* home."

"Not just yet." Gritti walked over to one the green chairs and turned it so he could include Vasco in his field of view. "First I want answers to a couple of questions."

"As you please," the Maestro said with unusual amiability.

He hobbled to his red chair, leaning on furniture because he had left his staff there. I went to my side of the desk and sat. *Missier Grande* remained standing. The two *fanti* were out in the *androne*, watching through the open door and within easy hail.

"Doctor Nostradamus," Gritti said, staring intently at him, "yesterday you did not know who Algol was. Do *not* interrupt me! If you had known you would have said so, and you didn't. You merely said you would tell me today, and this morning you sent your boy all the way to the Giudecca to accost a man who had not previously been mentioned in this case. To the best of my recollection, the name of Francesco Guarini has never been brought before the Ten. I grant you that his reaction to Zeno's summons was suspicious and his violence against the *vizio* will send him to the galleys, but where is your evidence that he has anything to do with either the Algol matter or the death of Danese Dolfin? Explain."

The Maestro leaned back, rested his elbows on the arms of his chair, and put his fingertips together, five and five. That almost always means that he is about to start lecturing, but for once it did not.

"The revered and mighty Council of Ten does not reveal all its methods, Your Excellency. I have my own professional secrets and need them to earn my living. I assure you that you have your man and a couple of witnesses are available. With a little encouragement, Guarini will confess to everything."

Inquisitors do not take kindly to defiance. Indeed, they take very cruelly to it, and Gritti's smile clotted my blood like butter. "But it is you I am presently encouraging. You will tell me how you learned his name. I will know who told you, and when. I am prepared to go to great lengths to get the truth."

There was the ultimatum. We were back to the question of how much torture a frail octogenarian could stand, and who else might be questioned in his stead. Gritti meant what he was saying. He was clearly prepared to accept as a working hypothesis that Guarini was Algol and would solve both the espionage case and the murder for him. Now he was investigating the problem of black magic. He had the scent of witchcraft in his nostrils and a true fanatic sees witchcraft as much worse than espionage.

"I am not prepared to tell you at this time," the Maestro said calmly, making as if to rise. "After we have eaten I may say more on the topic, but I believe it is irrelevant."

"It is relevant if I say it is!" The inquisitor's rubicund face darkened a few shades.

"But I know the details and you do not." If the Maestro was deliberately trying to get both himself and me arrested, he was certainly proceeding in the correct manner.

"Filippo Nostradamus, I am aware of your international reputation as a doctor. I am also aware of your reputation as a philosopher who dabbles in the dark arts, and I fear that this time you have dabbled much deeper than any Christian should, or can without selling his soul to the Enemy. I am aware that you have served *La Serenissima* well in the past, but I will not and cannot tolerate Satanism. How did you learn that Algol was Francesco Guarini?"

"Black magic," said Filiberto Vasco.

Heads turned. Now who was the life of the party?

"You have our attention, *Vizio*," the inquisitor said.

Judging by his gleeful expression, Vasco was rising above his pain. "When Zeno knocked on Guarini's door, Guarini called out to ask who he was." His voice was muffled and slurred by all the wine that he had consumed, but he was not too drunk to know what he was saying, and he was looking at me, not Gritti, gloating over worse tales he had yet to tell. "Zeno wouldn't tell him. First he asked for Guarini by name. Then he asked for 'Mirphak.' And finally he said that *the dead man sent him*!"

"Mirphak?" Gritti looked to me.

I hope my smile was debonair and not grotesque. "A shot in the dark, Your Excellency. Algol is the second brightest star in the constellation of Perseus. Mirphak is the brightest. If one was a code name, then the other might be. I was hoping it might provoke a guilty reaction."

Undeceived, the inquisitor shook his head contemptuously and looked back to Vasco, who probably tried to smile, because he winced with sudden pain.

"But when Zeno said, 'Danese Dolfin sent me,' Guarini threw the door open and attacked him."

"That one worked," I explained brightly.

And that one worked for Gritti, too. It would have been a believable ruse for me to try, and it had produced a convincing indication of guilt. He shrugged.

"It was true," Vasco protested. "Dolfin did send him! That was how they learned the name. Last night, Nostradamus and Zeno raised the ghost of Danese Dolfin and made it tell them who murdered him."

"Head injuries," the Maestro muttered sadly. "Difficult prognosis. Prolonged rest is indicated."

"No, he's just drunk," I said. "He never can hold his liquor. After all that lost blood, he's sprung his timbers."

"Over there?" Vasco pointed. "There's a spyhole beside the mirror. I watched from the dining room. I saw it all! I heard the ghost speak in Dolfin's voice!"

Missier Grande strode over to inspect. "That is correct," he announced. "There is a spyhole and the cover is currently open."

I felt as if I had been clubbed between the eyes. How had he done that? Someone might have opened it that morning, but I was certain I had seen it closed last night before we began our séance. Had Vasco himself used occult means to open the shutter so he could spy on us?

"Necromancy?" Gritti declaimed. "In all my years I have never heard a more terrible accusation. *Missier Grande*, take Nostradamus and Zeno to the palace and lock them in separate cells. They are to be charged with practicing Satanism."

"I'm ravenous," I said. "Providing first aid to critically wounded comrades is very hunger-making work and I need my breakfast. Mama Angeli has prepared a marvelous *prima colazione* in your honor, Excellency. Can't we eat first?"

The inquisitor stood up. "No," he said. "I will not sup at the table of a man I believe to be an agent of the Fiend."

"This is ridiculous!" roared the Maestro. "That boy is confused by concussion and also quite obviously drunk, and yet you accept his wild allegations as reliable testimony?

Am I an idiot that I would perform forbidden rites where he could overlook me, when I knew he was in the house? Do you think we don't know the spyhole is there? If you think I am so senile that I would forget about it, do you believe Alfeo would? Your Excellency, you are running a travesty of an investigation!"

Ignoring the tirade, Gritti had beckoned in the two *fanti*, but I reached the Maestro first and helped him up. I handed him his staff and gave him my arm to lean on. If he was going to be humiliated by being carried off like baggage to jail, then the least I could do was help him postpone the indignity as long as possible. Besides, I did not have my sword with me, so I couldn't put the time to better use by sending Vasco to hell with a warning I was coming.

I had always overestimated that dog's human qualities.

We shuffled out into the *salone*. The Angelis were emerging from the kitchen, just about all of them, and Bruno was with them. Bruno was going to be a problem. Already he was sensing the tension and frowning. The *fanti* would have to carry the Maestro downstairs and the moment they laid hands on him, Bruno was going to charge along the hall like my father's galley at Lepanto.

"Can you manage the stairs?" *Missier Grande* asked Vasco, eyeing the group of us. The Maestro must be carried, I must be watched, he had only two able-bodied men to assist him, and he must realize that Vasco would be in danger if he stayed around Ca' Barbolano unprotected.

"Do let me assist," I said. "I'll give him a helping foot."

Someone rapped the front door knocker.

33

Force of habit sent me to open the door and nobody moved to stop me. Outside, beaming, stood *sier* Alvise Barbolano in his formal *nobile homo* robe, or as much of it as the moths had left. At his side simpered madonna Maddalena compressed into a puce brocade gown that had been the fashion and perhaps her size about when I was born. She was ballasted by a display of jewelry that would have surprised the Sultan.

"We are not too late, I hope?" *sier* Alvise demanded.

I stopped gaping and bowed low to stimulate blood flow to my brain, but all too soon I had to straighten up and speak. "Right on time, I'd say, *clarissimo*. Oh, madonna, what a tragedy that Titian did not live to paint you!"

"He did," Alvise said, leading her past me. "Twice. So did Jacopo Palma il Vecchio. Ah! *Clarissimo!*" He swooped at the nonplused Ottone Gritti and embraced him fondly. "I did not expect you also, *messer*. My dear, of course you remember Orlando Grimani?" Despite his notorious savaging of names, the old aristocrat seemed unusually spry, worked up about something that totally escaped me.

Gritti kissed the lady's hand with a murmured pleasantry.

But then he fixed a rapier stare on Barbolano. "I understood that you were planning to evict your tenants, *clarissimo*. I was informed that Nostradamus would be thrown in the canal on Tuesday."

I caught the Maestro's eye and we exchanged slight nods. Vasco had been present when Barbolano gave me that ultimatum but had not had a chance to report it to Gritti. Renzo Marciana must have overheard it also, and would certainly have told the news to the rest of the Marciana tribe. At least two of them spy for the Council of Ten.

"What?" Alvise blinked. "Did I say that? Of course not! Have they arrived yet, Doctor?"

"They seem to have been delayed, *clarissimo*," the Maestro said. "But if you would care to wait over here, I—"

"They're here!" yelled Corrado Angeli, coming racing up the stairs.

I think Inquisitor Gritti guessed right away who *they* were, for he muttered something angrily under his breath, but I was still somewhere off in the paddy fields of Cathay. The Maestro was having trouble hiding a smirk. Had all his deliberate baiting of Gritti been merely a delaying tactic? A near-suicidal one, if it was. And I still could not see *whose* arrival could save us from the Three at this late date, except possibly the entire Turkish army's.

Nevertheless, moving with complete assurance that I knew what I was doing, I released the second flap of the double doors and swung them both wide. Let the Sultan ride through!

No. The head of the procession came into view on the first landing down, and the men leading it were Fulgentio Trau and another ducal equerry. Many voices drifted up to me. I turned and surveyed the reception party lining up to greet them—Alvise Barbolano and his wife, burning with excitement, savoring one of the greatest moments of their lives, perhaps *the* greatest; the Maestro leaning heavily on

his staff, but smirking at my nod of appreciation as I came
to understand the majestic coup he had pulled off; and State
Inquisitor Ottone Gritti, who was now redder than ever and
chewing his beard in fury. And Vasco blinking in drunken
confusion.

The equerries reached the top and took up position by
the door, Fulgentio flashing me a wink. I wanted to fall on
my knees and weep all over his feet in gratitude. He must
have done some very fast talking.

Then *Nasone* himself, *Il Serenissimo* Doge Pietro Moro, a
grizzled bear of a man in his ermine cape and cloth-of-gold
robes, with the horned *corno* on his head, pausing in the
doorway to catch his breath. Venetians live with stairs all
their lives, but he is old enough to be forgiven a little puffing after a long climb. We all bowed; republicans do not
kneel to their head of state.

"Sire, you are most welcome to our humble home," old
Barbolano bleated.

"The pleasure is mine, *sier* Alvise." The doge strode forward, leading in his six scarlet-clad ducal counselors, most
of them about as old as he. These seven were not quite the
full *Signoria*, for that includes the three chiefs of the *Quarantia*, but they are the seven who also belong to the Council of
Ten. Granted that seven is not a majority of seventeen, it is
very difficult to imagine the other ten overruling the doge
and his counselors when they have agreed on something,
and that day they had clearly agreed to sup with Maestro
Nostradamus. That may not be an unheard-of honor, but it
would be the talk of the city for weeks.

Gritti refused to eat at the table of a man he believed to
be an agent of the Fiend, but so would the *Signoria*. Therefore they did not believe that Nostradamus was a witch.
One of the counselors now embracing *sier* Alvise was a co-
member of the Three with Gritti.

I was certainly not part of the reception line, but a few

joyful minutes later I found myself eye to eye with Pietro Moro. I must be the only apprentice in Venice the doge knows by name.

"What have you done to your face, Alfeo?" he inquired softly.

"I fell downstairs, sire."

"And what happened to the *vizio*'s face, mm?"

"He was at the bottom of the stairs."

The ducal beard twitched as if trying to cover a smile. "Unfortunate! We shall hear more of this event, I trust?"

"I am sure my master will explain if you wish him to, sire." And probably if he didn't.

"I heard some curious rumors about books bursting into flames. I have warned you before, Alfeo, that chicanery like that would get you into trouble." He had not yet heard about Baphomet and I hoped fervently that he never would. His eyes twinkled. "But I admit I'm curious to know just how you pulled that one off."

"Well, sire . . . How would you suppose I did?"

"A silk thread to make the book move and a burning glass hidden in your hand?"

"It was very overcast yesterday, sire." Seeing his frown, I summoned my most mysterious smile. "The paper was incredibly old and dry, and both the *vizio* and I swiped at it with our rapiers a few times."

Now his eyes gleamed. "And the steel point scratching the terrazzo floor struck a spark?"

"It is good that everyone isn't as shrewd as you, sire."

Pietro Moro is shrewd enough to know that I could be lying by misdirection, but I am shrewd enough to know when he doesn't want to know any more. Although he is a total skeptic about magic, he is a good Christian, too, and aware of borderlands that should be left unexplored. He shook his head disbelievingly and turned away.

Terrazzo is made from powdered marble, cement, goat's

milk, and a few other things, but steel will not strike a spark from marble. It needs a harder rock, like flint. Oh, well . . .

A lowly apprentice should never presume to lead a conversation with his betters, especially a better so very much better than I than the doge is, but I could not resist whispering, "I am very grateful for your presence here today, sire."

He paused and eyed me narrowly. "There's more?"

"No, it's just that thanks to you, sire, I am confident that my chances of going up in smoke have just gone up in smoke."

The beard twitched again . . . this time accompanied by a ducal glare. "But those of a severe flogging have just increased dramatically!" Then he guffawed and moved on.

Moments later I found myself looking up into the jungle-thick beard of *sier* Zuanbattista Sanudo. That had been how the case had started, right here, just eight days ago. He acknowledged me with a nod. There might be a few more lines in his face and a droop to his eyelids, but he was bearing up amazingly under his burden.

"Well, *sier* Alfeo? Is your master going to denounce me as a traitor to the Republic?"

"I am certain he is not going to do that, *clarissimo*. Is the Council going to burn me at the stake for witchcraft?"

He snorted. "Of course not." He turned away to follow the doge.

Watching him going into the dining room, I remembered that he was due to preside over the Great Council that afternoon and was filled with admiration for his courage. His daughter had run away with a gigolo and now the gigolo had been murdered, so the opportunity for ridicule was obvious. His popularity would be severely tested. I wondered if he had tried to resign and the doge had insisted he stay on and fight. Or perhaps his wife had.

Not everyone dines with the doge. *Missier Grande* does not, nor his *vizio*, nor *fanti* like Amedeo Bolognetti and Marco Martini. Nor, alas, do astrologers' apprentices like Luca Alfeo Zeno, but some apprentices are quicker than others. As the dignitaries filed into the dining room, I slipped away to the atelier and locked myself in before *Missier Grande* could notice what I was up to or move to stop me. Quazza had been told to take the Maestro and me to jail, but he couldn't do that while the Maestro was with the doge, and he probably would not have taken his instructions so literally as to remove me only, because things had changed since Gritti issued those orders. Quazzo knew about the peephole, but I gambled that he would not interrupt the meeting to warn Gritti that I might be eavesdropping.

My stomach complained bitterly that I should have gone to the kitchen and found food, but I told it that fasting was good for our soul. Instead of eating, I watched as the guests settled in at the long table. The doge invited madonna Barbolano to sit at his right, the place of honor, and she looked ready to swoon. Alvise went on his left, of course, and the Maestro opposite, flanked by Gritti and Sanudo. The rest of the counselors were left on the edges, but the table could have held another forty. The two equerries stood in the background, in attendance.

Giorgio and Christoforo in their Sunday best acted as footmen. I could not see what they were serving, but it smelled wonderful and I marveled that Mama had managed to assemble a worthy repast at such short notice. She and her brood had fled the house right after her scream, you will recall, and on Saturday afternoon there would have been little left to buy on the stalls. Likely she had borrowed supplies from her enormous family and from Giorgio's, which is even larger. When the tale of the doge's visit got out, they would all bask in reflected glory.

I settled down to starve. Nothing of importance would be discussed until the Barbolanos were dismissed and possibly not even then, because the purpose of the gathering was merely to demonstrate to Ottone Gritti that the *Signoria* was not in favor of combusting the doge's personal physician.

34

Food was eaten with enjoyment, wine drunk with happy results, gossip and small talk tossed to and fro. Eventually the doge brought it all to an end by dismissing the Barbolanos.

"We have serious business to discuss with Maestro Nostradamus," he proclaimed. "Your tenant is an esteemed servant of the state, *clarissimo*. Sometimes I wonder what we should do without him."

That wrung a return flow of compliments from old *sier* Alvise. Not only was our tenancy safe now, he had probably already forgotten threatening it. Fulgentio escorted the Barbolanos out. I should have been at the front door to bow them on their way, but I stayed where I was. Now the meeting would get down to business.

"Now, Doctor," Moro said, leaning back. "Your message said you would introduce us to the man we have been seeking. I take this to mean that you have identified the notorious Algol?"

The Maestro beamed, bunching cheeks and very nearly showing his teeth. "Identified and delivered, Your Serenity. Inquisitor Gritti has him locked up already."

Eyes turned to Inquisitor Gritti, who alone looked as if he had not enjoyed the meal. "We have detained a man named Francesco Guarini, sire. He is charged with using violence against the *vizio*, who very nearly bled to death. He—"

"—would have bled to death, had Alfeo not known what to do," my master said.

The doge grunted annoyance at the interruption. "Sounds like Zeno. Continue, Inquisitor."

"We still have no evidence," Gritti said, "that Guarini and Algol are one and the same. Nostradamus refuses to justify his claims."

"It is fairly obvious." Taking silence as an invitation to lecture, the Maestro laid his forearms on the table and put his hands together, fingertip to fingertip. "Espionage, if I may be permitted to belabor the obvious, is a form of theft. It takes information belonging to A and transfers it to the buyer, whom we may call Z. Your Excellencies have not entrusted me with Z's identity, although you must know it because your own agents stole the information back again, albeit still in encoded form and therefore not identifiable with complete confidence until I broke its cipher for you. One report I saw was dated so recently that Z cannot be located far away, in say Paris or Constantinople. Most likely Z is an ambassador right here in Venice, and I shall assume for the sake of this discussion that he can be found in the Spanish Embassy. Which embassy does not matter, because my point is that espionage requires middlemen. It would be quite impossible for a senior magistrate to stroll along to any embassy without his own government knowing it."

The audience shifted uneasily at this allegation that the Ten spied upon its own, but none of them wasted breath to deny it.

"The same would be true, *messere*, if he sent his gondolier with a letter—very soon the Three would invite him in for a chat. It would be true also of the illustrious citizens who serve the Republic in high office and are privy to its secrets. So we must postulate B, who steals or buys the information from A and then delivers it, most likely to another middleman, C, who in turn passes it to D, and so on until it reaches Z. Of course Z probably hides behind one of his own subordinates, whom we may call X. Communication is the weak point in any espionage system, as you well know. Even on Thursday, when you entrusted me with the task of unmasking Algol, I was sure that the person I would catch would turn out to be a middleman, not a traitor within the government. The next day I learned that he was an amateur, not—"

"How?" barked Gritti.

The Maestro turned to him with an expression of bland surprise. "From the cipher, Excellency. He was using a most sophisticated method of enciphering—more subtle, I am certain, than the system used by *La Serenissima* herself—and yet he was using it very stupidly. A key only five letters long is absurd! Instead of *VIRTÙ*, he should have used something much longer: *LA SERENISSIMA*, or the paternoster, or a verse from Dante. He should certainly have employed a different key for each dispatch. Beginning every dispatch with a date is another incredible incompetence, a gift to the code breaker, but all ciphers are eventually betrayed by human stupidity.

"So B had to be an amateur, a local whom X had enlisted and taught to encipher. Fortunately, in spite of B's hamfisted, incompetent enciphering, the product was good enough to baffle most people." That was a nice dig at *Circospetto* and his minions. "As long as B continued to supply valuable information, X was content not to interrupt the flow. An alternative possibility was that B had taught himself the rudiments of enciphering by reading a book, and I admit that I found this theory attractive because Alfeo had

located a great library associated with a certain distinguished magistrate, but I discarded that as improbable as
soon as I identified *B* as Danese Dolfin."

"*What?*" The wintery blast came from Zuanbattista
Sanudo. "You dare suggest that I gave state secrets to that
slimy little thief? Or that my son did?"

"No, *messer*, I certainly do not." The Maestro shrugged.
"It is a complex story, which will be best understood if told
in a logical sequence. I may . . . ?" He accepted Zuanbattista's silent glare as assent. "The next link in the chain from
B to *X* was Francesco Guarini, of course, but I do not know
which of them masterminded their squalid conspiracy. I
suspect Dolfin, but Guarini may enlighten you, *messere*,
when he is motivated to explain."

I shivered. Gritti was showing his teeth, biding his time.
The Maestro might talk all he wanted, but he was not going
to escape the charge of necromancy.

"Dolfin's murder," Nostradamus said, "was in a sense a
lucky break for me as investigator, and for the Republic itself, although the Algol espionage was already ended before
that. The murder was bizarre. Why was the corpse brought
to Ca' Barbolano and left in the watergate with the impal-
ing sword still in place? Why not just drop it in a canal?
We have many murders in Venice, but few are deliberately
advertised as this one was. Why was he murdered at all?
One obvious motive, if *sier* Zuanbattista will forgive my
even mentioning it to dismiss it, is that someone in his family resented the way Dolfin had inveigled himself in by se-
ducing madonna Grazia. But the last thing Ca' Sanudo
would want would be publicity, so the grotesque spectacle
made of the corpse was not the work of any family member."

"I am so relieved to hear that!" Zuanbattista growled.

"Nor could his death be a random slaying during a rob-
bery," the Maestro continued unabashed, "because the killer
would not have known to bring him here, to Ca' Barbolano.

It could not be an effort to distract me from investigating the espionage case by involving me in murder, as I speculated at first, because publicity is the last thing a spy ever wants. For the same reason I do not believe that Dolfin was slain to silence him. Besides, the espionage was ended. Dolfin not only *would* not continue his treason, he *could* not, as I shall demonstrate. So why did his killer make an exhibition of him, a public scandal, the talk of the town?"

"Enough of this!" snapped the doge. "You are supposed to be telling us how you identified Guarini as the spy. And Dolfin, for that matter. Give us the facts and stop boasting how clever you are."

"Sire, forgive me!" the Maestro said, bowing in his seat. "The facts? The salient facts? The lightning flash that illuminates the truth? Yesterday Danese Dolfin's body was found in our watergate. A week ago yesterday, *sier* Zuanbattista and his noble lady came to our house in search of their daughter. One of the Algol documents you let me examine was dated the eleventh of August and another the fifteenth of September!"

Silence.

He looked around with the maddening pretense of puzzled innocence he adopts sometimes.

"Fridays," he explained patiently. "Last Friday night, Dolfin was murdered. The Friday before that he climbed over the wall of Ca' Sanudo, from which he had been expelled a few days earlier. Every Friday *B* wrote his report and met with *C*, who was either his letter box or his handler, in the argot of the espionage world, depending on which of them was senior. To abduct Grazia, Dolfin used a ladder. A week later Dolfin's corpse was brought to Ca' Barbolano's watergate, which has no true land access. Does this not scream at you that *C* must be a gondolier? In Venice, what else could he be? Only trained gondoliers can handle our narrow, unstable boats, and what gondolier would transport a ladder by night for a stranger? Or convey a corpse?

"Undoubtedly X would have ordered B and C to limit their meetings to their weekly rendezvous and avoid all other contact. They broke this rule once and thereby brought about their downfall, as I shall reveal. When Guarini arrived at the rendezvous near Ca' Sanudo on Friday the fifteenth of September, Dolfin explained that the golden goose had turned broody—he had been evicted from Ca' Sanudo and cut off from his source of information. He proposed a backup plan. He would carry off Grazia and marry her, gambling that her parents would eventually bow to the inevitable and accept the serpent back into their garden. Guarini agreed, took Dolfin to fetch his ladder, and then transported him and his victim to some nest where they spent the night. Possibly madonna Grazia will be able to identify the boatman, although she had other things on her mind and we tend not to notice gondoliers. The next day the lovers went to a priest and explained that they would be driven to sin unless he united them in holy matrimony.

"Compounding his error, Guarini had agreed to meet the couple again on Sunday morning and transport them over to the mainland, where they would hide out until her parents had no option but to accept Dolfin as the father of a future grandchild. Alfeo intervened to rescue Grazia. Guarini countered by trying to stun Alfeo—he is clearly prone to violence. My porter picked Guarini up by the scruff of the neck and threw him bodily into the Grand Canal. When Alfeo turned up on his doorstep this morning, it was not Alfeo who recognized Guarini, although he did so later, *it was Guarini who recognized Alfeo.* Realizing that the game was up, he reacted for a third time with excessive violence."

The Maestro beamed around his audience, and there was no fidgeting now. He had them enthralled.

"With your gracious permission, sire, I will speculate a

little about what happened right after that scuffle on the Riva del Vin last Sunday. I think Guarini, anxious to know what had gone wrong and who Alfeo was or represented, followed him and his charges back here to Ca' Barbolano. Speculating even further, he may have kept an eye on this house all week, wondering whether Dolfin had sold out to the Council of Ten. If so, he may have seen Dolfin freely coming and going, which would not have allayed his misgivings.

"They say that there is no honor among thieves, and there is certainly no trust among spies. When Friday came around again, it was two very nervous young men who went to their weekly rendezvous near Ca' Sanudo, as they had done for the past two months. Dolfin had first come here to Ca' Barbolano to retrieve his sword, so he foresaw trouble. Failing to find his own blade, he purloined Alfeo's. He arrived armed at the rendezvous, alarming Guarini even more, when he was already seeing agents of the Ten in every shadow. Dolfin announced that the dance was ended; he would deliver no more reports. Now that he was one of the family, he was buttering his bread on the other side.

"There were words, a fight, Dolfin died. Then Guarini must have thought that there was no one to betray his espionage, all he had to worry about was a murder."

The Maestro sighed. "Why did he not just rob the corpse, remove the sword, and go, leaving us to assume a random killing? I admit I do not know, and I should be very interested to hear what he says when you ask him. I have not met him, except for a few moments this morning. I posit that he is a stupid, violent man, given to rages, and craving revenge on the people in Ca' Barbolano who ruined his profitable avocation. Or he may be sly enough to see what I said earlier, that publicity is the last thing a spy ever wants. A sword is the weapon of a gentleman or a professional bravo, not a simple gondolier, so perhaps he thought his treatment

of the body would deflect attention away from him. Whatever the reason, he carried the corpse—it showed no signs of
having been dragged—to his boat, laying it face up there
because that way it would stain his boat less. On his way
home from Cannaregio to Giudecca, he had to pass fairly
close to San Remo anyway.

"If there is no rational explanation for an event, Your Excellencies, there must be an irrational one. In his fear and
murderous rage, Guarini lifted the corpse ashore, and left it
lying face up in our loggia. *So perish all the enemies of Francesco
Guarini!*"

"Ingenious as always," the doge conceded. "But you have
made grave accusations against a noble member of the *Signoria*. This is a serious offence."

The rest of the faces around the table were as grim as his,
but what had they expected? They had known from the beginning that the source of Algol's information must stand
close to *La Serenissima*'s heart. Were they about to kill the
messenger?

The Maestro spread his hands disarmingly. "Six years
ago, sire, when I was not as halt as I have become since, I attended Nicolò Morosini in his last illness. I had never seen
such a case, nor have I since. His entire hand was rotting. It
had begun with an insignificant paper cut, he said, but
those were almost his dying words. The poison spreading up
his arm killed him before sunset."

I held my breath, wondering if he would now dare mention the jinx, the cause of all the Sanudos' miseries. The
skeptics would not accept that argument and it would remind his audience of the strange events of the previous day's
inexplicable self-combustion. He did, but only obliquely.

"Disasters come in groups, it seems, sire. Since then, ill
luck has continued to dog Nicolò's family. Of course I know
his widow, madonna Fortunata, *sier* Zuanbattista's sister-in-
law, although I have not met her since her husband's death.

Last week she was mentioned as a resident of Ca' Sanudo, but later Alfeo spoke of her as if she were a very elderly woman and madonna Eva's aunt, not Grazia's. Alfeo is a sharp lad, who rarely makes such mistakes. He does tend to waste time staring at paintings, but when he described a portrait of her and her husband, I remembered it, and noted that he had recognized *sier* Nicolò's likeness but not hers, although she had been present in the room."

The doge was showing dangerous signs of impatience, and the Maestro abandoned his dissertation on the workings of curses.

"It has been a very hot summer, sire. *Sier* Zuanbattista was newly reunited with the family he had not seen in three years, including his son, and both of them were newly elected to very high office. What would be more natural than that they would sit out on their balcony on those sweltering evenings, overlooking their garden—"

"*Gesù bambino!*" Zuanbattista covered his face with his hands.

After a moment the Maestro completed his sentence, "—talking? Talking directly above the windows of the room assigned to Danese Dolfin, the lute-playing, poetry-reading, hair-brushing, light-fingered *cavaliere servente?*"

"Enough!" Zuanbattista rose from his chair. "It is true, sire! My son and I did sit and talk on that balcony in the evenings, after the ladies had retired. I see now that we were criminally careless not to realize that we could be overheard. We—Venetians! Natives of a city where hardly a door fits its frame. *Now*, will you let me resign?"

"No," said the doge. "Sit down. We sympathize with your troubles, but there must be no gossip about dissension within the *Signoria* or rumors of espionage. Carry on, Doctor."

The Maestro scowled and put his fingertips together again. "Let us consider for a moment, sire, the situation of this wretch, Danese Dolfin. Since boyhood he has lived by charm, good looks, and a total lack of morals. In the last three years in a palace at Celeseo, he acquired a taste for the good life—note that when he was evicted from Ca' Sanudo, he promptly weaseled his way into Ca' Barbolano. But now his mistress's husband had returned, he was billeted in a much smaller house, where he might easily become a nuisance underfoot, and—worst of all!—the useful body was aging. He was no longer a beautiful boy. Knowing his honeyed days were numbered, he began building a reserve by stealing his employer's jewelry, which is surely a sign of desperation.

"And then, a miracle! Gold rains down outside his window. Danese grabs a pen and takes notes. He gathers secrets, although in his haste and lack of education he makes mistakes. He gets some of his information wrong, as eavesdroppers will do. Then what? Run to the nearest embassy and open negotiations?"

The Maestro chuckled and answered his own question.

"Ah no! I surmise that such a course smelled too risky for *sier* Danese. He is still a *nobile homo* and he has returned to the city; the Ten's eyes will be on him again. No, Dolfin enlists the help of a friend, a gondolier because gondoliers go everywhere and are part of the scenery of Venice, rarely noticed. And, because a fish schools with its own, Dolfin knows just the sort of ruffian he needs—Francesco Guarini. It would have been Guarini who took the notes to the embassy and met with a flunky, the one I have called X. But lowly X knew a chance when he saw it, and he was loyal to whichever monarch he serves. He suspected, quite rightly, that someone in the embassy was not, so he instructed Guarini in how to encipher his reports before delivering them. He taught him, too, the rudiments of espionage, such as keeping meetings to a minimum. He paid him and promised more if the information proved reliable and kept coming.

"I do not know if Guarini then taught ciphering to Dolfin; I suspect not. Dolfin had little privacy in that intimate family home, and the villains would feel safer if he just kept his plaintext notes in a safe place and handed them over to his weekly contact. Guarini enciphered them later, I think . . . but you can establish that." The Maestro pulled a face. It is never pleasant to think that you have sent a man to his doom, however well deserved that doom may be.

"To the sage!" The doge raised his glass in a toast and the entire *Signoria* copied him. After they had all drunk he said, "*Lustrissimo dottore*, your explanation is impressive. Your apprentice confirms that Guarini was the man who attacked him on the Riva del Vin?"

The Maestro nodded. "He does, and so does my gondolier."

"Well, then, are our two inquisitors satisfied? Have you questions to ask him?"

Gritti now looked less grandfatherly and more avuncular—the wicked uncle who stole the throne. "No and yes, sire. Not satisfied, several questions. I agree Doctor Nostradamus has made an excellent case against Francesco Guarini, and Guarini must be closely questioned. But, Doctor, you have still not told us how you identified which of our ten thousand gondoliers was the one you sought. Perhaps you will elucidate your procedures for us?"

No, no! Don't!

The Maestro filled his glass and took a drink of wine.

He wiped his lips and leaned back.

"My apprentice had mentioned that Dolfin had several sisters. My first thought was that one of them might have married a gondolier, so that Dolfin, when he discovered his gold mine in the sky, took his proposal to a brother-in-law. I sent a boy, actually two boys, to ask Father Equiano in San Barnaba for the names and occupations of the Dolfin girls' husbands. Unfortunately not all brilliant hunches work out, and that one did not."

At that point I might have dived out the atelier door and made a break for freedom down the stairs, except that the old mountebank treated himself to another sip of wine. I know him well enough to know when he is letting the suspense build.

"My next idea worked better," he continued. "Ten thousand gondoliers are a small city all to themselves, but they are a very close fraternity, or perhaps two fraternities—the public-hire men despise those who work for wages. No matter, my own gondolier had seen the fight and watched Guarini clambering out of the water, so yesterday I asked him if he knew the man. He did not, but he said the story had been the joke of the week among the city's boatmen, because Guarini was not popular with those who did. I sent Giorgio out to ask some questions. He soon learned that the man we wanted belonged to the *traghetto* of the Ponte della Paglia, and then it was easy to learn his name and address."

Only fools tell outright lies, the Maestro says. *The wise use truth selectively.* An icy droplet ran down my ribs. I hoped the Maestro had primed Giorgio well in what to say when he was questioned.

The nobles of the *Signoria* were frowning, puzzled by the sudden tension.

"You swear by your immortal soul that this is the truth?" Gritti said, fondling the words like a silken cord.

"Certainly I do! I am not in the—"

"It is not what *Vizio* Vasco reports,"

The Maestro sighed. "What does *Vizio* Vasco report, Your Excellency?"

"Perhaps we should hear it from his own lips," Gritti smiled. "If Their Excellencies permit?"

"I can't see how it matters if he led us to the right man," the doge said impatiently. "But let's get it over with."

The inquisitor rose and went to the door. He spoke for a few moments with persons outside, then moved aside to let the *vizio* enter. Vasco was still pale and probably felt very shaky, but a healthy man will recover quickly from loss of blood if he is going to recover at all. Gritti led him to the table and pulled out a chair for him. He blinked uncertainly, sat down unsteadily and peered around the company. Excess of wine was affecting him more than shortage of blood now.

"Filiberto Vasco," the inquisitor said as he returned to his own seat, "do you swear to tell the truth?"

"I do, Your Excellency."

"Then tell us how Doctor Nostradamus learned the name of the man who murdered Danese Dolfin."

This was my cue to dive out the window and swim away along the canal.

I didn't.

"Yesh, Your Shereenit'tee . . ." Vasco's speech was slurred by the wine and tangled up by the packing in his grossly distended nose, but what he was trying to say was, "Yes. Your Serenity, Your Excellencies, last night I was present in this room. There's a spyhole in that wall and I could watch what Doctor Nostradamus and Alfeo Zeno were doing; and hear them, too."

"And what were they doing?" Gritti was literally rubbing his hands, not a gesture one often sees outside the theater.

The *vizio* smiled as well as he could with his face the way it was. He would have managed better had I been there for him to smile *at*. "They were performing a Satanic rite, worshiping a human head. They were summoning the soul of Danese Dolfin back from death to tell them the name of his murderer."

Several patricians gasped. Others crossed themselves. The doge and a couple of others rolled their eyes.

"Tell us more," the inquisitor said.

"They had the thing on a table, Excellency. They were

burning incense around it and they had laid out offerings to it. They put a lock of Dolfin's hair on it—on the head. Nostradamus read a long speech in a foreign tongue to the skull and then Zeno questioned it in *Veneziano* and it spoke to him. It was Dolfin! He had a very memorable voice. I knew it at once. Zeno asked him, er, it who killed him and he . . . it . . . the voice named Guarini and where he lived." Vasco smiled bravely. I would be toasted and he could dance around the pyre.

The inquisitor was just as happy. His old eyes held a youthful sparkle. "Did they give this talking head a name?"

"They called it Baphomet, Your Excellency."

The doge muttered something I was glad not to be able to hear, but he did not interrupt. The wily old man had learned half a century ago to judge the tone of a meeting, and the tide was running hard against Nostradamus now.

"Well, Doctor?" Gritti demanded triumphantly.

Nostradamus seemed to have shrunk. He shook his head sadly. "I confess," he said.

More gasps.

"I confess that both Alfeo and I had become very tired of having Filiberto Vasco underfoot all the time, prying and spying. He was only doing his job, I know, but . . . Well, I admit that I let my apprentice talk me into a most undignified prank. Yes, there is a spyhole in that wall, through to my atelier, and Vasco had found it. We set up a masquerade, *messere*! It was most unprofessional."

"What sort of masquerade?" Gritti demanded angrily.

Sometimes my master throws things at me without any warning whatsoever. One of these days he will outsmart himself by over-smarting me, but that morning I was able to rise to the occasion.

He turned to face me, spread his arms and cried, "Danese Dolfin! I summon you!"

I dropped my voice to the lowest register I could manage

and moaned back through the spyhole in my best attempt at Danese Dolfin's sepulchral bass. *"Who are you that calls to me in the darkness?"*

The audience jumped. *Sier* Zuanbattista, who knew that voice, knocked over his wine glass with an oath. For a moment the world seemed to stop breathing. Then the doge leaned back and bellowed with laughter, so everyone did— even Gritti, coming in last. That was an admission of defeat. *Ridicule is the deadliest weapon in the world*, the Maestro says.

Poor Vasco stared around in dismay, wondering why everyone was laughing. I did wish I could go and comfort him.

35

They could have arrested me for spying on their meeting, but I had taken the same oath of secrecy as the Maestro. What mattered more was that he had solved their espionage problem for them in record time. It would be more true to say that the weather had solved it for them by driving the Sanudos indoors, or Danese had, by getting himself transferred to a bedroom where he would not have had the option of sitting by the window and taking notes. No matter, the Maestro could take the credit and look forward to a handsome fee; the *Signoria* could go away happy and prepare for the Sunday afternoon meeting of the Great Council. It is to the Great Council that the Ten report their activities, but the Algol case would obviously not be reported to anyone.

The Maestro's stellar performance had tired him, though. When I had bowed the last guest off along the canal, I went back upstairs and found him already planted in his favorite chair. He glowered at me, which I took to be a good sign.

"Bring me the Dee papers."

That was an even better sign, because he has been running a savage argument with the heretic sage for years, and nothing would restore him like a good upsurge of choler. I could confidently expect to find several pages of venom and vilification lying on my side of the desk in the morning, waiting to be enciphered.

I headed over to the wall of books. John Dee, of course, is not merely a heretic and a skilled practitioner of the occult, but also a close confidant of the English queen, so his correspondence must be kept in one of the secret compartments. I knelt and began to empty a shelf of its books, stacking them on the floor beside me. "Thank you very much, master."

"For what?"

"For setting Vasco up by opening the spyhole so he could watch the séance. I wish you'd warned me, though."

"If I'd warned you beforehand, you might have started to giggle in the middle. And I had no chance to warn you afterward with the bat-eared *vizio* skulking around."

"But you took a terrible risk," I said, "letting him watch us practice necromancy."

"Bah! We didn't! That was the whole point. What I did was mere mummery. You saw how easy it was to burst that bubble. You, though, used the Word, which is authentic thaumaturgy. They might have let Gritti have you for that, but the doge's physician is too valuable to burn."

And I wasn't. He had saved me at no small risk to himself, so I must not sound ungrateful. "Yes, master. Thanks anyway."

I slid aside the panel at the back of the shelf and retrieved the Dee bundles, which occupy three pigeon holes. Having delivered them, I went back to replace the panel and the screen of books.

"If you don't need me this fine Sunday, I think I'll go and have a chat with Father Farsetti."

"*Why? Is something troubling you?*" Danese Dolfin demanded behind me.

I was squatting. In trying to spin around, I lost my

balance, dropped a pile of books in my lap, and sat down heavily. "That's a much better imitation than I did," I said, glowering.

The Maestro smirked. "Keep practicing! Oh, leave that. Go see the priest if you want, but I'd say you'd do better to visit that woman of yours and collect a few sins worth confessing."

I was supposed to look stunned, which wasn't difficult. "You really did get Guarini's name from Giorgio?"

"I said so, didn't I? You think I would lie under oath?"

"Then where did Mirphak come from?"

"Ah, yes. Mirphak? *Ahem!* Well, as you told Gritti, it was a shot in the dark. I invented it to use up one of your three questions. I wanted you to ask for Algol's name and address. I didn't want you asking something else that Dolfin would have known and I did not. As a matter of principle, apprentice: *A deception should be demarcated in advance so that it does not wander out of control.*"

"Thank you for that apophthegm, master. And no Baphomet?"

"None. The book's a total fake. It doesn't work. I've tried it before. Either it was put together by the Inquisition to scare some of the other Templars into confessing, or Raymbaud held back some of the spell. Now get out of here! Go!"

"Yes, master." I went.

A week or so later, Marco Martini dropped by again, this time to deliver a draft on the *Banco della Piazza*, whose size made my eyes pop, and for which I wrote him a most beautiful receipt in black letter gothic. Surprisingly, Zuanbattista Sanudo eventually paid the rest of the fee the Maestro had charged him for almost getting me murdered on the Riva del Vin.

And Francesco Guarini? Francesco Guarini was tried in

secret and sentenced to five years in the galleys. Francesco Guarini escaped from his cell in the palace and fled to Egypt. Francesco Guarini was tried in secret, strangled, and his body dumped in the Orfano Canal, where the tide could take it away. Believe whichever you like, because Francesco Guarini was never heard from again, at least not by me. I'd bet on the third ending, were I a gambling lad.

Close to Christmas, I saw the Sanudo gondola going by with Fabricio wielding the oar, so his exile had not lasted long. Just after Christmas, Girolamo Sanudo resigned from the *Collegio* and took the Franciscan habit and the name of Brother Pio. Zuanbattista served out his term as ducal counselor and thereafter declined office, indicating that if the Great Council elected him, he would refuse and pay whatever fine it levied. It did not nominate him after that, and he has reputedly been concentrating on his business interests ever since.

The following summer, Grazia sent me a polite note asking if I, as Danese's best friend, would stand as godfather for their son. I had never been a friend of his, best or worst, but I accepted. In my old age, I may have need of a very rich godson, which Alfeo Dolfin will certainly be. His great-aunt Fortunata came to the ceremony, looking twenty years younger. She stayed well away from me, though.

AFTERWORD

A book can have too much reality. I used modern time-keeping because the Venetian day began half an hour after sunset, which meant that noon varied from about fifteen o'clock to about eighteen. Yes, they used a twenty-four hour day, but clocks never struck more than twelve. Clocks were rare. The pendulum clock was not invented until sixty years later.

Polyalphabetic ciphers were known in the sixteenth century, but governments continued to use their cumbersome nomenclators. The reason may be that spelling and alphabets were not yet standardized. (The present English alphabet was introduced by Noah Webster in 1826 but was not universally adopted for another fifty years.) Thus it is anachronistic to describe Alfeo or Vasco writing out their alphabet—they might have come to blows over what the correct Venetian alphabet was. Without such agreement, substitution ciphers would easily have degenerated into nonsense. Codebooks, in contrast, did not rely on spelling.

Veneziano, by the way, was a language in its own right in which the laws of a sovereign state were recorded. Its modern equivalent is still spoken today, although commonly regarded as a dialect of Italian.

The traditional date for the election of the first doge of Venice was 697 A.D. In 1297, the aristocracy "closed" the Golden Book, restricting the vote and public office to men recorded there and their legitimate sons after them. Venice was not a democracy as we understand the word, but it kept its independence for eleven hundred years, the longest-surviving Republic in history. Hostile armies could not cross the lagoon, and navies could not sail it when the Venetians removed the markers showing navigable channels, as they did in time of war. By Alfeo's time, *La Serenissima*'s great days were over and it had entered into its long decay, but it was not until 1797, two centuries later, that a French army under Napoleon Bonaparte arrived on the shore with artillery that could reach across the lagoon to bombard the city. Rather than see Venice destroyed, the Great Council voted itself out of existence and Lodovico Manin, the only mainlander ever elected doge, removed the *corno* as a sign of his abdication. Napoleon was born in Ajaccio, Corsica, which explains the Maestro's quatrain on page 246. Bonaparte gave the city to Austria, and it did not become part of a united Italy for another seventy years.

GLOSSARY

altana a roof-top platform

androne a ground-floor hall used for business in a merchant's palace

atelier a studio or workshop

barnabotti impoverished nobles, named for the parish of San Barnaba

Basilica of San Marco the great church alongside the Doges' Palace; burial place of St. Mark and center of the city

broglio the area of the Piazzetta just outside the palace where the nobles meet and intrigue; by extension the political intrigue itself

ca' (short for *casa*) a house

calle an alley

campo an open space in front of a parish church

casa a noble house, meaning either the palace or the family itself *cavaliere servente* a married woman's male attendant (and frequently gigolo)

Circospetto popular nickname for the chief secretary to the Council of Ten

clarissimo "most illustrious," form of address for a nobleman

Collegio the executive, roughly equivalent to a modern cabinet—the doge, his six counselors, and the sixteen ministers

Constantinople the capital of the Ottoman (Turkish) Empire, now Istanbul

corno the distinctive cap worn by the doge

Council of Ten the intelligence and security arm of the government, made up of the doge, his six counselors, and ten elected noblemen

dogaressa the doge's wife

doge ("duke" in Venetian dialect) the head of state, elected for life

ducat a silver coin, equal to 8 lira or 160 *soldi*, and roughly a week's wages for a married journeyman laborer with children (unmarried men were paid less)

fante (pl: *fanti*) a minion of the Ten

felze a canopy on a gondola (no longer used)

fondamenta a footpath alongside a canal

Great Council the noblemen of Venice in assembly, the ultimate authority in the state

lira (pl: **lire**) a coin equal to 20 *soldi*

lustrissimo "most illustrious," honorific given to wealthy or notable citizens

magazzen a tavern that does not sell food and stays open around the clock

marangona the great bell in the campanile San Marco, which marked the main divisions of the day

messer my lord or sir

Missier Grande the chief of police, who carries out the orders of the Ten

Molo the waterfront of the Piazzetta, on the Grand Canal

moresca a popular Venetian sword dance

Piazza the city square in front of the Basilica of San Marco

Piazzetta an extension of the Piazza, flanking the palace

Porte or Sublime Porte, the Sultan's government in Constantinople

Quarantia the Council of Forty, very roughly equal to a supreme court but with administrative duties also. The three chiefs of the *Quarantia* are also members of the *Signoria*

salone a reception hall

salotto a living room

sbirro (pl: *sbirri*) a police constable

scuola (pl: *scuole*) a confraternity (restricted to commoners)

sequin a gold coin equal to 440 *soldi* (22 lire)

Serenissima, La the Republic of Venice

Signori di Notte young aristocrats elected to run the local *sbirri*

Signoria the doge and his six counselors, plus the three chiefs of the *Quarantia*

soldo (pl: *soldi*) see DUCAT

Ten see COUNCIL OF TEN

Three the state inquisitors, a subcommittee of the Council of Ten

traghetto a permanent mooring station for public-hire gondolas; also the association of gondoliers that owns it

Tuscan the language of Florence, which became modern Italian

Veneziano the language of Venice

vizio *Missier Grande*'s deputy

Wells the prison cells on the ground floor of the Doges' Palace

zonta a group of extra members added to a committee